OXFORD WORLD'S CLASSICS

THE DEAD SECRET

WILKIE COLLINS was born in London in 1824, the elder son of
a successful painter, William Collins. He left school at 17, and after
an unhappy spell as a clerk in a tea broker's office, during which he
wrote his first, unpublished novel, he entered Lincoln's Inn as a law
student in 1846. He considered a career as a painter, but after the
publication, in 1848, of his life of his father, and a novel, *Antonina*,
in 1850, his future as a writer was assured. His meeting with
Dickens in 1851 was perhaps the turning-point of his career. The
two became collaborators, and lifelong friends. Collins contributed
to Dickens's magazines *Household Words* and *All the Year Round*,
and his two best-known novels, *The Woman in White* and *The Moonstone*, were first published in *All the Year Round*. Collins's private
life was as complex and turbulent as his novels. He never married,
but lived with a widow, Mrs Caroline Graves, from 1859 until his
death. He also had three children by a younger woman, Martha
Rudd, whom he kept in a separate establishment. Collins suffered
from 'rheumatic gout', a form of arthritis which made him an
invalid in his later years, and he became addicted to the laudanum
he took to ease the pain of the illness. He died in 1889.

IRA B. NADEL, Professor of English at the University of British
Columbia, is author of *Biography: Fiction, Fact & Form* (1984),
Joyce and the Jews (1989), and *Various Positions: A Life of Leonard
Cohen* (1966). He has edited critical collections on Gertrude
Stein and George Orwell (1988), the letters of Ezra Pound to Alice
Corbin Henderson (1993) and the Oxford World's Classics edition
of Adams's *The Education of Henry Adams*. He is currently
completing an edition of Wilkie Collins's formerly lost first novel,
Iolani.

OXFORD WORLD'S CLASSICS

*For over 100 years Oxford World's Classics have brought
readers closer to the world's great literature. Now with over 700
titles—from the 4,000-year-old myths of Mesopotamia to the
twentieth century's greatest novels—the series makes available
lesser-known as well as celebrated writing.*

*The pocket-sized hardbacks of the early years contained
introductions by Virginia Woolf, T. S. Eliot, Graham Greene,
and other literary figures which enriched the experience of reading.
Today the series is recognized for its fine scholarship and
reliability in texts that span world literature, drama and poetry,
religion, philosophy and politics. Each edition includes perceptive
commentary and essential background information to meet the
changing needs of readers.*

OXFORD WORLD'S CLASSICS

WILKIE COLLINS

The Dead Secret

Edited with an Introduction and Notes by
IRA B. NADEL

OXFORD
UNIVERSITY PRESS

OXFORD
UNIVERSITY PRESS

Great Clarendon Street, Oxford OX2 6DP

Oxford University Press is a department of the University of Oxford.
It furthers the University's objective of excellence in research, scholarship,
and education by publishing worldwide in

Oxford New York

Athens Auckland Bangkok Bogotá Buenos Aires Cape Town
Chennai Dar es Salaam Delhi Florence Hong Kong Istanbul Karachi
Kolkata Kuala Lumpur Madrid Melbourne Mexico City Mumbai Nairobi
Paris São Paulo Shanghai Singapore Taipei Tokyo Toronto Warsaw

with associated companies in Berlin Ibadan

Oxford is a registered trade mark of Oxford University Press
in the UK and in certain other countries

Published in the United States
by Oxford University Press Inc., New York

Introduction, Note on the Text, and Explanatory Notes © Ira B. Nadel 1997
Select Bibliography and Chronology © Catherine Peters 1993,
chronology revised 1999 Norman Page

The moral rights of the author have been asserted

Database right Oxford University Press (maker)

First published as a World's Classics paperback 1997
Reissued as an Oxford World's Classics paperback 1999

British Library Cataloguing in Publication Data

Data available

Library of Congress Cataloging in Publication Data
Collins, Wilkie, 1824–1889.
The dead secret / Wilkie Collins; edited with an introduction
and notes by Ira B. Nadel.
(Oxford world's classics)
Includes bibliographical references (p.).
I. Nadel, Ira Bruce. II. Title. III. Series.
PR4494.D43 1997 823'.8—dc21 96–40167

ISBN 0–19–283841–5

6

Printed in Great Britain by
Clays Ltd, St Ives plc

CONTENTS

INTRODUCTION

Readers who do not wish to learn details of the plot will prefer to treat the Introduction as an Afterword.

Wilkie Collins wrote *The Dead Secret* between promise and fame. The last of his apprentice novels, it was succeeded by his first major success, *The Woman in White*. Up to that point, Collins was known as a writer of daring novels that challenged social behaviour through his presentation of domestic crime or bohemian artists. *The Dead Secret* only slightly altered that view, confronting such issues as the fallen woman, false inheritance, and mistaken identity, all on the wild coast of Cornwall.

Collins began his career by flirting with romance: an exotic novel titled *Iolani* and set in Tahiti, written at 20 and lost until 1991. He turned next to historical fiction with *Antonina*, located in ancient Rome and written in the manner of Bulwer-Lytton; the novel was an early if limited hit. He then turned to contemporary material: his third novel, *Basil*, dealt with the startling topic of a wife's infidelity. His fourth, *Hide and Seek*, expanded his belief that one must defy society to survive through the story of a painter and his rebellious friend. In 1856 he published a series of tales entitled *After Dark* and continued with his journalism, which mostly appeared in Dickens's *Household Words*, where he first published in 1852. In the nine years since his first printed work, an account of his father, the artist William Collins, Wilkie Collins had established himself as a writer whose narratives created suspense but, above all, told a story. *The Dead Secret* is no exception.

A tempered but encouraging reception greeted *The Dead Secret* when it was serialized in twenty-three parts in *Household Words* between January and June 1857, and published in book-form later that year. Reviews were at first tepid and complained about the flat style, slow action, and thin characters. 'Too much is made of too little mystery', the reviewer in the *Athenaeum* announced.[1] The *Saturday Review* complained that there was too much emphasis on unearthing the secret: nearly a hundred pages are spent managing its discovery.

The most stinging criticism was that Collins had allowed the secret to be known too quickly, a problem he addressed in his 1861 preface: 'If this was a mistake (which I venture to doubt), I committed it with both eyes open. After careful consideration, and after trying the experiment both ways, I thought it most desirable to let the effect of the story depend on expectation rather than surprise' (p. 5).

But not every critic found the novel disappointing. Edmund Yates praised Collins's power as a narrator and placed him as a novelist ahead of all his contemporaries except for Dickens, Thackeray, and Charlotte Brontë. 'As a story-teller,' he declared, 'he has no equal . . . he possesses the *art de conter* above all living writers.' Later critics found *The Dead Secret* one of Collins's most important works, an 1889 obituary proclaiming that *The Dead Secret* and *The Woman in White* 'are the general favourites, among his novels, with the majority of the reading public'.[2] Partial proof took the form of Russian and French translations of *The Dead Secret* within a year of its first appearance.

While *Hide and Seek*, his commercially disappointing but critically successful novel of 1854, displayed Collins's knowledge of the artistic world, a result of his father's career as a Royal Academician, his brother's artistic efforts, his friendship with painters like Holman Hunt and Augustus Egg, and his own early efforts as a painter, *The Dead Secret* drew on his new interest, the theatre. A year after the publication of *Hide and Seek*, on 16 June 1855, Collins had his first play performed. Entitled *The Lighthouse*, the melodrama was presented by Dickens's theatrical company at Tavistock House, with Dickens, Collins, Augustus Egg, and Mark Lemon taking parts. It

---

[1] [Horace St John], 'The Dead Secret', *Athenaeum* (20 June 1857), 788, in Norman Page (ed.), *Wilkie Collins: The Critical Heritage* (London: Routledge & Kegan Paul, 1974), 69.

[2] Edmund Yates, 'W. Wilkie Collins', *The Train*, 3 (June 1857), 354, in *Collins, The Critical Heritage*, 68; J. Ashby-Sterry, 'English Notes', *The Book-Buyer* (5 Oct. 1889), 361.

was a success and two years later was professionally produced at the Olympic Theatre, London.

Collins met Dickens in March 1851. Collins had just published a travel account of Cornwall, *Rambles Beyond Railways,* which followed his first novel, *Antonina* (1850). In contrast to the neophyte writer, Dickens—twelve years older—was basking in the popularity of *David Copperfield.* Collins was invited to play a part in Dickens's production of *Not So Bad As We Seem* by Bulwer-Lytton. A close friendship soon flourished which lasted until the death of Dickens in 1870. Collins began what he called his own 'dramatic experiments' in the summer of 1854 when he and Dickens spent several weeks together touring France.[3] But journalism—principally contributions to *Household Words* and *The Leader*—rather than playwriting provided his income.

In November 1855 a long essay by Émile Forgues praising the work of Collins appeared in the *Revue des deux mondes.* The essay contained advice as well as admiration: for example, Collins should curb the optimism of his invention, develop more psychologically penetrating characters, and stop imitating the style of Dickens. Collins listened, and by the 1860s consciously sought to disassociate his writing from Dickens's. *The Dead Secret* is a transitional novel in that process, marking a change from a fiction entirely dependent on setting, melodrama, and eccentrics to one focusing on suspense, locale, and psychological aberration.

When not thinking about the theatre, Collins gathered together five of the stories he published in *Household Words* between 1852 and 1855, added a new work, 'The Lady of Glenwith Grange', plus a framing narrative entitled 'Leaves from Leah's Diary', drawn from his mother's autobiographical fragment about her life as the wife of an artist, and published the stories in a two-volume collection entitled *After Dark* (1856). The narrative frame is that of a partially blind, travelling portrait painter—blindness figures importantly in *The Dead Secret*—who, to save his sight, must give up his painting for six

[3] Collins to Charles Ward, in Catherine Peters, *The King of Inventors: A Life of Wilkie Collins* (London: Minerva, 1992), 144.

months and who spends his time reciting the tales of his sitters. Among the stories is one of Collins's finest, 'A Terribly Strange Bed' (1852), which combines a Poe-like adventure in a dangerous Paris bedroom with gambling. The story introduces the theme of the mysterious room with a secret which forms a crucial part of the plot in *The Dead Secret*. Public response to the book was strong when it appeared in February 1856.

Following the publication of *After Dark*, Collins joined Dickens in Paris in the spring of 1856; Dickens had gone there in November 1855 to work on *Little Dorrit*, although he sporadically returned to London. While visiting France, Collins completed 'A Rogue's Life' for *Household Words*, a satire of Victorian middle-class taste where a rogue succeeds as an art forger. He also began to work out the plot of *The Dead Secret*—which Dickens thought the most exciting and successful of his works to date. Buttressing this creativity, heightened by many discussions with Dickens on the nature of fiction, were trips to theatres, literary salons, galleries, and bookstalls, where, amid various titles, Collins found a series of records of French crimes, one of which became the source of *The Woman in White*.

After his return to London in April 1856 and recovery from one of his recurrent bouts of illness, Collins went on a sailing trip with his friend Edward Pigott to France in June. In August he was again with Dickens, this time working on his new play, *The Frozen Deep*. The original suggestion for the story was Dickens's, based on an 1854 report of the ill-fated Franklin expedition to discover the North West Passage. The première at Tavistock House in January 1857 was reviewed by seven London papers and coincided with the appearance of *The Dead Secret* in *Household Words*. Collins memorialized his involvement with *The Frozen Deep* through his attachment to the name Franklin, derived from the Franklin expedition: with a different spelling, Leonard Frankland is the name of the blind hero of *The Dead Secret*, while Franklin Blake becomes the hero of *The Moonstone*.

Earlier, in September 1856, Collins had been offered a position as a permanent member of the *Household Words* staff. At first he had balked, not wanting to be tied down to a series of short pieces anonymously published in the house style imposed by Dickens. He would agree to the post only if the journal would serialize his next novel under his own name. After some debate, W. H. Wills, the editor, agreed to his demand at Dickens's direction; Collins joined the staff in October.

During this period of theatrical frenzy, with rewrites, rehearsals, and then performances of *The Frozen Deep*, Collins was writing *The Dead Secret*, which began to appear weekly in *Household Words* on 3 January 1857 and ran until June. The magazine advertised his work with his name in early December—not done for any other contributor except Dickens. Although Collins always worked out the plots of his novels in advance, Dickens assured him that he would not have to have more than a portion of the story written in advance of the start of its weekly publication in his journal. But Collins had difficulty staying ahead of his deadlines and frequently disappeared to the Richmond home of Edward Pigott to catch up on episodes; at times he remained only two weeks ahead of the printer's deadlines.

The Dead Secret was also being serialized in the United States and instalments had to be written to coincide with the sailings of transatlantic steamers; at the same time concerns with the Tavistock production of *The Frozen Deep* increased the pressure on his time—intensified by his secret involvement with Caroline Graves whom he dramatically met one evening in Hampstead in May 1854, an encounter the opening of *The Woman in White* recaptures. Soon, supporting (and, after 1859, living with) the young widow and her daughter in London became a lifelong preoccupation for Collins.

The impact of Collins's theatrical activities appears throughout *The Dead Secret*. Porthgenna Tower itself is the dimly lit stage on which the dramatic actions of 'Act I'—the dictation of the note by the former actress Mrs Rosamond Treverton to her maid (who subsequently disappears)—are succeeded by 'Act II's' development of plot: some fifteen years later, the disturbed Sarah Leeson, in disguise, acts as the suspicious Mrs Jazeph, nurse to Mrs Treverton's daughter; after her dismissal, she unsuccessfully searches for the note buried years earlier in the abandoned north wing of the tower. 'Act III' leads to the dramatic discovery of the secret by Rosamond and her husband, with 'Act IV' the denouement, the recovery of the fallen Sarah Leeson. 'Act V' marks the restoration of fortune to Rosamond and her husband.

Not only in structure but in individual scenes does the theatrical influence hold sway: from the opening and very staged setting of the dying Mrs Treverton lying in her four-poster bed rereading prompt copies of plays she acted in, insisting, in an inverted parody of the Ghost in *Hamlet* I. v, that her maid 'Swear!' that she will *reveal* the secret to Captain Treverton, to the prolonged but none the less dramatic discovery of the dead secret in the locked Myrtle Room of the north wing, the sense of theatre dominates the novel.

Beyond these individual moments, Mrs Treverton and Sarah Leeson remain actresses throughout their lives. They each mask the past and at one point exchange 'costumes', when Sarah gives birth to Rosamond. Such actions elaborate on a remark by the narrator early in the novel: 'the ineradicable theatrical instinct showed' (p. 21).

Despite the distractions of *The Frozen Deep* and Caroline Graves, Collins often found himself deeply affected by his story as he wrote it. To a correspondent years later who complimented him on a section of the novel, he wrote: 'I cried so myself over that passage in writing it, that I was obliged to make a fair copy of the page, when I was able to compose myself.'[4] In the text, Collins sustained a constant awareness of his readers' interests, providing a story that he hoped they could not put down, understanding that the construction of plot remained his primary strength. His flair for narrative made for well-told stories uninterrupted by digressions, sub-plots, or incidental detail.

Dickens, meanwhile, continued to influence his work, Collins telling his mother in April 1856 that if his friends 'knew that I had been reading my idea [of *The Dead Secret*] to

---

[1] Collins, quoted in Sue Lonoff, *Wilkie Collins and His Victorian Readers* (New York: AMS Press, 1982), 36. Source is a letter in the Parrish Collection at Princeton University dated 27 Apr. 1883.

Dickens—they would be sure to say when the book was published, that I had got all the good things in it from him'.[5] This, of course, was not the case, although Uncle Joseph, the Mozart-loving, German relative of Sarah Leeson in the novel is a gentle eccentric in the Dickens mould, while the misogynistic Andrew Treverton is a miser in the tradition of Scrooge and Grandfather Smallweed, while anticipating the miserly Michael and Noel Vanstone in Collins's own *No Name*. Yet Collins learned from Dickens's narrative experiments. *Basil*, for example, uses a first-person narrator, as found in *David Copperfield*, while *The Dead Secret* draws on such varied narrative voices as journals, letters, and autobiographical records as seen in *Bleak House*. He also learned not to control the reader too strongly; one should only '*suggest*, until the fulfilment comes' in the development of plot, concealing the mechanical.[6] Suspense and humour also began to blend in Collins's work, a quality seen in Dickens's own writing. But in the same letter, Collins wrote to his mother urging her *not* to reveal Dickens's role in the writing of *The Dead Secret*: '[Dickens] found out, as I had hoped, all the weak points in the story, and gave me the most inestimable hints for strengthening them.'[7]

Collaboration with Dickens between 1854 and 1856, however, led to various confusions, comic and otherwise. Collins, for example, appears to have written six of the eight parts of *The Seven Poor Travellers*, a comic short story of 1854 printed as an extra Christmas number of *Household Words*. 'Sister Rose', a story by Collins reprinted in his collection *After Dark*, appeared in America as a single volume by Charles Dickens in 1855. Critics frequently claimed for Dickens stories written or partially written by Collins, and admired stories by Collins when they were, in fact, written by Dickens. The two writers seemed more amused than troubled by the mix-ups, although Collins had hesitated to join the staff of *Household Words* because he felt his work might be thought to be Dickens's.

---

[5] Ibid. 44.

[6] Charles Dickens, in ibid. 46, from *The Letters of Charles Dickens*, ed. Walter Dexter (London: Constable, 1938), iii. 124–5.

[7] Lonoff, 46 (5 Apr. 1856).

In *The Dead Secret* too there are passages that, not surprisingly, seem Dickensian. One such moment is a description of a London evening when carriages fill the streets

with people in full dress, on their way to dinner, or on their way to the opera. The hawkers were shouting proclamations of news in the neighbouring square, with the second editions of the evening papers under their arms. People who had been serving behind the counter all day, were standing at the shop door to get a breath of fresh air . . . Idlers, who had come out after dinner, were lighting cigars at corners of streets, and looking about them, uncertain which way they should turn their steps next. It was just that transitional period of the evening at which the street-life of the day is almost over, and the street-life of the night has not quite begun. (p. 319)

While Dickens finished *Little Dorrit* in early May and tempted Collins with excursions to Brighton and beyond, Collins continued to struggle with *The Dead Secret* until he completed the final episode by the end of the month. It appeared in *Household Words* on 13 June 1857, and in the same month Bradbury & Evans issued the two-volume library edition.

Set in Cornwall at the mysterious Porthgenna Tower, *The Dead Secret* opens in 1829 with the dramatic death of Mrs Treverton, a former actress, who, moments before she expires, dictates a secret to her maid to be passed on to her husband. Sarah Leeson, the prematurely grey and mentally distracted maid, takes down her mistress's words, swearing to pass on the document; but inexplicably she decides to hide it in the Myrtle Room of the ruined north wing of Porthgenna Tower. She then flees, although not before stopping at the grave of one Hugh Polwheal, killed at the age of 26 in a mining accident. For added realism, Collins reproduces the inscription of the headstone (p. 36), as he will do later in *The Woman in White*. Fifteen years later Rosamond, the 'daughter' of Mrs Treverton, marries the blind Leonard Frankland, whose father had purchased Porthgenna Tower after Mrs Treverton's death.

Rosamond and Leonard plan to live at the Tower, although the death of her father delays their return. The premature birth of their child, occurring during their journey to Cornwall, further delays their arrival at the ancestral home. In the small village of West Winston, where the birth occurs, they encounter the disguised Sarah Leeson, now a housekeeper to a West Winston family. Calling herself Mrs Jazeph, she offers her services as nurse and a curious twenty-four hour period follows. 'An odd woman with an odd name', Mrs Jazeph acts suspiciously and dangerously, threatening Rosamond with a warning: 'When you go to Porthgenna, *keep out of the Myrtle Room!*' (pp. 102, 127). This, of course, has the opposite effect and outlines the plot for the balance of the novel.

Such a coincidence of events—that in a small Somerset town Sarah Leeson should turn up to become the nurse of Rosamond, despite her unusual behaviour, and offer such a bizarre warning about Porthgenna Tower—naturally makes the reader uneasy. Her warning to Rosamond not to enter the ironically named Myrtle Room (myrtle being the emblem of love and sacred to the goddess Venus) frightens the young woman, who, naturally, disregards it, but not before Sarah Leeson has fruitlessly searched for the hidden letter. Following various adventures, Rosamond, with the blind Leonard at her side, uncovers the 'dead secret': she is the illegitimate child of Sarah Leeson and the deceased miner, Hugh Polwheal. Mrs Treverton had deceived her husband into believing Rosamond was his child to sustain their love and satisfy his desperate desire for a child. She acted nobly in bringing up the girl, providing her with a good name and social status. But Rosamond suddenly feels she has deceived her own husband in marrying him, because she is low-born and illegitimate.

In a dramatic scene involving the telling of a story within the story, a meta-fictional moment that anticipates the remainder of the plot, Rosamond outlines a possible novel she might write about a woman who discovers a staggering truth: that she is not who she thought she was. She even scripts the ending in which the husband accepts the love and character of the woman. At that point, she reads the newly discovered letter to her husband, detailing the deception of Captain Treverton and the reason for it. She herself is referred to in the document as 'a love-child' (p. 286). Leonard nevertheless accepts her but, as a man of principle, he also tells Rosamond that since she is no longer the legitimate heir of the Treverton fortune, she must renounce it and pass it on to the miserly brother of the Captain, Andrew Treverton.

Reconciled to this sacrificial act, Rosamond soon realizes the need for compassion toward her mother and, through the assistance of the comic but kindly Uncle Joseph, she and her husband travel to London to locate the now gravely ill Sarah Leeson, who is using yet another alias, Mrs James. In a scene full of pathos, daughter and mother are reconciled as Rosamond nurses Sarah, inverting the earlier scene when the mother, as Mrs Jazeph, nursed the daughter and her infant son (pp. 337–41, 115–19). Granted forgiveness by her daughter, Sarah Leeson—a fallen woman now redeemed—dies, but not before confronting and defeating the ghost of the threatening Mrs Treverton (pp. 349–51). The reclusive Andrew Treverton, brother of the Captain, returns to the Franklands their falsely inherited fortune in a strange twist of the plot, and all concludes in relative happiness with a celebration of the verities love and truth in the sunshine of a summer's day.

Revealing long-hidden secrets was not a new ploy in Collins's fiction. In *Basil* and *Hide and Seek*, secrets were instrumental to his story. In the former it was the secret marriage of Basil with Margaret Sherwin. In *Hide and Seek*, Matthew Marksman uncovers the secret past of Zackary's father, once the mysterious 'Arthur Carr'. Secrets, whether in short stories like 'Brother Griffith's Story of the Family Secret' (first published in May 1857) or elaborated in Sir Percivale Glyde's parentage in *The Woman in White*, fascinated Collins who, at the time of *The Dead Secret*, was himself leading a secret private life with Caroline Graves.

Complementing secrets is setting. As in Collins's first three published novels, setting is significant for *The Dead Secret*, although it is not overly detailed despite the striking Cornish locale. His descriptions of the coast are full of foreboding but limited, drawing on his summer trip to Cornwall in 1850 which he recounted in 1851 as *Rambles Beyond Railways*. Travelling about Cornwall on foot, he and his companion, the artist

Henry Brandling, discovered unusual people, startling land-
scapes, and remarkable food. His account mixed history, leg-
end, and statistics with social commentary and humour. One
of the highlights was a descent into a mine under the sea, his
miner's outfit uncommonly large: 'The same mysterious dis-
pensation of fate, which always awards tall wives to short men,
decreed that a suit of the big miner's should be reserved for me.
He stood six feet two inches—I stand five feet six inches.'[8] The
walking tour of Cornwall was the principal source of his Cornish information for his next novel, *Basil* (1852) and later for
The Dead Secret.

Despite its Cornish setting and use of local geographical
terms—'Porth' in Cornish means harbour, cove, or landing
place; in the novel, Porthgenna Tower is both a building and a
village to mark a harbour or cove—no characters use Cornish
dialect. Cornish servants, residents, and workers, regardless of
class, speak with the same diction as those from other parts of
England. Collins's only experimentation with language occurs
with Uncle Joseph, the Mozart-loving German cabinet-maker
who owns a shop in Truro, and who speaks a Germanized English replete with mistakes that only enhances his amiability.

No single country house is the source of Porthgenna Tower;
it is probably an amalgamation of a series of buildings Collins
remembered from his 1850 sojourn. Pengersick Castle, of
which only a tower still stands, and its association with a mur-
der, may be one location; another is Lanhydrock House, a
great seventeenth-century home with a north gallery 116 feet
long, facing a large, three-sided court. As Porthgenna Tower
has only its west, south, and north sides standing, so, too, does
Lanhydrock House, whose east wing was demolished in 1780.
The principal entrance to the Porthgenna Tower was the west
front, 'approached by a terrace road that overlooked the sea'
(p. 171). The smaller entrance on the south side of the building, however, was generally used; it 'led through the servants'
office to the great hall and the west staircase' (p. 171).

---

[8] Wilkie Collins, *Rambles Beyond Railways, or, Notes in Cornwall taken A-
Foot*, new edn. (London: Bentley, 1861), 159. All further references to this
edition.

Another—and perhaps the most likely—source for Collins's Porthgenna Tower is Lanherne House, located near the sea in the Vale of Mawgan (as Collins called it), today the Vale of Lanherne, near the town of St Columb Major. Described at length in *Rambles Beyond Railways* because of its unusual history and use as a Carmelite nunnery since 1794 (an engraving of the building is included in the 2nd edition of *Rambles*, 1852), Lanherne House is impregnated with mystery. Once owned by the Arundels, one of the few Cornish families of Norman origin, the house is situated next to a small church above the centre of a scattered village. Almost anticipating the plot of *The Dead Secret*, Collins writes in *Rambles*, 'imagine the externals of the life which those massy walls keep secret', urging one to 'look deeper than the surface . . . to strip the inner life of the convent of all its mysteries and coverings . . . anatomising it inch by inch, search[ing] it through down to the very heart'. 'Should we pry into the dread and secret processes by which . . . one human emotion after another may be suffering, first ossification, then death?', he asks.[9] With its combination of ancient and modern sections, the manor house possesses a remarkable power to evoke a mysterious past, and may have suggested the central location of the novel.

In the text, the steward, Mr Munder, celebrates the reputation of Porthgenna Tower when he responds to a casual reference to it being a 'fine big house, [with] a very good staircase' by Uncle Joseph:

'We are not accustomed to hear either the house or the staircase spoken of in these terms, sir,' said Mr Munder, resolving to nip the foreigner's familiarity in the bud. 'The Guide to West Cornwall, which you would have done well to make yourself acquainted with before you came here, describes Porthgenna Tower as a Mansion, and uses the word Spacious in speaking of the west staircase. I regret to find, sir, that you have not consulted the Guide Book to West Cornwall.' (p. 183)

Collins made up the name of the reference work, but he likely found its origin in *A Handbook for Travellers in Cornwall*, the last in John Murray's popular series of travel handbooks for England, and possible source of the details of Cornish geography

---

[9] Ibid. 228–9.

Collins constantly refers to, enhancing the realism of his fiction.

Polwheal, the family name of the miner whose grave Sarah Leeson visits twice in the book, reveals another source for the novel. The name derives from Richard Polwhele, a Cornish man of letters who published a multi-volume *History of Cornwall* between 1803 and 1808, cited by Collins in the *Rambles*. (Polwhele also wrote *The Art of Eloquence: A Didactic Poem* (1785) and *A Cornish–English Vocabulary* (1808). His three-volume *Biographical Sketches in Cornwall* appeared in 1831.) The borrowing shows how Collins relied heavily on factual sources for his early fictional material, and that while his plots involved invention, his content often drew more from history and historical figures.

In *The Dead Secret*, descriptions of Porthgenna Tower, and its crumbling north section with its low tower, take precedence over landscape or any emphasis on natural details. The ruined state of the house indicates its moral as well as physical decay, while the intended repairs, the physical changes necessary for the building to survive, mirror the moral changes necessary to renew the life within its walls.

Of further importance to the novel is the Gothic element, which is gradually blended with the domestic to form what is particularly 'sensational' in Collins's fiction. A ruined home with a mysterious past supplemented by a possible ghost—that of Mrs Treverton—and the hint of a crime, are all features of Gothic fiction since Mrs Radcliffe's *Mysteries of Udolpho*, linked to the domestic and repeated throughout the novel. The representation of the house itself is sinister and suggestive, bordering on the sensational:

There, below them, was the dark, lonesome, spacious structure of Porthgenna Tower, with the sunlight already stealing round towards the windows of the west front! There was the path winding away to it gracefully over the brown moor, in curves of dazzling white! There, lower down, was the solitary old church, with the peaceful burial-ground nestling by its side! . . . there, beyond all, was the changeless glory of the sea, with its old seething lines of white foam, with the old winding margin of its yellow shores! (p. 167)

An exception to the architectural focus is a descriptive

passage on landscape displaying Collins's painterly skills. Returning to the drawing room of the house in possession of the secret, Rosamond considers how to tell her husband what she has discovered. But Collins diverts the reader, prolonging the suspense with Rosamond's gaze out the window and suggestive reading of the gloomy landscape:

The heat-mist still hid the horizon. Nearer, the oily, colourless surface of the water was just visible, heaving slowly from time to time in one vast monotonous wave that rolled itself out smoothly and endlessly till it was lost in the white obscurity of the mist. Close on the shore, the noisy surf was hushed. No sound came from the beach except at long, wearily long intervals, when a quick thump, and a still splash, just audible and no more, announced the fall of one tiny, mimic wave upon the parching sand . . . Not a human figure was to be seen anywhere on the shore. (pp. 279–80)

The suggestion in the novel that the north rooms could not be visited because of a ghost only intensifies the anxiety of the characters and suspicion of the readers. Uncle Joseph, accompanying his niece Sarah Leeson on a tour of the house on their return, nervously remarks, 'As I am a living sinner, this going over the house is like going to a funeral!' (p. 182).

Suspense is everywhere in this novel, despite Collins's revelation of the secret early in the text. And although he manages to exclude or omit the moments of danger, he never lessens the threat. In the opening we do not actually witness how Sarah Leeson hides the note dictated by Mrs Treverton when she secretly visits the Myrtle Room. But neither do we attend the actual wedding of Rosamond Treverton and Leonard Frankland, or participate in the curious history of Porthgenna Tower which had been sold to Leonard Frankland's father after the death of Mrs Treverton. Events are reported, not enacted for the reader. This form of narrative creates a mystery in the story-telling itself, which must rely on second-hand and sometimes circumstantial details. The reader has to reconstruct the actions of Sarah Leeson from evidence gradually revealed in the text. Only in Book V, Chapter V, when Rosamond and Leonard carefully scrutinize the Myrtle Room for the secret, does the reader discover the truth. In making the reader part of the action of discovery, Collins intensifies the suspense.

The Dead Secret also enlarges Collins's fascination with physical handicaps. In *Hide and Seek*, it was the deafness of Mary or 'Madonna' Grice; in *After Dark*, the temporary blindness of the narrator, the portrait painter William Kerby. In *The Dead Secret*, it is the blindness of Leonard Frankland, explained in Book II, Chapter I, as the result of poor health and eye-strain caused by his career as a watchmaker. There is also a criticism of medical practice, which is unable to prevent his blindness, despite visits to oculists in London and Paris—and a treatment which involves blistering him behind the ears and between the shoulders, drenching him with mercury, and keeping him in a dark room (p. 48). Later, the newly appointed doctor in the village of West Winston, Mr Orridge, successful in delivering Rosamond's baby, is less acute in his diagnosis of Sarah Leeson: 'at first glance, his medical eye detected that some of the intricate machinery of the nervous system had gone wrong with Mrs Jazeph.' A tic in her facial muscles and unusual flush to her cheeks lead to a study of her eyes: 'He observed a strangely scared look in her eyes, and remarked that it did not leave them when the rest of her face became gradually composed. "That woman has had some dreadful fright, some great grief, or some wasting complaint," he thought to himself. "I wonder which it is?"' (pp. 102–3). These suspicions anticipate the suppositional nature of medical knowledge in both *The Woman in White*, with its discussion of mental illness and scene at the sanatorium where the kidnapped Laura, Lady Glyde, is mistakenly imprisoned, and *The Moonstone* with Ezra Jennings and the doctor, Mr Candy.

Deepening the reader's interest and focusing the concern with mental illness is the character of the disturbed servant, Sarah Leeson, Rosamond's real mother. She is the most complex character yet to appear in Collins's fiction. Middle-aged and on the verge of a nervous breakdown, she is plagued by anxieties and insecurities. An unusual character for a Victorian novel in that her instability is so carefully detailed, she is also the centre of the plot as keeper of the 'dead secret', although thematically, of course, Collins shows that no secret can ever remain 'dead'.

Love for her child enforces silence on the maid, but her obligation to carry out her mistress's command to tell her husband the truth about their daughter after her death forces a painful decision to protect her child's position. Class, not truth, compels her to remain silent. But Sarah Leeson seems too challenging a character for Collins at this stage in his career. Instead of remaining the compelling figure of the opening chapters, physically distinctive and uniquely attractive—'few men, at first sight of her, could have resisted the desire to find out who she was' (p. 10)—she distracts the reader and dulls the plot in the second half of the book because of her secondary role, subordinate to the aggressive Rosamond and the likeable Uncle Joseph. Except for her description of being haunted by the dead Mrs Treverton and her deathbed confession at the end of the novel, which successfully dramatizes why and how she hid the secret (pp. 155–6, 334–51), Sarah becomes a minor figure.

Rosamond Treverton, her illegitimate daughter, is the opposite of her nervous, uncertain mother. She is decisive, quick-tempered, confident. She masterfully consoles and controls her blind husband. She is quick to anger and yet quick to forgive, while never hesitant in her determination and curiosity to locate the secret in the prohibited Myrtle Room. And through her ingenuity, she finds the secret hidden in the picture frame of a small, oval portrait of a wicked-looking woman, supposedly the Porthgenna ghost, a portrait hated by Mrs Treverton because 'the painted face had a strange likeness to hers' (p. 349).

Rosamond is one of Collins's earliest strong-minded and active heroines: she guides the blind Leonard Frankland emotionally as well as physically, and like a series of other women, from Marian Halcombe in *The Woman in White* to Rachel Verinder in *The Moonstone* and Lucilla Finch, the blind heroine of *Poor Miss Finch*, demonstrates independence and determination. Collins's heroines are forthright explorers who do not tolerate deception and often dominate their men. The only masters of women in Collins's fiction are the reprobates and rogues: Count Fosco in *The Woman in White*, who supervises his wife, Captain Wragge from *No Name*, who rules the gigantic Matilda, or Miserrimus Dexter from *The Law and The Lady*, who commands his servant.

The role of women in *The Dead Secret* is reinforced by the way their writing, reading, and action structure the novel: Sarah Leeson writes down and then hides the words of Mrs Treverton; Rosamond, not her husband, is the detective who locates the hidden record. Illegitimacy, a theme which will recur in *The Woman in White* and *No Name*, can be obscured but never lost. Buried writing is the focus of the novel—writing dictated, composed, and concealed by women—and kept secret from men. Hidden texts haunt *The Woman in White* too, where secret diaries and altered parish records influence the plot. In *The Moonstone*, Ezra Jennings requests that all his papers, including his new book on psychology, be buried with him in an unmarked grave, while Rosanna Spearman records her transgressive love for an upper-class man in a letter that sinks beneath the surface of the quicksand into which she later throws herself. Through literally hidden narratives, Collins uncovers the subversive that lurks beneath the surface of the conventional.

Sarah Leeson, figuring as 'the Other' in *The Dead Secret*, is threatening, unknown, dangerous. When Rosamond discovers that she is Sarah's daughter, she, too, is dispossessed. She loses not only her fortune and status, but also her identity, anticipating Laura, Lady Glyde's misfortune, in *The Woman in White*. Rosamond also forecasts a later illegitimate heroine in Collins's work, Magdalen Vanstone, who similarly has 'no name'.

Prefiguring the issue of mistaken identity in *The Dead Secret* is a scene where Sarah and Mrs Treverton, just before the child is born, exchange clothes and positions: 'You are the married lady, Mrs Treverton, and I am your maid who waits on you, Sarah Leeson', Mrs Treverton explains to the surprised young woman (p. 331). In this way, the servant will be saved from disgrace and ruin and her mistress will have a child to present to her husband, who has for so long cherished the wish to be a father. His declaration to his wife on his return from a lengthy sea voyage to discover his child confirms this view: 'I have never loved you, Rosamond, as I love you now' (p. 287).[10]

---

[10] The 1873 American reprint of the novel contains a significant misprint at this passage. It reads: 'I have never loved you, Rosamond, as I love you know.' See the Dover reprint of the 1873 Harper & Brothers edition, p. 283.

Collins clearly found such a switch in identity fascinating. In *The Woman in White* he shows the manipulative use of such an exchange in the abduction and imprisonment of Laura as the disturbed Anne Catherick, rescued by Marian Halcombe and Walter Hartright from a London asylum. In Collins's next novel, *No Name* (1862), the adventurous Magdalen Vanstone, once an actress (as was Mrs Treverton), alters her identity twice: first, when she successfully disguises herself as Miss Garth, the governess of the Vanstone sisters, and gains an interview with the sinister Mrs Lecount and the weak Noel Vanstone; second, when she exchanges her identity with her maid Louisa in order to be hired as a parlour-maid at the isolated manor house of St Crux where she hopes to locate a hidden document. 'Instead of your waiting on me, as usual, I will wait on you,' she tells the maid. 'When the week is over . . . we will leave this place, and go into other lodgings—you as the mistress; and I as the maid.'[11] A fortune revoked and a potentially illegimate child (that of the servant Louisa) are further parallels between *The Dead Secret* and *No Name*. Clearly, the themes of the former novel held sway over Collins as he constructed his later work.

Offsetting the tension of discovery and danger that encompasses *The Dead Secret* are a series of comic figures: Mr Phippen, 'A Martyr to Dyspepsia', whose grey eyes rolled from side to side 'in a moist state of admiration of something or somebody' (p. 41); the perpetually smiling governess, Miss Sturch, whose 'inexhaustible vocabulary of commonplace talk' dribbled 'placidly out of her lips whenever it was called for' (pp. 41–2); and the cabinet-maker who adores Mozart, Uncle Joseph. Action too is sometimes comically presented. As the steward Mr Munder and the housekeeper Mrs Pentreath show the returning Sarah Leeson and her Uncle Joseph about Porthgenna Tower, the housekeeper walks in a slow, stately manner, 'adapting her pace with feminine pliancy to the pace of the steward, [and] walked the national Sabbatarian Polonaise by his side, as if she was out with him for a mouthful of fresh air

---

[11] Wilkie Collins, *No Name*, ed. Virginia Blain (Oxford: Oxford World's Classics, 1987), 453.

between the services' (p. 182). Such comic characters anticipate later figures like the governess Mrs Vesey in *The Woman in
White*, or Gabriel Betteredge or Miss Clack in *The Moonstone*.

Music is another feature of *The Dead Secret* which Collins
later elaborated. Uncle Joseph's love of Mozart anticipates
Count Fosco's love of Rossini, especially *The Barber of Seville*.
Uncle Joseph's constant companion is a music-box that plays
the minuet from Mozart's *Don Giovanni*; repeatedly, he listens
to the air, 'Batti, Batti'. Rosamond plays Weber for her husband. Music actually accelerates the plot: Uncle Joseph's
enthusiasm for a music-box in Porthgenna Tower diverts the
housekeeper and steward, allowing Sarah Leeson to escape
into the mysterious north wing. Collins enlarges his love of
music in *The Woman in White*, where Laura also admires and
performs Mozart, apparently Collins's favourite composer.[12]

An 1877 stage adaptation of *The Dead Secret* marked its continued appeal. On 29 August 1877 it premièred at the Royal
Lyceum Theatre in London under the direction of Henry Irv-
ing. Miss Bateman starred as Sarah Leeson. Adapted by E. W.
Bramwell with the permission of Collins, the novel became a
three-act play with a prologue, although unlike the stage suc-
cesses of *The New Magdalen*, *Miss Gwilt* (the stage version of
Armadale), or *The Moonstone*, the stage version of *The Dead
Secret* made little impression on the public and closed shortly
after it opened.

Kathleen Tillotson once identified the 'purest type of sensation novel' as 'the novel-with-a-secret; a secret of whose effects
the reader is made aware just so far as to excite his continued
curiosity'.[13] Wilkie Collins's *The Dead Secret* is a critical step in
the evolution of this genre, possessing at its centre a dark secret
and, at its edge, enough curiosity to propel the reader onward.

---

[12] Kenneth Robinson, *Wilkie Collins: A Biography* (London: Bodley Head,
1951), 155.

[13] Kathleen Tillotson, 'Introduction: The Lighter Reading of the Eighteen-
Sixties', in Collins, *The Woman in White*, ed. Anthea Trodd (Boston: Riverside,
1969), p. xv.

NOTE ON THE TEXT

The text of this edition is that of the one-volume edition published by Sampson Low in January 1861 with a new preface, and an engraved frontispiece by the noted Victorian artist John Gilbert. It is the latest version of the novel reviewed, although not revised, by Collins and contains his important preface contradicting his critics. The title-page of this edition lists the work as a 'New Edition', although other than the addition of the preface, no substantial textual changes occurred. The title of the frontispiece, 'Timon of London', refers to the miserly Andrew Treverton and his servant Shrowl and is taken from Book III, Chapter I. It depicts an accusatory Andrew Treverton pointing to his servant and exclaiming 'What do you mean by that? You ugly brute, you've got a clean shirt on!'

The novel originally appeared in twenty-three parts in Dickens's *Household Words* from 3 January 1857 to 13 June 1857. It simultaneously appeared in the United States, first in *Harper's Weekly* from 24 January to 27 June 1857 and then, without the author's name, in *Littell's Living Age* (Boston) in fourteen parts between 28 February 1857 and 18 July 1857. Bradbury & Evans published the first edition in two volumes in June 1857, coinciding with its serial completion, followed by the one-volume edition in 1861. The novel was reprinted more than twelve times before the end of the nineteenth century. The first US edition (in one volume) appeared in 1857, published in New York by Miller & Curtis, and was reprinted in America throughout Collins's lifetime. Translations into Russian appeared in 1857 and 1861; into French in 1858. The 1877 adaptation for the London stage was by E. B. Bramwell.

SELECT BIBLIOGRAPHY

BIOGRAPHIES

The most recent and comprehensive biography is *King of Inventors: A Life of Wilkie Collins* by Catherine Peters (London, 1991, 1992). William M. Clarke's *The Secret Life of Wilkie Collins* (London, 1988, 1996) details Collins's unorthodox private life and two households, citing his work only when it pertains to the events of his life. The earlier biography by Kenneth Robinson, *Wilkie Collins* (London, 1951; repr. 1974) is still of interest, as are the four chapters of Dorothy Sayers's unfinished *Wilkie Collins: A Biographical and Critical Study*, ed. E. R. Gregory (Toledo, Ohio, 1977). Nuel Pharr Davis's *The Life of Wilkie Collins* (Urbana, Ill., 1956) attempts to give equal attention to the life and work.

CRITICAL AND BACKGROUND STUDIES

The Dead Secret received only modest attention from critics when it appeared, although journalists reviewed it extensively. For contemporary reviews see those collected by Norman Page in *Wilkie Collins: The Critical Heritage* (London, 1974; 1985), which also includes an extract from Émile Forgues's essay on Collins in the *Revue des deux mondes* from 1855. There are several pages on *The Dead Secret* by Robert Ashley in *Wilkie Collins* (London, 1952), as well as discussions of the novel in William H. Marshall, *Wilkie Collins* (New York, 1970); Sue Lonoff, *Wilkie Collins and His Victorian Readers* (New York, 1982); Tamar Heller, *Dead Secrets: Wilkie Collins and The Female Gothic* (New Haven, Conn., 1992); and Peter Thoms, *The Windings of the Labyrinth, Quest and Structure in the Major Novels of Wilkie Collins* (Athens, Ohio, 1992). A useful essay is Robert Ashley's 'A Second Look at *The Dead Secret*', *Wilkie Collins Society Journal* (1983), 21–5. For background on Cornwall, see Wilkie Collins, *Rambles Beyond Railways*.

BIBLIOGRAPHIES

There is no exhaustive and accurate bibliography of Wilkie Collins's writings; however, the following are useful. R. V. Andrew, *Wilkie Collins: A Critical Survey of his Prose Fiction, with a Bibliography* (New York, 1979); R. Ashley, 'Wilkie Collins', *Victorian Fiction: A Second Guide to Research* (New York, 1978); K. H. Beetz, *Wilkie Collins: An Annotated Bibliography, 1889–1976* (London, 1978), and 'Wilkie Collins Studies, 1972–1983', *Dickens Studies Annual*, 13 (1984), 333–55; Andrew Gasson, 'Wilkie Collins: A Collector's and Bibliographer's Challenge', *Private Library* (Summer 1980), 3: 51–77; M. L. Parrish, *Wilkie Collins and Charles Reade: First Editions Described with Notes* (London, 1940; repr. 1968); M. Sadleir, *XIX Century Fiction* (London, 1951), i. 376–7, and ii. 27; Robert L. Wolff, 'Wilkie Collins', *Nineteenth Century Fiction: A Bibliographical Catalogue* (New York, 1981–6).

A CHRONOLOGY OF WILKIE COLLINS

Life	*Historical and Cultural Background*
1824 (8 Jan.) Born at 11 New Cavendish Street, St Marylebone, London, elder son of William Collins, RA (1788–1847), artist, and Harriet Collins, née Geddes (1790–1868).	Death of Byron. Scott, *Redgauntlet*
1825	Stockton–Darlington railway opened. Hazlitt *Spirit of the Age*
1826 (Spring) Family moves to Pond Street, Hampstead	
1827	Death of Blake; University College London founded.
1828 (25 Jan.) Brother, Charles Allston Collins, born.	Birth of Meredith, D. G. Rossetti; Catholic Emancipation Act.
1829 (Autumn) Family moves to Hampstead Square.	Balzac's *La Comédie humaine* begins publication
1830 Family moves to Porchester Terrace, Bayswater.	Death of George IV and accession of William IV; July Revolution in France. Hugo, *Hernani* Tennyson, *Poems Chiefly Lyrical*
1831	British Association for the Advancement of Science founded; Britain annexes Mysore.
1832	Deaths of Bentham, Crabbe, Goethe, Scott; First Reform Bill passed.
1833	Slavery abolished throughout British Empire. Carlyle, *Sartor Resartus*
1834	Deaths of Coleridge, Lamb; new Poor Law comes into effect; Tolpuddle Martyrs.
1835 (13 Jan.) Starts school, the Maida Hill Academy.	Dickens, *Sketches by Boz* (1st series)
1836 (19 Sept.–15 Aug. 1838) Family visits France and Italy.	
1837	Death of William IV and accession of Victoria. Carlyle, *The French Revolution* Dickens, *Pickwick Papers*

Life	Historical and Cultural Background
1838 (Aug.) Family moves to 20 Avenue Road, Regent's Park. Attends Mr Cole's boarding school, Highbury Place, until Dec. 1840.	Anti-Corn Law League founded; Chartist petitions published; London–Birmingham railway opened; Anglo-Afghan War Dickens, *Oliver Twist*
1840 (Summer) Family moves to 85 Oxford Terrace, Bayswater.	Birth of Hardy; marriage of Victoria and Albert; penny postage introduced. Browning, *Sordello* Darwin, *Voyage of H.M.S. Beagle* Dickens, *The Old Curiosity Shop*
1841 (Jan.) Apprenticed to Antrobus & Co., tea merchants, Strand.	Carlyle, *Heroes and Hero-Worship*
1842 (June–July) Trip to Highlands of Scotland, and Shetland, with William Collins.	Child and female underground labour becomes illegal; Chartist riots; Act for inspection of asylums. Browning, *Dramatic Lyrics* Comte, *Cours de philosophie positive*, Macaulay, *Lays of Ancient Rome*, Tennyson, *Poems*
1843 (Aug.) First signed publication 'The Last Stage Coachman' in the *Illuminated Magazine*.	Birth of Henry James; Thames Tunnel opened. Carlyle, *Past and Present* Dickens, *A Christmas Carol* Ruskin, *Modern Painters* begins publication
1844 Writes his first (unpublished) novel, 'Iolani; or Tahiti as it was; a Romance'.	Factory Act. Chambers, *Vestiges of the Natural History of Creation* Elizabeth Barrett, *Poems*
1845 (Jan.) 'Iolani' submitted to Chapman & Hall, rejected (8 Mar.).	Boom in railway speculation; Newman joins Church of Rome. Disraeli, *Sybil* Engels, *Condition of the Working Class in England in 1844* Poe, *Tales of Mystery and Imagination*
1846 (17 May) Admitted student of Lincoln's Inn.	Repeal of Corn Laws; Irish potato famine. Lear, *Book of Nonsense*
1847 (17 Feb.) Death of William Collins.	Ten-hour Factory Act; California gold rush. Emily Brontë, *Wuthering Heights* Charlotte Brontë, *Jane Eyre* Tennyson, *The Princess*

Life	*Historical and Cultural Background*
1848 (Summer) Family move to 38 Blandford Square. (Nov.) First book, *Memoirs of the Life of William Collins, Esq., R.A.* published.	Death of Emily Brontë; Pre-Raphaelite Brotherhood founded; Chartist Petition; cholera epidemic; Public Health Act; revolutions in Europe. Dickens, *Dombey and Son* Gaskell, *Mary Barton* Marx and Engels, *Communist Manifesto* Thackeray, *Vanity Fair*
1849 Exhibits a painting at the Royal Academy summer exhibition.	Thackeray, *Pendennis* Ruskin, *Seven Lamps of Architecture*
1850 (27 Feb.) First published novel, *Antonina*. (Summer) Family move to 17 Hanover Terrace.	Deaths of Balzac, Wordsworth; Tennyson becomes Poet Laureate; Public Libraries Act. Dickens, *David Copperfield* Charles Kingsley, *Alton Locke* Tennyson, *In Memoriam* Wordsworth, *The Prelude* Dickens starts *Household Words*
1851 (Jan.) Travel book on Cornwall, *Rambles Beyond Railways*, published. (Mar.) Meets Dickens for the first time. (May) Acts with Dickens in Bulwer-Lytton's *Not So Bad as We Seem*.	Death of Turner; Great Exhibition in Hyde Park; Australian gold rush. Ruskin, *The Stones of Venice*
1852 (Jan.) *Mr Wray's Cash Box* published, with frontispiece by Millais. (24 Apr.) 'A Terribly Strange Bed', first contribution to *Household Words*. (May) Goes on tour with Dickens's company of amateur actors. (16 Nov.) *Basil* published.	Death of Wellington; Louis Napoleon becomes Emperor of France. Stowe, *Uncle Tom's Cabin* Thackeray, *Henry Esmond*
1853 (Oct.–Dec.) Tours Switzerland and Italy with Dickens and Augustus Egg.	Arnold, *Poems* Charlotte Brontë, *Villette* Dickens, *Bleak House* Gaskell, *Cranford*
1854 (5 June) *Hide and Seek* published.	Birth of Wilde; outbreak of Crimean War; Working Men's College founded. Dickens, *Hard Times*

Life

Historical and Cultural Background

1855 (Feb.) Spends a holiday in Paris with Dickens. (16 June) First play, *The Lighthouse*, performed by Dickens's theatrical company at Tavistock House. (Nov.–Dec.) *Mad Monkton* serialized.

Death of Charlotte Brontë.
Browning, *Men and Women*
Gaskell, *North and South*
Trollope, *The Warden*

1856 (Feb.) *After Dark*, a collection of short stories, published. (Feb.–Apr.) Spends six weeks in Paris with Dickens. (Mar.) *A Rogue's Life* serialized in *Household Words*. (Oct.) Joins staff of *Household Words* and begins collaboration with Dickens in *The Wreck of the Golden Mary* (Dec.).

Birth of Freud, Shaw; Crimean War ends.
E. B. Browning, *Aurora Leigh*

1857 (Jan.–June) *The Dead Secret* serialized in *Household Words*, published in volume form (June). (6 Jan.) *The Frozen Deep* performed by Dickens's theatrical company at Tavistock House. (Aug.) *The Lighthouse* performed at the Olympic Theatre. (Sept.) Spends a working holiday in the Lake District with Dickens, their account appearing as *The Lazy Tour of Two Idle Apprentices*, serialized in *Household Words*. (Oct.) Collaborates with Dickens on *The Perils of Certain English Prisoners*.

Birth of Conrad; Matrimonial Causes Act establishes divorce courts; Indian Mutiny.
Dickens, *Little Dorrit*
Flaubert, *Madame Bovary*
Trollope, *Barchester Towers*

1858 (May) Dickens separates from his wife. (Oct.) *The Red Vial* produced at the Olympic Theatre; a failure.

Victoria proclaimed Empress of India.
Eliot, *Scenes of Clerical Life*

Life	*Historical and Cultural Background*
1859 From this year no longer living with his mother; lives for the rest of his life (with one interlude) with Mrs Caroline Graves. (Jan.–Feb.) Living at 124 Albany Street. (May–Dec.) Living at 2a Cavendish Street. (Apr.) *All the Year Round* begins publication. (Oct.) *The Queen of Hearts*, a collection of short stories, published. (26 Nov.–25 Aug. 1860) *The Woman in White* serialized in *All the Year Round*. (Dec.) Moves to 12 Harley Street.	War of Italian Liberation. Darwin, *Origin of Species* Eliot, *Adam Bede* Meredith, *The Ordeal of Richard Feverel* Mill, *On Liberty* Samuel Smiles, *Self-Help* Tennyson, *Idylls of the King*
1860 (Aug.) *The Woman in White* published in volume form: a bestseller in Britain and the United States, and rapidly translated into most European languages.	British Association meeting at Oxford (Huxley–Wilberforce debate). Eliot, *The Mill on the Floss*
1861 (Jan.) Resigns from *All the Year Round*.	Death of Albert, Prince Consort; Offences Against the Person Act (includes provisions on bigamy); outbreak of American Civil War. Dickens, *Great Expectations* Eliot, *Silas Marner* Palgrave, *Golden Treasury* Reade, *The Cloister and the Hearth*
1862 (15 Mar.–17 Jan. 1863) *No Name* serialized in *All the Year Round*, published in volume form 31 Dec.	Clough, *Poems*
1863 *My Miscellanies*, a collection of journalism from *Household Words* and *All the Year Round*, published.	Death of Thackeray. Eliot, *Romola* Huxley, *Man's Place in Nature* Lyell, *Antiquity of Man* Mill, *Utilitarianism*
1864 (Nov.–June 1866) *Armadale* serialized in *The Cornhill*. (Dec.) Moves to 9 Melcombe Place, Dorset Square.	Albert Memorial constructed. Newman, *Apologia pro Vita Sua*

Life	*Historical and Cultural Background*
1865	Birth of Kipling, Yeats; death of Gaskell. Arnold, *Essays in Criticism* (1st series) Carroll, *Alice's Adventures in Wonderland* Dickens, *Our Mutual Friend* Tolstoy, *War and Peace* Wagner, *Tristan und Isolde*
1866 (May) *Armadale* published in two volumes. (Oct.) *The Frozen Deep* produced at the Olympic Theatre.	Birth of Wells. Dostoyevsky, *Crime and Punishment* Swinburne, *Poems and Ballads*
1867 (Sept.) Moves to 90 Gloucester Place, Portman Square. Collaborates with Dickens on *No Thoroughfare*, published as Christmas Number of *All the Year Round*; dramatic version performed at the Adelphi Theatre (Christmas Eve).	Second Reform Bill passed; Paris Exhibition. Bagehot, *English Constitution* Marx, *Das Kapital*
1868 (4 Jan.–8 Aug.) *The Moonstone* serialized in *All the Year Round*; published in three volumes (July). (19 Mar.) Mother, Harriet Collins, dies; Collins forms liaison with Martha Rudd ('Mrs Dawson'). (4 Oct.) Caroline Graves marries Joseph Charles Clow.	Report of Royal Commission on the Laws of Marriage. Browning, *The Ring and the Book*
1869 (Mar.) *Black and White*, written in collaboration with Charles Fechter, produced at the Adelphi Theatre. (4 July) Daughter, Marian Dawson, born to Collins and Martha Rudd, at 33 Bolsover Street, Portland Place.	Suez Canal opened. Arnold, *Culture and Anarchy* Mill, *On the Subjection of Women*
1870 (June) *Man and Wife* published in volume form. (9 June) Dickens dies. (Aug.) Dramatic version of *The Woman in White* tried out in Leicester.	Education Act; Married Woman's Property Act; Franco-Prussian War; fall of Napoleon III. D. G. Rossetti, *Poems* Spencer, *Principles of Psychology*

Life	*Historical and Cultural Background*
1871 (14 May) Second daughter, Harriet Constance Dawson, born at 33 Bolsover Street. (May) Caroline Graves again living with Collins. (Oct.) *The Woman in White* produced at the Olympic Theatre. (Oct.–Mar. 1872) *Poor Miss Finch* serialized in *Cassell's Magazine*. (25 Dec.) *Miss or Mrs?* published.	Trades unions become legal; first Impressionist Exhibition held in Paris; religious tests abolished at Oxford, Cambridge, Durham. Darwin, *Descent of Man* Eliot, *Middlemarch*
1872 (Feb.) *Poor Miss Finch* published in volume form.	Butler, *Erewhon*
1873 (Feb.) Dramatic version of *Man and Wife* performed at the Prince of Wales Theatre. (9 Apr.) Brother, Charles Allston Collins, dies. (May) *The New Magdalen* published in volume form; dramatic version performed at the Olympic Theatre. *Miss or Mrs? And Other Stories in Outline* published. (Sept.–Mar. 1874) Tours United States and Canada, giving readings from his work.	Mill, *Autobiography* Pater, *Studies in the Renaissance*
1874 (Nov.) *The Frozen Deep and Other Stories*. (25 Dec.) Son, William Charles Dawson, born, 10 Taunton Place, Regent's Park.	Factory Act; Public Worship Act. Hardy, *Far from the Madding Crowd*
1875 Copyrights in Collins's work transferred to Chatto & Windus, who become his main publisher. *The Law and the Lady* serialized in *The London Graphic*; published in volume form.	Artisans' Dwellings Act; Public Health Act.
1876 (Apr.) *Miss Gwilt* (dramatic version of *Armadale*) performed at the Globe Theatre. *The Two Destinies* published in volume form.	Invention of telephone and phonograph. Eliot, *Daniel Deronda* James, *Roderick Hudson* Lombroso, *The Criminal*

Life	*Historical and Cultural Background*
1877 (Sept.) Dramatic version of *The Moonstone* performed at the Olympic Theatre. *My Lady's Money* and *Percy and the Prophet*, short stories, published.	Annexation of Transvaal. Ibsen, *The Pillars of Society* Tolstoy, *Anna Karenina*
1878 (June–Nov.) *The Haunted Hotel* serialized.	Whistler–Ruskin controversy; Congress of Berlin; Edison invents the incandescent electric lamp. Hardy, *The Return of the Native*
1879 *The Haunted Hotel* published in volume form. *The Fallen Leaves—First Series* published in volume form. *A Rogue's Life* published in volume form.	Birth of E. M. Forster. Ibsen, *A Doll's House*
1880 *Jezebel's Daughter* published in volume form.	Death of George Eliot, Flaubert; Bradlaugh, an atheist, becomes an MP. Gissing, *Workers in the Dawn* Zola, *Nana*
1881 *The Black Robe* published in volume form; A. P. Watt becomes Collins's literary agent.	Death of Carlyle; Democratic Federation founded. Ibsen, *Ghosts* James, *Portrait of a Lady*
1882	Birth of Joyce, Woolf; death of Darwin, D. G. Rossetti, Trollope; Married Woman's Property Act; Daimler invents the petrol engine.
1883 *Heart and Science* published in volume form. *Rank and Riches* produced at the Adelphi Theatre: a theatrical disaster.	Deaths of Marx, Wagner. Trollope, *An Autobiography*
1884 *'I Say No'* published in volume form.	Fabian Society founded; Third Reform Bill; birth of Lawrence; Criminal Law
1885	Amendment Act (raising age of consent to 16). Maupassant, *Bel-Ami* Pater, *Marius the Epicurean* Zola, *Germinal*
1886 *The Evil Genius* published in volume form. *The Guilty River* published in *Arrowsmith's Christmas Annual*.	Irish Home Rule Act; Contagious Diseases Acts repealed. Hardy, *The Mayor of Casterbridge*

Life	*Historical and Cultural Background*
1887 *Little Novels*, a collection of short stories, published.	Victoria's Golden Jubilee; Independent Labour Party founded. Hardy, *The Woodlanders* Strindberg, *The Father*
1888 *The Legacy of Cain* published in volume form. (Feb.) Moves to 82 Wimpole Street.	Death of Arnold; birth of T. S. Eliot. Kipling, *Plain Tales from the Hills*
1889 (23 Sept.) Dies at 82 Wimpole Street.	Deaths of Browning, Hopkins; dock strike in London. Booth, *Life and Labour of the People in London* Shaw, *Fabian Essays in Socialism* Ibsen's *A Doll's House* staged in London
1890 *Blind Love* (completed by Walter Besant) published in volume form.	Death of Newman; Parnell case; first underground railway in London. Booth, *In Darkest England* Frazer, *The Golden Bough* William James, *Principles of Psychology* Morris, *News from Nowhere*
1895 (June) Caroline Graves dies and is buried in Wilkie Collins's grave.	
1919 Martha Rudd (Dawson) dies.	

THE DEAD SECRET

Affectionately Dedicated to

EDWARD FREDERICK SMYTH PIGOTT

PREFACE TO THE PRESENT EDITION

'The Dead Secret' made its first appeal to readers, in periodical portions, week by week. On its completion, it was reprinted in two Volumes. The edition so produced having been exhausted, the story makes its public appearance, for the third time, in the present form.*

Having previously tried my hand at short serial stories (collected and reprinted in 'After Dark,' and 'The Queen of Hearts'), I ventured on my first attempt, in this book, to produce a sustained work of fiction, intended for periodical publication during many successive weeks.* The experiment proved successful both in this country and in America. Two of the characters which appear in these pages—'Rosamond,' and 'Uncle Joseph'—had the good fortune to find friends everywhere who took a hearty liking to them. A more elaborately drawn personage in the story—'Sarah Leeson'—was, I think less generally understood. The idea of tracing, in this character, the influence of a heavy responsibility on a naturally timid woman, whose mind was neither strong enough to bear it, nor bold enough to drop it altogether, was a favourite idea with me, at the time, and is so much a favourite still, that I privately give 'Sarah Leeson' the place of honour in the little portrait-gallery which my story contains. Perhaps, in saying this, I am only acknowledging, in other words, that the parents of literary families share the well-known inconsistencies of parents in general, and are sometimes unreasonably fond of the child who has always given them the most trouble.

It may not be out of place, here, to notice a critical objection which was raised, in certain quarters, against the construction of the narrative. I was blamed for allowing the 'Secret' to glimmer on the reader at an early period of the story, instead of keeping it in total darkness till the end.* If this was a mistake (which I venture to doubt), I committed it with both eyes open. After careful consideration, and after trying the experiment both ways, I thought it most desirable to let the effect of the story depend on expectation rather than surprise; believing that the reader would be all the more interested in watching the progress of 'Rosamond' and her husband towards the discovery of the Secret, if he previously held some clue to the mystery in his own hand. So far as I am enabled to judge, from the opinions which reached me through various channels, this peculiar treatment of the narrative presented one of the special attractions of the book to a large variety of readers.

I may add, in conclusion, that 'The Dead Secret' was admirably rendered into French by Monsieur E. D. Forgues, of Paris. The one difficulty which neither the accomplished translator nor any one else proved able to overcome, was presented, oddly enough, by the English title. When the work was published in Paris, its name was of necessity shortened to 'Le Secret'—because no French equivalent could be found for such an essentially English phrase as a '*dead* secret.'

Harley Street, London,
January, 1861.

CONTENTS

8 CONTENTS

BOOK VI

THE DEAD SECRET

BOOK I

CHAPTER I

THE TWENTY-THIRD OF AUGUST, 1829

'WILL she last out the night, I wonder?'

'Look at the clock, Mathew.'

'Ten minutes past twelve! She *has* lasted the night out. She has lived, Robert, to see ten minutes of the new day.'

These words were spoken in the kitchen of a large country-house situated on the west coast of Cornwall.* The speakers were two of the men-servants composing the establishment of Captain Treverton, an officer in the navy, and the eldest male representative of an old Cornish family. Both the servants communicated with each other restrainedly, in whispers—sitting close together, and looking round expectantly towards the door whenever the talk flagged between them.

'It's an awful thing,' said the elder of the men, 'for us two to be alone here, at this dark time, counting out the minutes that our mistress has left to live!'

'Robert,' said the other, 'you have been in the service here since you were a boy—did you ever hear that our mistress was a play-actress when our master married her?'

'How came you to know that?' inquired the elder servant, sharply.

'Hush!' cried the other, rising quickly from his chair.

A bell rang in the passage outside.

'Is that for one of us?' asked Mathew.

'Can't you tell, by the sound, which is which of those bells yet?' exclaimed Robert, contemptuously. 'That bell is for Sarah Leeson. Go out into the passage and look.'

The younger servant took a candle and obeyed. When he opened the kitchen-door, a long row of bells met his eye on the wall opposite. Above each of them was painted, in neat black letters, the distinguishing title of the servant whom it was specially intended to summon. The row of letters began with Housekeeper and Butler, and ended with Kitchenmaid and Footman's Boy.

Looking along the bells, Mathew easily discovered that one of them was still in motion. Above it were the words, Lady's Maid. Observing this, he passed quickly along the passage, and knocked at an old-fashioned oak door at the end of it. No answer being given, he opened the door and looked into the room. It was dark and empty.

'Sarah is not in the housekeeper's room,' said Mathew, returning to his fellow-servant in the kitchen.

'She is gone to her own room, then,' rejoined the other. 'Go up and tell her that she is wanted by her mistress.'

The bell rang again as Mathew went out.

'Quick!—quick!' cried Robert. 'Tell her she is wanted directly. Wanted,' he continued to himself in lower tones, 'perhaps for the last time!'

Mathew ascended three flights of stairs—passed half-way down a long arched gallery—and knocked at another old-fashioned oak door. This time the signal was answered. A low, clear, sweet voice, inside the room, inquired who was waiting without? In a few hasty words Mathew told his errand. Before he had done speaking, the door was quietly and quickly opened, and Sarah Leeson confronted him on the threshold, with her candle in her hand.

Not tall, not handsome, not in her first youth—shy and irresolute in manner—simple in dress to the utmost limits of plainness—the lady's maid, in spite of all these disadvantages, was a woman whom it was impossible to look at without a feeling of curiosity, if not of interest. Few men, at first sight of her, could have resisted the desire to find out who she was; few would have been satisfied with receiving for answer, She is Mrs Treverton's maid; few would have refrained from the attempt to extract some secret information for themselves from her face and manner: and none, not even the most patient and practised of observers, could have succeeded in discovering more than that she must have passed through the ordeal of some great suffering, at some former period of her life. Much in her manner, and more in her face, said plainly and sadly: I am the wreck of something that you might once have liked to see; a wreck that can never be repaired—that must drift on through life unnoticed, unguided, unpitied—drift till the fatal shore is touched, and the waves of Time have swallowed up these broken relics of me for ever. This was the story that was told in Sarah Leeson's face—this, and no more.

No two men interpreting that story for themselves, would probably have agreed on the nature of the suffering which this woman had undergone. It was hard to say, at the outset, whether the past pain that had set its ineffaceable mark on her, had been pain of the body or pain of the mind. But whatever the nature of the affliction she had suffered, the traces it had left were deeply and strikingly visible in every part of her face.

Her cheeks had lost their roundness and their natural colour; her lips, singularly flexible in movement and delicate in form, had faded to an unhealthy paleness; her eyes, large and black and overshadowed by unusually thick lashes, had contracted an anxious startled look, which never left them, and which piteously expressed the painful acuteness of her sensibility, the inherent timidity of her disposition. So far, the marks which sorrow or sickness had set on her, were the marks common to most victims of mental or physical suffering. The one extraordinary personal deterioration which she had undergone, consisted in the unnatural change that had passed over the colour of her hair. It was as thick and soft, it grew as gracefully, as the hair of a young girl; but it was as grey as the hair of an old woman. It seemed to contradict, in the most startling manner, every personal assertion of youth that still existed in her face. With all its haggardness and paleness, no one could have looked at it and supposed for a moment that it was the face of an elderly woman. Wan as they might be, there was not a wrinkle in her cheeks. Her eyes, viewed apart from their prevailing expression of uneasiness and timidity, still preserved that bright, clear moisture which is never seen in the eyes of the old. The skin about her temples was as delicately smooth as the skin of a child. These and other physical signs which never mislead, showed that she was still, as to years, in the very prime of her life. Sickly and sorrow-stricken as she was, she looked, from the eyes downwards, a woman who had barely reached thirty years of age. From the eyes upwards, the effect of her abundant grey hair, seen in connection with her face, was not simply incongruous—it was absolutely startling; so startling as to make it no paradox to say that she would have looked most natural, most like herself, if her hair had been dyed. In her case, Art would have seemed to be the truth, because Nature looked like falsehood.

What shock had stricken her hair, in the very maturity of its luxuriance, with the hue of an unnatural old age? Was it a serious illness, or a dreadful grief, that had turned her grey in the prime of her womanhood? That question had often been agitated among her fellow-servants, who were all struck by the peculiarities of her personal appearance, and rendered a little suspicious of her, as well, by an inveterate habit that she had of talking to herself. Inquire as they might, however, their curiosity was always baffled. Nothing more could be discovered than that Sarah Leeson was, in the common phrase, touchy on the subject of her grey hair and her habit of talking to herself, and that Sarah Leeson's mistress had long since forbidden every one, from her husband downwards, to ruffle her maid's tranquillity by inquisitive questions.

She stood for an instant speechless, on that momentous morning of the twenty-third of August, before the servant who summoned her to her mistress's death-bed—the light of the candle flaring brightly over her large, startled, black eyes, and the luxuriant, unnatural, grey hair above them. She stood a moment silent—her hand trembling while she held the candlestick, so that the extinguisher lying loose in it rattled incessantly—then thanked the servant for calling her. The trouble and fear in her voice, as she spoke, seemed to add to its sweetness; the agitation of her manner took nothing away from its habitual gentleness, its delicate, winning, feminine restraint. Mathew, who, like the other servants, secretly distrusted and disliked her for differing from the ordinary pattern of professed ladies' maids, was, on this particular occasion, so subdued by her manner and her tone as she thanked him, that he offered to carry her candle for her to the door of her mistress's bed-chamber. She shook her head, and thanked him again, then passed before him quickly on her way out of the gallery.

The room in which Mrs Treverton lay dying, was on the floor beneath. Sarah hesitated twice, before she knocked at the door. It was opened by Captain Treverton.

The instant she saw her master, she started back from him. If she had dreaded a blow, she could hardly have drawn away more suddenly, or with an expression of greater alarm. There was nothing in Captain Treverton's face to warrant the suspicion of ill-treatment, or even of harsh words. His countenance was kind, hearty, and open; and the tears were still trickling down it, which he had shed by his wife's bed-side.

'Go in,' he said, turning away his face. 'She does not wish the nurse to attend; she only wishes for you. Call me, if the doctor'——His voice faltered, and he hurried away without attempting to finish the sentence.

Sarah Leeson, instead of entering her mistress's room, stood looking after her master attentively, with her pale cheeks turned to a deathly whiteness,—with an eager, doubting, questioning terror in her eyes. When he had disappeared round the corner of the gallery, she listened for a moment outside the door of the sick-room—whispered affrightedly to herself, 'Can she have told him?'—then opened the door, with a visible effort to recover her self-control; and, after lingering suspiciously on the threshold for a moment, went in.

Mrs Treverton's bed-chamber was a large, lofty room, situated in the western front of the house, and consequently overlooking the sea-view. The night-light burning by the bed-side, displayed rather than dispelled the darkness in the corners of the room. The bed was of the old-fashioned pattern, with heavy hangings and thick curtains drawn all round it. Of the other objects in the chamber, only those of the largest and most solid kind were prominent enough to be tolerably visible in the dim light. The cabinets, the wardrobe, the full-length looking-glass, the high-backed arm-chair, these, with the great shapeless bulk of the bed itself, towered up heavily and gloomily into view. Other objects were all merged together in the general obscurity. Through the open window—opened to admit the fresh air of the new morning after the sultriness of the

August night—there poured monotonously into the room, the dull, still, distant roaring of the surf on the sandy coast. All outer noises were hushed at that first dark hour of the new day. Inside the room, the one audible sound was the slow, toilsome breathing of the dying woman, raising itself in its mortal frailness, awfully and distinctly, even through the far thunder-breathing from the bosom of the everlasting sea.

'Mistress,' said Sarah Leeson, standing close to the curtains, but not withdrawing them, 'my master has left the room, and has sent me here in his place.'

'Light!—give me more light.'*

The feebleness of mortal sickness was in the voice; but the accent of the speaker sounded resolute even yet—doubly resolute by contrast with the hesitation of the tones in which Sarah had spoken. The strong nature of the mistress and the weak nature of the maid came out, even in that short inter-change of words, spoken through the curtain of a death-bed.

Sarah lit two candles with a wavering hand—placed them hesitatingly on a table by the bedside—waited for a moment, looking all round her with suspicious timidity—then undrew the curtains.

The disease of which Mrs Treverton was dying, was one of the most terrible of all the maladies that afflict humanity—one to which women are especially subject—and one which under-mines life, without, in most cases, showing any remarkable traces of its corroding progress in the face. No uninstructed person, looking at Mrs Treverton when her attendant undrew the bed-curtain, could possibly have imagined that she was past all help that mortal skill could offer to her. The slight marks of illness in her face, the inevitable changes in the grace and roundness of its outline, were rendered hardly noticeable by the marvellous preservation of her complexion in all the light and delicacy of its first girlish beauty. There lay her face on the pillow—tenderly framed in by the rich lace of her cap; softly crowned by her shining brown hair—to all outward appearance, the face of a beautiful woman recovering from a slight illness, or reposing after unusual fatigue. Even Sarah Leeson, who had watched her all through her malady, could hardly believe, as she looked at her mistress, that the Gates of

Life had closed behind her, and that the beckoning hand of Death was signing to her already from the Gates of the Grave.

Some dogs'-eared books in paper covers lay on the counterpane of the bed. As soon as the curtain was drawn aside, Mrs Treverton ordered her attendant by a gesture to remove them. They were plays,* underscored in certain places by ink lines, and marked with marginal annotations referring to entrances, exits, and places on the stage. The servants, talking down stairs of their mistress's occupation before her marriage, had not been misled by false reports. Their master, after he had passed the prime of life, had, in very truth, taken his wife from the obscure stage of a country theatre, when little more than two years had elapsed since her first appearance in public. The dogs'-eared old plays had been once her treasured dramatic library; she had always retained a fondness for them from old associations; and, during the latter part of her illness, they had remained on her bed for days and days together.

Having put away the plays, Sarah went back to her mistress; and, with more of dread and bewilderment in her face than grief, opened her lips to speak. Mrs Treverton held up her hand, as a sign that she had another order to give.

'Bolt the door,' she said, in the same enfeebled voice, but with the same accent of resolution which had so strikingly marked her first request to have more light in the room. 'Bolt the door. Let no one in, till I give you leave.'

'No one?' repeated Sarah, faintly. 'Not the doctor? not even my master?'

'Not the doctor—not even your master,' said Mrs Treverton, and pointed to the door. The hand was weak; but even in that momentary action of it, there was no mistaking the gesture of command.

Sarah bolted the door, returned irresolutely to the bedside, fixed her large, eager, startled eyes inquiringly on her mistress's face, and, suddenly bending over her, said in a whisper:

'Have you told my master?'

'No,' was the answer. 'I sent for him, to tell him—I tried hard to speak the words—it shook me to my very soul, only to think how I should best break it to him—I am so fond of him! I love him so dearly! But I should have spoken in spite of that, if he had not talked of the child. Sarah! he did nothing but talk of the child—and that silenced me.'

Sarah, with a forgetfulness of her station which might have appeared extraordinary even in the eyes of the most lenient of mistresses, flung herself back in a chair when the first word of Mrs Treverton's reply was uttered, clasped her trembling hands over her face, and groaned to herself:—'O, what will happen! what will happen now!'

Mrs Treverton's eyes had softened and moistened when she spoke of her love for her husband. She lay silent for a few minutes; the working of some strong emotion in her being expressed by her quick, hard, laboured breathing, and by the painful contraction of her eyebrows. Ere long, she turned her head uneasily towards the chair in which her attendant was sitting, and spoke again—this time, in a voice which had sunk to a whisper.

'Look for my medicine,' said she, 'I want it.'

Sarah started up, and with the quick instinct of obedience brushed away the tears that were rolling fast over her cheeks.

'The doctor,' she said. 'Let me call the doctor.'

'No! The medicine—look for the medicine.'

'Which bottle? The opiate——'

'No. Not the opiate. The other.'

Sarah took a bottle from the table, and looking attentively at the written direction on the label, said that it was not yet time to take that medicine again.

'Give me the bottle.'

'O, pray don't ask me. Pray wait. The doctor said it was as bad as dram-drinking, if you took too much.'

Mrs Treverton's clear grey eyes began to flash; the rosy flush deepened on her cheeks; the commanding hand was raised again, by an effort, from the counterpane on which it lay.

'Take the cork out of the bottle,' she said, 'and give it to me. I want strength. No matter whether I die in an hour's time, or a week's. Give me the bottle.'

'No, no—not the bottle!' said Sarah, giving it up, nevertheless, under the influence of her mistress's look. 'There are two doses left. Wait, pray wait till I get a glass.'

She turned again towards the table. At the same instant

Mrs Treverton raised the bottle to her lips, drained it of its contents, and flung it from her on the bed.

'She has killed herself!' cried Sarah, running in terror to the door.

'Stop!' said the voice from the bed, more resolute than ever, already. 'Stop! Come back and prop me up higher on the pillows.'

Sarah put her hand on the bolt.

'Come back,' reiterated Mrs Treverton. 'While there is life in me, I will be obeyed. Come back.' The colour began to deepen perceptibly all over her face, and the light to grow brighter in her widely-opened eyes.

Sarah came back; and with shaking hands, added one more to the many pillows which supported the dying woman's head and shoulders. While this was being done, the bed-clothes became a little discomposed. Mrs Treverton shuddered, and drew them up to their former position, close round her neck.

'Did you unbolt the door?' she asked.

'No.'

'I forbid you to go near it again. Get my writing-case, and the pen and ink, from the cabinet near the window.'

Sarah went to the cabinet and opened it; then stopped, as if some sudden suspicion had crossed her mind, and asked what the writing materials were wanted for.

'Bring them, and you will see.'

The writing-case, with a sheet of note-paper on it, was placed upon Mrs Treverton's knees; the pen was dipped into the ink, and given to her; she paused, closed her eyes for a minute, and sighed heavily; then began to write, saying to her waiting-maid, as the pen touched the paper: 'Look.'

Sarah peered anxiously over her shoulder, and saw the pen slowly and feebly form these three words:—*To my Husband.*

'O, no! no! For God's sake, don't write it!' she cried, catching at her mistress's hand—but suddenly letting it go again the moment Mrs Treverton looked at her.

The pen went on; and more slowly, more feebly, formed words enough to fill a line—then stopped. The letters of the last syllable were all blotted together.

'Don't!' reiterated Sarah, dropping on her knees at the bed-side. 'Don't write it to him if you can't tell it to him. Let me go on bearing what I have borne so long already. Let the Secret die with you and die with me, and be never known in this world—never, never, never!'

'The Secret must be told,' answered Mrs Treverton. 'My husband ought to know it, and must know it. I tried to tell him, and my courage failed me. I cannot trust you to tell him, after I am gone. It must be written. Take you the pen; my sight is failing, my touch is dull. Take the pen, and write what I tell you.'

Sarah, instead of obeying, hid her face in the bed-cover, and wept bitterly.

'You have been with me ever since my marriage,' Mrs Treverton went on. 'You have been my friend more than my servant. Do you refuse my last request? You do! Fool! look up and listen to me. On your peril, refuse to take the pen. Write, or I shall not rest in my grave. *Write, or as true as there is a Heaven above us, I will come to you from the other world!*'

Sarah started to her feet with a faint scream.

'You make my flesh creep!' she whispered, fixing her eyes on her mistress's face with a stare of superstitious horror.

At the same instant, the overdose of the stimulating medicine began to affect Mrs Treverton's brain. She rolled her head restlessly from side to side of the pillow—repeated vacantly a few lines from one of the old play-books which had been removed from her bed—and suddenly held out the pen to the servant, with a theatrical wave of the hand, and a glance upward at an imaginary gallery of spectators.

'Write!' she cried, with an awful mimicry of her old stage voice. 'Write!' And the weak hand was waved again with a forlorn, feeble imitation of the old stage gesture.

Closing her fingers mechanically on the pen that was thrust between them, Sarah, with her eyes still expressing the superstitious terror which her mistress's words had aroused, waited for the next command. Some minutes elapsed before Mrs Treverton spoke again. She still retained her senses sufficiently to be vaguely conscious of the effect which the medicine was producing on her, and to be desirous of combating its further progress before it succeeded in utterly confusing her ideas. She asked first for the smelling-bottle, next for some Eau de Cologne.

This last, poured on to her handkerchief, and applied to her forehead, seemed to prove successful in partially clearing her faculties. Her eyes recovered their steady look of intelligence; and, when she again addressed her maid, reiterating the word 'Write,' she was able to enforce the direction by beginning immediately to dictate in quiet, deliberate, determined tones. Sarah's tears fell fast; her lips murmured fragments of sentences in which entreaties, expressions of penitence, and exclamations of fear were all strangely mingled together: but she wrote on submissively, in wavering lines, until she had nearly filled the two first sides of the note-paper. Then Mrs Treverton paused, looked the writing over, and, taking the pen, signed her name at the end of it. With this effort, her powers of resistance to the exciting effect of the medicine seemed to fail her again. The deep flush began to tinge her cheeks once more, and she spoke hurriedly and unsteadily when she handed the pen back to her maid.

'Sign!' she cried, beating her hand feebly on the bed-clothes. 'Sign Sarah Leeson, witness. No!—write Accomplice. Take your share of it; I won't have it shifted on me. Sign, I insist on it! Sign as I tell you.'*

Sarah obeyed; and Mrs Treverton taking the paper from her, pointed to it solemnly, with a return of the stage gesture which had escaped her a little while back.

'You will give this to your master,' she said, 'when I am dead; and you will answer any questions he puts to you as truly as if you were before the judgment-seat.'

Clasping her hands fast together, Sarah regarded her mistress, for the first time, with steady eyes, and spoke to her for the first time in steady tones.

'If I only knew that I was fit to die,' she said, 'O, how gladly I would change places with you!'

'Promise me that you will give the paper to your master,' repeated Mrs Treverton. 'Promise—No! I won't trust your promise: I'll have your oath. Get the Bible—the Bible the clergyman used when he was here this morning. Get it, or

I shall not rest in my grave. Get it, *or I will come to you from the other world.*'

The mistress laughed, as she reiterated that threat. The maid shuddered, as she obeyed the command which it was designed to impress on her.

'Yes, yes—the Bible the clergyman used,' continued Mrs Treverton, vacantly, after the book had been produced. 'The clergyman—a poor weak man—I frightened him, Sarah. He said, "Are you at peace with all the world?" and I said, "All but one." You know who.'

'The Captain's brother? O, don't die at enmity with anybody. Don't die at enmity even with *him*,' pleaded Sarah.

'The clergyman said so too,' murmured Mrs Treverton, her eyes beginning to wander childishly round the room, her tones growing suddenly lower and more confused. ' "You must forgive him," the clergyman said. And I said, "No, I forgive all the world, but not my husband's brother." The clergyman got up from the bedside, frightened, Sarah. He talked about praying for me, and coming back. Will he come back?'

'Yes, yes,' answered Sarah. 'He is a good man—he will come back—and O! tell him that you forgive the Captain's brother! Those vile words he spoke of you, when you were married, will come home to him some day. Forgive him—forgive him before you die!'

Saying those words, she attempted to remove the Bible softly out of her mistress's sight. The action attracted Mrs Treverton's attention, and roused her sinking faculties into observation of present things.

'Stop!' she cried, with a gleam of the old resolution flashing once more over the dying dimness of her eyes. She caught at Sarah's hand with a great effort, placed it on the Bible, and held it there. Her other hand wandered a little over the bed-clothes, until it encountered the written paper addressed to her husband. Her fingers closed on it; and a sigh of relief escaped her lips.

'Ah!' she said, 'I know what I wanted the Bible for. I'm dying with all my senses about me, Sarah; you can't deceive me even yet.' She stopped again, smiled a little, whispered to herself rapidly, 'Wait, wait, wait!' then added aloud, with the old stage voice and the old stage gesture: 'No! I won't trust you on your promise. I'll have your oath. Kneel down. These are my last words in this world—disobey them if you dare!'

Sarah dropped on her knees by the bed. The breeze outside, strengthening just then with the slow advance of the morning, parted the window-curtains a little, and wafted a breath of its sweet fragrance joyously into the sick room. The heavy-beating hum of the distant surf came in at the same time, and poured out its unresting music in louder strains. Then the window-curtains fell to again heavily, the wavering flame of the candle grew steady once more, and the awful silence in the room sank deeper than ever.

'Swear!'* said Mrs Treverton. Her voice failed her when she had pronounced that one word. She struggled a little, recovered the power of utterance, and went on: 'Swear that you will not destroy this paper, after I am dead.'

Even while she pronounced these solemn words, even at that last struggle for life and strength, the ineradicable theatrical instinct showed, with a fearful inappropriateness, how firmly it kept its place in her mind. Sarah felt the cold hand that was still laid on hers lifted for a moment—saw it waving gracefully towards her—felt it descend again, and clasp her own hand with a trembling, impatient pressure. At that final appeal, she answered faintly:—

'I swear it.'

'Swear that you will not take this paper away with you, if you leave the house, after I am dead.'

Again Sarah paused before she answered—again the trembling pressure made itself felt on her hand, but more weakly this time—and again the words dropped affrightedly from her lips;—

'I swear it.'

'Swear!' Mrs Treverton began for the third time. Her voice failed her once more; and she struggled vainly to regain the command over it.

Sarah looked up, and saw signs of convulsion beginning to disfigure the beautiful face—saw the fingers of the white, delicate hand getting crooked as they reached over towards the table on which the medicine-bottles were placed.

'You drank it all,' she cried, starting to her feet, as she

comprehended the meaning of that gesture. 'Mistress, dear mistress, you drank it all—there is nothing but the opiate left. Let me go—let me go and call——'

A look from Mrs Treverton stopped her before she could utter another word. The lips of the dying woman were moving rapidly. Sarah put her ear close to them. At first she heard nothing but panting, quick-drawn breaths—then a few broken words mingled confusedly with them:

'I hav'n't done—you must swear—close, close, come close—a third thing—your master—swear to give it——'

The last words died away very softly. The lips that had been forming them so laboriously, parted on a sudden and closed again no more. Sarah sprang to the door, opened it, and called into the passage for help; then ran back to the bed-side, caught up the sheet of note-paper on which she had written from her mistress's dictation, and hid it in her bosom. The last look of Mrs Treverton's eyes fastened sternly and reproachfully on her as she did this, and kept their expression unchanged, through the momentary distortion of the rest of the features, for one breathless moment. That moment passed, and, with the next, the shadow which goes before the presence of death, stole up, and shut out the light of life, in one quiet instant, from all the face.

The doctor, followed by the nurse and by one of the servants, entered the room; and, hurrying to the bed-side, saw at a glance that the time for his attendance there had passed away for ever. He spoke first to the servant who had followed him.

'Go to your master,' he said, 'and beg him to wait in his own room until I can come and speak to him.'

Sarah still stood—without moving, or speaking, or noticing any one—by the bed-side.

The nurse, approaching to draw the curtains together, started at the sight of her face, and turned to the doctor.

'I think this person had better leave the room, sir?' said the nurse, with some appearance of contempt in her tones and looks. 'She seems unreasonably shocked and terrified by what has happened.'

'Quite right,' said the doctor. 'It is best that she should withdraw. Let me recommend you to leave us for a little while,' he added, touching Sarah on the arm.

She shrank back suspiciously, raised one of her hands to the place where the letter lay hidden in her bosom, and pressed it there firmly, while she held out the other hand for a candle.

'You had better rest for a little in your own room,' said the doctor, giving her a candle. 'Stop, though,' he continued, after a moment's reflection. 'I am going to break the sad news to your master, and I may find that he is anxious to hear any last words that Mrs Treverton may have spoken in your presence. Perhaps you had better come with me, and wait while I go into Captain Treverton's room.'

'No! no!—oh, not now—not now, for God's sake!' Speaking those words in low, quick, pleading tones, and drawing back affrightedly to the door, Sarah disappeared without waiting a moment to be spoken to again.

'A strange woman!' said the doctor, addressing the nurse. 'Follow her, and see where she goes to, in case she is wanted and we are obliged to send for her. I will wait here until you come back.'

When the nurse returned she had nothing to report, but that she had followed Sarah Leeson to her own bed-room, had seen her enter it, had listened outside, and had heard her lock the door.

'A strange woman!' repeated the doctor. 'One of the silent, secret sort.'

'One of the wrong sort,' said the nurse. 'She is always talking to herself, and that is a bad sign, in my opinion. I distrusted her, sir, the very first day I entered the house.'

CHAPTER II

THE CHILD

THE instant Sarah Leeson had turned the key of her bedroom door, she took the sheet of note-paper from its place of concealment in her bosom—shuddering, when she drew it out, as if the mere contact of it hurt her—placed it open on her little dressing table, and fixed her eyes eagerly on the lines which the note contained. At first they swam and mingled together before her. She pressed her hands over her eyes, for a few minutes, and then looked at the writing again.

The characters were clear now—vividly clear, and, as she fancied, unnaturally large and near to view. There was the address: 'To my husband;' there the first blotted line beneath, in her dead mistress's handwriting; there the lines that followed, traced by her own pen, with the signature at the end—Mrs Treverton's first, and then her own. The whole amounted to but very few sentences, written on one perishable fragment of paper, which the flame of a candle would have consumed in a moment. Yet there she sat, reading, reading, reading, over and over again; never touching the note, except when it was absolutely necessary to turn over the first page; never moving, never speaking, never raising her eyes from the paper. As a condemned prisoner might read his death-warrant, so did Sarah Leeson now read the few lines which she and her mistress had written together not half-an-hour since.

The secret of the paralysing effect of that writing on her mind lay, not only in itself, but in the circumstances which had attended the act of its production.

The oath which had been proposed by Mrs Treverton under no more serious influence than the last caprice of her disordered faculties, stimulated by confused remembrances of stage words and stage situations, had been accepted by Sarah Leeson as the most sacred and inviolable engagement to which she could bind herself. The threat of enforcing obedience to her last commands from beyond the grave, which the mistress had uttered in mocking experiment on the superstitious fears of the maid, now hung darkly over the weak mind of Sarah, as a judgment which might descend on her, visibly and inexorably, at any moment of her future life. When she roused herself at last, and pushed away the paper, and rose to her feet, she stood quite still for an instant, before she ventured to look behind her. When she did look, it was with an effort and a start, with a searching distrust of the empty dimness in the remoter corners of the room.

Her old habit of talking to herself began to resume its influence, as she now walked rapidly backwards and forwards, sometimes along the room and sometimes across it. She repeated incessantly such broken phrases as these: 'How can I give him the letter?—Such a good master; so kind to us all.—Why did she die, and leave it all to *me?*—I can't bear it alone; it's too much for me.' While reiterating these sentences, she vacantly occupied herself in putting things about the room in order, which were set in perfect order already. All her looks, all her actions, betrayed the vain struggle of a weak mind to sustain itself under the weight of a heavy responsibility. She arranged and rearranged the cheap china ornaments on her chimney-piece a dozen times over—put her pin-cushion first on the looking-glass, then on the table in front of it—changed the position of the little porcelain dish and tray on her wash-hand-stand, now to one side of the basin, and now to the other. Throughout all these trifling actions, the natural grace, delicacy, and prim neat-handedness of the woman still waited mechanically on the most useless and aimless of her occupations of the moment. She knocked nothing down, she put nothing awry, her footsteps at the fastest made no sound—the very skirts of her dress were kept as properly and prudishly composed as if it was broad daylight and the eyes of all her neighbours were looking at her.

From time to time the sense of the words she was murmuring confusedly to herself changed. Sometimes they disjointedly expressed bolder and more self-reliant thoughts. Once they seemed to urge her again to the dressing-table and the open letter on it, against her own will. She read aloud the address: 'To my Husband,' and caught the letter up sharply, and spoke in firmer tones. 'Why give it to him at all? Why not let the secret die with her and die with me, as it ought? Why should he know it? He shall *not* know it!'

Saying those last words, she desperately held the letter within an inch of the flame of the candle. At the same moment the white curtain over the window before her stirred a little, as the freshening air found its way through the old-fashioned, ill-fitting sashes. Her eye caught sight of it, as it waved gently backwards and forwards. She clasped the letter suddenly to her breast with both hands, and shrank back against the wall of the room, her eyes still fastened on the curtain with the same blank look of horror which they had exhibited when

Mrs Treverton had threatened to claim her servant's obedience from the other world.

'Something moves,' she gasped to herself, in a breathless whisper. 'Something moves in the room.'

The curtain waved slowly to and fro for the second time. Still fixedly looking at it over her shoulder, she crept along the wall to the door.

'Do you come to me already?' she said, her eyes riveted on the curtain while her hand groped over the lock for the key. 'Before your grave is dug? Before your coffin is made? Before your body is cold?'

She opened the door and glided into the passage; stopped there for a moment, and looked back into the room.

'Rest!' she said. 'Rest, mistress—he shall have the letter.'

The staircase-lamp guided her out of the passage. Descending hurriedly, as if she feared to give herself time to think, she reached Captain Treverton's study, on the ground-floor, in a minute or two. The door was wide open, and the room was empty.

After reflecting a little, she lighted one of the chamber-candles standing on the hall-table, at the lamp in the study, and ascended the stairs again to her master's bed-room. After repeatedly knocking at the door and obtaining no answer, she ventured to go in. The bed had not been disturbed, the candles had not been lit—to all appearance the room had not even been entered during the night.

There was but one other place to seek him in—the chamber in which his wife lay dead. Could she summon the courage to give him the letter there? She hesitated a little—then whispered, 'I must! I must!'

The direction she now compelled herself to take, led her a little way down the stairs again. She descended very slowly this time, holding cautiously by the banisters, and pausing to take breath almost at every step. The door of what had been Mrs Treverton's bed-room was opened, when she ventured to knock at it, by the nurse, who enquired roughly and suspiciously, what she wanted there.

'I want to speak to my master.'

'Look for him somewhere else. He was here half an hour ago. He is gone now.'

'Do you know where he has gone?'

'No. I don't pry into other people's goings and comings. I mind my own business.'

With that discourteous answer, the nurse closed the door again. Just as Sarah turned away from it, she looked towards the inner end of the passage. The door of the nursery was situated there. It was ajar, and a dim gleam of candle-light was flickering through it.

She went in immediately, and saw that the candle-light came from an inner room, usually occupied, as she well knew, by the nursery-maid and by the only child of the house of Treverton; a little girl, named Rosamond, aged, at that time, nearly five years.

'Can he be there?—in that room, of all the rooms in the house!'

Quickly as the thought arose in her mind, Sarah raised the letter (which she had hitherto carried in her hand) to the bosom of her dress, and hid it for the second time, exactly as she had hidden it on leaving her mistress's bed-side.

She then stole across the nursery on tiptoe towards the inner room. The entrance to it, to please some caprice of the child's, had been arched, and framed with trellis-work, gaily-coloured, so as to resemble the entrance to a summer-house. Two pretty chintz curtains, hanging inside the trellis-work, formed the only barrier between the day-room and the bed-room. One of these was looped up, and towards the opening thus made, Sarah now advanced, after cautiously leaving her candle in the passage outside.

The first object that attracted her attention in the child's bed-room, was the figure of the nurse-maid, leaning back, fast asleep, in an easy chair by the window. Venturing, after this discovery, to look more boldly into the room, she next saw her master sitting with his back towards her, by the side of the child's crib. Little Rosamond was awake, and was standing up in bed with her arms round her father's neck. One of her hands held over his shoulder the doll that she had taken to bed with her, the other was twined gently in his hair. The child had been crying bitterly, and had now exhausted herself, so that she was only moaning a little from time to time, with her head laid wearily on her father's bosom.

The tears stood thick in Sarah's eyes as they looked on her master and on the little hands that lay round his neck. She lingered by the raised curtain, heedless of the risk she ran, from moment to moment, of being discovered and questioned—lingered until she heard Captain Treverton say soothingly to the child:

'Hush, Rosie, dear! hush, my own love! Don't cry any more for poor mamma. Think of poor papa, and try to comfort him.'

Simple as the words were, quietly and tenderly as they were spoken, they seemed instantly to deprive Sarah Leeson of all power of self-control. Reckless whether she was heard or not, she turned and ran into the passage as if she had been flying for her life. Passing the candle she had left there, without so much as a look at it, she made for the stairs, and descended them with headlong rapidity to the kitchen-floor. There, one of the servants who had been sitting up met her, and, with a face of astonishment and alarm, asked what was the matter.

'I'm ill—I'm faint—I want air,' she answered, speaking thickly and confusedly. 'Open the garden door, and let me out.'

The man obeyed, but doubtfully, as if he thought her unfit to be trusted by herself.

'She gets stranger than ever in her ways,' he said, when he rejoined his fellow-servant, after Sarah had hurried past him into the open air. 'Now our mistress is dead, she will have to find another place, I suppose. I, for one, shan't break my heart when she's gone. Shall you?'

CHAPTER III

THE HIDING OF THE SECRET

THE cool, sweet air in the garden blowing freshly over Sarah's face, seemed to calm the violence of her agitation. She turned down a side walk, which led to a terrace and overlooked the church of the neighbouring village.

The daylight out of doors was clear already. The misty auburn light that goes before sunrise, was flowing up, peaceful and lovely, behind a line of black-brown moorland, over all the eastern sky. The old church, with the hedge of myrtle* and fuchsia growing round the little cemetery in all the luxuriance which is only seen in Cornwall, was clearing and brightening to view, almost as fast as the morning firmament itself. Sarah leaned her arms heavily on the back of a garden-seat, and turned her face towards the church. Her eyes wandered from the building itself to the cemetery by its side—rested there— and watched the light growing warmer and warmer over the lonesome refuge where the dead lay at rest.

'O, my heart! my heart!' she said. 'What must it be made of not to break?'

She remained for some time leaning on the seat, looking sadly towards the churchyard, and pondering over the words which she had heard Captain Treverton say to the child. They seemed to connect themselves, as everything else now appeared to connect itself in her mind, with the letter that had been written on Mrs Treverton's death-bed. She drew it from her bosom once more, and crushed it up angrily in her fingers.

'Still in my hands! still not seen by any eyes but mine!' she said, looking down at the crumpled pages. 'Is it all my fault? If she was alive now—if she had seen what I saw, if she had heard what I heard in the nursery—could she expect me to give him the letter?'

Her mind was apparently steadied by the reflection which her last words expressed. She moved away thoughtfully from the garden-seat, crossed the terrace, descended some wooden steps, and followed a shrubbery path, which led round by a winding track from the east to the north side of the house.

This part of the building had been uninhabited and neglected for more than half a century past. In the time of Captain Treverton's father the whole range of the north rooms had been stripped of their finest pictures and their most valuable furniture, to assist in re-decorating the west rooms, which now formed the only inhabited part of the house, and which were amply sufficient for the accommodation of the family and of any visitors who came to stay with them. The mansion had been originally built in the form of a square, and had been strongly fortified. Of the many defences of the place, but one

now remained—a heavy, low tower (from which and from the
village near, the house derived its name of Porthgenna
Tower),* standing at the southern extremity of the west front.
The south side itself consisted of stables and out-houses, with
a ruinous wall in front of them, which, running back, eastward,
at right angles, joined the north side, and so completed the
square which the whole outline of the building represented.

The outside view of the range of north rooms, from the
weedy, deserted garden below, showed plainly enough that
many years had passed since any human creature had inhabited them. The window-panes were broken in some places, and
covered thickly with dirt and dust in others. Here, the shutters
were closed—there, they were only half-opened. The
untrained ivy, the rank vegetation growing in fissures of the
stone-work, the festoons of spiders' webs, the rubbish of wood,
bricks, plaster, broken glass, rags, and strips of soiled cloth,
which lay beneath the windows, all told the same tale of
neglect. Shadowed by its position, this ruinous side of the
house had a dark, cold, wintry aspect, even on the sunny
August morning, when Sarah Leeson strayed into the deserted
northern garden. Lost in the labyrinth of her own thoughts, she
moved slowly past flower-beds, long since rooted up, and
along gravel-walks overgrown by weeds; her eyes wandering
mechanically over the prospect, her feet mechanically carrying
her on wherever there was a trace of a footpath, lead where it
might.

The shock which the words spoken by her master in the
nursery had communicated to her mind, had set her whole
nature, so to speak, at bay, and had roused in her, at last, the
moral courage to arm herself with a final and desperate resolution. Wandering more and more slowly along the pathways of
the forsaken garden, as the course of her ideas withdrew her
more and more completely from all outward things, she
stopped insensibly on an open patch of ground, which had
once been a well-kept lawn, and which still commanded a full
view of the long range of uninhabited north rooms.

'What binds me to give the letter to my master at all?' she
thought to herself, smoothing out the crumpled paper dream-
ily in the palm of her hand. 'My mistress died without making

me swear to do that. Can she visit it on me from the other world, if I keep the promises I swore to observe, and do no more? May I not risk the worst that can happen, so long as I hold religiously to all that I undertook to do on my oath?'

She paused here in reasoning with herself; her superstitious fears still influencing her out of doors, in the daylight, as they had influenced her in her own room, in the time of darkness. She paused—then fell to smoothing the letter again, and began to recal the terms of the solemn engagement which Mrs Treverton had forced her to contract.

What had she actually bound herself to do? Not to destroy the letter, and not to take it away with her if she left the house. Beyond that, Mrs Treverton's desire had been that the letter should be given to her husband. Was that last wish binding on the person to whom it had been confided? Yes. As binding as an oath? No.

As she arrived at that conclusion, she looked up.

At first, her eyes rested vacantly on the lonely, deserted north front of the house; gradually, they became attracted by one particular window exactly in the middle, on the floor above the ground—the largest and the gloomiest of all the row; suddenly, they brightened with an expression of intelligence. She started; a faint flush of colour flew into her cheeks, and she hastily advanced closer to the wall of the house.

The panes of the large window were yellow with dust and dirt, and festooned about fantastically with cobwebs. Below it was a heap of rubbish, scattered over the dry mould of what might once have been a bed of flowers or shrubs. The form of the bed was still marked out by an oblong boundary of weeds and rank grass. She followed it irresolutely all round, looking up at the window at every step—then stopped close under it, glanced at the letter in her hand, and said to herself abruptly:—

'I'll risk it!'

As the words fell from her lips, she hastened back to the inhabited part of the house, followed the passage on the kitchen-floor which led to the housekeeper's room, entered it, and took down from a nail in the wall a bunch of keys, having a large ivory label attached to the ring that connected them, on which was inscribed, 'Keys of the North Rooms.'

She placed the keys on a writing-table near her, took up a pen, and rapidly added these lines on the blank side of the letter which she had written under her mistress's dictation:—

'If this paper should ever be found (which I pray with my whole heart it never may be), I wish to say that I have come to the resolution of hiding it, because I dare not show the writing that it contains to my master, to whom it is addressed. In doing what I now propose to do, though I am acting against my mistress's last wishes, I am not breaking the solemn engagement which she obliged me to make before her on her death-bed. That engagement forbids me to destroy this letter, or to take it away with me if I leave the house. I shall do neither,—my purpose is to conceal it in the place, of all others, where I think there is least chance of its ever being found again. Any hardship or misfortune which may follow as a consequence of this deceitful proceeding on my part, will fall on myself. Others, I believe in my conscience, will be the happier for the hiding of the dreadful Secret which this letter contains.'

She signed those lines with her name,—pressed them hurriedly over the blotting-pad that lay with the rest of the writing materials on the table,—took the note in her hand, after first folding it up,—and then, snatching at the bunch of keys with a look all round her, as if she dreaded being secretly observed, left the room. All her actions since she had entered it had been hasty and sudden; she was evidently afraid of allowing herself one leisure moment to reflect.

On quitting the housekeeper's room, she turned to the left, ascended a back staircase, and unlocked a door at the top of it. A cloud of dust flew all about her, as she softly opened the door; a mouldy coolness made her shiver as she crossed a large stone hall, with some black old family portraits hanging on the walls, the canvases of which were bulging out of the frames. Ascending more stairs, she came upon a row of doors, all leading into rooms on the first floor of the north side of the house.

She knelt down, putting the letter on the boards beside her, opposite the keyhole of the fourth door she came to after reaching the top of the stairs, peered in distrustfully for an instant, then began to try the different keys till she found one that fitted the lock. She had great difficulty in accomplishing this, from the violence of her agitation, which made her hands tremble to such a degree that she was hardly able to keep the keys separate one from the other. At length she succeeded in opening the door. Thicker clouds of dust than she had yet met with flew out the moment the interior of the room was visible; a dry, airless, suffocating atmosphere almost choked her as she stooped to pick up the letter from the floor. She recoiled from it at first, and took a few steps back towards the staircase. But she recovered her resolution immediately.

'I can't go back now!' she said, desperately, and entered the room.

She did not remain in it more than two or three minutes. When she came out again, her face was white with fear, and the hand which had held the letter when she went into the room, held nothing now but a small rusty key.

After locking the door again, she examined the large bunch of keys which she had taken from the housekeeper's room, with closer attention than she had yet bestowed on them. Besides the ivory label attached to the ring that connected them, there were smaller labels, of parchment, tied to the handles of some of the keys, to indicate the rooms to which they gave admission. The particular key which she had used had one of these labels hanging to it. She held the little strip of parchment close to the light, and read on it, in written characters faded by time,

'*The Myrtle Room.*'

The room in which the letter was hidden had a name, then! A prettily sounding name that would attract most people, and keep pleasantly in their memories. A name to be distrusted by her, after what she had done, on that very account.

She took her housewife* from its usual place in the pocket of her apron, and, with the scissors which it contained, cut the label from the key. Was it enough to destroy that one only? She lost herself in a maze of useless conjecture; and ended by cutting off the other labels, from no other motive than instinctive suspicion of them.

Carefully gathering up the strips of parchment from the floor, she put them, along with the little rusty key which she had brought out of the Myrtle Room, in the empty pocket of her apron. Then, carrying the large bunch of keys in her hand,

and carefully locking the doors that she had opened on her way to the north side of Porthgenna Tower, she retraced her steps to the housekeeper's room, entered it without seeing anybody, and hung up the bunch of keys again on the nail in the wall.

Fearful, as the morning hours wore on, of meeting with some of the female servants, she next hastened back to her bed-room. The candle she had left there was still burning feebly in the fresh daylight. When she drew aside the window-curtain, after extinguishing the candle, a shadow of her former fear passed over her face, even in the broad daylight that now flowed in upon it. She opened the window, and leaned out eagerly into the cool air.

Whether for good or for evil, the fatal Secret was hidden now—the act was done. There was something calming in the first consciousness of that one fact. She could think more com-posedly, after that, of herself, and of the uncertain future that lay before her.

Under no circumstances could she have expected to remain in her situation, now that the connection between herself and her mistress had been severed by death. She knew that Mrs Treverton, in the last days of her illness, had earnestly recommended her maid to Captain Treverton's kindness and protection, and she felt assured that the wife's last entreaties, in this as in all other instances, would be viewed as the most sacred of obligations by the husband. But could she accept protection and kindness at the hand of the master whom she had been accessory to deceiving, and whom she had now committed herself to deceiving still? The bare idea of such baseness was so revolting, that she accepted, almost with a sense of relief, the one sad alternative that remained—the alter-native of leaving the house immediately.

And how was she to leave it? By giving formal warning, and so exposing herself to questions which would be sure to con-fuse and terrify her? Could she venture to face her master again, after what she had done—to face him, when his first inquiries would refer to her mistress, when he would be certain to ask for the last mournful details, for the slightest word that had been spoken during the death-scene that she alone had witnessed? She started to her feet, as the certain consequences of submitting herself to that unendurable trial all crowded together warningly on her mind, took her cloak from its place on the wall, and listened at her door in sudden suspicion and fear. Had she heard footsteps? Was her master sending for her already?

No: all was silent outside. A few tears rolled over her cheeks, as she put on her bonnet, and felt that she was facing, by the performance of that simple action, the last, and perhaps the hardest to meet, of the cruel necessities in which the hiding of the Secret had involved her. There was no help for it. She must run the risk of betraying everything, or brave the double trial of leaving Porthgenna Tower, and leaving it secretly.

Secretly—as a thief might go? Without a word to her master; without so much as one line of writing to thank him for his kindness, and to ask his pardon? She had unlocked her desk, and had taken from it her purse, one or two letters, and a little book of Wesley's Hymns,* before these considerations occurred to her. They made her pause in the act of shutting up the desk. 'Shall I write?' she asked herself, 'and leave the letter here, to be found when I am gone?'

A little more reflection decided her in the affirmative. As rapidly as her pen could form the letters, she wrote a few lines addressed to Captain Treverton, in which she confessed to having kept a secret from his knowledge which had been left in her charge to divulge; adding, that she honestly believed no harm could come to him, or to any one in whom he was interested, by her failing to perform the duty entrusted to her; and ending by asking his pardon for leaving the house secretly, and by begging, as a last favour, that no search might ever be made for her. Having sealed this short note, and left it on her table, with her master's name written outside, she listened again at the door; and, after satisfying herself that no one was yet stirring, began to descend the stairs at Porthgenna Tower for the last time.

At the entrance of the passage leading to the nursery, she stopped. The tears which she had restrained since leaving her room, began to flow again. Urgent as her reasons now were for effecting her departure without a moment's loss of time, she advanced, with the strangest inconsistency, a few steps towards the nursery-door. Before she had gone far, a slight noise in the lower part of the house caught her ear, and instantly checked her further progress.

While she stood doubtful, the grief at her heart—a greater grief than any she had yet betrayed—rose irresistibly to her lips, and burst from them in one deep gasping sob. The sound of it seemed to terrify her into a sense of the danger of her position, if she delayed a moment longer. She ran out again to the stairs, reached the kitchen-floor in safety, and made her escape by the garden-door which the servant had opened for her at the dawn of the morning.

On getting clear of the premises at Porthgenna Tower, instead of taking the nearest path over the moor that led to the high road, she diverged to the church; but stopped before she came to it, at the public well of the neighbourhood, which had been sunk near the cottages of the Porthgenna fishermen. Cautiously looking round her, she dropped into the well the little rusty key which she had brought out of the Myrtle Room; then hurried on, and entered the churchyard. She directed her course straight to one of the graves, situated a little apart from the rest. On the headstone were inscribed these words:—

SACRED TO THE MEMORY
OF
HUGH POLWHEAL,*
AGED 26 YEARS.
HE MET WITH HIS DEATH
THROUGH THE FALL OF A ROCK
IN
PORTHGENNA MINE,
DECEMBER 17TH, 1823.

Gathering a few leaves of grass from the grave, Sarah opened the little book of Wesley's Hymns which she had brought with her from the bed-room at Porthgenna Tower, and placed the leaves delicately and carefully between the pages. As she did this, the wind blew open the title-page of the Hymns, and displayed this inscription on it, written in large clumsy characters:—'Sarah Leeson, her book. The gift of Hugh Polwheal.'

Having secured the blades of grass between the pages of the

book, she retraced her way towards the path leading to the high road. Arrived on the moor, she took out of her apron-pocket the parchment labels that had been cut from the keys, and scattered them under the furze-bushes.

'Gone,' she said, 'as I am gone! God help and forgive me, it is all done and over now!'

With those words she turned her back on the old house and the sea-view below it, and followed the moorland path on her way to the high road.

Four hours afterwards, Captain Treverton desired one of the servants at Porthgenna Tower to inform Sarah Leeson that he wished to hear all she had to tell him of the dying moments of her mistress. The messenger returned with looks and words of amazement, and with the letter that Sarah had addressed to her master in his hand.

The moment Captain Treverton had read the letter, he ordered an immediate search to be made after the missing woman. She was so easy to describe and to recognise by the premature greyness of her hair, by the odd, scared look in her eyes, and by her habit of constantly talking to herself, that she was traced with certainty as far as Truro.* In that large town the track of her was lost, and never recovered again.

Rewards were offered; the magistrates of the district were interested in the case; all that wealth and power could do to discover her, was done—and done in vain. No clue was found to suggest a suspicion of her whereabouts, or to help in the slightest degree towards explaining the nature of the secret at which she had hinted in her letter. Her master never saw her again; never heard of her again, after the morning of the twenty-third of August, eighteen hundred and twenty-nine.

BOOK II

CHAPTER I

FIFTEEN YEARS AFTER

THE church of Long Beckley (a large agricultural village in one of the midland counties of England), although a building in no way remarkable either for its size, its architecture, or its antiquity, possesses, nevertheless, one advantage which mercantile London has barbarously denied to the noble cathedral church of St Paul. It has plenty of room to stand in, and it can consequently be seen with perfect convenience from every point of view, all round the compass.

The large open space around the church can be approached in three different directions. There is a road from the village, leading straight to the principal door. There is a broad gravel-walk, which begins at the vicarage gates, crosses the church-yard, and stops, as in duty bound, at the vestry entrance. There is a footpath over the fields, by which the lord of the manor, and the gentry in general who live in his august neighbourhood, can reach the side door of the building, whenever their natural humility may incline them to encourage Sabbath observance in the stables, by going to church, like the lower sort of worshippers, on their own legs.

At half-past seven o'clock, on a certain fine summer morning, in the year eighteen hundred and forty-four, if any observant stranger had happened to be standing in some unnoticed corner of the churchyard, and to be looking about him with sharp eyes, he would probably have been the witness of proceedings which might have led him to believe that there was a conspiracy going on in Long Beckley, of which the church was the rallying-point, and some of the most respectable inhabitants the principal leaders. Supposing him to have been looking towards the vicarage as the clock chimed the half-hour, he would have seen the Vicar of Long Beckley, the Reverend Doctor Chennery, leaving his house suspiciously, by the back way, glancing behind him guiltily as he approached the gravel-walk that led to the vestry, stopping mysteriously just outside the door, and gazing anxiously down the road that led from the village.

Assuming that our observant stranger would, upon this, keep out of sight, and look down the road, like the vicar, he would next have seen the clerk of the church—an austere, yellow-faced man—a Protestant Loyola* in appearance, and a working shoemaker by trade—approaching with a look of unutterable mystery in his face, and a bunch of big keys in his hands. He would have seen the vicar nod in an abstracted manner to the clerk, and say, 'Fine morning, Thomas. Have you had your breakfast yet?' He would have heard Thomas reply, with a suspicious regard for minute particulars: 'I have had a cup of tea and a crust, sir.' And he would then have seen these two local conspirators, after looking up with one accord at the church clock, draw off together to the side door which commanded a view of the footpath across the fields.

Following them —as our inquisitive stranger could not fail to do—he would have detected three more conspirators advancing along the footpath. The leader of this treasonable party was an elderly gentleman, with a weather-beaten face, and a bluff hearty manner. His two followers were a young gentleman and a young lady, walking arm-in-arm, and talking together in whispers. They were dressed in the plainest morning costume. The faces of both were rather pale, and the manner of the lady was a little flurried. Otherwise, there was nothing remarkable to observe in them, until they came to the wicket-gate leading into the churchyard; and there the conduct of the young gentleman seemed, at first sight, rather inexplicable. Instead of holding the gate open for the lady to pass through, he hung back, allowed her to open it for herself, waited till she had got to the churchyard side, and then, stretching out his hand over the gate, allowed her to lead him through the entrance, as if he had suddenly changed from a grown man to a helpless little child.

Noting this, and remarking also that, when the party from the fields had arrived within greeting distance of the vicar, and when the clerk had used his bunch of keys to open the church-door, the young lady's companion was led into the building (this time by Doctor Chennery's hand), as he had been previously led through the wicket-gate, our observant stranger must have arrived at one inevitable conclusion—that the person requiring such assistance as this, was suffering under the affliction of blindness. Startled a little by that discovery, he would have been still further amazed, if he had looked into the church, by seeing the blind man and the young lady standing together before the altar rails, with the elderly gentleman in parental attendance. Any suspicions he might now entertain that the bond which united the conspirators at that early hour of the morning was of the hymeneal sort, and that the object of their plot was to celebrate a wedding with the strictest secresy, would have been confirmed in five minutes by the appearance of Doctor Chennery from the vestry in full canonicals, and by the reading of the marriage service in the reverend gentleman's most harmonious officiating tones. The ceremony concluded, the attendant stranger must have been more perplexed than ever, by observing that the persons concerned in it all separated, the moment the signing, the kissing, and congratulating duties proper to the occasion had been performed, and quickly retired in the various directions by which they had approached the church.

Leaving the clerk to return by the village road, the bride, bridegroom, and elderly gentleman to turn back by the footpath over the fields, and the visionary stranger of these pages to vanish out of them, in any direction that he pleases;—let us follow Doctor Chennery to the vicarage breakfast-table, and hear what he has to say about his professional exertions of the morning, in the familiar atmosphere of his own family circle.

The persons assembled at the breakfast were, first, Mr Phippen, a guest; secondly, Miss Sturch, a governess; thirdly, fourthly, and fifthly, Miss Louisa Chennery (aged eleven years), Miss Amelia Chennery (aged nine years), and Master Robert Chennery (aged eight years). There was no mother's face present, to make the household picture complete. Doctor Chennery had been a widower since the birth of his youngest child.

The guest was an old college acquaintance of the vicar's, and he was supposed to be now staying at Long Beckley for the benefit of his health. Most men of any character at all contrive to get a reputation of some sort which individualises them in the social circle amid which they move. Mr Phippen was a man of some little character, and he lived with great distinction in the estimation of his friends, on the reputation of being A Martyr to Dyspepsia.

Wherever Mr Phippen went, the woes of Mr Phippen's stomach went with him. He dieted himself publicly, and physicked himself publicly. He was so intensely occupied with himself and his maladies, that he would let a chance acquaintance into the secret of the condition of his tongue, at five minutes' notice; being just as perpetually ready to discuss the state of his digestion as people in general are to discuss the state of the weather. On this favourite subject, as on all others, he spoke with a wheedling gentleness of manner, sometimes in softly mournful, sometimes in languidly sentimental tones. His politeness was of the oppressively affectionate sort, and he used the word 'dear' continually, in addressing himself to others. Personally, he could not be called a handsome man. His eyes were watery, large, and light grey; they were always rolling from side to side in a state of moist admiration of something or somebody. His nose was long, drooping, profoundly melancholy,— if such an expression may be permitted in reference to that particular feature. For the rest, his lips had a lachrymose twist; his stature was small; his head, large, bald, and loosely set on his shoulders; his manner of dressing himself eccentric, on the side of smartness; his age about five-and forty; his condition that of a single man. Such was Mr Phippen, the Martyr to Dyspepsia, and the guest of the vicar of Long Beckley.

Miss Sturch, the governess, may be briefly and accurately described as a young lady who had never been troubled with an idea or a sensation since the day when she was born. She was a little, plump, quiet, white-skinned, smiling, neatly-dressed girl, wound up accurately to the performance of certain duties at certain times; and possessed of an inexhaustible vocabulary of common-place talk, which dribbled placidly out of her lips whenever it was called for, always in the same quantity, and always of the same quality, at every hour in the day, and through every change in the seasons. Miss Sturch never laughed, and never cried, but took the safe middle course of smiling perpetually. She smiled when she came down on a morning in January, and said it was very cold. She smiled when she came down on a morning in July, and said it was very hot. She smiled when the bishop came once a-year to see the vicar; she smiled when the butcher's boy came every morning for orders. Let what might happen at the vicarage, nothing ever jerked Miss Sturch out of the one smooth groove in which she ran perpetually, always at the same pace. If she had lived in a royalist family, during the civil wars in England, she would have rung for the cook, to order dinner, on the morning of the execution of Charles the First.* If Shakespeare had come back to life again, and had called at the vicarage at six o'clock on Saturday evening, to explain to Miss Sturch exactly what his views were in composing the tragedy of Hamlet, she would have smiled and said it was extremely interesting, until the striking of seven o'clock; at which time she would have left him in the middle of a sentence, to superintend the housemaid in the verification of the washing-book. A very estimable young person, Miss Sturch (as the ladies of Long Beckley were accustomed to say); so judicious with the children and so attached to her household duties; such a well-regulated mind, and such a crisp touch on the piano; just nice-looking enough, just well-dressed enough, just talkative enough; not quite old enough, perhaps, and a little too much inclined to be embraceably plump about the region of the waist—but, on the whole, a most estimable young person,—very much so, indeed.

On the characteristic peculiarities of Miss Sturch's pupils, it is not necessary to dwell at very great length. Miss Louisa's habitual weakness was an inveterate tendency to catch cold. Miss Amelia's principal defect was a disposition to gratify her palate by eating supplementary dinners and breakfasts at unauthorised times and seasons. Master Robert's most noticeable failings were caused by alacrity in tearing his clothes, and obtuseness in learning the Multiplication Table. The virtues of all three were of much the same nature—they were well grown, they were genuine children, and they were boisterously fond of Miss Sturch.

To complete the gallery of family portraits, an outline, at the least, must be attempted of the vicar himself. Doctor Chennery was, in a physical point of view, a credit to the Establishment to which he was attached. He stood six feet two in his shooting-shoes; he weighed fifteen stone; he was the best bowler in the Long Beckley cricket-club; he was a strictly orthodox man in the matter of wine and mutton; he never started disagreeable theories about people's future destinies in the pulpit, never quarrelled with anybody out of the pulpit, never buttoned up his pockets when the necessities of his poor brethren (dis-senters included) pleaded with him to open them. His course through the world was a steady march along the high and dry middle of a safe turnpike-road. The serpentine side-paths of controversy might open as alluringly as they pleased on his right hand and on his left, but he kept on his way sturdily, and never regarded them. Innovating young recruits in the Church army might entrappingly open the Thirty-nine Articles* under his very nose, but the veteran's wary eye never looked a hair's-breadth further than his own signature at the bottom of them. He knew as little as possible of theology, he had never given the Privy Council* a minute's trouble in the whole course of his life, he was innocent of all meddling with the reading or writing of pamphlets, and he was quite incapable of finding his way to the platform of Exeter Hall.* In short, he was the most uncler-ical of clergymen—but, for all that, he had such a figure for a surplice as is seldom seen. Fifteen stone weight of upright mus-cular flesh, without an angry spot or a sore place in any part of it, has the merit of suggesting stability, at any rate,—an excellent virtue in pillars of all kinds, but an especially precious quality, at the present time, in a pillar of the Church.

As soon as the vicar entered the breakfast-parlour, the children assailed him with a chorus of shouts. He was a severe disciplinarian in the observance of punctuality at meal times; and he now stood convicted by the clock of being too late for breakfast by a quarter of an hour.

'Sorry to have kept you waiting, Miss Sturch,' said the vicar; 'but I have a good excuse for being late this morning.'

'Pray don't mention it, sir,' said Miss Sturch, blandly rubbing her plump little hands one over the other. 'A beautiful morning. I fear we shall have another warm day. Robert, my love, your elbow is on the table. A beautiful morning, indeed!'

'Stomach still out of order—eh, Phippen?' asked the vicar, beginning to carve the ham.

Mr Phippen shook his large head dolefully, placed his yellow forefinger, ornamented with a large turquoise ring, on the centre cheek of his light green summer waistcoat—looked piteously at Doctor Chennery, and sighed—removed the finger, and produced from the breast-pocket of his wrapper a little mahogany case—took out of it a neat pair of apothecary's scales, with the accompanying weights, a morsel of ginger, and a highly-polished silver nutmeg-grater. 'Dear Miss Sturch will pardon an invalid?' said Mr Phippen, beginning to grate the ginger feebly into the nearest tea-cup.

'Guess what has made me a quarter of an hour late this morning,' said the vicar, looking mysteriously all round the table.

'Lying in bed, papa,' cried the three children, clapping their hands in triumph.

'What do *you* say, Miss Sturch?' asked Doctor Chennery.

Miss Sturch smiled as usual, rubbed her hands as usual, cleared her throat softly as usual, looked at the tea-urn, and begged, with the most graceful politeness, to be excused if she said nothing.

'Your turn now, Phippen,' said the vicar. 'Come, guess what has kept me late this morning.'

'My dear friend,' said Mr Phippen, giving the Doctor a brotherly squeeze of the hand, 'don't ask me to guess—I know! I saw what you eat at dinner yesterday—I saw what you drank after dinner. No digestion could stand it—not even yours. Guess what has made you late this morning? Pooh! pooh! I know. You dear, good soul, you have been taking physic!'

'Hav'n't touched a drop, thank God, for the last ten years!' said Doctor Chennery, with a look of devout gratitude. 'No, no; you're all wrong. The fact is, I have been to church; and what do you think I have been doing there? Listen,

Miss Sturch—listen, girls, with all your ears. Poor blind young Frankland is a happy man at last—I have married him to our dear Rosamond Treverton this very morning!'

'Without telling us, papa!' cried the two girls together in their shrillest tones of vexation and surprise. 'Without telling us, when you know how we should have liked to see it!'

'That was the very reason why I did not tell you, my dears,' answered the vicar. 'Young Frankland has not got so used to his affliction yet, poor fellow, as to bear being publicly pitied and stared at in the character of a blind bridegroom. He had such a nervous horror of being an object of curiosity on his wedding-day, and Rosamond, like a kind-hearted girl as she is, was so anxious that his slightest caprices should be humoured, that we settled to have the wedding at an hour in the morning when no idlers were likely to be lounging about the neighbour-hood of the church. I was bound over to the strictest secresy about the day, and so was my clerk, Thomas. Excepting us two, and the bride and bridegroom, and the bride's father, Captain Treverton, nobody knew——'

'Treverton!' exclaimed Mr Phippen, holding his tea-cup, with the grated ginger in the bottom of it to be filled by Miss Sturch. 'Treverton! (No more tea, dear Miss Sturch.) How very remarkable! I know the name. (Fill up with water, if you please.) Tell me, my dear doctor (many, many thanks; no sugar, it turns acid on the stomach), is this Miss Treverton whom you have been marrying (many thanks again; no milk, either) one of the Cornish Trevertons?'

'To be sure she is!' rejoined the vicar. 'Her father, Captain Treverton, is the head of the family. Not that there's much family to speak of now. The Captain, and Rosamond, and that whimsical old brute of an uncle of hers, Andrew Treverton, are the last left now, of the old stock—a rich family, and a fine family, in former times—good friends to Church and State, you know, and all that——'

'Do you approve, sir, of Amelia having a second helping of bread and marmalade?' asked Miss Sturch, appealing to Doctor Chennery with the most perfect unconsciousness of interrupting him. Having no spare room in her mind for putting things away in until the appropriate time came for bringing them out, Miss Sturch always asked questions and made remarks the moment they occurred to her, without waiting for the beginning, middle, or end of any conversations that might be proceeding in her presence. She invariably looked the part of a listener to perfection, but she never acted it except in the case of talk that was aimed point-blank at her own ears.

'O, give her a second helping, by all means!' said the vicar, carelessly; 'if she must over-eat herself, she may as well do it on bread and marmalade as on anything else.'

'My dear good soul,' exclaimed Mr Phippen, 'look what a wreck I am, and don't talk in that shockingly thoughtless way of letting our sweet Amelia over-eat herself. Load the stomach in youth, and what becomes of the digestion in age? The thing which vulgar people call the inside—I appeal to Miss Sturch's interest in her charming pupil as an excuse for going into physiological particulars—is, in point of fact, an Apparatus. Digestively considered, Miss Sturch, even the fairest and youngest of us is an Apparatus. Oil our wheels, if you like; but clog them at your peril. Farinaceous puddings and mutton-chops: mutton-chops and farinaceous puddings— those should be the parents' watch-words, if I had my way, from one end of England to the other. Look here, my sweet child, look at me. There is no fun, dear, about these little scales, but dreadful earnest. See! I put in the balance on one side, dry bread (stale, dry bread, Amelia!), and on the other, some ounce weights. "Mr Phippen, eat by weight, Mr Phippen! eat the same quantity, day by day, to a hair's-breadth. Mr Phippen! exceed your allowance (though it is only stale, dry bread) if you dare!" Amelia, love, this is not fun—this is what the doctors tell me—the doctors, my child, who have been searching my Apparatus through and through for thirty years past, with little pills, and have not found out where my wheels are clogged yet. Think of that, Amelia—think of Mr Phippen's clogged Apparatus—and say "No, thank you," next time. Miss Sturch, I beg a thousand pardons for intruding on your province; but my interest in that sweet child—Chennery, you dear good soul, what were we talking about? Ah! the bride—the interesting bride!

And so she is one of the Cornish Trevertons? I knew something of Andrew, years ago. He was a bachelor, like myself,
Miss Sturch. His Apparatus was out of order, like mine, dear
Amelia. Not at all like his brother, the captain, I should suppose? And so, she is married? A charming girl, I have no
doubt. A charming girl!'

'No better, truer, prettier girl in the world,' said the vicar.

'A very lively, energetic person,' remarked Miss Sturch.

'How I shall miss her!' cried Miss Louisa. 'Nobody else
amused me as Rosamond did, when I was laid up with that last
bad cold of mine.'

'She used to give us such nice little early supper-parties,' said
Miss Amelia.

'She was the only girl I ever saw who was fit to play with
boys,' said Master Robert. 'She could catch a ball, Mr Phippen,
sir, with one hand, and go down a slide with both her legs
together.'

'Bless me!' said Mr Phippen. 'What an extraordinary wife for
a blind man! You said he was blind from his birth, my dear
doctor, did you not? Let me see, what was his name? You will
not bear too hardly on my loss of memory, Miss Sturch? When
indigestion has done with the body, it begins to prey on the
mind. Mr Frank Something, was it not?'

'No, no—Frankland,' answered the vicar. 'Leonard Frankland. And not blind from his birth by any means. It is not much
more than a year ago since he could see almost as well as any of
us.'

'An accident, I suppose!' said Mr Phippen. 'You will excuse
me if I take the armchair?—a partially reclining posture is of
great assistance to me, after meals. So an accident happened to
his eyes? Ah, what a delightfully easy chair to sit in!'

'Scarcely an accident,' said Doctor Chennery. 'Leonard
Frankland was a difficult child to bring up: great constitutional weakness, you know, at first. He seemed to get over that
with time, and grew into a quiet, sedate, orderly sort of boy—
as unlike my son there as possible—very amiable, and what
you call easy to deal with. Well, he had a turn for mechanics
(I am telling you all this to make you understand about his
blindness), and after veering from one occupation of that sort

to another, he took at last to watchmaking. Curious amusement for a boy, but anything that required delicacy of touch and plenty of patience and perseverance, was just the thing to amuse and occupy Leonard. I always said to his father and mother, "Get him off that stool, break his magnifying-glasses, send him to me, and I'll give him a back at Leap Frog, and teach him the use of a bat." But it was no use. His parents knew best, I suppose, and they said he must be humoured. Well, things went on smoothly enough for some time, till he got another long illness—as I believe, from not taking exercise enough. As soon as he began to get round, back he went to his old watchmaking occupations again. But the bad end of it all was coming. About the last work he did, poor fellow, was the repairing of my watch—here it is; goes as regular as a steam engine. I hadn't got it back into my fob very long before I heard that he was getting a bad pain at the back of his head, and that he saw all sorts of moving spots before his eyes. String him up with lots of port wine, and give him three hours a day on the back of a quiet pony—that was my advice. Instead of taking it, they sent for doctors from London, and blistered him behind the ears and between the shoulders, and drenched the lad with mercury, and moped him up in a dark room. No use. The sight got worse and worse, flickered and flickered, and went out at last like the flame of a candle. His mother died—luckily for her, poor soul—before that happened. His father was half out of his mind: took him to oculists in London, and oculists in Paris. All they did was to call the blindness by a long Latin name, and to say that it was hopeless and useless to try an operation. Some of them said it was the result of the long weaknesses from which he had twice suffered after illness. Some said it was an apoplectic effusion in his brain. All of them shook their heads when they heard of the watchmaking. So they brought him back home, blind; blind he is now; and blind he will remain, poor dear fellow, for the rest of his life.'

'You shock me; my dear Chennery, you shock me dreadfully,' said Mr Phippen. 'Especially when you state that theory about long weakness after illness. Good Heavens! Why *I* have had long weaknesses—I have got them now. Spots did he see before his eyes? I see spots, black spots, dancing black spots, dancing black bilious spots. Upon my word of honour, Chennery, this comes home to me—my sympathies are painfully acute—I feel this blind story in every nerve of my body; I do indeed!'

'You would hardly know that Leonard was blind, to look at him,' said Miss Louisa, striking into the conversation with a view to restoring Mr Phippen's equanimity. 'Except that his eyes look quieter than other people's, there seems no difference in them now. Who was that famous character you told us about, Miss Sturch, who was blind, and didn't show it any more than Leonard Frankland?'

'Milton, my love. I begged you to remember that he was the most famous of British epic poets,' answered Miss Sturch with suavity. 'He poetically describes his blindness as being caused by "so thick a drop serene."* You shall read about it, Louisa. After we have had a little French, we will have a little Milton, this morning. Hush, love, your papa is speaking.'

'Poor young Frankland!' said the vicar, warmly. 'That good, tender, noble creature I married him to this morning, seems sent as a consolation to him in his affliction. If any human being can make him happy for the rest of his life, Rosamond Treverton is the girl to do it.'

'She has made a sacrifice,' said Mr Phippen; 'but I like her for that, having made a sacrifice myself in remaining single. It seems indispensable, indeed, on the score of humanity, that I should do so. How could I conscientiously inflict such a digestion as mine on a member of the fairer portion of creation? No: I am a sacrifice in my own proper person, and I have a fellow-feeling for others who are like me. Did she cry much, Chennery, when you were marrying her?'

'Cry!' exclaimed the vicar, contemptuously. 'Rosamond Treverton is not one of the puling, sentimental sort, I can tell you. A fine, buxom, warm-hearted, quick-tempered girl, who looks what she means when she tells a man she is going to marry him. And, mind you, she has been tried. If she hadn't loved him with all her heart and soul, she might have been free months ago to marry anybody she pleased. They were engaged long before this cruel affliction befel young

Frankland—the fathers, on both sides, having lived as near neighbours in these parts for years. Well, when the blindness came, Leonard at once offered to release Rosamond from her engagement. You should have read the letter she wrote to him, Phippen, upon that. I don't mind confessing that I blubbered like a baby over it, when they showed it to me. I should have married them at once the instant I read it, but old Frankland was a fidgety, punctilious kind of man, and he insisted on a six months' probation, so that she might be certain of knowing her own mind. He died before the term was out, and that caused the marriage to be put off again. But no delays could alter Rosamond—six years, instead of six months, would not have changed her. There she was this morning as fond of that poor patient blind fellow as she was the first day they were engaged. "You shall never know a sad moment, Lenny, if I can help it, as long as you live," these were the first words she said to him when we all came out of church. "I hear you, Rosamond," said I. "And you shall judge me, too, doctor," says she, quick as lightning. "We will come back to Long Beckley, and you shall ask Lenny if I have not kept my word." With that, she gave me a kiss that you might have heard down here at the vicarage, bless her heart! We'll drink her health after dinner, Miss Sturch—we'll drink both their healths, Phippen, in a bottle of the best wine I have in my cellar.'

'In a glass of toast-and-water, so far as I am concerned, if you will allow me,' said Mr Phippen, mournfully. 'But, my dear Chennery, when you were talking of the fathers of these two interesting young people, you spoke of their living as near neighbours here, at Long Beckley. My memory is impaired, as I am painfully aware; but I thought Captain Treverton was the eldest of the two brothers, and that he always lived, when he was on shore, at the family place in Cornwall?'

'So he did,' returned the vicar, 'in his wife's lifetime. But since her death, which happened as long ago as the year 'twenty-nine—let me see, we are now in the year forty-four—and that makes——'

The vicar stopped for an instant to calculate, and looked at Miss Sturch.

'Fifteen years ago, sir,' said Miss Sturch, offering the accommodation of a little simple subtraction to the vicar, with her blandest smile.

'Of course,' continued Doctor Chennery. 'Well, since Mrs Treverton died, fifteen years ago, Captain Treverton has never been near Porthgenna Tower. And, what is more, Phippen, at the first opportunity he could get, he sold the place—sold it, out and out, mine, fisheries, and all—for forty thousand pounds.'

'You don't say so!' exclaimed Mr Phippen. 'Did he find the air unhealthy? I should think the local produce, in the way of food, must be coarse now, in those barbarous regions? Who bought the place?'

'Leonard Frankland's father,' said the vicar. 'It is rather a long story, that sale of Porthgenna Tower, with some curious circumstances involved in it. Suppose we take a turn in the garden, Phippen? I'll tell you all about it over my morning cigar. Miss Sturch, if you want me, I shall be on the lawn somewhere. Girls! mind you know your lessons. Bob! remember that I've got a cane in the hall, and a birchrod in my dressing-room. Come, Phippen, rouse up out of that arm-chair. You won't say, no, to a turn in the garden?'

'My dear fellow, I will say yes—if you will kindly lend me an umbrella, and allow me to carry my camp-stool in my hand,' said Mr Phippen. 'I am too weak to encounter the sun, and I can't go far without sitting down. The moment I feel fatigued, Miss Sturch, I open my camp-stool, and sit down anywhere, without the slightest regard for appearances. I am ready, Chennery, whenever you are—equally ready, my good friend, for the garden and the story about the sale of Porthgenna Tower. You said it was a curious story, did you not?'

'I said there was some curious circumstances connected with it,' replied the vicar. 'And when you hear about them, I think you will say so, too. Come along! you will find your camp-stool, and a choice of all the umbrellas in the house, in the hall.'

With those words, Doctor Chennery opened his cigar-case, and led the way out of the breakfast parlour.

CHAPTER II

THE SALE OF PORTHGENNA TOWER

'How charming! how pastoral! how exquisitely soothing!' said Mr Phippen, sentimentally surveying the lawn at the back of the vicarage-house, under the shadow of the lightest umbrella he could pick out of the hall. 'Three years have passed, Chennery, since I last stood on this lawn. There is the window of your old study, where I had my attack of heartburn last time,—in the strawberry season; don't you remember? Ah! and there is the school-room! Shall I ever forget dear Miss Sturch coming to me out of that room—a ministering angel with soda and ginger—so comforting, so sweetly anxious about stirring it up, so unaffectedly grieved that there was no sal-volatile in the house! I do so enjoy these pleasant recollections, Chennery; they are as great a luxury to me as your cigar is to you. Could you walk on the other side, my dear fellow? I like the smell, but the smoke is a little too much for me. Thank you. And now about the story? What was the name of the old place—I am so interested in it—it began with a P, surely?'

'Porthgenna Tower,' said the vicar.

'Exactly,' rejoined Mr Phippen, shifting the umbrella tenderly from one shoulder to the other. 'And what in the world made Captain Treverton sell Porthgenna Tower?'

'I believe the reason was that he could not endure the place after the death of his wife,' answered Doctor Chennery. 'The estate, you know, has never been entailed; so the Captain had no difficulty in parting with it, except, of course, the difficulty of finding a purchaser.'

'Why not his brother?' asked Mr Phippen. 'Why not our eccentric friend, Andrew Treverton?'

'Don't call him my friend,' said the vicar. 'A mean, grovelling, cynical, selfish old wretch! It's no use shaking your head, Phippen, and trying to look shocked. I know Andrew Treverton's early history as well as you do. I know that he was treated with the basest ingratitude by a college friend, who took all he had to give, and swindled him at last in the grossest manner. I know all about that. But one instance of ingratitude does not justify a man in shutting himself up from society, and railing against all mankind as a disgrace to the earth they walk on. I myself have heard the old brute say that the greatest benefactor to our generation would be a second Herod,* who could prevent another generation from succeeding it. Ought a man who can talk in that way, to be the friend of any human being with the slightest respect for his species or himself?'

'My friend!' said Mr Phippen, catching the vicar by the arm, and mysteriously lowering his voice, 'My dear and reverend friend! I admire your honest indignation against the utterer of that exceedingly misanthropical sentiment; but—I confide this to you, Chennery, in the strictest secresy—there are moments—morning moments generally—when my digestion is in such a state, that I have actually agreed with that annihi-lating person, Andrew Treverton! I have woke up with my tongue like a cinder—I have crawled to the glass and looked at it—and I have said to myself, Let there be an end of the human race rather than a continuance of this!'

'Pooh! pooh!' cried the vicar, receiving Mr Phippen's confession with a burst of irreverent laughter. 'Take a glass of cool small beer next time your tongue is in that state, and you will pray for a continuance of the brewing part of the human race, at any rate. But let us go back to Porthgenna Tower, or I shall never get on with my story. When Captain Treverton had once made up his mind to sell the place, I have no doubt that, under ordinary circumstances, he would have thought of offering it to his brother, with a view, of course, to keeping the estate in the family. Andrew was rich enough to have bought it; for, though he got nothing at his father's death, but the old gentleman's rare collection of books, he inherited his mother's fortune, as the second son. However, as things were at that time (and are still, I am sorry to say), the Captain could make no personal offers of any kind to Andrew; for the two were not then, and are not now, on speaking, or even on writing terms. It is a shocking thing to say, but the worst quarrel of the kind I ever heard of, is the quarrel between those two brothers.'

'Pardon me, my dear friend,' said Mr Phippen, opening his camp-stool, which had hitherto dangled by its silken tassel from the hooked handle of the umbrella. 'May I sit down before you go any further? I am getting a little excited about this part of the story, and I dare not fatigue myself. Pray go on. I don't think the legs of my camp-stool will make holes in the lawn. I am so light—a mere skeleton, in fact. Do go on!'

'You must have heard,' pursued the vicar, 'that Captain Treverton, when he was advanced in life, married an actress—rather a violent temper, I believe; but a person of spotless character, and as fond of her husband as a woman could be; therefore, according to my view of it, a very good wife for him to marry. However, the Captain's friends, of course, made the usual senseless outcry, and the Captain's brother, as the only near relation, took it on himself to attempt breaking off the marriage in the most offensively indelicate way. Failing in that, and hating the poor woman like poison, he left his brother's house, saying, among many other savage speeches, one infamous thing about the bride, which—which, upon my honour, Phippen, I am ashamed to repeat. Whatever the words were, they were unluckily carried to Mrs Treverton's ears, and they were of the kind that no woman—let alone a quick-tempered woman like the Captain's wife—ever forgives. An interview followed between the two brothers—and it led, as you may easily imagine, to very unhappy results. They parted in the most deplorable manner. The Captain declared, in the heat of his passion, that Andrew had never had one generous impulse in his heart since he was born, and that he would die without one kind feeling towards any living soul in the world. Andrew replied, that if he had no heart, he had a memory, and that he should remember those farewell words as long as he lived. So they separated. Twice afterwards, the Captain made overtures of reconciliation. The first time, when his daughter Rosamond was born; the second time, when Mrs Treverton died. On each occasion, the elder brother wrote to say, that if the younger would retract the atrocious words he had spoken against his sister-in-law, every atonement should be offered to him for the harsh language which the Captain had used, in the hastiness of anger, when they last met. No answer was received from Andrew to either letter; and the estrangement between the two brothers has continued to the present time. You understand now why Captain Treverton could not privately consult

Andrew's inclinations, before he publicly announced his intention of parting with Porthgenna Tower.'

Although Mr Phippen declared, in answer to this appeal, that he understood perfectly, and although he begged with the utmost politeness that the vicar would go on, his attention seemed, for the moment, to be entirely absorbed in inspecting the legs of his camp-stool, and in ascertaining what impression they made on the vicarage lawn. Doctor Chennery's own interest, however, in the circumstances that he was relating, seemed sufficiently strong to make up for any transient lapse of attention on the part of his guest. After a few vigorous puffs at his cigar (which had been several times in imminent danger of going out while he was speaking), he went on with his narrative in these words:—

'Well, the house, the estate, the mine, and the fisheries of Porthgenna were all publicly put up for sale, a few months after Mrs Treverton's death; but no offers were made for the property which it was possible to accept. The ruinous state of the house, the bad cultivation of the land, legal difficulties in connection with the mine, and quarter-day difficulties in the collection of the rents, all contributed to make Porthgenna what the auctioneers would call a bad lot to dispose of. Failing to sell the place, Captain Treverton could not be prevailed on to change his mind, and live there again. The death of his wife almost broke his heart—for he was, by all accounts, just as fond of her as she had been of him—and the very sight of the place that was associated with the greatest affliction of his life, became hateful to him. He removed, with his little girl and a relative of Mrs Treverton, who was her governess, to our neighbourhood, and rented a pretty little cottage across the church-fields. The house nearest to it was inhabited at that time by Leonard Frankland's father and mother. The new neighbours soon became intimate; and thus it happened that the couple whom I have been marrying this morning were brought up together as children, and fell in love with each other, almost before they were out of their pinafores.

'Chennery, my dear fellow, I don't look as if I was sitting all on one side, do I?' cried Mr Phippen, suddenly breaking into the vicar's narrative, with a look of alarm. 'I am shocked to interrupt you; but surely your grass is amazingly soft in this part of the country. One of my camp-stool legs is getting shorter and shorter every moment. I'm drilling a hole! I'm toppling over! Gracious Heavens! I feel myself going—I shall be down, Chennery; upon my life, I shall be down!'

'Stuff!' cried the vicar, pulling up, first Mr Phippen and then Mr Phippen's camp-stool, which had rooted itself in the grass, all on one side. 'Here, come on to the gravel-walk; you can't drill holes in that. What's the matter now?'

'Palpitations,' said Mr Phippen, dropping his umbrella, and placing his hand over his heart; 'and bile. I see those black spots again—those infernal, lively, black spots, dancing before my eyes. Chennery, suppose you consult some agricultural friend about the quality of your grass. Take my word for it, your lawn is softer than it ought to be.—Lawn!' repeated Mr Phippen to himself, contemptuously, as he turned round to pick up his umbrella. 'It isn't a lawn—it is a Bog!'

'There, sit down,' said the vicar, 'and don't pay the palpitations and the black spots the compliment of bestowing the smallest attention on them. Do you want anything to drink? Shall it be physic, or beer, or what?'

'No, no! I am so unwilling to give trouble,' answered Mr Phippen. 'I would rather suffer—rather, a great deal. I think if you would go on with your story, Chennery, it would compose me. I have not the faintest idea of what led to it, but I think you were saying something interesting on the subject of pinafores!'

'Nonsense!' said Doctor Chennery. 'I was only telling you of the fondness between the two children who have now grown up to be man and wife. And I was going on to tell you that Captain Treverton, shortly after he settled in our neighbourhood, took to the active practice of his profession again. Nothing else seemed to fill up the gap that the loss of Mrs Treverton had made in his life. Having good interest with the Admiralty, he can always get a ship when he applies for one; and up to the present time, with intervals on shore, he has resolutely stuck to the sea—though he is getting, as his daughter and his friends think, rather too old for it now. Don't look puzzled, Phippen; I am not going so wide of the mark as you think. These are some of the necessary particulars that must be stated first. And now they are comfortably disposed of, I can get round at last to the main part of my story—the sale of Porthgenna Tower.—What is it now? Do you want to get up again?'

Yes, Mr Phippen did want to get up again, for the purpose of composing the palpitations and dispersing the black spots, by trying the experiment of a little gentle exercise. He was most unwilling to occasion any trouble, but would his worthy friend Chennery give him an arm, and carry the camp-stool, and walk slowly in the direction of the school-room window, so as to keep Miss Sturch within easy hailing distance, in case it became necessary to try the last resource of taking a composing draught? The vicar, whose inexhaustible good nature was proof against every trial that Mr Phippen's dyspeptic infirmities could inflict on it, complied with all these requests, and went on with his story, unconsciously adopting the tone and manner of a good-humoured parent who was doing his best to soothe the temper of a fretful child.

'I told you,' he said, 'that the elder Mr Frankland and Captain Treverton were near neighbours here. They had not been long acquainted before the one found out from the other that Porthgenna Tower was for sale. On first hearing this, old Frankland asked a few questions about the place, but said not a word on the subject of purchasing it. Soon after that, the Captain got a ship, and went to sea. During his absence, old Frankland privately set off for Cornwall, to look at the estate, and to find out all he could about its advantages and defects from the persons left in charge of the house and lands. He said nothing when he came back, until Captain Treverton returned from his first cruise; and then the old gentleman spoke out one morning, in his quiet, decided way.

' "Treverton," said he, "if you will sell Porthgenna Tower at the price at which you bought it in, when you tried to dispose of it by auction, write to your lawyer, and tell him to take the title-deeds to mine, and ask for the purchase-money."

'Captain Treverton was naturally a little astonished at the readiness of this offer; but people, like myself, who knew old Frankland's history, were not so surprised. His fortune had been made by trade, and he was foolish enough to be always a little ashamed of acknowledging that one simple and creditable fact. The truth was, that his ancestors had been landed gentry of importance, before the time of the Civil War, and the old gentleman's great ambition was to sink the merchant in the landed grandee, and to leave his son to succeed him in the character of a Squire of large estate and great county influence. He was willing to devote half his fortune to accomplish this scheme; but half his fortune would not buy him such an estate as he wanted, in an important agricultural county like ours. Rents are high, and land is made the most of with us. An estate as extensive as the estate at Porthgenna, would fetch more than double the money which Captain Treverton could venture to ask for it, if it was situated in these parts. Old Frankland was well aware of that fact, and attached all possible importance to it. Besides, there was something in the feudal look of Porthgenna Tower, and in the right over the mine and fisheries, which the purchase of the estate included, that flattered his notions of restoring the family greatness. Here, he and his son after him, could lord it, as he thought, on a large scale, and direct at their sovereign will and pleasure, the industry of hundreds of poor people, scattered along the coast, or huddled together in the little villages inland. This was a tempting prospect, and it could be secured for forty thousand pounds—which was just ten thousand pounds less than he had made up his mind to give, when he first determined to metamorphose himself from a plain merchant into a magnificent landed gentleman. People who knew these facts were, as I have said, not much surprised at Mr Frankland's readiness to purchase Porthgenna Tower; and Captain Treverton, it is hardly necessary to say, was not long in clenching the bargain on his side. The estate changed hands; and away went old Frankland with a tail of wiseacres from London at his heels, to work the mine and the fisheries on new scientific principles, and to beautify the old house from top to bottom with bran-new mediæval decorations under the direction of a gentleman who was said to be an architect, but who looked, to my mind, the very image of a Popish priest* in disguise. Wonderful plans and projects, were they not? And how do you think they succeeded?'

'Do tell me, my dear fellow!' was the answer that fell from Mr Phippen's lips. 'I wonder whether Miss Sturch keeps a bottle of camphor julep in the family medicine chest?' was the thought that passed through Mr Phippen's mind.

'Tell you!' exclaimed the vicar. 'Why, of course, every one of his plans turned out a complete failure. His Cornish tenantry received him as an interloper. The antiquity of his family made no impression upon them. It might be an old family, but it was not a Cornish family, and, therefore, it was of no importance in their eyes. They would have gone to the world's end for the Trevertons; but not a man would move a step out of his way for the Franklands. As for the mine, it seemed to be inspired with the same mutinous spirit that possessed the tenantry. The wiseacres from London blasted in all directions on the profoundest scientific principles, and brought about sixpennyworth of ore to the surface for every five pounds spent in getting it up. The fisheries turned out little better. A new plan for curing pilchards, which was a marvel of economy in theory, proved to be a perfect phenomenon of extravagance in practice. The only item of luck in old Frankland's large sum of misfortunes was produced by his quarrelling in good time with the mediæval architect, who was like a Popish priest in disguise. This fortunate event saved the new owner of Porthgenna all the money he might otherwise have spent in restoring and re-decorating the whole suite of rooms on the north side of the house, which had been left to go to rack and ruin for more than fifty years past, and which remain in their old neglected condition to this day. To make a long story short, after uselessly spending more thousands of pounds at Porthgenna than I should like to reckon up, old Frankland gave in at last, left the place in disgust to the care of his steward, who was charged never to lay out another farthing on it, and returned to this neighbourhood. Being in high dudgeon, and happening to catch Captain Treverton on shore when he got back, the first thing he did was to abuse Porthgenna and all the people about it, a little too vehemently in the Captain's presence. This led to a coolness between the two neighbours, which might have ended in the breaking off of all intercourse, but for the children on either side, who would

see each other just as often as ever, and who ended, by dint of
wilful persistency, in putting an end to the estrangement
between the fathers, by making it look simply ridiculous.
Here, in my opinion, lies the most curious part of the story.
Important family interests depended on those two young
people falling in love with each other; and, wonderful to relate,
that (as you know, after my confession at breakfast-time) was
exactly what they did. Here is a case of the most romantic
love-match, which is also the marriage, of all others, that the
parents on both sides had the strongest worldly interest in
promoting. Shakespeare may say what he pleases, the course
of true love does run smooth sometimes. Never was the
marriage service performed to better purpose than when
I read it this morning. The estate being entailed on Leonard,
Captain Treverton's daughter now goes back, in the capacity of mistress, to the house and lands which her father
sold. Rosamond being an only child, the purchase-money of
Porthgenna, which old Frankland once lamented as money
thrown away, will now, when the Captain dies, be the
marriage-portion of young Frankland's wife. I don't know
what you think of the beginning and middle of my story,
Phippen, but the end ought to satisfy you, at any rate. Did you
ever hear of a bride and bridegroom who started with fairer
prospects in life than our bride and bridegroom of to-day?'

Before Mr Phippen could make any reply, Miss Sturch put
her head out of the school-room window: and seeing the two
gentlemen approaching, beamed on them with her invari-
able smile. Then addressing the vicar, said in her softest
tones:

'I regret extremely to trouble you, sir, but I find Robert very
intractable, this morning, with his multiplication table.'

'Where does he stick now?' asked Doctor Chennery.

'At seven times eight, sir,' replied Miss Sturch.

'Bob!' shouted the vicar through the window. 'Seven times
eight?'

'Forty-three,' answered the whimpering voice of the invisible Bob.

'You shall have one more chance before I get my cane,' said
Doctor Chennery. 'Now, then, look out! Seven times——'

'My dear, good friend,' interposed Mr Phippen, 'if you cane that very unhappy boy, he will scream. My nerves have been tried once this morning by the camp-stool. I shall be totally shattered if I hear screams. Give me time to get out of the way, and allow me also to spare dear Miss Sturch the sad spectacle of correction (so shocking to sensibilities like hers) by asking her for a little camphor julep, and so giving her an excuse for getting out of the way like me. I think I could have done without the camphor julep under any other circumstances; but I ask for it unhesitatingly now, as much for Miss Sturch's sake, as for the sake of my own poor nerves. Have you got camphor julep, Miss Sturch? Say yes, I beg and entreat, and give me an opportunity of escorting you out of the way of the screams.'

While Miss Sturch—whose well-trained sensibilities were proof against the longest paternal caning and the loudest filial acknowledgment of it in the way of screams—tripped up-stairs to fetch the camphor julep, as smiling and self-possessed as ever, Master Bob, finding himself left alone with his sisters in the school-room, sidled up to the youngest of the two, produced from the pocket of his trowsers three frowsy acidulated drops looking very much the worse for wear, and, attacking Miss Amelia on the weak, or greedy side of her character, artfully offered the drops, in exchange for information on the subject of seven times eight. 'You like 'em?' whispered Bob. 'Oh, don't I!' answered Amelia. 'Seven times eight?' asked Bob. 'Fifty-six,' answered Amelia. 'Sure?' said Bob. 'Certain,' said Amelia.—The drops changed hands, and the catastrophe of the domestic drama changed with them. Just as Miss Sturch appeared with the camphor julep at the garden door, in the character of medical Hebe* to Mr Phippen, her intractable pupil showed himself to his father at the school-room window, in the character, arithmetically speaking, of a reformed son. The cane reposed for the day; and Mr Phippen drank his glass of camphor julep with a mind at ease on the twin-subjects of Miss Sturch's sensibilities and Master Bob's screams.

'Most gratifying in every way,' said the Martyr to Dyspepsia, smacking his lips with great relish, as he drained the last drops

out of the glass. 'My nerves are spared, Miss Sturch's feelings
are spared, and the dear boy's back is spared. You have no idea
how relieved I feel, Chennery. Whereabouts were we in that
delightful story of yours when this little domestic interruption
occurred?'

'At the end of it, to be sure,' said the vicar. 'The bride
and bridegroom are some miles on their way, by this time,
to spend the honeymoon at St Swithin's-on-Sea. Captain
Treverton is only left behind for a day. He received his sailing
orders on Monday, and he will be off to Portsmouth to-
morrow morning to take command of his ship. Though
he won't admit it in plain words, I happen to know that
Rosamond has persuaded him to make this his last cruise. She
has a plan for getting him back to Porthgenna, to live there
with her husband, which I hope and believe will succeed. The
west rooms at the old house, in one of which Mrs Treverton
died, are not to be used at all by the young married couple.
They have engaged a builder—a sensible, practical man, this
time—to survey the neglected north rooms, with a view to
their redecoration and thorough repair in every way. This part
of the house cannot possibly be associated with any melancholy recollections in Captain Treverton's mind; for neither
he nor any one else ever entered it during the period of his
residence at Porthgenna. Considering the change in the look
of the place which this project of repairing the north rooms is
sure to produce, and taking into account also the softening
effect of time on all painful recollections, I should say there
was a fair prospect of Captain Treverton's returning to pass
the end of his days, among his old tenantry. It will be a great
chance for Leonard Frankland if he does, for he would be sure
to dispose the people at Porthgenna kindly towards their
new master. Introduced amongst his Cornish tenants under
Captain Treverton's wing, Leonard is sure to get on well with
them, provided he abstains from showing too much of the
family pride which he has inherited from his father. He is a
little given to over-rate the advantages of birth and the importance of rank—but that is really the only noticeable defect
in his character. In all other respects I can honestly say of him
that he deserves what he has got—the best wife in the world.

What a life of happiness, Phippen, seems to be awaiting these lucky young people! It is a bold thing to say of any mortal creatures, but, look as far as I may, not a cloud can I see anywhere on their future prospects.'

'You excellent creature!' exclaimed Mr Phippen, affectionately squeezing the vicar's hand. 'How I enjoy hearing you! how I luxuriate in your bright view of life!'

'And is it not the true view—especially in the case of young Frankland and his wife?' inquired the vicar.

'If you ask me,' said Mr Phippen, with a mournful smile, and a philosophic calmness of manner, 'I can only answer that the direction of a man's speculative views depends—not to mince the matter—on the state of his secretions. Your biliary secretions, dear friend, are all right, and you take bright views. My biliary secretions are all wrong, and I take dark views. You look at the future prospects of this young married couple, and say there is no cloud over them. I don't dispute the assertion, not having the pleasure of knowing either bride or bridegroom. But I look up at the sky over our heads—I remember that there was not a cloud on it when we first entered the garden—I now see, just over those two trees growing so close together, a cloud that has appeared unexpectedly from nobody knows where—and I draw my own conclusions. Such,' said Mr Phippen, ascending the garden steps on his way into the house, 'is my philosophy. It may be tinged with bile, but it is philosophy for all that.'

'All the philosophy in the world,' said the vicar, following his guest up the steps, 'will not shake my conviction that Leonard Frankland and his wife have a happy future before them.'

Mr Phippen laughed, and, waiting on the steps till his host joined him, took Doctor Chennery's arm in the friendliest manner.

'You have told a charming story, Chennery,' he said, 'and you have ended it with a charming sentiment. But, my dear friend, though your healthy mind (influenced by an enviably easy digestion) despises my bilious philosophy, don't quite forget the cloud over the two trees. Look up at it now—it is getting darker and bigger already.'

CHAPTER III

THE BRIDE AND BRIDEGROOM

UNDER the roof of a widowed mother, Miss Mowlem lived humbly at St Swithin's-on-Sea. In the spring of the year eighteen hundred and forty-four, the heart of Miss Mowlem's widowed mother was gladdened by a small legacy. Turning over in her mind the various uses to which the money might be put, the discreet old lady finally decided on investing it in furniture, on fitting up the first floor and the second floor of her house in the best taste, and on hanging a card in the parlour window to inform the public that she had furnished apartments to let. By the summer the apartments were ready, and the card was put up. It had hardly been exhibited a week before a dignified personage in black applied to look at the rooms, expressed himself as satisfied with their appearance, and engaged them for a month certain, for a newly-married lady and gentleman, who might be expected to take possession in a few days. The dignified personage in black was Captain Treverton's servant, and the lady and gentleman, who arrived in due time to take possession, were Mr and Mrs Frankland.

The natural interest which Mrs Mowlem felt in her youthful first lodgers was necessarily vivid in its nature; but it was apathy itself compared to the sentimental interest which her daughter took in observing the manners and customs of the lady and gentleman in their capacity of bride and bridegroom. From the moment when Mr and Mrs Frankland entered the house, Miss Mowlem began to study them with all the ardour of an industrious scholar who attacks a new branch of knowledge. At every spare moment of the day, this industrious young lady occupied herself in stealing up-stairs to collect observations, and in running down-stairs to communicate them to her mother. By the time the married couple had been in the house a week, Miss Mowlem had made such good use of her eyes, ears, and opportunities that she could have written a seven days' diary of the lives of Mr and Mrs Frankland, with the truth and minuteness of Mr Samuel Pepys himself.

But, learn as much as we may, the longer we live the more information there is to acquire. Seven days' patient accumulation of facts in connection with the honeymoon had not placed Miss Mowlem beyond the reach of further discoveries. On the morning of the eighth day, after bringing down the breakfast tray, this observant spinster stole up-stairs again, according to custom, to drink at the spring of knowledge through the key-hole channel of the drawing-room door. After an absence of five minutes she descended to the kitchen, breathless with excitement, to announce a fresh discovery in connection with Mr and Mrs Frankland to her venerable mother.

'Whatever do you think she's doing now?' cried Miss Mowlem, with widely-opened eyes and highly elevated hands.

'Nothing that's useful,' answered Mrs Mowlem, with sarcastic readiness.

'She's actually sitting on his knee! Mother, did you ever sit on father's knee when you were married?'

'Certainly not, my dear. When me and your poor father married, we were neither of us flighty young people, and we knew better.'

'She's got her head on his shoulder,' proceeded Miss Mowlem more and more agitatedly, 'and her arms round his neck—both her arms, mother, as tight as can be.'

'I won't believe it,' exclaimed Mrs Mowlem, indignantly. 'A lady like her, with riches, and accomplishments, and all that, demean herself like a housemaid with a sweetheart. Don't tell me, I won't believe it!'

It was true though, for all that. There were plenty of chairs in Mrs Mowlem's drawing-room; there were three beautifully bound books on Mrs Mowlem's Pembroke table (the Antiquities of St Swithin's, Smallridge's Sermons, and Klopstock's Messiah in English prose)*—Mrs Frankland might have sat on purple morocco leather, stuffed with the best horse-hair, might have informed and soothed her mind with archæological diversions, with orthodox native theology, and with devotional poetry of foreign origin—and yet, so frivolous is the nature of women, she was perverse enough to prefer doing nothing, and perching herself uncomfortably on her husband's knee!

She sat for some time in the undignified position which Miss Mowlem had described with such graphic correctness to her mother—then drew back a little, raised her head, and looked earnestly into the quiet, meditative face of the blind man.

'Lenny, you are very silent this morning,' she said. 'What are you thinking about? If you will tell me all your thoughts, I will tell you all mine.'

'Would you really care to hear all my thoughts?' asked Leonard.

'Yes; all. I shall be jealous of any thoughts that you keep to yourself. Tell me what you were thinking of just now! Me?'

'Not exactly of you.'

'More shame for you. Are you tired of me in eight days? I have not thought of anybody but you ever since we have been here. Ah! you laugh. O, Lenny, I do love you so; how can I think of anybody but you? No! I shan't kiss you. I want to know what you were thinking about first.'

'Of a dream, Rosamond, that I had last night. Ever since the first days of my blindness—Why, I thought you were not going to kiss me again till I had told you what I was thinking about!'

'I can't help kissing you, Lenny, when you talk of the loss of your sight. Tell me, my poor love, do I help to make up for that loss? Are you happier than you used to be? and have I some share in making that happiness, though it is ever so little?'

She turned her head away as she spoke, but Leonard was too quick for her. His inquiring fingers touched her cheek. 'Rosamond, you are crying,' he said.

'I crying!' she answered, with a sudden assumption of gaiety. 'No,' she continued, after a moment's pause. 'I will never deceive you, love, even in the veriest trifle. My eyes serve for both of us now, don't they? you depend on me for all that your touch fails to tell you, and I must never be unworthy of my trust—must I? I did cry, Lenny—but only a very little. I don't know how it was, but I never, in all my life, seemed to pity you, and feel for you as I did just at that moment. Never mind, I've done now. Go on—do go on with what you were going to say.'

'I was going to say, Rosamond, that I have observed one curious thing about myself since I lost my sight. I dream a great deal, but I never dream of myself as a blind man. I often visit in my dreams places that I saw, and people whom I knew when I had my sight, and though I feel as much myself, at those visionary times, as I am now when I am wide-awake, I never by any chance feel blind. I wander about all sorts of old walks in my sleep, and never grope my way. I talk to all sorts of old friends in my sleep, and see the expression in their faces which, waking, I shall never see again. I have lost my sight more than a year now, and yet it was like the shock of a new discovery to me to wake up last night from my dream, and remember suddenly that I was blind.'

'What dream was it, Lenny?'

'Only a dream of the place where I first met you when we were both children. I saw the glen, as it was years ago, with the great twisted roots of the trees, and the blackberry bushes twining about them in a still shadowed light that came through thick leaves from the rainy sky. I saw the mud on the walk in the middle of the glen, with the marks of the cows' hoofs in some places, and the sharp circles in others where some country-women had been lately trudging by on pattens. I saw the muddy water running down on either side of the path after the shower; and I saw you, Rosamond, a naughty girl, all covered with clay and wet—just as you were in the reality—soiling your bright blue pelisse and your pretty little chubby hands by making a dam to stop the running water, and laughing at the indignation of your nursemaid when she tried to pull you away, and take you home. I saw all that exactly as it really was in the bygone time; but, strangely enough, I did not see myself as the boy I then was. You were a little girl, and the glen was in its old neglected state, and yet, though I was all in the past so far, I was in the present as regarded myself. Throughout the whole dream I was uneasily conscious of being a grown man—of being, in short, exactly what I am now, excepting always that I was not blind.'

'What a memory you must have, love, to be able to recall all those little circumstances, after the years that have passed since that wet day in the glen! How well you recollect what I was as a child! Do you remember in the same vivid way, what I looked like a year ago, when you saw me—O, Lenny, it almost breaks my heart to think of it!—when you saw me for the last time?'

'Do I remember, Rosamond! My last look at your face has painted your portrait on my memory in colours that can never change. I have many pictures in my mind, but your picture is the clearest and brightest of all.'

'And it is the picture of me at my best—painted in my youth, dear, when my face was always confessing how I loved you, though my lips said nothing. There is some consolation in that thought. When years have passed over us both, Lenny, and when time begins to set his mark on me, you will not say to yourself, "My Rosamond is beginning to fade; she grows less and less like what she was when I married her." I shall never grow old, love, for you! The bright young picture in your mind will still be my picture when my cheeks are wrinkled and my hair is grey.'

'Still your picture—always the same, grow as old as I may.'

'But are you sure it is clear in every part? Are there no doubtful lines, no unfinished corners anywhere? I have not altered yet, since you saw me—I am just what I was a year ago. Suppose I ask you what I am like now, could you tell me without making a mistake?'

'Try me.'

'May I? You shall be put through a complete catechism! I don't tire you sitting on your knee, do I? Well, in the first place, how tall am I when we both stand up side by side?'

'You just reach to my ear.'

'Quite right, to begin with. Now for the next question. What does my hair look like in your portrait?'

'It is dark brown—there is a great deal of it—and it grows rather too low on your forehead for the taste of some people—'

'Never mind about "some people;" does it grow too low for your taste?'

'Certainly not. I like it to grow low; I like all those little natural waves that it makes against your forehead; I like it taken back, as you wear it, in plain bands which leave your ears and your cheeks visible; and above all things, I like that big glossy knot that it makes where it is all gathered up together at the back of your head.'

'O, Lenny, how well you remember me, so far! Now go a little lower.'

'A little lower is down to your eyebrows. They are very nicely shaped eyebrows in my picture—'

'Yes, but they have a fault. Come! tell me what the fault is?'

'They are not quite so strongly marked as they might be.'

'Right again! And my eyes?'

'Brown eyes, large eyes, wakeful eyes, that are always looking about them. Eyes that can be very soft at one time, and very bright at another. Eyes tender and clear, just at the present moment, but capable, on very slight provocation, of opening rather too widely, and looking rather too brilliantly resolute.'

'Mind you don't make them look so now! What is there below the eyes?'

'A nose that is not quite big enough to be in proper proportion with them. A nose that has a slight tendency to be—'

'Don't say the horrid English word! Spare my feelings by putting it in French. Say retroussé, and skip over my nose as fast as possible.'

'I must stop at the mouth, then, and own that it is as near perfection as possible. The lips are lovely in shape, fresh in colour, and irresistible in expression. They smile in my portrait, and I am sure they are smiling at me now.'

'How could they do otherwise when they are getting so much praise? My vanity whispers to me that I had better stop the catechism here. If I talk about my complexion, I shall only hear that it is of the dusky sort; and that there is never red enough in it, except when I am walking, or confused, or angry. If I ask a question about my figure, I shall receive the dreadful answer, "You are dangerously inclined to be fat." If I say, how do I dress? I shall be told, not soberly enough; you are as fond as a child of gay colours—No! I will venture no more questions. But, vanity apart, Lenny, I am so glad, so proud, so happy to find that you can keep the image of me clearly in your mind. I shall do my best now to look and dress like your last remembrance of me. My love of loves! I will do you credit—I will try if I can't make you envied for your wife. You deserve a hundred thousand kisses for saying your catechism so well—and there they are!'

While Mrs Frankland was conferring the reward of merit on her husband, the sound of a faint, small, courteously-significant cough, made itself timidly audible in a corner of the room. Turning round instantly with the quickness that characterised all her actions, Mrs Frankland, to her horror and indignation, confronted Miss Mowlem standing just inside the door with a letter in her hand, and a blush of sentimental agitation on her simpering face.

'You wretch! how dare you come in without knocking at the door?' cried Rosamond, starting to her feet with a stamp, and passing in an instant from the height of fondness to the height of indignation.

Miss Mowlem shook guiltily before the bright, angry eyes that looked through and through her, turned very pale, held out the letter apologetically, and said in her meekest tones that she was very sorry.

'Sorry!' exclaimed Rosamond, getting even more irritated by the apology than she had been by the intrusion, and showing it by another stamp of the foot; 'who cares whether you are sorry? I don't want your sorrow—I won't have it. I never was so insulted in my life—never, you mean, prying, inquisitive creature!'

'Rosamond! Rosamond! pray don't forget yourself!' interposed the quiet voice of Mr Frankland.

'Lenny, dear, I can't help it! That creature would drive a saint mad. She has been prying after us ever since we have been here—you have, you ill-bred, indelicate woman!—I suspected it before—I am certain of it now! Must we lock our doors to keep you out?—we won't lock our doors! Fetch the bill! We give you warning. Mr Frankland gives you warning—don't you, Lenny? I'll pack up all your things, dear; she shan't touch one of them. Go down-stairs and make out your bill, and give your mother warning. Mr Frankland says he won't have his rooms burst into, and his doors listened at by inquisitive women—and I say so too. Put that letter down on the table—unless you want to open it and read it—put it down, you audacious woman, and fetch the bill, and tell your mother we are going to leave the house directly!'

At this dreadful threat, Miss Mowlem, who was soft and

timid, as well as curious, by nature, wrung her hands in despair, and overflowed meekly in a shower of tears.

'O! good gracious Heavens above!' cried Miss Mowlem, addressing herself distractedly to the ceiling, 'what will mother say! whatever will become of me now! O, Mam, I thought I knocked—I did, indeed! O, Mam! I humbly beg pardon, and I'll never intrude again. O, Mam! mother's a widow, and this is the first time we have let the lodgings, and the furniture's swallowed up all our money, and, O, Mam! Mam! how I shall catch it if you go!' Here words failed Miss Mowlem, and hysterical sobs pathetically supplied their place.

'Rosamond!' said Mr Frankland. There was an accent of sorrow in his voice this time, as well as an accent of remonstrance. Rosamond's quick ear caught the alteration in his tone. As she looked round at him, her colour changed, her head drooped a little, and her whole expression altered on the instant. She stole gently to her husband's side with softened, saddened eyes, and put her lips caressingly close to his ear.

'Lenny,' she whispered, 'have I made you angry with me?'

'I can't be angry with you, Rosamond,' was the quiet answer. 'I only wish, love, that you could have controlled yourself a little sooner.'

'I am so sorry—so very, very sorry!' The fresh, soft lips came closer still to his ear as they whispered these penitent words; and the cunning little hand crept up tremblingly round his neck and began to play with his hair. 'So sorry, and so ashamed of myself! But it was enough to make almost anybody angry, just at first—wasn't it, dear? And you will forgive me—won't you, Lenny?—if I promise never to behave so badly again? Never mind that wretched whimpering fool at the door,' said Rosamond, undergoing a slight relapse as she looked round at Miss Mowlem, standing immovably repentant against the wall, with her face buried in a dingy-white pocket-handkerchief. 'I'll make it up with her; I'll stop her crying; I'll take her out of the room; I'll do anything in the world that's kind to her, if you will only forgive me.'

'A polite word or two is all that is wanted—nothing more than a polite word or two,' said Mr Frankland, rather coldly and constrainedly.

'Don't cry any more, for goodness sake!' said Rosamond, walking straight up to Miss Mowlem, and pulling the dingy-white pocket-handkerchief away from her face without the least ceremony. 'There! leave off, will you? I am very sorry I was in a passion—though you had no business to come in without knocking—I never meant to distress you, and I'll never say a hard word to you again, if you will only knock at the door for the future, and leave off crying now. *Do* leave off crying, you tiresome creature! We are not going away. We don't want your mother, or the bill, or anything. Here! here's a present for you, if you'll leave off crying. Here's my neck-ribbon—I saw you trying it on yesterday afternoon, when I was lying down on the bed-room sofa, and you thought I was asleep. Never mind; I'm not angry about that. Take the ribbon—take it as a peace-offering, if you won't as a present. You *shall* take it!—No, I don't mean that—I mean, please take it! There, I've pinned it on. And now, shake hands and be friends, and go up-stairs and see how it looks in the glass.' With these words, Mrs Frankland opened the door, administered, under the pretence of a pat on the shoulder, a good-humoured shove to the amazed and embarrassed Miss Mowlem, closed the door again, and resumed her place in a moment on her husband's knee.

'I've made it up with her, dear. I've sent her away with my bright green ribbon, and it makes her look as yellow as a guinea, and as ugly as——' Rosamond stopped, and looked anxiously into Mr Frankland's face. 'Lenny!' she said, sadly, putting her cheek against his, 'are you angry with me still?'

'My love, I was never angry with you. I never can be.'

'I will always keep my temper down for the future, Lenny!'

'I am sure you will, Rosamond. But never mind that. I am not thinking of your temper now.'

'Of what, then?'

'Of the apology you made to Miss Mowlem.'

'Did I not say enough? I'll call her back if you like—I'll make another penitent speech—I'll do anything but kiss her. I really can't do that—I can't kiss anybody now, but you.'

'My dear, dear love, how very much like a child you are still, in some of your ways! You said more than enough to Miss Mowlem—far more. And if you will pardon me for making the

remark, I think in your generosity and good-nature, you a little
forgot yourself with the young woman. I don't so much allude
to your giving her the ribbon—though, perhaps, that might
have been done a little less familiarly—but, from what I heard
you say, I infer that you actually went the length of shaking
hands with her.'

'Was that wrong? I thought it was the kindest way of making
it up.'

'My dear, it is an excellent way of making it up between
equals. But consider the difference between your station in
society and Miss Mowlem's.'

'I will try and consider it, if you wish me, love. But I think I
take after my father, who never troubles his head (dear old
man!) about differences of station. I can't help liking people
who are kind to me, without thinking whether they are above
my rank or below it; and when I got cool, I must confess I felt
just as vexed with myself for frightening and distressing that
unlucky Miss Mowlem, as if her station had been equal to
mine. I will try to think as you do, Lenny; but I am very much
afraid that I have got, without knowing exactly how, to be what
the newspapers call, a Radical.'*

'My dear Rosamond! don't talk of yourself in that way, even
in joke. You ought to be the last person in the world to confuse
those distinctions in rank on which the whole well-being of
society depends.'

'Does it really? And yet, dear, we don't seem to have been
created with such very wide distinctions between us. We have
all got the same number of arms and legs; we are all hungry and
thirsty, and hot in the summer and cold in the winter; we all
laugh when we are pleased, and cry when we are distressed;
and, surely, we have all got very much the same feelings,
whether we are high or whether we are low. I could not have
loved you better, Lenny, than I do now, if I had been a duchess,
or less than I do now, if I had been a servant-girl.'

'My love, you are not a servant-girl. And, as to what you say
about being a duchess, let me remind you that you are not so
much below a duchess as you seem to think. Many a lady of
high title, cannot look back on such a line of ancestors as yours.
Your father's family, Rosamond, is one of the oldest in

England: even *my* father's family hardly dates back so far; and we were landed gentry when many a name in the peerage was not heard of. It is really almost laughably absurd to hear you talking of yourself as a Radical.'

'I won't talk of myself so again, Lenny—only don't look so serious. I will be a Tory*, dear, if you will give me a kiss, and let me sit on your knee a little longer.'

Mr Frankland's gravity was not proof against his wife's change of political principles, and the conditions which she annexed to it. His face cleared up, and he laughed almost as gaily as Rosamond herself.

'By the bye,' he said, after an interval of silence had given him time to collect his thoughts, 'did I not hear you tell Miss Mowlem to put a letter down on the table? Is it a letter for you, or for me?'

'Ah! I forgot all about the letter,' said Rosamond, running to the table. 'It is for you, Lenny—and, goodness me! here's the Porthgenna postmark on it.'

'It must be from the builder whom I sent down to the old house about the repairs. Lend me your eyes, love, and let us hear what he says.'

Rosamond opened the letter, drew a stool to her husband's feet, and, sitting down with her arms on his knees, read as follows:-

TO LEONARD FRANKLAND, ESQ.

SIR,—Agreeably to the instructions with which you favoured me, I have proceeded to survey Porthgenna Tower, with a view to ascertaining what repairs the house in general, and the north side of it in particular, may stand in need of.

As regards the outside, a little cleaning and new-pointing is all that the building wants. The walls and foundations seem made to last for ever. Such strong solid work I never set eyes on before.

Inside the house, I cannot report so favourably. The rooms in the west front, having been inhabited during the period of Captain Treverton's occupation, and having been well looked after since, are in tolerably sound condition. I should say two hundred pounds would cover the expense of all repairs in my line, which these rooms need. This sum would not include the restoration of the west staircase, which has given a little in some places, and the banisters of which are decidedly insecure, from the first to the second landing. From twenty-five to thirty pounds would suffice to set this all right.

In the rooms on the north front, the state of dilapidation, from top to bottom, is as bad as can be. From all that I could ascertain, nobody ever went near these rooms in Captain Treverton's time, or has ever entered them since. The people who now keep the house have a superstitious dread of opening any of the north doors, in consequence of the time that has elapsed since any living being has passed through them. Nobody would volunteer to accompany me in my survey, and nobody could tell me which keys fitted which room doors in any part of the north side. I could find no plan containing the names or numbers of the rooms; nor, to my surprise, were there any labels attached separately to the keys. They were given to me, all hanging together on a large ring, with an ivory label to it, which was only marked   Keys of the North Rooms. I take the liberty of mentioning these particulars in order to account for my having, as you might think, delayed my stay at Porthgenna Tower longer than is needful. I lost nearly a whole day in taking the keys off the ring, and fitting them at hazard to the right doors. And I occupied some hours of another day in marking each door with a number on the outside, and putting a corresponding label to each key, before I replaced it on the ring, in order to prevent the possibility of future errors and delays.

As I hope to furnish you, in a few days, with a detailed estimate of the repairs needed in the north part of the house, from basement to roof, I need only say here that they will occupy some time, and will be of the most extensive nature. The beams of the staircase and the flooring of the first storey have got the dry rot. The damp in some rooms, and the rats in others, have almost destroyed the wainscottings. Four of the mantelpieces have given out from the walls, and all the ceilings are either stained, cracked, or peeled away in large patches. The flooring is, in general, in a better condition than I had anticipated; but the shutters and window-sashes are so warped as to be useless. It is only fair to acknowledge that the expense of setting all these things to rights that is to say, of making the rooms safe and habitable, and of putting them in proper condition for the upholsterer will be considerable. I would respectfully suggest, in the event of your feeling any surprise or dissatisfaction at the amount of my estimate, that you should name a friend in whom you place confidence, to go over the north rooms with me, keeping my estimate in his hand. I will undertake to prove, if needful, the necessity of each separate repair, and the justice of each separate charge for the same, to the satisfaction of any competent and impartial person whom you may please to select.

Trusting to send you the estimate in a few days,
I remain, sir,
Your humble servant,
THOMAS HORLOCK.

'A very honest, straightforward letter,' said Mr Frankland.

'I wish he had sent the estimate with it,' said Rosamond. 'Why could not the provoking man tell us at once in round numbers what the repairs will really cost?'

'I suspect, my dear, he was afraid of shocking us, if he mentioned the amount in round numbers.'

'That horrid money! It is always getting in one's way, and upsetting one's plans. If we haven't got enough, let us go and borrow of somebody who has. Do you mean to despatch a friend to Porthgenna to go over the house with Mr Horlock? If you do, I know who I wish you would send.'

'Who?'

'Me, if you please—under your escort, of course. Don't laugh, Lenny. I would be very sharp with Mr Horlock; I would object to every one of his charges, and beat him down without mercy. I once saw a surveyor go over a house, and I know exactly what to do. You stamp on the floor, and knock at the walls, and scrape at the brickwork, and look up all the chimneys, and out of all the windows—sometimes you make notes in a little book, sometimes you measure with a foot-rule, sometimes you sit down all of a sudden, and think profoundly—and the end of it is that you say the house will do very well indeed, if the tenant will pull out his purse, and put it in proper repair.'

'Well done, Rosamond! You have one more accomplishment than I knew of; and I suppose I have no choice now but to give you an opportunity of displaying it. If you don't object, my dear, to being associated with a professional assistant in the important business of checking Mr Horlock's estimate, I don't object to paying a short visit to Porthgenna whenever you please—especially now I know that the west rooms are still habitable.'

'O, how kind of you! how pleased I shall be! how I shall enjoy seeing the old place again before it is altered! I was only five years old, Lenny, when we left Porthgenna, and I am so anxious to see what I can remember of it, after such a long, long absence as mine. Do you know, I never saw anything of that ruinous north side of the house—and I do so dote on old rooms? We will go all through them, Lenny. You shall have hold of my hand, and look with my eyes, and make as many discoveries as I do. I prophesy that we shall see ghosts, and find treasures, and hear mysterious noises—and, oh heavens! what clouds of dust we shall have to go through. Pouf! the very anticipation of them chokes me already!'

'Now we are on the subject of Porthgenna, Rosamond, let us be serious for one moment. It is clear to me that these repairs of the north rooms will cost a large sum of money. Now, my love, I consider no sum of money misspent, however large it may be, if it procures you pleasure. I am with you heart and soul——'

He paused. His wife's caressing arms were twining round his neck again, and her cheek was laid gently against his. 'Go on, Lenny,' she said, with such an accent of tenderness in the utterance of those three simple words, that his speech failed him for the moment, and all his sensations seemed absorbed in the one luxury of listening. 'Rosamond,' he whispered, 'there is no music in the world that touches me as your voice touches me now! I feel it all through me, as I used sometimes to feel the sky at night, in the time when I could see.' As he spoke, the caressing arms tightened round his neck, and the fervent lips softly took the place which the cheek had occupied. 'Go on, Lenny,' they repeated happily as well as tenderly now, 'you said you were with me, heart and soul. With me in what?'

'In your project, love, for inducing your father to retire from his profession after this last cruise, and in your hope of prevailing on him to pass the evening of his days happily with us at Porthgenna. If the money spent in restoring the north rooms, so that we may all live in them for the future, does indeed so alter the look of the place to his eyes as to dissipate his old sorrowful associations with it, and to make his living there again a pleasure instead of a pain to him, I shall regard it as money well laid out. But, Rosamond, are you sure of the success of your plan before we undertake it? Have you dropped any hint of the Porthgenna project to your father?'

'I told him, Lenny, that I should never be quite comfortable unless he left the sea, and came to live with us—and he said that he would. I did not mention a word about Porthgenna—nor did he—but he knows that we shall live there when we are settled, and he made no conditions when he promised that our home should be his home.'

'Is the loss of your mother the only sad association he has with the place?'

'Not quite. There is another association, which has never been mentioned, but which I may tell you, because there are no secrets between us. My mother had a favourite maid who lived with her from the time of her marriage, and who was, accidentally, the only person present in her room when she died. I remember hearing of this woman as being odd in her look and manner, and no great favourite with anybody but her mistress. Well, on the morning of my mother's death, she disappeared from the house in the strangest way, leaving behind her a most singular and mysterious letter to my father, asserting that in my mother's dying moments, a Secret had been confided to her which she was charged to divulge to her master when her mistress was no more; and adding that she was afraid to mention this secret, and that, to avoid being questioned about it, she had resolved on leaving the house for ever. She had been gone some hours when the letter was opened—and she has never been seen or heard of since that time. This circumstance seemed to make almost as strong an impression on my father's mind as the shock of my mother's death. Our neighbours and servants all thought (as I think) that the woman was mad; but he never agreed with them, and I know that he has neither destroyed nor forgotten the letter from that time to this.'

'A strange event, Rosamond,—a very strange event. I don't wonder that it has made a lasting impression on him.'

'Depend upon it, Lenny, the servants and the neighbours were right—the woman was mad. Any way, however, it was certainly a singular event in our family. All old houses have their romance—and that is the romance of our house. But years and years have passed since then; and, what with time, and what with the changes we are going to make, I have no fear that my dear, good father will spoil our plans. Give him a new north garden at Porthgenna, where he can walk the decks, as I call it,—give him new north rooms to live in—and I will answer for the result. But all this is in the future; let us get back to the present time. When shall we pay our flying visit to Porthgenna, Lenny, and plunge into the important business of checking Mr Horlock's estimate for the repairs?'

'We have three weeks more to stay here, Rosamond.'

'Yes; and then we must go back to Long Beckley. I promised that best and biggest of men, the vicar, that we would pay our first visit to him. He is sure not to let us off under three weeks or a month.'

'In that case, then, we had better say two months hence for the visit to Porthgenna. Is your writing-case in the room, Rosamond?'

'Yes; close by us, on the table.'

'Write to Mr Horlock then, love—and appoint a meeting in two months' time at the old house. Tell him also, as we must not trust ourselves on unsafe stairs—especially considering how dependent I am on banisters—to have the west staircase repaired immediately. And, while you have the pen in your hand, perhaps it may save trouble if you write a second note to the housekeeper at Porthgenna, to tell her when she may expect us.'

Rosamond sat down gaily at the table and dipped her pen in the ink with a little flourish of triumph.

'In two months,' she exclaimed joyfully, 'I shall see the dear old place again! In two months, Lenny, our profane feet will be raising the dust in the solitudes of the North Rooms.'

BOOK III

CHAPTER I

TIMON OF LONDON

TIMON of Athens* retreated from an ungrateful world to a cavern by the sea-shore, vented his misanthropy in magnificent poetry, and enjoyed the honour of being called 'My Lord.' Timon of London took refuge from his species in a detached house at Bayswater—expressed his sentiments in shabby prose—and was only addressed as 'Mr Treverton.' The one point of resemblance which it is possible to set against these points of contrast between the two Timons, consisted in this: that their misanthropy was, at least, genuine. Both were incorrigible haters of mankind.

There is probably no better proof of the accuracy of that definition of man which describes him as an imitative animal, than is to be found in the fact, that the verdict of humanity is always against any individual member of the species who presumes to differ from the rest. A man is one of a flock, and his wool must be of the general colour. He must drink when the rest drink, and graze where the rest graze. Let him walk at noonday with perfect composure of countenance and decency of gait, with not the slightest appearance of vacancy in his eyes or wildness in his manner, from one end of Oxford Street* to the other, without his hat, and let every one of the thousands of hat-wearing people whom he passes be asked separately what they think of him, how many will abstain from deciding instantly that he is mad, on no other evidence than the evidence of his bare head? Nay, more; let him politely stop each one of those passengers, and let him explain in the plainest form of words, and in the most intelligible manner, that his head feels more easy and comfortable without a hat than with one, how many of his fellow mortals who decided that he was mad on first meeting him, will change their opinion when they part from him after hearing his explanation? In the vast majority of cases, the very explanation itself would be accepted as an excellent additional proof that the intellect of the hatless man was indisputably deranged.

Starting at the beginning of the march of life out of step with the rest of the mortal regiment, Andrew Treverton paid the penalty of his irregularity from his earliest days. He was a phenomenon in the nursery, a butt at school, and a victim at college. The ignorant nursemaid reported him as a queer child; the learned schoolmaster genteelly varied the phrase, and described him as an eccentric boy; the college tutor, harping on the same string, facetiously likened his head to a roof, and said there was a slate loose in it. When a slate is loose, if nobody fixes it in time, it ends by falling off. In the roof of a house we view that consequence as a necessary result of neglect; in the roof of a man's head we are generally very much shocked and surprised by it.

Overlooked in some directions and misdirected in others, Andrew's uncouth capacities for good tried helplessly to shape themselves. The better side of his eccentricity took the form of friendship. He became violently and unintelligibly fond of one among his schoolfellows—a boy, who treated him with no especial consideration in the play-ground, and who gave him no particular help in the class. Nobody could discover the smallest reason for it, but it was nevertheless a notorious fact, that Andrew's pocket money was always at this boy's service, that Andrew ran about after him like a dog, and that Andrew over and over again took the blame and punishment on his own shoulders which ought to have fallen on the shoulders of his friend. When, a few years afterwards, that friend went to college, the lad petitioned to be sent to college too, and attached himself there more closely than ever to the strangely-chosen comrade of his schoolboy days. Such devotion as this must have touched any man possessed of ordinary generosity of disposition. It made no impression whatever on the inherently base nature of Andrew's friend. After three years of intercourse at college—intercourse which was all selfishness on one side and all self-sacrifice on the other—the end came, and the light was let in cruelly on Andrew's eyes. When his purse grew light in his friend's hand, and when his acceptances were most numerous on his friend's bills, the brother of his honest affection, the hero of his simple admiration, abandoned him to embarrassment, to ridicule, and to solitude, without the faintest affectation of penitence—without so much even as a word of farewell.

He returned to his father's house, a soured man at the outset of life—returned to be upbraided for the debts that he had contracted to serve the man who had heartlessly outraged and shamelessly cheated him. He left home in disgrace, to travel on a small allowance. The travels were protracted, and they ended, as such travels often do, in settled expatriation. The life he led, the company he kept, during his long residence abroad, did him permanent and fatal harm. When he at last returned to England, he presented himself in the most hopeless of all characters—the character of a man who believes in nothing. At this period of his life, his one chance for the future lay in the good results which his brother's influence over him might have produced. The two had hardly resumed their intercourse of early days, when the quarrel occasioned by Captain Treverton's marriage broke it off for ever. From that time, for all social interests and purposes, Andrew was a lost man. From that time, he met the last remonstrances that were made to him by the last friends who took any interest in his fortunes, always with the same bitter and hopeless form of reply: 'My dearest friend forsook and cheated me,' he would say. 'My only brother has quarrelled with me for the sake of a play-actress. What am I to expect of the rest of mankind after that? I have suffered twice for my belief in others—I will never suffer a third time. The wise man is the man who does not disturb his heart at its natural occupation of pumping blood through his body. I have gathered my experience abroad and at home; and have learnt enough to see through the delusions of life which look like realities to other men's eyes. My business in this world is to eat, drink, sleep, and die. Everything else is superfluity—and I have done with it.'

The few people who ever cared to inquire about him again, after being repulsed by such an avowal as this, heard of him three or four years after his brother's marriage, in the neighbourhood of Bayswater. Local report described him as having bought the first cottage he could find which was cut off from other houses by a wall all round it. It was further rumoured that he was living like a miser; that he had got an old man-servant, named Shrowl, who was even a greater enemy to mankind than himself; that he allowed no living soul, not even an occasional charwoman, to enter the house; that he was letting his beard grow,* and that he had ordered his servant Shrowl to follow his example. In the year eighteen hundred and forty-four, the fact of a man's not shaving was regarded by the enlightened majority of the English nation as a proof of unsoundness of intellect. At the present time, Mr Treverton's beard would only have interfered with his reputation for respectability. Seventeen years ago, it was accepted as so much additional evidence in support of the old theory that his intellects were deranged. He was at that very time, as his stock-broker could have testified, one of the sharpest men of business in London; he could argue on the wrong side of any question with an acuteness of sophistry and sarcasm that Dr Johnson* himself might have envied; he kept his household accounts right to a farthing—but what did these advantages avail him, in the estimation of his neighbours, when he presumed to live on another plan than theirs, and when he wore a hairy certificate of lunacy on the lower part of his face? We have advanced a little in the matter of partial toleration of beards since that time; but we have still a good deal of ground to get over. In the present year of progress, eighteen hundred and sixty-one, would the most trustworthy banker's clerk in the whole metropolis have the slightest chance of keeping his situation if he left off shaving his chin?

Common report, which calumniated Mr Treverton as mad, had another error to answer for in describing him as a miser. He saved more than two-thirds of the income derived from his comfortable fortune, not because he liked hoarding up money; but because he had no enjoyment of the comforts and luxuries which money is spent in procuring. To do him justice, his contempt for his own wealth was quite as hearty as his contempt for the wealth of his neighbours. Thus characteristically wrong in endeavouring to delineate his character, report was, nevertheless, for once in a way, inconsistently right in describing his manner of life. It was true that he had bought the first cottage he could find that was secluded within its own walls—true that nobody was allowed, on any pretence whatever, to enter his doors—and true that he had met with a servant, who was even bitterer against all mankind than himself, in the person of Mr Shrowl.

The life these two led approached as nearly to the existence of the primitive man (or savage) as the surrounding conditions of civilisation would allow. Admitting the necessity of eating and drinking, the first object of Mr Treverton's ambition was to sustain life with the least possible dependence on the race of men who professed to supply their neighbours' bodily wants, and who, as he conceived, cheated them infamously on the strength of their profession.

Having a garden at the back of the house, Timon of London dispensed with the greengrocer altogether by cultivating his own vegetables. There was no room for growing wheat, or he would have turned farmer also on his own account; but he could outwit the miller and the baker, at any rate, by buying a sack of corn, grinding it in his own hand-mill, and giving the flour to Shrowl to make into bread. On the same principle, the meat for the house was bought wholesale of the City salesmen—the master and servant eating as much of it in the fresh state as they could, salting the rest, and setting butchers at defiance. As for drink, neither brewer nor publican ever had the chance of extorting a farthing from Mr Treverton's pocket. He and Shrowl were satisfied with beer—and they brewed for themselves. With bread, vegetables, meat, and malt liquor, these two hermits of modern days achieved the great double purpose of keeping life in, and keeping the tradesmen out.

Eating like primitive men, they lived in all other respects like primitive men also. They had pots, pans, and pipkins, two deal tables, two chairs, two old sofas, two short pipes, and two long cloaks. They had no stated meal-times, no carpets and bedsteads, no cabinets, bookcases, or ornamental knick-knacks of any kind, no laundress, and no charwoman. When either of the two wanted to eat and drink, he cut off his crust of bread, cooked his bit of meat, drew his drop of beer, without the slightest reference to the other. When either of the two thought he wanted a clean shirt, which was very seldom, he went and washed one for himself. When either of the two discovered that any part of the house was getting very dirty indeed, he took a bucket of water and a birch-broom, and washed the place out like a dog-kennel. And lastly, when either of the two wanted to go to sleep, he wrapped himself up in his cloak, lay down on one of the sofas, and took what repose he required, early in the evening, or late in the morning, just as he pleased.

When there was no baking, brewing, gardening, or cleaning to be done, the two sat down opposite each other, and smoked for hours, generally without uttering a word. Whenever they did speak, they quarrelled. Their ordinary dialogue was a species of conversational prize-fight, beginning with a sarcastic affectation of good-will on either side, and ending in hearty exchanges of violent abuse—just as the boxers go through the feeble formality of shaking hands before they enter on the serious practical business of beating each other's faces out of all likeness to the image of man. Not having so many disadvantages of early refinement and education to contend against as his master, Shrowl generally won the victory in these engagements of the tongue. Indeed, though nominally the servant, he was really the ruling spirit in the house—acquiring unbounded influence over his master by dint of outmarching Mr Treverton in every direction on his own ground. Shrowl's was the harshest voice; Shrowl's were the bitterest sayings; and Shrowl's was the longest beard. The surest of all retributions is the retribution that lies in wait for a man who boasts. Mr Treverton was rashly given to boasting of his independence, and when retribution overtook him, it assumed a personal form, and bore the name of Shrowl.

On a certain morning, about three weeks after Mrs Frankland had written to the housekeeper at Porthgenna Tower to mention the period at which her husband and herself might be expected there, Mr Treverton descended, with his sourest face and his surliest manner, from the upper regions of the cottage to one of the rooms on the ground-floor, which civilised tenants would probably have called the parlour. Like his elder brother, he was a tall, well-built man; but his bony, haggard, sallow face bore not the slightest resemblance to the handsome, open, sunburnt face of the Captain. No one, seeing them together, could possibly have guessed that they were brothers—so completely did they differ in expression as well as in feature. The heart-aches that he had suffered in youth; the reckless, wandering, dissipated life that he had led in manhood; the petulance, the disappointment, and the physical exhaustion of his latter days, had so wasted and worn him away that he looked his brother's elder by almost twenty years. With unbrushed hair and unwashed face, with a tangled grey beard, and an old patched dirty flannel dressing-gown that hung about him like a sack, this descendant of a wealthy and ancient family looked as if his birth-place had been the workhouse, and his vocation in life the selling of cast-off clothes.

It was breakfast-time with Mr Treverton—that is to say it was the time at which he felt hungry enough to think about eating something. In the same position, over the mantelpiece, in which a looking-glass would have been placed in a household of ordinary refinement, there hung in the cottage of Timon of London a side of bacon. On the deal table by the fire, stood half a loaf of heavy-looking brown bread; in a corner of the room was a barrel of beer, with two battered pewter pots hitched on to nails in the wall above it; and under the grate lay a smoky old gridiron, left just as it had been thrown down when last used and done with. Mr Treverton took a greasy clasp-knife out of the pocket of his dressing-gown, cut off a rasher of bacon, jerked the gridiron on to the fire, and began to cook his breakfast. He had just turned the rasher, when the door opened, and Shrowl entered the room, with his pipe in his mouth, bent on the same eating errand as his master.

In personal appearance, Shrowl was short, fat, flabby, and perfectly bald, except at the back of his head, where a ring of bristly iron-grey hair projected like a collar that had got hitched out of its place. To make amends for the scantiness of his hair, the beard which he had cultivated by his master's desire, grew far over his cheeks, and drooped down on his chest in two thick jagged peaks. He wore a very old long-tailed dress-coat, which he had picked up a bargain in Petticoat Lane*—a faded yellow shirt, with a large torn frill—velveteen trousers, turned up at the ancles—and Blucher boots that had never been blacked since the day when they last left the cobbler's stall. His colour was unhealthily florid, his thick lips curled upward with a malicious grin, and his eyes were the nearest approach, in form and expression, to the eyes of a bull terrier which those features are capable of achieving when they are placed in the countenance of a man. Any painter wanting to express strength, insolence, ugliness, coarseness, and cunning, in the face and figure of one and the same individual, could have discovered no better model for the purpose, all the world over, than he might have found in the person of Mr Shrowl.

Neither master nor servant exchanged a word, or took the smallest notice of each other, on first meeting. Shrowl stood stolidly contemplative, with his hands in his pockets, waiting for his turn at the gridiron. Mr Treverton finished his cooking, took his bacon to the table, and cutting a crust of bread, began to eat his breakfast. When he had disposed of the first mouthful, he condescended to look up at Shrowl, who was at that moment opening his clasp-knife and approaching the side of bacon with slouching steps and sleepily greedy eyes.

'What do you mean by that?' asked Mr Treverton, pointing with indignant surprise at Shrowl's breast. 'You ugly brute, you've got a clean shirt on!'

'Thankee, sir, for noticing it,' said Shrowl, with a sarcastic affectation of humility. 'This is a joyful occasion, this is. I couldn't do no less than put a clean shirt on, when it's my master's birthday. Many happy returns, sir. Perhaps you thought I should forget that to-day was your birthday? Lord bless your sweet face, I wouldn't have forgot it on any account. How old are you to-day? It's a long time ago, sir, since you was a plump smiling little boy, with a frill round your neck, and marbles in your pocket, and trousers and waistcoat all in one, and kisses and presents from Pa and Ma and uncle and aunt, on your birthday. Don't you be afraid of me wearing out this shirt by too much washing. I mean to put it away in lavender against your next birthday; or against your funeral, which is just as likely at your time of life—isn't it, sir?'

'Don't waste a clean shirt on my funeral,' retorted Mr Treverton. 'I hav'n't left you any money in my will, Shrowl. You'll be on your way to the workhouse, when I'm on my way to the grave.'

'Have you really made your will, at last, sir?' enquired Shrowl, pausing, with an appearance of the greatest interest, in the act of cutting off his slice of bacon. 'I humbly beg pardon, but I always thought you was afraid to do it.'

The servant had evidently touched intentionally on one of the master's sore points. Mr Treverton thumped his crust of bread on the table, and looked up angrily at Shrowl.

'Afraid of making my will, you fool!' said he. 'I don't make it, and I won't make it, on principle.'

Shrowl slowly sawed off his slice of bacon, and began to whistle a tune.

'On principle,' repeated Mr Treverton. 'Rich men who leave money behind them are the farmers who raise the crop of human wickedness. When a man has any spark of generosity in his nature, if you want to put it out, leave him a legacy. When a man is bad, if you want to make him worse, leave him a legacy. If you want to collect a number of men together for the purpose of perpetuating corruption and oppression on a large scale, leave them a legacy under the form of endowing a public charity. If you want to give a woman the best chance in the world of getting a bad husband, leave her a legacy. *Make my will!* I have a pretty strong dislike of my species, Shrowl, but I don't quite hate mankind enough yet, to do such mischief among them as that!' Ending his diatribe in those words, Mr Treverton took down one of the battered pewter pots, and refreshed himself with a pint of beer.

Shrowl shifted the gridiron to a clear place in the fire, and chuckled sarcastically.

'Who the devil would you have me leave my money to?' cried Mr Treverton, overhearing him. 'To my brother, who thinks me a brute now; who would think me a fool then; and who would encourage swindling, anyhow, by spending all my money among doxies and strolling players? To the child of that player-woman, whom I have never set eyes on, who has been brought up to hate me, and who would turn hypocrite directly by pretending, for decency's sake, to be sorry for my death? To *you*, you human baboon!—you, who would set up an usury-office directly, and prey upon the widow, the fatherless, and the unfortunate, generally, all over the world? Your good health, Mr Shrowl! I can laugh as well as you—especially when I know I'm not going to leave you sixpence.'

Shrowl, in his turn, began to get a little irritated now. The jeering civility which he had chosen to assume on first entering the room, gave place to his habitual surliness of manner and his natural growling intonation of voice.

'You just let me alone—will you?' he said, sitting down sulkily to his breakfast. 'I've done joking for to-day; suppose you finish, too. What's the use of talking nonsense about your money? You must leave it to somebody.'

'Yes, I will,' said Mr Treverton. 'I will leave it, as I have told you over and over again, to the first Somebody I can find who honestly despises money, and who can't be made the worse, therefore, by having it.'

'That means nobody,' grunted Shrowl.

'I know it does!' retorted his master.

Before Shrowl could utter a word of rejoinder, there was a ring at the gate-bell of the cottage.

'Go out,' said Mr Treverton, 'and see what that is. If it's a woman-visitor, show her what a scarecrow you are, and frighten her away. If it's a man-visitor——'

'If it's a man-visitor,' interposed Shrowl, 'I'll punch his head for interrupting me at my breakfast.'

Mr Treverton filled and lit his pipe during his servant's absence. Before the tobacco was well a-light, Shrowl returned, and reported a man-visitor.

'Did you punch his head?' asked Mr Treverton.

'No,' said Shrowl, 'I picked up his letter. He poked it under the gate, and went away. Here it is.'

The letter was written on foolscap paper, superscribed in a round legal hand. As Mr Treverton opened it, two slips cut from newspapers dropped out. One fell on the table before which he was sitting; the other fluttered to the floor. This last slip Shrowl picked up and looked over its contents, without troubling himself to go through the ceremony of first asking leave.

After slowly drawing in and slowly puffing out again one mouthful of tobacco-smoke, Mr Treverton began to read the letter. As his eye fell on the first lines, his lips began to work round the mouth-piece of the pipe in a manner that was very unusual with him. The letter was not long enough to require him to turn over the first leaf of it—it ended at the bottom of the opening sheet. He read it down to the signature—then looked up to the address, and went through it again from the beginning. His lips still continued to work round the mouth-piece of the pipe, but he smoked no more. When he had finished the second reading, he set the letter down very gently on the table, looked at his servant with an unaccustomed vacancy in the expression of his eyes, and took the pipe out of his mouth with a hand that trembled a little.

'Shrowl,' he said, very quietly, 'my brother, the Captain, is drowned.'

'I know he is,' answered Shrowl, without looking up from the newspaper-slip. 'I'm reading about it here.'

'The last words my brother said to me when we quarrelled about the player-woman,' continued Mr Treverton, speaking as much to himself as to his servant, 'were, that I should die without one kind feeling in my heart towards any living creature.'

'So you will,' muttered Shrowl, turning the slip over to see if there was anything worth reading at the back of it.

'I wonder what he thought about me when he was dying?' said Mr Treverton, abstractedly, taking up the letter again from the table.

'He didn't waste a thought on you or anybody else,' remarked Shrowl. 'If he thought at all, he thought about how he could save his life. When he had done thinking about that, he had done living, too.' With this expression of opinion Mr Shrowl went to the beer-barrel, and drew his morning draught.

'Damn that player-woman!' muttered Mr Treverton. As he said the words his face darkened and his lips closed firmly. He smoothed the letter out on the table. There seemed to be some doubt in his mind whether he had mastered all its contents yet— some idea that there ought to be more in it than he had yet discovered. In going over it for the third time, he read it to himself aloud and very slowly, as if he was determined to fix every separate word firmly in his memory. This was the letter:—

'SIR,—As the old legal adviser and faithful friend of your family, I am desired by Mrs Frankland, formerly Miss Treverton, to acquaint you with the sad news of your brother's death. This deplorable event occurred on board the ship of which he was captain, during a gale of wind in which the vessel was lost on a reef of rocks off the island of Antigua. I enclose a detailed account of the shipwreck, extracted from the Times, by which you will see that your brother died nobly in the performance of his duty towards the officers and men whom he commanded. I also send a slip from the local Cornish paper, containing a memoir of the deceased gentleman.

'Before closing this communication, I must add that no will has been found, after the most rigorous search, among the papers of the late Captain Treverton. Having disposed, as you know, of Porthgenna, the only property of which he was possessed at the time of his death was personal property, derived from the sale of his estate; and this, in consequence of his dying intestate, will go in due course of law to his daughter, as his nearest of kin.

'I am, Sir,

'Your obedient servant,

'ALEXANDER NIXON.'

The newspaper-slip, which had fallen on the table, contained the paragraph from the Times. The slip from the Cornish paper, which had dropped to the floor, Shrowl poked under his master's eyes, in a fit of temporary civility, as soon as he had done reading it. Mr Treverton took not the slightest notice either of the one paragraph or the other. He still sat looking at the letter, even after he had read it for the third time.

'Why don't you give the strip of print a turn, as well as the sheet of writing?' asked Shrowl. 'Why don't you read about what a great man your brother was, and what a good life he led, and what a wonderful handsome daughter he's left behind him, and what a capital marriage she's made along with the man that's owner of your old family estate? *She* don't want your money now, at any rate! The ill wind that blowed her father's ship on the rocks has blowed forty thousand pounds of good into her lap. Why don't you read about it? She and her husband have got a better house in Cornwall than you have got here. Ain't you glad of that? They were going to have repaired the place from top to bottom for your brother to go and live along with 'em in clover when he came back from sea. Who will ever repair a place for you? I wonder whether your niece would knock the old house about for your sake, now, if you was to clean yourself up and go and ask her?'

At the last question, Shrowl paused in the work of aggravation—not for want of more words, but for want of encouragement to utter them. For the first time since they had kept house together, he had tried to provoke his master and had failed. Mr Treverton listened, or appeared to listen, without moving a muscle—without the faintest change to anger in his face. The only words he said when Shrowl had done, were these two—

'Go out!'

Shrowl was not an easy man to move, but he absolutely changed colour when he heard himself suddenly ordered to leave the room.

'Go out!' reiterated Mr Treverton. 'And hold your tongue henceforth and for ever, about my brother and my brother's daughter. I never *have* set eyes upon the player-woman's child, and I never will. Hold your tongue—leave me alone—go out!'

'I'll be even with him for this,' thought Shrowl as he slowly withdrew from the room.

When he had closed the door, he listened outside it, and heard Mr Treverton push aside his chair, and walk up and down, talking to himself. Judging by the confused words that escaped him, Shrowl concluded that his thoughts were still running on the 'player-woman' who had set his brother and himself at variance. He seemed to feel a barbarous sense of relief in venting his dissatisfaction with himself, after the news of Captain Treverton's death, on the memory of the woman whom he hated so bitterly, and on the child whom she had left behind her.

After a while, the low rumbling tones of his voice ceased altogether. Shrowl peeped through the keyhole, and saw that he was reading the newspaper-slips which contained the account of the shipwreck, and the Memoir of his brother. The latter adverted to some of those family particulars which the vicar of Long Beckley had mentioned to his guest; and the writer of the Memoir concluded by expressing a hope that the bereavement which Mr and Mrs Frankland had suffered would not interfere with their project for repairing Porthgenna

Tower, after they had gone the length already of sending a builder to survey the place. Something in the wording of that paragraph seemed to take Mr Treverton's memory back to his youthtime when the old family house had been his home. He whispered a few words to himself which gloomily referred to the days that were gone, rose from his chair impatiently, threw both the newspaper-slips into the fire, watched them while they were burning, and sighed when the black gossamer ashes floated upward on the draught, and were lost in the chimney.

The sound of that sigh startled Shrowl as the sound of a pistol-shot might have startled another man. His bull-terrier's eyes opened wide in astonishment, and he shook his head ominously as he walked away from the door.

CHAPTER II

WILL THEY COME?

THE housekeeper at Porthgenna Tower had just completed the necessary preparations for the reception of her master and mistress, at the time mentioned in Mrs Frankland's letter from St Swithin's-on-Sea, when she was startled by receiving a note sealed with black wax, and surrounded by a thick mourning border. The note briefly communicated the news of Captain Treverton's death, and informed her that the visit of Mr and Mrs Frankland to Porthgenna was deferred for an indefinite period.

By the same post, the builder who was superintending the renovation of the west staircase also received a letter, requesting him to send in his account as soon as the repairs on which he was then engaged were completed; and telling him that Mr Frankland was unable, for the present, to give any further attention to the project for making the north rooms habitable. On the receipt of this communication, the builder withdrew himself and his men as soon as the west stairs and banisters had been made secure; and Porthgenna Tower was again left to the care of the housekeeper and her servant, without master or mistress, friends or strangers, to thread its solitary passages or enliven its empty rooms.

From this time, eight months passed away, and the house-keeper heard nothing of her master and mistress, except through the medium of paragraphs in the local newspaper, which dubiously referred to the probability of their occupying the old house, and interesting themselves in the affairs of their tenantry, at no very distant period. Occasionally, too, when business took him to the post-town, the steward collected reports about his employers among the old friends and dependants of the Treverton family.

From these sources of information, the housekeeper was led to conclude that Mr and Mrs Frankland had returned to Long Beckley, after receiving the news of Captain Treverton's death, and had lived there for some months in strict retirement. When they left that place, they moved (if the newspaper report was to be credited) to the neighbourhood of London, and occupied the house of some friends who were travelling on the continent. Here they must have remained for some time, for the new year came and brought no rumours of any change in their place of abode. January and February passed without any news of them. Early in March the steward had occasion to go to the post-town. When he returned to Porthgenna, he came back with a new report relating to Mr and Mrs Frankland, which excited the housekeeper's interest in an extraordinary degree. In two different quarters, each highly respectable, the steward had heard it facetiously announced that the domestic responsi-bilities of his master and mistress were likely to be increased by their having a nurse to engage and a crib to buy at the end of the spring or the beginning of the summer. In plain English, among the many babies who might be expected to make their appearance in the world in the course of the next three months, there was one who would inherit the name of Frankland, and who (if the infant luckily turned out to be a boy) would cause a sensation throughout West Cornwall as heir to the Porthgenna estate.

In the next month, the month of April, before the house-keeper and the steward had done discussing their last and most important fragment of news, the postman made his welcome appearance at Porthgenna Tower, and brought another note from Mrs Frankland. The housekeeper's face brightened with unaccustomed pleasure and surprise as she read the first line. The letter announced that the long-deferred visit of her master and mistress to the old house would take place early in May, and that they might be expected to arrive any day from the first to the tenth of the month.

The reasons which had led the owners of Porthgenna to fix a period, at last, for visiting their country seat, were connected with certain particulars into which Mrs Frankland had not thought it advisable to enter in her letter. The plain facts of the case were, that a little discussion had arisen between the husband and wife in relation to the next place of residence which they should select, after the return from the continent of the friends whose house they were occupying. Mr Frankland had very reasonably suggested returning again to Long Beckley—not only because all their oldest friends lived in the neighbourhood, but also (and circumstances made this an important consideration) because the place had the advantage of possessing an excellent resident medical man. Unfortunately this latter advantage, so far from carrying any weight with it in Mrs Frankland's estimation, actually prejudiced her mind against the project of going to Long Beckley. She had always, she acknowledged, felt an unreasonable antipathy to the doctor there. He might be a very skilful, an extremely polite, and an undeniably respectable man; but she never had liked him, and never should, and she was resolved to oppose the plan for living at Long Beckley, because the execution of it would oblige her to commit herself to his care.

Two other places of residence were next suggested: but Mrs Frankland had the same objection to oppose to both—in each case, the resident doctor would be a stranger to her, and she did not like the notion of being attended by a stranger. Finally, as she had all along anticipated, the choice of the future abode was left entirely to her own inclinations; and then, to the amazement of her husband and her friends, she immediately decided on going to Porthgenna. She had formed this strange project, and was now resolved on executing it, partly because she was more curious than ever to see the place again;

partly, because the doctor who had been with her mother in
Mrs Treverton's last illness, and who had attended her through
all her own little maladies, when she was a child, was still living
and practising in the Porthgenna neighbourhood. Her father
and the doctor had been old cronies, and had met for years at
the same chess-board every Saturday night. They had kept up
their friendship, when circumstances separated them, by
exchanges of Christmas presents every year; and when the sad
news of the Captain's death had reached Cornwall, the doctor
had written a letter of sympathy and condolence to Rosamond,
speaking in such terms of his former friend and patron as she
could never forget. He must be a nice, fatherly old man, now,
the man of all others who was fittest, on every account, to
attend her. In short, Mrs Frankland was just as strongly
prejudiced in favour of employing the Porthgenna doctor, as
she was prejudiced against employing the Long Beckley
doctor; and she ended, as all young married women, with
affectionate husbands, may, and do, end, whenever they
please—by carrying her own point, and having her own way.

On the first of May, the west rooms were all ready for the
reception of the master and mistress of the house. The beds
were aired, the carpets cleaned, the sofas and chairs uncovered.
The housekeeper put on her satin gown and her garnet brooch;
the maid followed suit, at a respectful distance, in brown
merino and a pink ribbon; and the steward, determining not
to be outdone by the women, arrayed himself in a black
brocaded waistcoat, which almost rivalled the gloom and
grandeur of the housekeeper's satin gown. The day wore on,
evening closed in, bed-time came, and there were no signs yet
of Mr and Mrs Frankland.

But the first was an early day on which to expect them. The
steward thought so, and the housekeeper added that it would
be foolish to feel disappointed, even if they did not arrive until
the fifth. The fifth came, and still nothing happened. The sixth,
seventh, eighth, and ninth followed, and no sound of the
expected carriage-wheels came near the lonely house.

On the tenth, and last day, the housekeeper, the steward,
and the maid, all three rose earlier than usual; all three opened
and shut doors, and went up and down stairs oftener than was

needful; all three looked out perpetually towards the moor and the high road, and thought the view flatter, and duller, and emptier than ever it had appeared to them before. The day waned, the sunset came; darkness changed the perpetual looking out of the housekeeper, the steward, and the maid, into perpetual listening; ten o'clock struck, and still there was nothing to be heard when they went to the open window, but the wearisome beating of the surf on the sandy shore.

The housekeeper began to calculate the time that would be consumed on the railway journey from London to Exeter, and on the posting journey afterwards through Cornwall to Porthgenna. When had Mr and Mrs Frankland left Exeter?— that was the first question. And what delays might they have encountered afterwards in getting horses?—that was the second. The housekeeper and the steward differed in debating these points; but both agreed that it was necessary to sit up until midnight, on the chance of the master and mistress arriving late. The maid, hearing her sentence of banishment from bed for the next two hours, pronounced by the superior authorities, yawned and sighed mournfully—was reproved by the steward—and was furnished by the housekeeper with a book of Hymns to read, to keep up her spirits.

Twelve o'clock struck, and still the monotonous beating of the surf, varied occasionally by those loud, mysterious, cracking noises which make themselves heard at night in an old house, were the only audible sounds. The steward was dozing; the maid was fast asleep under the soothing influence of the Hymns; the housekeeper was wide awake, with her eyes fixed on the window, and her head shaking forebodingly from time to time. At the last stroke of the clock she left her chair, listened attentively, and still hearing nothing, shook the maid irritably by the shoulder, and stamped on the floor to arouse the steward.

'We may go to bed,' she said. 'They are not coming. This is the second time they have disappointed us. The first time, the Captain's death stood in the way. What stops them now? Another death? I shouldn't wonder if it was.'

'Now I think of it, no more should I,' said the steward, ominously knitting his brows.

'Another death!' repeated the housekeeper, superstitiously. 'If it *is* another death, I should take it, in their place, as a warning to keep away from the house.'

CHAPTER III

MRS JAZEPH

IF, instead of hazarding the guess that a second death stood in the way of Mr and Mrs Frankland's arrival at Porthgenna, the housekeeper had, by way of variety, surmised, this time, that a birth was the obstacle which delayed them, she might have established her character as a wise woman, by hitting at random on the actual truth. Her master and mistress had started from London on the ninth of May, and had got through the greater part of their railway journey, when they were suddenly obliged to stop, on Mrs Frankland's account, at the station of a small town in Somersetshire. The little visitor, who was destined to increase the domestic responsibilities of the young married couple, had chosen to enter on the scene in the character of a robust boy-baby, a month earlier than he had been expected, and had modestly preferred to make his first appearance in a small Somersetshire inn, rather than wait to be ceremoniously welcomed to life in the great house of Porthgenna, which he was one day to inherit.

Very few events had ever produced a greater sensation in the town of West Winston, than the one small event of the unexpected stoppage of Mr and Mrs Frankland's journey at that place. Never, since the last election, had the landlord and landlady of the Tiger's Head Hotel bustled about their house in such a fever of excitement as possessed them, when Mr Frankland's servant and Mrs Frankland's maid drew up at the door in a fly* from the station, to announce that their master and mistress were behind, and that the largest and quietest rooms in the hotel were wanted immediately, under the most unexpected circumstances. Never, since he had triumphantly passed his examination, had young Mr Orridge, the new doctor, who had started in life by purchasing the West Winston practice, felt such a thrill of pleasurable agitation pervade him from top to toe, as when he heard that the wife of a blind gentleman of great fortune had been taken ill on the railway journey from London to Devonshire, and required all that his skill and attention could do for her, without a moment's delay. Never, since the last archery meeting and fancy fair, had the ladies of the town been favoured with such an all-absorbing subject for conversation as was now afforded to them by Mrs Frankland's mishap. Fabulous accounts of the wife's beauty and the husband's fortune poured from the original source of the Tiger's Head, and trickled through the highways and byways of the little town. There were a dozen different reports, one more elaborately false than the other, about Mr Frankland's blindness, and the cause of it; about the lamentable condition in which his wife had arrived at the hotel; and about the painful sense of responsibility which had unnerved the inexperienced Mr Orridge from the first moment when he set eyes on his patient. It was not till eight o'clock in the evening that the public mind was relieved at last from all suspense by an announcement that the child was born, and screaming lustily; that the mother was wonderfully well, considering all things; and that Mr Orridge had covered himself with distinction by the skill, tenderness, and attention with which he had performed his duties.

On the next day, and the next, and for a week after that, the accounts were still favourable. But on the tenth day, a catastrophe was reported. The nurse who was in attendance on Mrs Frankland had been suddenly taken ill, and was rendered quite incapable of performing any further service for at least a week to come, and perhaps for a much longer period.

In a large town this misfortune might have been readily remedied, but in a place like West Winston it was not so easy to supply the loss of an experienced nurse at a few hours' notice. When Mr Orridge was consulted in the new emergency, he candidly acknowledged that he required a little time for consideration before he could undertake to find another professed nurse of sufficient character and experience to wait on a lady like Mrs Frankland. Mr Frankland suggested telegraphing to a medical friend in London for a nurse, but the doctor was unwilling for many reasons to adopt that plan, except as a last resource. It would take some time to find the right person, and to send her to West Winston; and, moreover, he would infinitely prefer employing a woman with whose character and capacity he was himself acquainted. He therefore proposed that Mrs Frankland should be trusted for a few hours to the care of her maid, under supervision of the landlady of the Tiger's Head, while he made enquiries in the neighbourhood. If the enquiries produced no satisfactory result, he should be ready, when he called in the evening, to adopt Mr Frankland's idea of telegraphing to London for a nurse.

On proceeding to make the investigation that he had proposed, Mr Orridge, although he spared no trouble, met with no success. He found plenty of volunteers for the office of nurse, but they were all loud-voiced, clumsy-handed, heavy-footed countrywomen, kind and willing enough, but sadly awkward, blundering attendants to place at the bedside of such a lady as Mrs Frankland. The morning hours passed away, and the afternoon came, and still Mr Orridge had found no substitute for the invalided nurse whom he could venture to engage.

At two o'clock he had half-an-hour's drive before him to a country-house, where he had a child-patient to see. 'Perhaps I may remember somebody who may do, on the way out, or on the way back again,' thought Mr Orridge, as he got into his gig. 'I have some hours at my disposal still, before the time comes for my evening visit at the inn.'

Puzzling his brains, with the best intention in the world, all along the road to the country house, Mr Orridge reached his destination without having arrived at any other conclusion than that he might just as well state his difficulty to Mrs Norbury, the lady whose child he was about to prescribe for. He had called on her when he bought the West Winston practice, and had found her one of those frank, good-humoured, middle-aged women, who are generally designated by the epithet 'motherly.' Her husband was a country squire, famous for his old politics, his old stories, and his old wine. He had seconded his wife's hearty reception of the new doctor, with all the usual jokes about never giving him any employment, and never letting any bottles into the house, except the bottles that went down into the cellar. Mr Orridge had been amused by the husband and pleased with the wife; and he thought it might be at least worth while, before he gave up all hope of finding a fit nurse, to ask Mrs Norbury, as an old resident in the West Winston neighbourhood, for a word of advice.

Accordingly, after seeing the child, and pronouncing that there were no symptoms about the little patient which need cause the slightest alarm to anybody, Mr Orridge paved the way for a statement of the difficulty that beset him, by asking Mrs Norbury if she had heard of the 'interesting event' that had happened at the Tiger's Head.

'You mean,' answered Mrs Norbury, who was a downright woman, and a resolute speaker of the plainest possible English, 'you mean, have I heard about that poor unfortunate lady who was taken ill on her journey, and who had a child born at the inn? We have heard so much, and no more—living as we do (thank Heaven!) out of reach of the West Winston gossip. How is the lady? Who is she? Is the child well? Is she tolerably comfortable? poor thing! Can I send her anything, or do anything for her?'

'You would do a great thing for her, and render a great assistance to me,' said Mr Orridge, 'if you could tell me of any respectable woman in this neighbourhood who would be a proper nurse for her.'

'You don't mean to say that the poor creature has not got a nurse!' exclaimed Mrs Norbury.

'She has had the best nurse in West Winston,' replied Mr Orridge. 'But, most unfortunately, the woman was taken ill this morning, and was obliged to go home. I am now at my wit's end for somebody to supply her place. Mrs Frankland has been used to the luxury of being well waited on; and where I am to find an attendant, who is likely to satisfy her, is more than I can tell.'

'Frankland, did you say, her name was?' enquired Mrs Norbury.

'Yes. She is, I understand, a daughter of that Captain Treverton, who was lost with his ship, a year ago, in the West

Indies. Perhaps you may remember the account of the disaster in the newspapers?'

'Of course I do! and I remember the Captain too. I was acquainted with him when he was a young man, at Portsmouth. His daughter and I ought not to be strangers, especially under such circumstances as the poor thing is placed in now. I will call at the inn, Mr Orridge, as soon as you will allow me to introduce myself to her. But, in the mean time, what is to be done in this difficulty about the nurse? Who is with Mrs Frankland now?'

'Her maid; but she is a very young woman, and doesn't understand nursing-duties. The landlady of the inn is ready to help when she can; but then she has constant demands on her time and attention. I suppose we shall have to telegraph to London and get somebody sent here by railway.'

'And that will take time, of course. And the new nurse may turn out to be a drunkard, or a thief, or both—when you have got her here,' said the outspoken Mrs Norbury. 'Dear, dear me! can't we do something better than that? I am ready, I am sure, to take any trouble, or make any sacrifice, if I can be of use to Mrs Frankland. Do you know, Mr Orridge, I think it would be a good plan if we consulted my housekeeper, Mrs Jazeph. She is an odd woman, with an odd name, you will say; but she has lived with me in this house more than five years, and she may know of somebody in our neighbourhood who might suit you, though I don't.' With those words, Mrs Norbury rang the bell, and ordered the servant who answered it, to tell Mrs Jazeph that she was wanted up-stairs immediately.

After the lapse of a minute or so, a soft knock was heard at the door, and the housekeeper entered the room.

Mr Orridge looked at her, the moment she appeared, with an interest and curiosity for which he was hardly able to account. He judged her, at a rough guess, to be a woman of about fifty years of age. At the first glance, his medical eye detected that some of the intricate machinery of the nervous system had gone wrong with Mrs Jazeph. He noted the painful working of the muscles of her face, and the hectic flush that flew into her cheeks when she entered the room and found a visitor there. He observed a strangely scared look in her eyes, and remarked that it did not leave them when the rest of her face became gradually composed. 'That woman has had some dreadful fright, some great grief, or some wasting complaint,' he thought to himself. 'I wonder which it is?'

'This is Mr Orridge, the medical gentleman who has lately settled at West Winston,' said Mrs Norbury, addressing the housekeeper. 'He is in attendance on a lady, who was obliged to stop, on her journey westward, at our station, and who is now staying at the Tiger's Head. You have heard something about it, have you not, Mrs Jazeph?'

Mrs Jazeph, standing just inside the door, looked respectfully towards the doctor, and answered in the affirmative. Although she only said the two common words, 'Yes, ma'am,' in a quiet, uninterested way, Mr Orridge was struck by the sweetness and tenderness of her voice. If he had not been looking at her, he would have supposed it to be the voice of a young woman. His eyes remained fixed on her after she had spoken, though he felt that they ought to have been looking towards her mistress. He, the most unobservant of men in such things, found himself noticing her dress, so that he remembered, long afterwards, the form of the spotless muslin cap that primly covered her smooth grey hair, and the quiet brown colour of the silk dress that fitted so neatly and hung around her in such spare and disciplined folds. The little confusion which she evidently felt at finding herself the object of the doctor's attention, did not betray her into the slightest awkwardness of gesture or manner. If there can be such a thing, physically speaking, as the grace of restraint, that was the grace which seemed to govern Mrs Jazeph's slightest movements; which led her feet smoothly over the carpet, as she advanced when her mistress next spoke to her; which governed the action of her wan right hand as it rested lightly on a table by her side, while she stopped to hear the next question that was addressed to her.

'Well,' continued Mrs Norbury, 'this poor lady was just getting on comfortably, when the nurse, who was looking after her, fell ill this morning; and there she is now, in a strange place, with a first child, and no proper attendance—no woman of age and experience to help her as she ought to be helped. We want somebody fit to wait on a delicate woman who has seen nothing of the rough side of humanity. Mr Orridge can find nobody at a day's notice, and I can tell him of nobody. Can you help us, Mrs Jazeph? Are there any women down in the village, or among Mr Norbury's tenants, who understand nursing, and have some tact and tenderness to recommend them into the bargain?'

Mrs Jazeph reflected for a little while, and then said, very respectfully, but very briefly also, and still without any appearance of interest in her manner, that she knew of no one whom she could recommend.

'Don't make too sure of that till you have thought a little longer,' said Mrs Norbury. 'I have a particular interest in serving this lady, for Mr Orridge told me just before you came in, that she is the daughter of Captain Treverton, whose shipwreck——'

The instant those words were spoken, Mrs Jazeph turned round with a start, and looked at the doctor. Apparently forgetting that her right hand was on the table, she moved it so suddenly that it struck against a bronze statuette of a dog placed on some writing materials. The statuette fell to the ground, and Mrs Jazeph stooped to pick it up with a cry of alarm which seemed strangely exaggerated by comparison with the trifling nature of the accident.

'Bless the woman! what is she frightened about?' exclaimed Mrs Norbury. 'The dog is not hurt—put it back again! This is the first time, Mrs Jazeph, that I ever knew you do an awkward thing. You may take that as a compliment, I think. Well, as I was saying, this lady is the daughter of Captain Treverton, whose dreadful shipwreck we all read about in the papers. I knew her father in my early days, and on that account I am doubly anxious to be of service to her now. Do think again. Is there nobody within reach who can be trusted to nurse her?'

The doctor, still watching Mrs Jazeph with that secret medical interest of his in her case, had seen her turn so deadly pale when she started and looked towards him, that he would not have been surprised if she had fainted on the spot. He now observed that she changed colour again when her mistress left off speaking. The hectic red tinged her cheeks once more with two bright spots. Her timid eyes wandered uneasily about the room; and her fingers, as she clasped her hands together, interlaced themselves mechanically. 'That would be an interesting case to treat,' thought the doctor, following every nervous movement of the housekeeper's hands with watchful eyes.

'Do think again,' repeated Mrs Norbury. 'I am so anxious to help this poor lady through her difficulty, if I can.'

'I am very sorry,' said Mrs Jazeph, in faint, trembling tones, but still always with the same sweetness in her voice; 'very sorry that I can think of no one who is fit; but——'

She stopped. No shy child on its first introduction to the society of strangers could have looked more disconcerted than she looked now. Her eyes were on the ground; her colour was deepening; the fingers of her clasped hands were working together faster and faster every moment.

'But what?' asked Mrs Norbury.

'I was about to say, ma'am,' answered Mrs Jazeph, speaking with the greatest difficulty and uneasiness, and never raising her eyes to her mistress's face, 'that, rather than this lady should want for a nurse, I would—considering the interest, ma'am, which you take in her—I would, if you thought you could spare me——'

'What, nurse her yourself!' exclaimed Mrs Norbury. 'Upon my word, although you have got to it in rather a roundabout way, you have come to the point at last, in a manner which does infinite credit to your kindness of heart and your readiness to make yourself useful. As to sparing you, of course I am not so selfish, under the circumstances, as to think twice of the inconvenience of losing my housekeeper. But the question is, are you competent as well as willing? Have you ever had any practice in nursing?'

'Yes, ma'am,' answered Mrs Jazeph, still without raising her eyes from the ground. 'Shortly after my marriage' (the flush disappeared, and her face turned pale again as she said those words), 'I had some practice in nursing, and continued it at intervals until the time of my husband's death. I only presume to offer myself, sir,' she went on, turning towards the doctor, and becoming more earnest and self-possessed in her manner as she did so; 'I only presume to offer myself, with my mistress's permission, as a substitute for a nurse until some better qualified person can be found.'

'What do you say, Mr Orridge?' asked Mrs Norbury.

It had been the doctor's turn to start when he first heard Mrs Jazeph propose herself for the office of nurse. He hesitated before he answered Mrs Norbury's question, then said:

'I can have but one doubt about the propriety of thankfully accepting Mrs Jazeph's offer.'

Mrs Jazeph's timid eyes looked anxiously and perplexedly at him as he spoke. Mrs Norbury, in her downright, abrupt way, asked immediately what the doubt was.

'I feel some uncertainty,' replied Mr Orridge, 'as to whether Mrs Jazeph—she will pardon me, as a medical man, for mentioning it—as to whether Mrs Jazeph is strong enough, and has her nerves sufficiently under control to perform the duties which she is so kindly ready to undertake.'

In spite of the politeness of the explanation, Mrs Jazeph was evidently disconcerted and distressed by it. A certain quiet, uncomplaining sadness, which it was very touching to see, overspread her face as she turned away, without another word, and walked slowly to the door.

'Don't go yet!' cried Mrs Norbury, kindly, 'or, at least, if you do go, come back again in five minutes. I am quite certain we shall have something more to say to you then.'

Mrs Jazeph's eyes expressed her thanks in one grateful glance. They looked so much brighter than usual while they rested on her mistress's face, that Mrs Norbury half doubted whether the tears were not just rising in them at that moment. Before she could look again, Mrs Jazeph had curtseyed to the doctor, and had noiselessly left the room.

'Now we are alone, Mr Orridge,' said Mrs Norbury, 'I may tell you, with all submission to your medical judgment, that you are a little exaggerating Mrs Jazeph's nervous infirmities. She looks poorly enough, I own—but, after five years' experience of her, I can tell you that she is stronger than she looks, and I honestly think you will be doing good service to Mrs Frankland if you try our volunteer nurse, at least, for a day or two. She is the gentlest, tenderest creature I ever met with, and conscientious to a fault in the performance of any duty that she undertakes. Don't be under any delicacy about taking her away. I gave a dinner-party last week, and shall not give another for some time to come. I never could have spared my housekeeper more easily than I can spare her now.'

'I am sure I may offer Mrs Frankland's thanks to you as well as my own,' said Mr Orridge. 'After what you have said, it would be ungracious and ungrateful in me not to follow your advice. But will you excuse me if I ask one question? Did you ever hear that Mrs Jazeph was subject to fits of any kind?'

'Never.'

'Not even to hysterical affections, now and then?'

'Never, since she has been in this house.'

'You surprise me, there is something in her look and manner——'

'Yes, yes; everybody remarks that at first; but it simply means that she is in delicate health, and that she has not led a very happy life (as I suspect) in her younger days. The lady from whom I had her (with an excellent character) told me that she had married unhappily, when she was in a sadly poor unprotected state. She never says anything about her married troubles herself; but I believe her husband ill-used her. However, it does not seem to me that this is our business. I can only tell you again that she has been an excellent servant here for the last five years, and that, in your place, poorly as she may look, I should consider her as the best nurse that Mrs Frankland could possibly wish for, under the circumstances. There is no need for me to say any more. Take Mrs Jazeph, or telegraph to London for a stranger—the decision of course rests with you.'

Mr Orridge thought he detected a slight tone of irritability in Mrs Norbury's last sentence. He was a prudent man; and he suppressed any doubts he might still feel in reference to Mrs Jazeph's physical capacities for nursing, rat er than risk offending the most important lady in the neighbourhood at the outset of his practice in West Winston as a medical man.

'I cannot hesitate a moment after what you have been good enough to tell me,' he said. 'Pray believe that I gratefully accept your kindness and your housekeeper's offer.'

Mrs Norbury rang the bell. It was answered on the instant by the housekeeper herself.

The doctor wondered whether she had been listening outside the door, and thought it rather strange, if she had, that she should be so anxious to learn his decision.

'Mr Orridge accepts your offer with thanks,' said Mrs Norbury, beckoning to Mrs Jazeph to advance into the room. 'I have persuaded him that you are not quite so weak and ill as you look.'

A gleam of joyful surprise broke over the housekeeper's face. It looked suddenly younger by years and years, as she smiled and expressed her grateful sense of the trust that was about to be reposed in her. For the first time, also, since the doctor had seen her, she ventured on speaking before she was spoken to.

'When will my attendance be required, sir?' she asked.

'As soon as possible,' replied Mr Orridge. How quickly and brightly her dim eyes seemed to clear as she heard that answer! How much more hasty than her usual movements was the movement with which she now turned round and looked appealingly at her mistress!

'Go whenever Mr Orridge wants you,' said Mrs Norbury. 'I know your accounts are always in order, and your keys always in their proper places. You never make confusion and you never leave confusion. Go, by all means, as soon as the doctor wants you.'

'I suppose you have some preparations to make?' said Mr Orridge.

'None, sir, that need delay me more than half-an-hour,' answered Mrs Jazeph.

'This evening will be early enough,' said the doctor, taking his hat, and bowing to Mrs Norbury. 'Come to the Tiger's Head, and ask for me. I shall be there between seven and eight. Many thanks again, Mrs Norbury.'

'My best wishes and compliments to your patient, doctor.'

'At the Tiger's Head, between seven and eight this evening,' reiterated Mr Orridge, as the housekeeper opened the door for him.

'Between seven and eight, sir,' repeated the soft, sweet voice, sounding younger than ever, now that there was an under-note of pleasure running through its tones.

CHAPTER IV

THE NEW NURSE

As the clock struck seven, Mr Orridge put on his hat to go to the Tiger's head. He had just opened his own door, when he was met on the step by a messenger, who summoned him immediately to a case of sudden illness in the poor quarter of the town. The inquiries he made satisfied him that the appeal was really of an urgent nature, and that there was no help for it but to delay his attendance for a little while at the inn. On reaching the bedside of the patient, he discovered symptoms in the case which rendered an immediate operation necessary. The performance of this professional duty occupied some time. It was a quarter to eight before he left his house, for the second time, on his way to the Tiger's Head.

On entering the inn door, he was informed that the new nurse had arrived as early as seven o'clock, and had been waiting for him in a room by herself, ever since. Having received no orders from Mr Orridge, the landlady had thought it safest not to introduce the stranger to Mrs Frankland before the doctor came.

'Did she ask to go up into Mrs Frankland's room?' inquired Mr Orridge.

'Yes, sir,' replied the landlady. 'And I thought she seemed rather put out when I said that I must beg her to wait till you got here. Will you step this way, and see her at once, sir? She is in my parlour.'

Mr Orridge followed the landlady into a little room at the back of the house, and found Mrs Jazeph sitting alone in the corner farthest from the window. He was rather surprised to see that she drew her veil down the moment the door was opened.

'I am sorry you should have been kept waiting,' he said; 'but I was called away to a patient. Besides, I told you between seven and eight, if you remember; and it is not eight o'clock yet.'

'I was very anxious to be in good time, sir,' said Mrs Jazeph.

There was an accent of restraint in the quiet tones in which she spoke which struck Mr Orridge's ear, and a little perplexed him. She was, apparently, not only afraid that her face might betray something, but apprehensive also that her voice might tell him more than her words expressed. What feeling was she anxious to conceal? Was it irritation at having been kept waiting so long by herself in the landlady's room?

'If you will follow me,' said Mr Orridge, 'I will take you to Mrs Frankland immediately.'

Mrs Jazeph rose slowly, and, when she was on her feet, rested her hand for an instant on a table near her. That action, momentary as it was, helped to confirm the doctor in his conviction of her physical unfitness for the position which she had volunteered to occupy.

'You seem tired,' he said, as he led the way out of the door. 'Surely, you did not walk all the way here?'

'No, sir. My mistress was so kind as to let one of the servants drive me in the pony-chaise.'* There was the same restraint in her voice, as she made that answer; and still she never attempted to lift her veil. While ascending the inn stairs Mr Orridge mentally resolved to watch her first proceedings in Mrs Frankland's room closely, and to send, after all, for the London nurse, unless Mrs Jazeph showed remarkable aptitude in the performance of her new duties.

The room which Mrs Frankland occupied was situated at the back of the house, having been chosen in that position, with the object of removing her as much as possible from the bustle and noise about the inn door. It was lighted by one window overlooking a few cottages, beyond which spread the rich grazing grounds of West Somersetshire, bounded by a long monotonous line of thickly-wooded hills. The bed was of the old-fashioned kind, with the customary four posts and the inevitable damask curtains. It projected from the wall into the middle of the room in such a situation, as to keep the door on the right hand of the person occupying it, the window on the left, and the fire-place opposite the foot of the bed. On the side of the bed nearest the window, the curtains were open, while at the foot, and on the side near the door, they were closely drawn. By this arrangement the interior of the bed was necessarily concealed from the view of any person on first entering the room.

'How do you find yourself to-night, Mrs Frankland?' asked Mr Orridge, reaching out his hand to undraw the curtains. 'Do you think you will be any the worse for a little freer circulation of air?'

'On the contrary, doctor, I shall be all the better,' was the answer. 'But I am afraid—in case you have ever been disposed to consider me a sensible woman—that my character will suffer a little in your estimation, when you see how I have been occupying myself for the last hour.'

Mr Orridge smiled as he undrew the curtains, and laughed outright when he looked at the mother and child.

Mrs Frankland had been amusing herself, and gratifying her taste for bright colours, by dressing out her baby with blue ribbons as he lay asleep. He had a necklace, shoulder-knots, and bracelets, all of blue ribbon; and to complete the quaint finery of his costume, his mother's smart little lace cap had been hitched comically on one side of his head. Rosamond herself, as if determined to vie with the baby in gaiety of dress, wore a light pink jacket, ornamented down the bosom and over the sleeves with bows of white satin ribbon. Laburnum blossoms, gathered that morning, lay scattered about over the white counterpane, intermixed with some flowers of the Lily of the Valley, tied up into two nosegays with strips of cherry-coloured ribbon. Over this varied assemblage of colours, over the baby's smoothly-rounded cheeks and arms, over his mother's happy, youthful face, the tender light of the May evening poured tranquil and warm. Thoroughly appreciating the charm of the picture which he had disclosed on undrawing the curtains, the doctor stood looking at it for a few moments, quite forgetful of the errand that had brought him into the room. He was only recalled to a remembrance of the new nurse by a chance question which Mrs Frankland addressed to him.

'I can't help it, doctor,' said Rosamond, with a look of apology. 'I really can't help treating my baby, now I am a grown woman, just as I used to treat my doll when I was a little girl. Did anybody come into the room with you? Lenny, are you there? Have you done dinner, darling, and did you drink my health when you were left at dessert all by yourself?'

'Mr Frankland is still at dinner,' said the doctor. 'But I certainly brought some one into the room with me. Where, in the name of wonder, has she gone to?—Mrs Jazeph!'

The housekeeper had slipped round to the part of the room between the foot of the bed and the fire-place, where she was hidden by the curtains that still remained drawn. When Mr Orridge called to her, instead of joining him where he stood, opposite the window, she appeared at the other side of the bed, where the window was behind her. Her shadow stole darkly over the bright picture which the doctor had been admiring. It stretched obliquely across the counterpane, and its dusky edges touched the figures of the mother and child.

'Gracious goodness! who are you?' exclaimed Rosamond. 'A woman or a ghost?'

Mrs Jazeph's veil was up at last. Although her face was necessarily in shadow in the position which she had chosen to occupy, the doctor saw a change pass over it when Mrs Frankland spoke. The lips dropped and quivered a little; the marks of care and age, about the mouth, deepened; and the eyebrows contracted suddenly. The eyes Mr Orridge could not see; they were cast down on the counterpane at the first word that Rosamond uttered. Judging by the light of his medical experience, the doctor concluded that she was suffering pain, and trying to suppress any outward manifestation of it. 'An affection of the heart, most likely,' he thought to himself. 'She has concealed it from her mistress, but she can't hide it from me.'

'Who are you?' repeated Rosamond. 'And what in the world do you stand there for—between us and the sunlight?'

Mrs Jazeph neither answered nor raised her eyes. She only moved back timidly to the farthest corner of the window.

'Did you not get a message from me this afternoon?' asked the doctor, appealing to Mrs Frankland.

'To be sure I did,' replied Rosamond. 'A very kind, flattering message about a new nurse.'

'There she is,' said Mr Orridge, pointing across the bed to Mrs Jazeph.

'You don't say so!' exclaimed Rosamond. 'But of course it must be. Who else could have come in with you? I ought to have known that. Pray come here—(what is her name, doctor? Joseph, did you say?—No?—Jazeph?)—pray come nearer, Mrs Jazeph, and let me apologise for speaking so abruptly to you. I am more obliged than I can say, for your kindness in coming here, and for your mistress's good-nature in resigning you to me. I hope I shall not give you much trouble, and I am sure you will find the baby easy to manage. He is a perfect angel, and sleeps like a dormouse. Dear me! now I look at you a little closer, I am afraid you are in very delicate health, yourself. Doctor! if Mrs Jazeph would not be offended with me, I should almost feel inclined to say that she looks in want of nursing, herself.'

Mrs Jazeph bent down over the laburnum blossoms on the bed, and began hurriedly and confusedly to gather them together.

'I thought as you do, Mrs Frankland,' said Mr Orridge. 'But I have been assured that Mrs Jazeph's looks belie her, and that her capabilities, as a nurse, quite equal her zeal.'

'Are you going to make all that laburnum into a nosegay?' asked Mrs Frankland, noticing how the new nurse was occupying herself. 'How thoughtful of you! and how magnificent it will be! I am afraid you will find the room very untidy. I will ring for my maid to set it to rights.'

'If you will allow me to put it in order, ma'am, I shall be very glad to begin being of use to you in that way,' said Mrs Jazeph. When she made the offer she looked up; and her eyes and Mrs Frankland's met. Rosamond instantly drew back on the pillow, and her colour altered a little.

'How strangely you look at me!' she said.

Mrs Jazeph started at the words, as if something had struck her, and moved away suddenly to the window.

'You are not offended with me, I hope?' said Rosamond, noticing the action. 'I have a sad habit of saying anything that comes uppermost. And I really thought you looked just now as if you saw something about me that frightened or grieved you. Pray put the room in order, if you are kindly willing to undertake the trouble. And never mind what I say, you will soon get used to my ways—and we shall be as comfortable and friendly—'

Just as Mrs Frankland said the words, 'comfortable' and 'friendly,' the new nurse left the window, and went back to the part of the room where she was hidden from view, between the fire-place and the closed curtains at the foot of the bed. Rosamond looked round to express her surprise to the doctor, but he turned away at the same moment so as to occupy a position which might enable him to observe what Mrs Jazeph was doing on the other side of the bed-curtains.

When he first caught sight of her, her hands were both raised to her face. Before he could decide whether he had surprised her in the act of clasping them over her eyes or not, they changed their position, and were occupied in removing her bonnet. After she had placed this part of her wearing apparel, and her shawl and gloves, on a chair in a corner of the room, she went to the dressing-table, and began to arrange the various useful and ornamental objects scattered about it. She set them in order with remarkable dexterity and neatness, showing a taste for arrangement, and a capacity for discriminating between things that were likely to be wanted and things that were not, which impressed Mr Orridge very favourably. He particularly noticed the carefulness with which she handled some bottles of physic, reading the labels on each, and arranging the medicine that might be required at night on one side of the table, and the medicine that might be required in the daytime on the other. When she left the dressing-table, and occupied herself in setting the furniture straight, and in folding up articles of clothing that had been thrown on one side, not the slightest movement of her thin wasted hands seemed ever to be made at hazard or in vain. Noiselessly, modestly, observantly, she moved from side to side of the room, and neatness and order followed her steps wherever she went. When Mr Orridge resumed his place at Mrs Frankland's bedside, his mind was at ease on one point at least—it was perfectly evident that the new nurse could be depended on to make no mistakes.

'What an odd woman she is!' whispered Rosamond.

'Odd, indeed,' returned Mr Orridge, 'and desperately broken in health, though she may not confess to it. However, she is wonderfully neat-handed and careful, and there can be no harm in trying her for one night—that is to say, unless you feel any objection.'

'On the contrary,' said Rosamond, 'she rather interests me. There is something in her face and manner—I can't say what—that makes me feel curious to know more of her. I must get her to talk, and try if I can't bring out all her peculiarities. Don't be afraid of my exciting myself, and don't stop here in this dull room on my account. I would much rather you went down-stairs, and kept my husband company over his wine. Do go and talk to him, and amuse him a little—he must be so dull, poor fellow, while I am up here; and he likes you, Mr Orridge—he does, very much. Stop one moment, and just look at the baby again. He doesn't take a dangerous quantity of sleep, does he? And, Mr Orridge, one word more: when you have done your wine, you will promise to lend my husband the use of your eyes, and bring him upstairs to wish me good-night, won't you?'

Willingly engaging to pay attention to Mrs Frankland's request, Mr Orridge left the bed-side.

As he opened the room door, he stopped to tell Mrs Jazeph that he should be downstairs if she wanted him, and that he would give her any instructions of which she might stand in need later in the evening, before he left the inn for the night. The new nurse, when he passed by her, was kneeling over one of Mrs Frankland's open trunks, arranging some articles of clothing which had been rather carelessly folded up. Just before he spoke to her, he observed that she had a chemisette* in her hand, the frill of which was laced through with ribbon.

One end of this ribbon she appeared to him to be on the point of drawing out, when the sound of his footsteps disturbed her. The moment she became aware of his approach, she dropped the chemisette suddenly in the trunk, and covered it over with some handkerchiefs. Although this proceeding on Mrs Jazeph's part rather surprised the doctor, he abstained from showing that he had noticed it. Her mistress had vouched for her character, after five years' experience of it, and the bit of ribbon was intrinsically worthless. On both accounts, it was impossible to suspect her of attempting to steal it; and yet, as Mr Orridge could not help feeling when he had left the room, her conduct, when he surprised her over the trunk, was exactly the conduct of a person who is about to commit a theft.

'Pray don't trouble yourself about my luggage,' said Rosamond, remarking Mrs Jazeph's occupation as soon as the doctor had gone. 'That is my idle maid's business, and you will only make her more careless than ever if you do it for her. I am sure the room is beautifully set in order. Come here and sit down and rest yourself. You must be a very unselfish, kind-hearted woman to give yourself all this trouble to serve a stranger. The doctor's message this afternoon told me that your mistress was a friend of my poor, dear father's. I suppose she must have known him before my time. Any way, I feel doubly grateful to her for taking an interest in me for my father's sake. But you can have no such feeling; you must have come here from pure good-nature and anxiety to help others. Don't go away, there, to the window. Come and sit down by me.'

Mrs Jazeph had risen from the trunk, and was approaching the bedside—when she suddenly turned away in the direction of the fire-place, just as Mrs Frankland began to speak of her father.

'Come and sit here,' reiterated Rosamond, getting impatient at receiving no answer. 'What in the world are you doing there at the foot of the bed?'

The figure of the new nurse again interposed between the bed and the fading evening light that glimmered through the window, before there was any reply.

'The evening is closing in,' said Mrs Jazeph, 'and the window is not quite shut. I was thinking of making it fast, and of drawing down the blind—if you had no objection, ma'am?'

'O, not yet! not yet! Shut the window, if you please, in case the baby should catch cold, but don't draw down the blind. Let me get my peep at the view as long as there is any light left to see it by. That long flat stretch of grazing-ground out there is just beginning, at this dim time, to look a little like my childish recollections of a Cornish moor. Do you know anything about Cornwall, Mrs Jazeph?'

'I have heard'——At those first three words of reply the nurse stopped. She was just then engaged in shutting the window, and she seemed to find some difficulty in closing the lock.

'What have you heard?' asked Rosamond.

'I have heard that Cornwall is a wild, dreary country,' said Mrs Jazeph, still busying herself with the lock of the window, and, by consequence, still keeping her back turned to Mrs Frankland.

'Can't you shut the window, yet?' said Rosamond. 'My maid always does it quite easily. Leave it till she comes up, I am going to ring for her directly. I want her to brush my hair and cool my face with a little Eau de Cologne and water.'

'I have shut it, ma'am,' said Mrs Jazeph, suddenly succeeding in closing the lock. 'And if you will allow me, I should be very glad to make you comfortable for the night, and save you the trouble of ringing for the maid.'

Thinking the new nurse the oddest woman she had ever met with, Mrs Frankland accepted the offer. By the time Mrs Jazeph had prepared the Eau de Cologne and water, the twilight was falling softly over the landscape outside, and the room was beginning to grow dark.

'Had you not better light a candle?' suggested Rosamond.

'I think not, ma'am,' said Mrs Jazeph, rather hastily. 'I can see quite well without.'

She began to brush Mrs Frankland's hair as she spoke; and, at the same time, asked a question which referred to the few words that had passed between them on the subject of Cornwall. Pleased to find that the new nurse had grown familiar enough at last to speak before she was spoken to, Rosamond desired nothing better than to talk about her recollections of her native country. But, from some inexplicable reason, Mrs Jazeph's touch, light and tender as it was, had such a strangely disconcerting effect on her, that she could not succeed, for the moment, in collecting her thoughts so as to reply, except in the briefest manner. The careful hands of the nurse lingered with a stealthy gentleness among the locks of her hair; the pale, wasted face of the new nurse approached, every now and then, more closely to her own than appeared at all needful. A vague sensation of uneasiness, which she could not trace to any particular part of her—which she could hardly say that she really felt, in a bodily sense, at all—seemed to be floating about her, to be hanging around and over her, like the air she breathed. She could not move, though she wanted to move in the bed; she could not turn her head so as to humour the action of the brush; she could not look round; she could not break the embarrassing silence which had been caused by her own short, discouraging answer. At last the sense of oppression—whether fancied or real—irritated her into snatching the brush out of Mrs Jazeph's hand. The instant she had done so, she felt ashamed of the discourteous abruptness of the action, and confused at the alarm and surprise which the manner of the nurse exhibited. With the strongest sense of the absurdity of her own conduct, and yet without the least power of controlling herself, she burst out laughing, and tossed the brush away to the foot of the bed.

'Pray don't look surprised, Mrs Jazeph,' she said, still laughing without knowing why, and without feeling in the slightest degree amused. 'I'm very rude and odd, I know. You have brushed my hair delightfully; but—I can't tell how—it seemed, all the time, as if you were brushing the strangest fancies into my head. I can't help laughing at them—I can't indeed! Do you know, once or twice, I absolutely fancied, when your face was closest to mine, that you wanted to kiss me! Did you ever hear of anything so ridiculous? I declare I am more of a baby, in some things, than the little darling here by my side!'

Mrs Jazeph made no answer. She left the bed while Rosamond was speaking, and came back, after an unaccountably long delay, with the Eau de Cologne and water. As she held the basin while Mrs Frankland bathed her face, she kept away at arm's length, and came no nearer when it was time to offer the towel. Rosamond began to be afraid that she had seriously offended Mrs Jazeph, and tried to soothe and propitiate her by asking questions about the management of the baby. There was a slight trembling in the sweet voice of the new nurse, but not the faintest tone of sullenness or anger, as she simply and quietly answered the inquiries addressed to her. By dint of keeping the conversation still on the subject of the child, Mrs Frankland succeeded, little by little, in luring her back to the bedside—in tempting her to bend down admiringly over the infant—in emboldening her, at last, to kiss him tenderly on the cheek. One kiss was all that she gave; and she turned away from the bed, after it, and sighed heavily.

The sound of that sigh fell very sadly on Rosamond's heart. Up to this time, the baby's little span of life had always been associated with smiling faces and pleasant words. It made her uneasy to think that anyone could caress him and sigh after it.

'I am sure you must be fond of children,' she said, hesitating a little from natural delicacy of feeling. 'But, will you excuse me for noticing that it seems rather a mournful fondness? Pray—pray don't answer my question if it gives you any pain—if you have any loss to deplore; but—but I do so want to ask if you have ever had a child of your own?'

Mrs Jazeph was standing near a chair when that question was put. She caught fast hold of the back of it, grasping it so firmly, or perhaps leaning on it so heavily, that the woodwork cracked. Her head drooped low on her bosom. She did not utter, or even attempt to utter, a single word.

Fearing that she must have lost a child of her own, and dreading to distress her unnecessarily by venturing to ask any more questions, Rosamond said nothing, as she stooped over the baby to kiss him in her turn. Her lips rested on his cheek a little above where Mrs Jazeph's lips had rested the moment before, and they touched a spot of wet on his smooth warm skin. Fearing that some of the water in which she had been bathing her face might have dropped on him, she passed her fingers lightly over his head, neck, and bosom, and felt no other spots of wet anywhere. The one drop that had fallen on him was the drop that wetted the cheek which the new nurse had kissed.

The twilight faded over the landscape, the room grew darker and darker; and still, though she was now sitting close to the table on which the candles and matches were placed, Mrs Jazeph made no attempt to strike a light. Rosamond did not feel quite comfortable at the idea of lying awake in the darkness, with nobody in the room but a person who was as yet almost a total stranger; and she resolved to have the candles lighted immediately.

'Mrs Jazeph,' she said, looking towards the gathering obscurity outside the window, 'I shall be much obliged to you, if you will light the candles, and pull down the blind. I can trace no more resemblances out there, now, to a Cornish prospect; the view has gone altogether.'

'Are you very fond of Cornwall, ma'am?' asked Mrs Jazeph, rising, in rather a dilatory manner, to light the candles.

'Indeed I am,' said Rosamond. 'I was born there; and my husband and I were on our way to Cornwall, when we were obliged to stop, on my account, at this place. You are a long time getting the candles lit. Can't you find the matchbox?'

Mrs Jazeph, with an awkwardness which was rather surprising in a person who had shown so much neat-handedness in setting the room to rights, broke the first match in attempting to light it, and let the second out the instant after the flame was kindled. At the third attempt she was more successful; but she only lit one candle, and that one she carried away from the table which Mrs Frankland could see, to the dressing-table, which was hidden from her by the curtains at the foot of the bed.

'Why do you move the candle?' asked Rosamond.

'I thought it was best for your eyes, ma'am, not to have the light too near them,' replied Mrs Jazeph; and then added hastily, as if she was unwilling to give Mrs Frankland time to make any objections, 'And so you were going to Cornwall, ma'am, when you stopped at this place? To travel about there a little, I suppose?' After saying these words, she took up the second candle, and passed out of sight as she carried it to the dressing-table.

Rosamond thought that the nurse, in spite of her gentle looks and manners, was a remarkably obstinate woman. But she was too good-natured to care about asserting her right to have the candles placed where she pleased; and when she answered Mrs Jazeph's question, she still spoke to her as cheerfully and familiarly as ever.

'O, dear no! Not to travel about,' she said, 'but to go straight to the old country house where I was born. It belongs to my husband now, Mrs Jazeph. I have not been near it since I was a little girl of five years of age. Such a ruinous, rambling old place! You, who talk of the dreariness and wildness of Cornwall, would be quite horrified at the very idea of living in Porthgenna Tower.'

The faintly rustling sound of Mrs Jazeph's silk dress, as she moved about the dressing-table, had been audible all the while Rosamond was speaking. It ceased instantaneously when she said the words, 'Porthgenna Tower;' and for one moment there was a dead silence in the room.

'You, who have been living all your life, I suppose, in nicely-repaired houses, cannot imagine what a place it is that we are going to, when I am well enough to travel again,' pursued Rosamond. 'What do you think, Mrs Jazeph, of a house with one whole side of it that has never been inhabited for sixty or seventy years past? You may get some notion of the size of Porthgenna Tower from that. There is a west side that we are to live in when we get there, and a north side, where the empty old rooms are, which I hope we shall be able to repair. Only think of the hosts of odd, old-fashioned things that we may find in those uninhabited rooms! I mean to put on the cook's apron and the gardener's gloves, and rummage all over them from top to bottom. How I shall astonish the housekeeper, when I get to Porthgenna, and ask her for the keys of the ghostly north rooms!'

A low cry, and a sound as if something had struck against the dressing-table, followed Mrs Frankland's last words. She started in the bed, and asked eagerly what was the matter.

'Nothing,' answered Mrs Jazeph, speaking so constrainedly that her voice dropped to a whisper. 'Nothing, ma'am— nothing, I assure you. I struck my side, by accident, against the table—pray don't be alarmed!—it's not worth noticing.'

'But you speak as if you were in pain,' said Rosamond.

'No, no, not in pain. Not hurt, not hurt, indeed.'

While Mrs Jazeph was declaring that she was not hurt, the door of the room was opened, and the doctor entered, leading in Mr Frankland.

'We come early, Mrs Frankland, but we are going to give you plenty of time to compose yourself for the night,' said Mr Orridge. He paused, and noticed that Rosamond's colour was heightened. 'I am afraid you have been talking and exciting yourself a little too much,' he went on. 'If you will excuse me for venturing on the suggestion, Mr Frankland, I think the sooner good-night is said the better. Where is the nurse?'

Mrs Jazeph sat down with her back to the lighted candle when she heard herself asked for. Just before that, she had been looking at Mr Frankland with an eager, undisguised curiosity, which, if anyone had noticed it, must have appeared surprisingly out of character with her usual modesty and refinement of manner.

'I am afraid the nurse has accidentally hurt her side more than she is willing to confess,' said Rosamond to the doctor, pointing, with one hand, to the place in which Mrs Jazeph was sitting, and raising the other to her husband's neck as he stooped over her pillow.

Mr Orridge, on inquiring what had happened, could not prevail on the new nurse to acknowledge that the accident was of the slightest consequence. He suspected, nevertheless, that she was suffering, or, at least, that something had happened to discompose her; for he found the greatest difficulty in fixing her attention, while he gave her a few needful directions in case her services were required during the night. All the time he was speaking, her eyes wandered away from him to the part of the room where Mr and Mrs Frankland were talking together. Mrs Jazeph looked like the last person in the world who would be guilty of an act of impertinent curiosity; and yet she openly betrayed all the characteristics of an inquisitive woman, while Mr Frankland was standing by his wife's pillow. The doctor was obliged to assume his most peremptory manner, before he could get her to attend to him at all.

'And now, Mrs Frankland,' said Mr Orridge, turning away from the nurse, 'as I have given Mrs Jazeph all the directions she wants, I shall set the example of leaving you in quiet, by saying good-night.'

Understanding the hint conveyed in these words, Mr Frankland attempted to say good-night, too, but his wife kept tight hold of both his hands, and declared that it was unreasonable to expect her to let him go for another half-hour at least. Mr Orridge shook his head, and began to expatiate on the evils of over-excitement, and the blessings of composure and sleep.

His remonstrances, however, would have produced very little effect, even if Rosamond had allowed him to continue them, but for the interposition of the baby, who happened to wake up at that moment, and who proved himself a powerful auxiliary on the doctor's side, by absorbing all his mother's attention immediately. Seizing his opportunity at the right moment, Mr Orridge quietly led Mr Frankland out of the room, just as Rosamond was taking the child up in her arms. He stopped before closing the door to whisper one last word to Mrs Jazeph.

'If Mrs Frankland wants to talk, you must not encourage her,' he said. 'As soon as she has quieted the baby, she ought to go to sleep. There is a chair-bedstead in that corner, which you can open for yourself when you want to lie down. Keep the candle where it is now, behind the curtain. The less light Mrs Frankland sees, the sooner she will compose herself to sleep.'

Mrs Jazeph made no answer: she only looked at the doctor and curtseyed. That strangely scared expression in her eyes, which he had noticed on first seeing her, was more painfully apparent than ever, when he left her alone for the night with the mother and child. 'She will never do,' thought Mr Orridge, as he led Mr Frankland down the inn stairs. 'We shall have to send to London for a nurse, after all.'

Feeling a little irritated by the summary manner in which her husband had been taken away from her, Rosamond fretfully rejected the offers of assistance which were made to her by Mrs Jazeph as soon as the doctor had left the room. The nurse said nothing when her services were declined; and yet, judging by her conduct, she seemed anxious to speak. Twice she advanced towards the bedside,—opened her lips—stopped— and retired confusedly, before she settled herself finally in her former place by the dressing-table. Here she remained, silent and out of sight, until the child had been quieted, and had fallen asleep in his mother's arms, with one little pink, half-closed hand resting on her bosom. Rosamond could not resist raising the hand to her lips, though she risked waking him again by doing so. As she kissed it, the sound of the kiss was followed by a faint, suppressed sob, proceeding from the other side of the curtains at the lower end of the bed.

'What is that?' she exclaimed.

'Nothing, ma'am,' said Mrs Jazeph, in the same constrained, whispering tones in which she had answered Mrs Frankland's former question. 'I think I was just falling asleep in the arm-chair, here; and I ought to have told you perhaps that, having had my troubles, and being afflicted with a heart complaint, I have a habit of sighing in my sleep. It means nothing, ma'am, and I hope you will be good enough to excuse it.'

Rosamond's generous instincts were aroused in a moment.

'Excuse it!' she said. 'I hope I may do better than that, Mrs Jazeph, and be the means of relieving it. When Mr Orridge comes to-morrow, you shall consult him, and I will take care that you want for nothing that he may order. No! no! Don't thank me until I have been the means of making you well—and keep where you are, if the arm-chair is comfortable. The baby is asleep again; and I should like to have half-an-hour's quiet, before I change to the night-side of the bed. Stop where you are for the present: I will call as soon as I want you.'

So far from exercising a soothing effect on Mrs Jazeph, these kindly-meant words produced the precisely opposite result of making her restless. She began to walk about the room, and confusedly attempted to account for the change in her conduct, by saying that she wished to satisfy herself that all her arrangements were properly made for the night. In a few minutes more, she began, in defiance of the doctor's prohibi-tion, to tempt Mrs Frankland into talking again, by asking questions about Porthgenna Tower, and by referring to the chances for and against its being chosen as a permanent residence by the young married couple.

'Perhaps, ma'am,' she said, speaking on a sudden, with an eagerness in her voice, which was curiously at variance with the apparent indifference of her manner—'Perhaps when you see Porthgenna Tower, you may not like it so well as you think you will now? Who can tell that you may not get tired and leave the place again after a few days—especially if you go into the empty rooms. I should have thought—if you will excuse my saying so, ma'am—I should have thought that a lady like you would have liked to get as far away as possible from dirt and dust, and disagreeable smells?'

'I can face worse inconveniences than those, where my curiosity is concerned,' said Rosamond. 'And I am more curious to see the uninhabited rooms at Porthgenna, than to see the Seven Wonders of the World.* Even if we don't settle altogether at the old house, I feel certain that we shall stay there for some time.'

At that answer, Mrs Jazeph abruptly turned away, and asked no more questions. She retired to a corner of the room near the door, where the chair-bedstead stood which the doctor had pointed out to her—occupied herself for a few minutes in making it ready for the night—then left it as suddenly as she had approached it, and began to walk up and down, once more. This unaccountable restlessness, which had already surprised Rosamond, now made her feel rather uneasy—especially when she once or twice overheard Mrs Jazeph talking to herself. Judging by words and fragments of sentences that were audible now and then, her mind was still running, with the most inexplicable persistency, on the subject of Porthgenna Tower. As the minutes wore on, and she continued to walk up and down, and still went on talking, Rosamond's uneasiness began to strengthen into something like alarm. She resolved to awaken Mrs Jazeph, in the least offensive manner, to a sense of the strangeness of her own conduct, by noticing that she was talking, but by not appearing to understand that she was talking to herself.

'What did you say?' asked Rosamond, putting the question at a moment when the nurse's voice was most distinctly betraying her in the act of thinking aloud.

Mrs Jazeph stopped, and raised her head vacantly, as if she had been awakened out of a heavy sleep.

'I thought you were saying something more about our old house,' continued Rosamond. 'I thought I heard you say that I ought not to go to Porthgenna, or that you would not go there in my place, or something of that sort.'

Mrs Jazeph blushed like a young girl. 'I think you must have been mistaken, ma'am,' she said, and stooped over the chair-bedstead again.

Watching her anxiously, Rosamond saw that, while she was affecting to arrange the bedstead, she was doing nothing whatever to prepare it for being slept in. What did that mean? What did her whole conduct mean for the last half-hour. As Mrs Frankland asked herself those questions, the thrill of a terrible suspicion turned her cold to the very roots of her hair. It had never occurred to her before, but it suddenly struck her now, with the force of positive conviction, that the new nurse was not in her right senses.

All that was unaccountable in her behaviour—her odd disappearances behind the curtains, at the foot of the bed; her lingering, stealthy, over-familiar way of using the hair-brush; her silence at one time, her talkativeness at another; her restlessness, her whispering to herself, her affectation of being deeply engaged in doing something which she was not doing at all—every one of her strange actions (otherwise incomprehensible) became intelligible in a moment on that one dreadful supposition that she was mad.

Terrified as she was, Rosamond kept her presence of mind. One of her arms stole instinctively round the child; and she had half-raised the other to catch at the bell-rope hanging above her pillow, when she saw Mrs Jazeph turn and look at her.

A woman possessed only of ordinary nerve would, probably, at that instant, have pulled at the bell-rope in the unreasoning desperation of sheer fright. Rosamond had courage enough to calculate consequences, and to remember that Mrs Jazeph would have time to lock the door, before assistance could arrive, if she betrayed her suspicions by ringing without first assigning some plausible reason for doing so. She slowly closed her eyes as the nurse looked at her, partly to convey the notion that she was composing herself to sleep,—partly to gain time to think of some safe excuse for summoning her maid. The flurry of her spirits, however, interfered with the exercise of her ingenuity. Minute after minute dragged on heavily, and still she could think of no assignable reason for ringing the bell.

She was just doubting whether it would not be safest to send Mrs Jazeph out of the room, on some message to her husband, to lock the door the moment she was alone, and then to ring— she was just doubting whether she would boldly adopt this course of proceeding, or not, when she heard the rustle of the nurse's silk dress approaching the bedside.

Her first impulse was to snatch at the bell-rope; but fear had paralysed her hand; she could not raise it from the pillow.

The rustling of the silk dress ceased. She half unclosed her eyes, and saw that the nurse was stopping midway between the part of the room from which she had advanced, and the bedside. There was nothing wild or angry in her look. The agitation which her face expressed, was the agitation of perplexity and alarm. She stood rapidly clasping and unclasping her hands, the image of bewilderment and distress—stood so for nearly a minute—then came forward a few steps more, and said inquiringly, in a whisper:—

'Not asleep? not quite asleep, yet?'

Rosamond tried to speak in answer, but the quick beating of her heart seemed to rise up to her very lips, and to stifle the words on them.

The nurse came on, still with the same perplexity and distress in her face, to within a foot of the bedside—knelt down by the pillow, and looked earnestly at Rosamond—shuddered a little, and glanced all round her, as if to make sure that the room was empty—bent forward—hesitated—bent nearer, and whispered into her ear these words:—

'When you go to Porthgenna, *keep out of the Myrtle Room!*'

The hot breath of the woman, as she spoke, beat on Rosamond's cheek, and seemed to fly in one fever-throb through every vein of her body. The nervous shock of that unutterable sensation burst the bonds of the terror that had hitherto held her motionless and speechless. She started up in bed with a scream, caught hold of the bell-rope, and pulled it violently.

'O, hush! hush!' cried Mrs Jazeph, sinking back on her knees, and beating her hands together despairingly with the helpless gesticulation of a child.

Rosamond rang again and again. Hurrying footsteps and eager voices were heard outside on the stairs. It was not ten o'clock yet—nobody had retired for the night—and the violent ringing had already alarmed the house.

The nurse rose to her feet, staggered back from the bedside, and supported herself against the wall of the room, as the footsteps and the voices reached the door. She said not another word. The hands that she had been beating together so violently, but an instant before, hung down nerveless at her side. The blank of a great ag ny spread over all her face, and stilled it awfully.

The first person who entered the roo n was Mrs Frankland's maid, and the landlady followed her.

'Fetch Mr Frankland,' said Rosamond, faintly, addressing the landlady. 'I want to speak to him directly. You,' she continued, beckoning to the maid, 'sit by me here, till your master comes. I have been dreadfully frightened. Don't ask me questions; but stop here.'

The maid stared at her mistress in amazement; then looked round with a disparaging frown at the nurse. When the landlady left the room to fetch Mr Frankland, she had moved a little away from the wall, so as to command a full view of the bed. Her eyes fixed with a look of breathless suspense, of devouring anxiety, on Rosamond's face. From all her other features the expression seemed to be gone. She said nothing, she noticed nothing. She did not start, she did not move aside an inch, when the landlady returned, and led Mr Frankland to his wife.

'Lenny! don't let the new nurse stop here to-night—pray, pray don't!' whispered Rosamond, eagerly catching her husband by the arm.

Warned by the trembling of her hand, Mr Frankland laid his fingers lightly on her temples and on her heart.

'Good heavens, Rosamond! what has happened? I left you quiet and comfortable, and now——'

'I've been frightened, dear—dreadfully frightened, by the new nurse. Don't be hard on her, poor creature; she is not in her right senses—I am certain she is not. Only get her away quietly—only send her back at once to where she came from. I shall die of the fright, if she stops here. She has been behaving so strangely, she has spoken such words to me—Lenny! Lenny! don't let go of my hand. She came stealing up to me so horribly, just where you are now; she knelt down at my ear, and whispered—Oh, such words!'

'Hush, hush, love!' said Mr Frankland, getting seriously alarmed by the violence of Rosamond's agitation. 'Never mind repeating the words now; wait till you are calmer—I beg and entreat of you, wait till you are calmer. I will do everything you wish, if you will only lie down and be quiet, and try to compose yourself before you say another word. It is quite enough for me to know that this woman has frightened you, and that you wish her to be sent away with as little harshness as possible. We will put off all further explanations till tomorrow morning. I deeply regret now that I did not persist in carrying out my own idea of sending for a proper nurse from London. Where is the landlady?'

The landlady placed herself by Mr Frankland's side.

'Is it late?' asked Leonard.

'Oh no, sir; not ten o'clock yet.'

'Order a fly to be brought to the door, then, as soon as possible, if you please. Where is the nurse?'

'Standing behind you, sir, near the wall,' said the maid.

As Mr Frankland turned in that direction, Rosamond whispered to him: 'Don't be hard on her, Lenny.'

The maid, looking with contemptuous curiosity at Mrs Jazeph, saw the whole expression of her countenance alter, as those words were spoken. The tears rose thick in her eyes, and flowed down her cheeks. The deathly spell of stillness that had lain on her face was broken in an instant. She drew back again, close to the wall, and leaned against it as before. 'Don't be hard on her!' the maid heard her repeat to herself, in a low sobbing voice. 'Don't be hard on her! Oh, my God! she said that kindly—she said that kindly, at least!'

'I have no desire to speak to you, or to use you unkindly,' said Mr Frankland, imperfectly hearing what she said. 'I know nothing of what has happened, and I make no accusations. I find Mrs Frankland violently agitated and frightened; I hear her connect that agitation with you—not angrily, but compassionately—and instead of speaking harshly, I prefer leaving it to your own sense of what is right, to decide whether your attendance here ought not to cease at once. I have provided the proper means for your conveyance from this place; and I would suggest that you should make our apologies to your mistress, and say nothing more than that circumstances have happened which oblige us to dispense with your services.'

'You have been considerate towards me, sir,' said Mrs Jazeph, speaking quietly, and with a certain gentle dignity in her manner, 'and I will not prove myself unworthy of your forbearance by saying what I might say in my own defence.' She advanced into the middle of the room, and stopped where she could see Rosamond plainly. Twice she attempted to speak, and twice her voice failed her. At the third effort she succeeded in controlling herself.

'Before I go, ma'am,' she said, 'I hope you will believe that I have no bitter feeling against you, for sending me away. I am not angry—pray remember always that I was not angry, and that I never complained.'

There was such a forlornness in her face, such a sweet, sorrowful resignation in every tone of her voice during the utterance of these few words, that Rosamond's heart smote her.

'Why did you frighten me?' she asked, half relenting.

'Frighten you? How could I frighten you? Oh me! of all the people in the world, how could *I* frighten you?'

Mournfully saying those words, the nurse went to the chair on which she had placed her bonnet and shawl, and put them on. The landlady and the maid, watching her with curious eyes, detected that she was again weeping bitterly, and noticed with astonishment, at the same time, how neatly she put on her bonnet and shawl. The wasted hands were moving mechanically, and were trembling while they moved,—and yet, slight thing though it was, the inexorable instinct of propriety guided their most trifling actions still.

On her way to the door, she stopped again at passing the bedside, looked through her tears at Rosamond and the child, struggled a little with herself, and then spoke her farewell words——

'God bless you, and keep you and your child happy and prosperous,' she said. 'I am not angry at being sent away. If you ever think of me again, after to-night, please to remember that I was not angry, and that I never complained.'

She stood for a moment longer, still weeping, and still looking through her tears at the mother and child—then turned away, and walked to the door. Something in the last tones of her voice caused a silence in the room. Of the four persons in it not one could utter a word, as the nurse closed the door gently, and went out from them alone.

CHAPTER V

A COUNCIL OF THREE

ON the morning after the departure of Mrs Jazeph, the news that she had been sent away from the Tiger's Head by Mr Frankland's directions, reached the doctor's residence from the inn, just as he was sitting down to breakfast. Finding that the report of the nurse's dismissal was not accompanied by any satisfactory explanation of the cause of it, Mr Orridge refused to believe that her attendance on Mrs Frankland had really ceased. However, although he declined to credit the news, he was so far disturbed by it that he finished his breakfast in a hurry, and went to pay his morning visit at the Tiger's Head, nearly two hours before the time at which he usually attended on his patient.

On his way to the inn, he was met and stopped by the one waiter attached to the establishment. 'I was just bringing you a message from Mr Frankland, sir,' said the man. 'He wants to see you as soon as possible.'

'Is it true that Mrs Frankland's nurse was sent away last night, by Mr Frankland's order?' asked Mr Orridge.

'Quite true, sir,' answered the waiter.

The doctor coloured, and looked seriously discomposed. One of the most precious things we have about us—especially if we happen to belong to the medical profession—is our dignity. It struck Mr Orridge that he ought to have been consulted before a nurse of his recommending was dismissed from her situation at a moment's notice. Was Mr Frankland presuming upon his position as a gentleman of fortune? The power of wealth may do much with impunity, but it is not privileged to offer any practical contradictions to a man's good opinion of himself. Never had the doctor thought more disrespectfully of rank and riches; never had he been conscious of reflecting on republican principles with such absolute impartiality, as when he now followed the waiter in sullen silence to Mr Frankland's room.

'Who is that?' asked Leonard, when he heard the door open.

'Mr Orridge, sir,' said the waiter.

'Good morning,' said Mr Orridge, with self-asserting abruptness and familiarity.

Mr Frankland was sitting in an arm-chair, with his legs crossed. Mr Orridge carefully selected another arm-chair, and crossed his legs on the model of Mr Frankland's the moment he sat down. Mr Frankland's hands were in the pockets of his dressing-gown. Mr Orridge had no pockets, except in his coat-tails, which he could not conveniently get at; but he put his thumbs into the arm-holes of his waistcoat, and asserted himself against the easy insolence of wealth, in that way. It made no difference to him—so curiously narrow is the range of a man's perceptions when he is insisting on his own importance—that Mr Frankland was blind, and consequently incapable of being impressed by the independence of his bearing. Mr Orridge's own dignity was vindicated in Mr Orridge's own presence; and that was enough.

'I am glad you have come so early, doctor,' said Mr Frankland. 'A very unpleasant thing happened here last night. I was obliged to send the new nurse away at a moment's notice.'

'Were you, indeed!' said Mr Orridge, defensively matching Mr Frankland's composure, by an assumption of the completest indifference. 'Aha! were you indeed?'

'If there had been time to send and consult you, of course I should have been only too glad to have done so,' continued Leonard; 'but it was impossible to hesitate. We were all alarmed by a loud ringing of my wife's bell; I was taken up to her room, and found her in a condition of the most violent agitation and alarm. She told me she had been dreadfully frightened by the new nurse; declared her conviction that the woman was not in her right senses; and entreated that I would get her out of the house with as little delay and as little harshness as possible. Under these circumstances, what could I do?

I may seem to have been wanting in consideration towards you, in proceeding on my own sole responsibility; but Mrs Frankland was in such a state of excitement that I could not tell what might be the consequence of opposing her, or of venturing on any delays; and after the difficulty had been got over, she would not hear of your being disturbed by a summons to the inn. I am sure you will understand this explanation, doctor, in the spirit in which I offer it.'

Mr Orridge began to look a little confused. His solid substructure of independence was softening and sinking from under him. He suddenly found himself thinking of the cultivated manners of the wealthy classes; his thumbs slipped mechanically out of the arm-holes of his waistcoat; and, before he well knew what he was about, he was stammering his way through all the choicest intricacies of a complimentary and respectful reply.

'You will naturally be anxious to know what the new nurse said, or did, to frighten my wife so,' pursued Mr Frankland. 'I can tell you nothing in detail; for Mrs Frankland was in such a state of nervous dread last night that I was really afraid of asking for any explanations; and I have purposely waited to make inquiries this morning, until you could come here and accompany me up-stairs. You kindly took so much trouble to secure this unlucky woman's attendance, that you have a right to hear all that can be alleged against her, now she has been sent away. Considering all things, Mrs Frankland is not so ill this morning as I was afraid she would be. She expects to see you with me; and if you will kindly give me your arm, we will go up to her immediately.'

On entering Mrs Frankland's room, the doctor saw, at a glance, that she had been altered for the worse by the events of the past evening. He remarked that the smile with which she greeted her husband was the faintest and saddest he had seen on her face. Her eyes looked dim and weary, her skin was dry, her pulse was irregular. It was plain that she had passed a wakeful night, and that her mind was not at ease. She dismissed the inquiries of her medical attendant as briefly as possible, and led the conversation immediately, of her own accord, to the subject of Mrs Jazeph.

'I suppose you have heard what has happened,' she said, addressing Mr Orridge. 'I can't tell you how grieved I am about it. My conduct must look in your eyes, as well as in the eyes of the poor unfortunate nurse, the conduct of a capricious, unfeeling woman. I am ready to cry with sorrow and vexation, when I remember how thoughtless I was, and how little courage I showed. O, Lenny, it is dreadful to hurt the feelings of anybody, but to have pained that unhappy, helpless woman, as we pained her, to have made her cry so bitterly, to have caused her such humiliation and wretchedness——'

'My dear Rosamond,' interposed Mr Frankland, 'you are lamenting effects, and forgetting causes altogether. Remember what a state of terror I found you in—there must have been some reason for that. Remember, too, how strong your conviction was, that the nurse was out of her senses. Surely, you have not altered your opinion on that point already?'

'It is that very opinion, love, that has been perplexing and worrying me all night. I can't alter it; I feel more certain than ever that there must be something wrong with the poor creature's intellect—and yet, when I remember how good-naturedly she came here to help me, and how anxious she seemed to make herself useful, I can't help feeling ashamed of my suspicions; I can't help reproaching myself for having been the cause of her dismissal last night. Mr Orridge, did you notice anything in Mrs Jazeph's face, or manner, which might lead you to doubt whether her intellects were quite as sound as they ought to be?'

'Certainly not, Mrs Frankland, or I should never have brought her here. I should not have been astonished to hear that she was suddenly taken ill, or that she had been seized with a fit, or that some slight accident, which would have frightened nobody else, had seriously frightened her; but to be told that there is anything approaching to derangement in her faculties, does, I own, fairly surprise me.'

'Can I have been mistaken!' exclaimed Rosamond, looking confusedly and self-distrustfully from Mr Orridge to her husband. 'Lenny! Lenny! if I have been mistaken, I shall never forgive myself.'

'Suppose you tell us, my dear, what led you to suspect that she was mad?' suggested Mr Frankland.

Rosamond hesitated. 'Things that are great in one's own mind,' she said, 'seem to get so little when they are put into words. I almost despair of making you understand what good reason I had to be frightened—and then, I am afraid, in trying to do justice to myself, that I may not do justice to the nurse.'

'Tell your own story, my love, in your own way, and you will be sure to tell it properly,' said Mr Frankland.

'And pray remember,' added Mr Orridge, 'that I attach no real importance to my opinion of Mrs Jazeph. I have not had time enough to form it. Your opportunities of observing her have been far more numerous than mine.'

Thus encouraged, Rosamond plainly and simply related all that had happened in her room on the previous evening, up to the time when she had closed her eyes, and had heard the nurse approaching her bedside. Before repeating the extraordinary words that Mrs Jazeph had whispered into her ear, she made a pause, and looked earnestly in her husband's face.

'Why do you stop?' asked Mr Frankland.

'I feel nervous and flurried still, Lenny, when I think of the words the nurse said to me, just before I rang the bell.'

'What did she say? Was it something you would rather not repeat?'

'No! no! I am most anxious to repeat it, and to hear what you think it means. As I have just told you, Lenny, we had been talking of Porthgenna, and of my project of exploring the north rooms, as soon as I got there; and she had been asking many questions about the old house; appearing, I must say, to be unaccountably interested in it, considering she was a stranger.'

'Yes?'

'Well, when she came to the bedside, she knelt down close at my ear, and whispered all on a sudden:—"When you go to Porthgenna, keep out of the Myrtle Room!" '

Mr Frankland started. 'Is there such a room at Porthgenna?' he asked, eagerly.

'I never heard of it,' said Rosamond.

'Are you sure of that?' inquired Mr Orridge. Up to this moment the doctor had privately suspected that Mrs Frankland must have fallen asleep soon after he left her the evening before; and that the narrative which she was now relating, with the sincerest conviction of its reality, was actually derived from nothing but a series of vivid impressions produced by a dream.

'I am certain I never heard of such a room,' said Rosamond. 'I left Porthgenna at five years old; and I had never heard of it then. My father often talked of the house in after-years; but I am certain that he never spoke of any of the rooms by any particular names; and I can say the same of your father, Lenny, whenever I was in his company after he had bought the place. Besides, don't you remember, when the builder we sent down to survey the house wrote you that letter, he complained that there were no names of the rooms on the different keys, to guide him in opening the doors, and that he could get no information from anybody at Porthgenna on the subject? How could I ever have heard of the Myrtle Room? Who was there to tell me?'

Mr Orridge began to look perplexed; it seemed by no means so certain that Mrs Frankland had been dreaming, after all.

'I have thought of nothing else,' said Rosamond to her husband, in low, whispering tones. 'I can't get those mysterious words off my mind. Feel my heart, Lenny—it is beating quicker than usual, only with saying them over to you. They are such very strange, startling words. What do you think they mean?'

'Who is the woman who spoke them?—that is the most important question,' said Mr Frankland.

'But why did she say the words to *me?* That is what I want to know—that is what I must know, if I am ever to feel easy in my mind again!'

'Gently, Mrs Frankland, gently!' said Mr Orridge. 'For your child's sake, as well as for your own, pray try to be calm, and to look at this very mysterious event as composedly as you can. If any exertions of mine can throw light upon this strange woman and her still stranger conduct, I will not spare them. I am going to-day to her mistress's house, to see one of the children; and, depend upon it, I will manage in some way to make Mrs Jazeph explain herself. Her mistress shall hear every word that you have told me; and I can assure you, she is just the sort of downright, resolute woman who will insist on having the whole mystery instantly cleared up.'

Rosamond's weary eyes brightened at the doctor's proposal. 'O, go at once, Mr Orridge!' she exclaimed, 'go at once!'

'I have a great deal of medical work to do in the town first,' said the doctor, smiling at Mrs Frankland's impatience.

'Begin it then, without losing another instant,' said Rosamond. 'The baby is quite well, and I am quite well—we need not detain you a moment. And, Mr Orridge, pray be as gentle and considerate as possible with the poor woman; and tell her that I never should have thought of sending her away, if I had not been too frightened to know what I was about. And say how sorry I am this morning, and say—'

'My dear, if Mrs Jazeph is really not in her right senses, what would be the use of overwhelming her with all these excuses?' interposed Mr Frankland. 'It will be more to the purpose if Mr Orridge will kindly explain and apologise for us to her mistress.'

'Go! Don't stop to talk—pray go at once!' cried Rosamond, as the doctor attempted to reply to Mr Frankland.

'Don't be afraid; no time shall be lost,' said Mr Orridge, opening the door. 'But remember, Mrs Frankland, I shall expect you to reward your ambassador, when he returns from his mission, by showing him that you are a little more quiet and composed than I find you this morning.' With that parting hint, the doctor took his leave.

' "When you go to Porthgenna, keep out of the Myrtle Room," ' repeated Mr Frankland, thoughtfully. 'Those are very strange words, Rosamond. Who can this woman really be? She is a perfect stranger to both of us; we are brought into contact with her by the merest accident; and we find that she knows something about our own house, of which we were both perfectly ignorant until she chose to speak!'

'But the warning, Lenny—the warning, so pointedly and mysteriously addressed to me? O, if I could only go to sleep at once, and not wake again till the doctor comes back!'

'My love, try not to count too certainly on our being enlightened, even then. The woman may refuse to explain herself to anybody.'

'Don't even hint at such a disappointment as that, Lenny—or I shall be wanting to get up, and go and question her myself!'

'Even if you could get up and question her, Rosamond, you might find it impossible to make her answer. She may be afraid of certain consequences which we cannot foresee; and, in that case, I can only repeat, that it is more than probable she will explain nothing—or, perhaps, still more likely that she will coolly deny her own words altogether.'

'Then, Lenny, we will put them to the proof for ourselves.'

'And how can we do that?'

'By continuing our journey to Porthgenna, the moment I am allowed to travel, and by leaving no stone unturned, when we get there, until we have discovered whether there is, or is not, any room in the old house that ever was known, at any time of its existence, by the name of the Myrtle Room.'

'And suppose it should turn out that there is such a room?' asked Mr Frankland, beginning to feel the influence of his wife's enthusiasm.

'If it does turn out so,' said Rosamond, her voice rising, and her face lighting up with its accustomed vivacity, 'how can you doubt what will happen next? Am I not a woman? And have I not been forbidden to enter the Myrtle Room? Lenny! Lenny! Do you know so little of my half of humanity, as to doubt what I should do, the moment the room was discovered? My darling, as a matter of course, I should walk into it immediately.'

CHAPTER VI

ANOTHER SURPRISE

WITH all the haste he could make, it was one o'clock in the afternoon before Mr Orridge's professional avocations allowed him to set forth in his gig for Mrs Norbury's house. He drove there with such good-will that he accomplished the half-hour's journey in twenty minutes. The footman having heard the rapid approach of the gig, opened the hall door the instant the horse was pulled up before it, and confronted the doctor with a smile of malicious satisfaction.

'Well,' said Mr Orridge, bustling into the hall, 'you were all rather surprised, last night, when the housekeeper came back, I suppose?'

'Yes, sir, we certainly were surprised when she came back last night,' answered the footman; 'but we were still more surprised when she went away again this morning.'

'Went away! You don't mean to say she is gone?'

'Yes, I do, sir—she has lost her place, and gone for good.' The footman smiled again, as he made that reply; and the housemaid, who happened to be on her way down stairs while he was speaking, and to hear what he said, smiled too. Mrs Jazeph had evidently been no favourite in the servants' hall.

Amazement prevented Mr Orridge from uttering another word. Hearing no more questions asked, the footman threw open the door of the breakfast-parlour, and the doctor followed him into the room. Mrs Norbury was sitting near the window in a rigidly upright attitude, inflexibly watching the proceedings of her invalid child over a basin of beef-tea.

'I know what you are going to talk about before you open your lips,' said the outspoken lady. 'But just look to the child first, and say what you have to say on that subject, if you please, before you enter on any other.'

The child was examined, was pronounced to be improving rapidly, and was carried away by the nurse to lie down and rest a little. As soon as the door of the room had closed, Mrs Norbury abruptly addressed the doctor, interrupting him, for the second time, just as he was about to speak.

'Now, Mr Orridge,' she said, 'I want to tell you something at the outset. I am a remarkably just woman, and I have no quarrel with *you*. You are the cause of my having been treated with the most audacious insolence by three people—but you are the innocent cause, and, therefore, I don't blame you.'

'I am really at a loss,' Mr Orridge began, 'quite at a loss, I assure you—'

'To know what I mean?' said Mrs Norbury. 'I will soon tell you. Were you not the original cause of my sending my housekeeper to nurse Mr Frankland?'

'Yes.' Mr Orridge could not hesitate to acknowledge that.

'Well,' pursued Mrs Norbury, 'and the consequence of my sending her is, as I said before, that I am treated with unparalleled insolence by no less than three people. Mrs Frankland takes an insolent whim into her head, and affects to be frightened by my housekeeper. Mr Frankland shows an insolent readiness to humour that whim, and hands me back my housekeeper as if she was a bad shilling; and last, and worst of all, my house-keeper herself insults me to my face, as soon as she comes back—insults me, Mr Orridge, to that degree, that I give her twelve hours' notice to leave the place. Don't begin to defend yourself! I know all about it; I know you had nothing to do with sending her back; I never said you had. All the mischief you have done is innocent mischief. I don't blame you, remember that—whatever you do, Mr Orridge, remember that!'

'I had no idea of defending myself,' said the doctor, 'for I have no reason to do so. But you surprise me beyond all power of expression, when you tell me that Mrs Jazeph treated you with incivility.'

'Incivility!' exclaimed Mrs Norbury. 'Don't talk about incivility—it's not the word. Impudence is the word; brazen impudence. The only charitable thing to say of Mrs Jazeph is that she is not right in her head. I never noticed anything odd about her myself; but the servants used to laugh at her for being as timid in the dark as a child, and for often running away to her candle in her own room, when they declined to light the lamps before the night had fairly set in. I never troubled my head about this before; but I thought of it last night, I can tell you, when I found her looking me fiercely in the face, and contra-dicting me flatly the moment I spoke to her.'

'I should have thought she was the very last woman in the world to misbehave herself in that way,' answered the doctor.

'Very well. Now hear what happened when she came back, last night,' said Mrs Norbury. 'She got here just as we were going up-stairs to bed. Of course, I was astonished; and, of course, I called her into the drawing-room for an explanation. There was nothing very unnatural in that course of proceeding, I suppose? Well, I noticed that her eyes were swollen and red, and that her looks were remarkably wild and queer; but I said nothing, and waited for the explanation. All that she had to tell me was, that something she had unintentionally said, or done, had frightened Mrs Frankland, and that Mrs Frankland's

husband had sent her away on the spot. I disbelieved this at
first—and very naturally, I think—but she persisted in the
story, and answered all my questions by declaring that she
could tell me nothing more. "So then," I said, "I am to believe
that, after I have inconvenienced myself by sparing you, and
after you have inconvenienced yourself by undertaking the
business of nurse, I am to be insulted, and you are to be
insulted, by your being sent away from Mrs Frankland on the
very day when you get to her, because she chooses to take a
whim into her head?" "I never accused Mrs Frankland of
taking a whim into her head," said Mrs Jazeph, and stares me
straight in the face, with such a look as I never saw in her eyes
before, after all my five years' experience of her. "What do you
mean?" I asked, giving her back her look, I can promise you.
"Are you base enough to take the treatment you have received
in the light of a favour?" "I am just enough," said Mrs Jazeph,
as sharp as lightning, and still with that same stare straight at
me, "I am just enough not to blame Mrs Frankland." "O, you
are, are you?" I said. "Then all I can tell you is, that I feel this
insult, if you don't; and that I consider Mrs Frankland's conduct to be the conduct of an ill-bred, impudent, capricious,
unfeeling woman." Mrs Jazeph takes a step up to me—takes a
step, I give you my word of honour—and says distinctly, in so
many words, "Mrs Frankland is neither ill-bred, impudent,
capricious, nor unfeeling." "Do you mean to contradict me,
Mrs Jazeph?" I asked. "I mean to defend Mrs Frankland
from unjust imputations," says she. Those were her words,
Mr Orridge—on my honour, as a gentlewoman, those were
exactly her words.'

The doctor's face expressed the blankest astonishment.
Mrs Norbury went on—

'I was in a towering passion—I don't mind confessing that,
Mr Orridge—but I kept it down. "Mrs Jazeph," I said, "this is
language that I am not accustomed to, and that I certainly
never expected to hear from your lips. Why you should take it
on yourself to defend Mrs Frankland for treating us both with
contempt, and to contradict me for resenting it, I neither know
nor care to know. But I must tell you, in plain words, that I will
be spoken to by every person in my employment, from my

housekeeper to my scullery-maid, with respect. I would have given warning on the spot to any other servant in this house who had behaved to me as you have behaved."—She tried to interrupt me there, but I would not allow her. "No," I said, "you are not to speak to me just yet; you are to hear me out. Any other servant, I tell you again, should have left this place to-morrow morning; but I will be more than just to *you*. I will give you the benefit of your five years' good conduct in my service. I will leave you the rest of the night to get cool, and to reflect on what has passed between us; and I will not expect you to make the proper apologies to me until the morning." You see, Mr Orridge, I was determined to act justly and kindly; I was ready to make allowances—and what do you think she said in return? "I am willing to make any apologies, ma'am, for offending you," she said, "without the delay of a single minute; but, whether it is to-night, or whether it is to-morrow morning, I cannot stand by silent when I hear Mrs Frankland charged with acting unkindly, uncivilly, or improperly, towards me or towards any one." "Do you tell me that deliberately, Mrs Jazeph?" I asked. "I tell it you sincerely, ma'am," she answered; "and I am very sorry to be obliged to do so." "Pray don't trouble yourself to be sorry," I said, "for you may consider yourself no longer in my service. I will order the steward to pay you the usual month's wages instead of the month's warning, the first thing to-morrow; and I beg that you will leave the house as soon as you conveniently can afterwards." "I will leave to-morrow, ma'am," says she, "but without troubling the steward. I beg respectfully, and with many thanks for your past kindness, to decline taking a month's money which I have not earned by a month's service." And, thereupon, she curtseys and goes out. That is, word for word, what passed between us, Mr Orridge. Explain the woman's conduct in your own way, if you can. I say that it is utterly incomprehensible, unless you agree with me, that she was not in her right senses when she came back to this house last night.'

The doctor began to think, after what he had just heard, that Mrs Frankland's suspicions in relation to the new nurse were not quite so unfounded as he had been at first disposed to consider them. He wisely refrained, however, from complicating matters, by giving utterance to what he thought; and, after answering Mrs Norbury in a few vaguely polite words, endeavoured to soothe her irritation against Mr and Mrs Frankland, by assuring her that he came as the bearer of apologies from both husband and wife, for the apparent want of courtesy and consideration in their conduct, which circumstances had made inevitable. The offended lady, however, absolutely refused to be propitiated. She rose up, and waved her hand with an air of great dignity.

'I cannot hear a word more from you, Mr Orridge,' she said, 'I cannot receive any apologies which are made indirectly. If Mr Frankland chooses to call, and if Mrs Frankland condescends to write to me, I am willing to think no more of the matter. Under any other circumstances, I must be allowed to keep my present opinions both of the lady and the gentleman. Don't say another word, and be so kind as to excuse me if I leave you, and go up to the nursery to see how the child is getting on. I am delighted to hear that you think her so much better. Pray call again to-morrow, or next day, if you conveniently can. Good morning!'

Half-amused at Mrs Norbury, half-displeased at the curt tone she adopted towards him, Mr Orridge remained for a minute or two alone in the breakfast-parlour, feeling rather undecided about what he should do next. He was, by this time, almost as much interested in solving the mystery of Mrs Jazeph's extraordinary conduct, as Mrs Frankland herself; and he felt unwilling, on all accounts, to go back to the Tiger's Head, and merely repeat what Mrs Norbury had told him, without being able to complete the narrative by informing Mr and Mrs Frankland of the direction that the housekeeper had taken on leaving her situation. After some pondering, he determined to question the footman, under the pretence of desiring to know if his gig was at the door. The man having answered the bell, and having reported the gig to be ready, Mr Orridge, while crossing the hall, asked him carelessly, if he knew at what time in the morning Mrs Jazeph had left her place.

'About ten o'clock, sir,' answered the footman. 'When the carrier came by from the village, on his way to the station for the eleven o'clock train.'

'O! I suppose he took her boxes?' said Mr Orridge.

'And he took her, too, sir,' said the man, with a grin. 'She had to ride, for once in her life, at any rate, in a carrier's cart.'

On getting back to West Winston, the doctor stopped at the station, to collect further particulars, before he returned to the Tiger's Head. No trains, either up or down, happened to be due just at that time. The station-master was reading the newspaper, and the porter was gardening on the slope of the embankment.

'Is the train at eleven in the morning an up-train, or a down-train?' asked Mr Orridge, addressing the porter.

'A down-train.'

'Did many people go by it?'

The porter repeated the names of some of the inhabitants of West Winston.

'Were there no passengers but passengers from the town?' inquired the doctor.

'Yes, sir. I think there was one stranger—a lady.'

'Did the station-master issue the tickets for that train?'

'Yes, sir.'

Mr Orridge went on to the station-master.

'Do you remember giving a ticket, this morning, by the eleven o'clock down-train, to a lady travelling alone?'

The station-master pondered. 'I have issued tickets, up and down, to half-a-dozen ladies to-day,' he answered, doubtfully.

'Yes, but I am speaking only of the eleven o'clock train,' said Mr Orridge. 'Try if you can't remember?'

'Remember? Stop! I do remember; I know who you mean. A lady who seemed rather flurried, and who put a question to me that I am not often asked at this station. She had her veil down, I recollect, and she got here for the eleven o'clock train. Crouch, the carrier, brought her trunk into the office.'

'That is the woman. Where did she take her ticket for?'

'For Exeter.'

'You said she asked you a question?'

'Yes: a question about what coaches met the rail at Exeter to take travellers into Cornwall. I told her we were rather too far off here to have the correct time-table, and recommended her to apply for information to the Devonshire people, when she got to the end of her journey. She seemed a timid, helpless kind of woman to travel alone. Anything wrong in connection with her, sir?'

'O, no! nothing,' said Mr Orridge, leaving the station-master and hastening back to his gig again.

When he drew up, a few minutes afterwards, at the door of the Tiger's Head, he jumped out of his vehicle with the confident air of a man who has done all that could be expected of him. It was easy to face Mrs Frankland with the unsatisfactory news of Mrs Jazeph's departure, now that he could add, on the best authority, the important supplementary information that she had gone to Cornwall.

BOOK IV

CHAPTER I

A PLOT AGAINST THE SECRET

TOWARDS the close of the evening, on the day after Mr Orridge's interview with Mrs Norbury, the Druid fast coach, running through Cornwall as far as Truro, set down three inside passengers at the door of the booking-office, on arriving at its destination. Two of these passengers were an old gentleman and his daughter; the third was Mrs Jazeph.

The father and daughter collected their luggage, and entered the hotel; the outside passengers branched off in different directions with as little delay as possible; Mrs Jazeph alone stood irresolute on the pavement, and seemed uncertain what she should do next. When the coachman good-naturedly endeavoured to assist her in arriving at a decision of some kind, by asking whether he could do anything to help her, she started, and looked at him suspiciously; then, appearing to recollect herself, thanked him for his kindness, and inquired, with a confusion of words and a hesitation of manner which appeared very extraordinary in the coachman's eyes, whether she might be allowed to leave her trunk at the booking-office for a little while, until she could return and call for it again.

Receiving permission to leave her trunk as long as she pleased, she crossed over the principal street of the town, ascended the pavement on the opposite side, and walked down the first turning she came to. On entering the bye-street to which the turning led, she glanced back, satisfied herself that nobody was following or watching her, hastened on a few yards, and stopped again at a small shop devoted to the sale of book-cases, cabinets, work-boxes, and writing-desks. After first looking up at the letters painted over the door—BUSCHMANN, CABINET-MAKER, &c.—she peered in at the shop window. A middle-aged man, with a cheerful face, sat behind the counter, polishing a rosewood bracket, and nodding briskly at regular intervals, as if he were humming a tune and keeping time to it with his head. Seeing no customers in the shop, Mrs Jazeph opened the door and walked in.

As soon as she was inside, she became aware that the cheerful man behind the counter was keeping time, not to a tune of his own humming, but to a tune played by a musical box. The clear ringing notes came from a parlour behind the shop, and the air the box was playing was the lovely 'Batti, Batti,'* of Mozart.

'Is Mr Buschmann at home?' asked Mrs Jazeph.

'Yes, ma'am,' said the cheerful man, pointing with a smile towards the door that led into the parlour. 'The music answers for him. Whenever Mr Buschmann's box, is playing, Mr Buschmann himself is not far off from it. Did you wish to see him, ma'am?'

'If there is nobody with him.'

'Oh, no, he is quite alone. Shall I give any name?'

Mrs Jazeph opened her lips to answer, hesitated, and said nothing. The shopman, with a quicker delicacy of perception than might have been expected from him, judging by outward appearances, did not repeat the question, but opened the door at once, and admitted the visitor to the presence of Mr Buschmann.

The shop parlour was a very small room, with an old three-cornered look about it, with a bright green paper on the walls, with a large dried fish in a glass case over the fireplace, with two meerschaum pipes hanging together on the wall opposite, and with a neat round table placed as accurately as possible in the middle of the floor. On the table were tea-things, bread, butter, a pot of jam, and a musical box in a quaint, old-fashioned case; and by the side of the table sat a little, rosy-faced, white-haired, simple-looking old man, who started up, when the door was opened, with an appearance of extreme confusion, and touched the stop of the musical box so that it might cease playing when it came to the end of the air.

'A lady to speak with you, sir,' said the cheerful shopman. 'That is Mr Buschmann, ma'am,' he added in a lower tone, seeing Mrs Jazeph stop in apparent uncertainty on entering the parlour.

'Will you please to take a seat, ma'am?' said Mr Buschmann, when the shopman had closed the door and gone back to his counter. 'Excuse the music; it will stop directly.' He spoke these words in a foreign accent, but with perfect fluency.

Mrs Jazeph looked at him earnestly while he was addressing her, and advanced a step or two before she said anything. 'Am I so changed?' she asked softly. 'So sadly, sadly changed, uncle Joseph?'

'Gott im Himmel! it's her voice—it's Sarah Leeson!' cried the old man, running up to his visitor as nimbly as if he was a boy again, taking both her hands, and kissing her with an odd brisk tenderness on the cheek. Although his niece was not at all above the average height of women, Uncle Joseph was so short that he had to raise himself on tiptoe to perform the ceremony of embracing her.

'To think of Sarah coming at last!' he said, pressing her into a chair. 'After all these years and years, to think of Sarah Leeson coming to see Uncle Joseph again!'

'Sarah still, but not Sarah Leeson,' said Mrs Jazeph, pressing her thin, trembling hands firmly together, and looking down on the floor while she spoke.

'Ah! married?' said Mr Buschmann, gaily. 'Married, of course. Tell me all about your husband, Sarah.'

'He is dead. Dead, and forgiven.' She murmured the last three words in a whisper to herself.

'Ah! I am so sorry for you! I spoke too suddenly, did I not, my child?' said the old man. 'Never mind! No, no; I don't mean that—I mean let us talk of something else. You will have a bit of bread and jam, won't you, Sarah?—ravishing raspberry jam that melts in your mouth. Some tea, then? So, so, she will have some tea, to be sure. And we won't talk of our troubles—at least, not just yet. You look very pale, Sarah, very much older than you ought to look—no, I don't mean that either; I don't mean to be rude. It was your voice I knew you by, my child— your voice that your poor uncle Max always said would have made your fortune if you would only have learnt to sing. Here's his pretty music box going still. Don't look so down-hearted—don't, pray! Do listen a little to the music: you remember the box—my brother Max's box? Why, how you look! Have you forgotten the box that the divine Mozart gave to my brother with his own hand, when Max was a boy in the music school at Vienna? Listen! I have set it going again. It's a song they call "Batti, Batti;" it's a song in an opera of Mozart's. Ah, beautiful! beautiful! your uncle Max said that all music was comprehended in that one song. I know nothing about music, but I have my heart and my ears, and they tell me that Max was right.'

Speaking these words with abundant gesticulation and amazing volubility, Mr Buschmann poured out a cup of tea for his niece, stirred it carefully, and patting her on the shoulder, begged that she would make him happy by drinking it all up directly. As he came close to her to press this request, he discovered that the tears were in her eyes, and that she was trying to take her handkerchief from her pocket without being observed.

'Don't mind me,' she said, seeing the old man's face sadden as he looked at her; 'and don't think me forgetful or ungrateful, Uncle Joseph. I remember the box—I remember everything that you used to take an interest in, when I was younger and happier than I am now. When I last saw you, I came to you in trouble; and I come to you in trouble once more. It seems neglectful in me never to have written to you for so many years past: but my life has been a very sad one, and I thought I had no right to lay the burden of my sorrow on other shoulders than my own.'

Uncle Joseph shook his head at these last words, and touched the stop of the musical box. 'Mozart shall wait a little,' he said, gravely, 'till I have told you something. Sarah, hear what I say, and drink your tea, and own to me whether I speak the truth or not. What did I, Joseph Buschmann, tell you, when you first came to me in trouble, fourteen, fifteen, ah more! sixteen years ago, in this town, and in this same house? I said then, what I say again, now: Sarah's sorrow is my sorrow, and Sarah's joy is my joy; and if any man asks me reasons for that, I have three to give him.'

He stopped to stir up his niece's tea for the second time, and to draw her attention to it, by tapping with the spoon on the edge of the cup.

'Three reasons,' he resumed. 'First you are my sister's child—some of her flesh and blood, and some of mine, therefore, also. Second, my sister, my brother, and lastly me myself, we owe to your good English father—all. A little word that means much, and may be said again and again—all. Your father's friends cry, Fie! Agatha Buschmann is poor, Agatha Buschmann is foreign! But your father loves the poor German girl, and he marries her in spite of their Fie, Fie. Your father's friends cry Fie! again; Agatha Buschmann has a musician brother, who gabbles to us about Mozart, and who cannot make to his porridge, salt. Your father says Good! I like his gabble; I like his playing: I shall get him people to teach; and while I have pinches of salt in my kitchen, he to his porridge shall have pinches of salt, too. Your father's friends cry Fie! for the third time. Agatha Buschmann has another brother, a little Stupid-Head, who to the other's gabble can only listen and say Amen. Send him trotting; for the love of Heaven, shut up all the doors and send Stupid-Head trotting, at least! Your father says, No! Stupid-Head has his wits in his hands; he can cut, and carve, and polish; help him a little at the starting; and, after, he shall help himself. They are all gone now but me! Your father, your mother, and Uncle Max—they are all gone. Stupid-Head alone remains to remember and to be grateful— to take Sarah's sorrow for his sorrow, and Sarah's joy for his joy.'

He stopped again, to blow a speck of dust off the musical box. His niece endeavoured to speak, but he held up his hand, and shook his forefinger at her warningly.

'No,' he said. 'It is yet my business to talk, and your business to drink tea. Have I not my third reason still? Ah! you look away from me; you know my third reason before I say a word. When I, in my turn, marry, and my wife dies, and leaves me alone with little Joseph, and when the boy falls sick, who comes then, so quiet, so pretty, so neat, with the bright young eyes, and the hands so tender and light? Who helps me with little Joseph by night and by day? Who makes a pillow for him on her arm when his head is weary? Who holds this box patiently at his ear?—yes! this box, that the hand of Mozart has touched—Who holds it closer, closer always, when little Joseph's sense grows dull, and he moans for the friendly music that he has known from a baby, the friendly music that he can now so hardly, hardly hear? Who kneels down by Uncle Joseph when his heart is breaking, and says, "Oh, hush! hush! The boy is gone where the better music plays, where the sickness shall never waste or the sorrow touch him more?" Who? Ah, Sarah! you cannot forget those days; you cannot forget the Long Ago! When the trouble is bitter, and the burden is heavy, it is cruelty to Uncle Joseph to keep away; it is kindness to him to come here.'

The recollections that the old man had called up, found their way tenderly to Sarah's heart. She could not answer him; she could only hold out her hand. Uncle Joseph bent down, with a quaint, affectionate gallantry, and kissed it; then stepped back again to his place by the musical box. 'Come!' he said, patting it cheerfully, 'we will say no more for a while. Mozart's box, Max's box, little Joseph's box, you shall talk to us again!'

Having put the tiny machinery in motion, he sat down by the table, and remained silent until the air had been played over twice. Then observing that his niece seemed calmer, he spoke to her once more.

'You are in trouble, Sarah,' he said, quietly. 'You tell me that, and I see it is true in your face. Are you grieving for your husband?'

'I grieve that I ever met him,' she answered. 'I grieve that I ever married him. Now that he is dead, I cannot grieve—I can only forgive him.'

'Forgive him? How you look, Sarah, when you say that! Tell me——'

'Uncle Joseph! I have told you that my husband is dead, and that I have forgiven him.'

'You have forgiven him? He was hard and cruel with you, then? I see; I see. That is the end, Sarah—but the beginning? Is the beginning that you loved him?'

Her pale cheeks flushed; and she turned her head aside. 'It is hard and humbling to confess it,' she murmured, without raising her eyes; 'but you force the truth from me, uncle. I had no love to give to my husband—no love to give to any man.'

'And yet, you married him! Wait! it is not for me to blame. It is for me to find out, not the bad, but the good. Yes, yes: I shall say to myself, she married him when she was poor and helpless; she married him when she should have come to Uncle Joseph, instead. I shall say that to myself, and I shall pity, but I shall ask no more.'

Sarah half reached her hand out to the old man again—then suddenly pushed her chair back, and changed the position in which she was sitting. 'It is true that I was poor,' she said, looking about her in confusion, and speaking with difficulty. 'But you are so kind and so good, I cannot accept the excuse that your forbearance makes for me. I did not marry him because I was poor, but——' She stopped, clasped her hands together, and pushed her chair back still farther from the table.

'So! so!' said the old man, noticing her confusion. 'We will talk about it no more.'

'I had no excuse of love; I had no excuse of poverty,' she said, with a sudden burst of bitterness and despair. 'Uncle Joseph, I married him because I was too weak to persist in saying No! The curse of weakness and fear has followed me all the days of my life! I said No to him once. I said No to him twice. Oh, uncle, if I could only have said it for the third time! But he followed me, he frightened me, he took away from me all the little will of my own that I had. He made me speak as he wished me to speak, and go where he wished me to go. No, no, no—don't come to me, uncle; don't say anything. He is gone; he is dead— I have got my release; I have given my pardon! Oh, if I could only go away and hide somewhere! All people's eyes seem to look through me; all people's words seem to threaten me. My heart has been weary ever since I was a young woman; and all these long, long years, it has never got any rest. Hush! the man in the shop—I forgot the man in the shop. He will hear us; let us talk in a whisper. What made me break out so? I'm always wrong. Oh me! I'm wrong when I speak; I'm wrong when I say nothing; wherever I go and whatever I do, I'm not like other people. I seem never to have grown up in my mind, since I was a little child. Hark! the man in the shop is moving—has he heard me? Oh, Uncle Joseph! do you think he had heard me?'

Looking hardly less startled than his niece, Uncle Joseph assured her that the door was solid, that the man's place in the shop was at some distance from it, and that it was impossible,

even if he heard voices in the parlour, that he could also distin-
guish any words that were spoken in it.

'You are sure of that?' she whispered, hurriedly. 'Yes, yes,
you are sure of that, or you would not have told me so, would
you? We may go on talking now. Not about my married life:
that is buried and past. Say that I had some years of sorrow and
suffering, which I deserved,—say that I had other years of
quiet, when I was living in service with masters and mistresses
who were often kind to me when my fellow-servants were
not,—say just that much about my life, and it is saying enough.
The trouble that I am in now, the trouble that brings me to you,
goes back further than the years we have been talking about—
goes back, back, back, Uncle Joseph, to the distant day when
we last met.'

'Goes back all through the sixteen years!' exclaimed the old
man, incredulously. 'Goes back, Sarah, even to the Long Ago!'

'Even to that time. Uncle, you remember where I was living,
and what had happened to me, when——'

'When you came here in secret? When you asked me to hide
you? That was the same week, Sarah, when your mistress died;
your mistress who lived away, west, in the old house. You were
frightened, then—pale and frightened as I see you now.'

'As every one sees me! People are always staring at me;
always thinking that I am nervous, always pitying me for being
ill.'

Saying these words with a sudden fretfulness, she lifted the
tea-cup by her side to her lips, drained it of its contents at a
draught, and pushed it across the table to be filled again. 'I have
come all over thirsty and hot,' she whispered. 'More tea, Uncle
Joseph—more tea.'

'It is cold,' said the old man. 'Wait till I ask for hot water.'

'No!' she exclaimed, stopping him as he was about to rise.
'Give it me cold; I like it cold. Let nobody else come in—I can't
speak if anybody else comes in.' She drew her chair close to her
uncle's, and went on:—'You have not forgotten how frightened I was, in that byegone time—do you remember why I was
frightened?'

'You were afraid of being followed—that was it, Sarah.
I grow old, but my memory keeps young. You were afraid of

your master, afraid of his sending servants after you. You had run away; you had spoken no word to anybody; and you spoke little—ah, very, very little—even to Uncle Joseph, even to me.'

'I told you,' said Sarah, dropping her voice to so faint a whisper that the old man could barely hear her—'I told you that my mistress had left me a Secret on her death-bed—a Secret in a letter, which I was to give to my master. I told you I had hidden the letter, because I could not bring myself to deliver it, because I would rather die a thousand times over than be questioned about what I knew of it. I told you so much, I know. Did I tell you no more? Did I not say that my mistress made me take an oath on the Bible?—Uncle! are there candles in the room? Are there candles we can light without disturbing anybody, without calling anybody in here?'

'There are candles and a match-box in my cupboard,' answered Uncle Joseph. 'But look out of window, Sarah. It is only twilight—it is not dark yet.'

'Not outside; but it is dark here.'

'Where?'

'In that corner. Let us have candles. I don't like the darkness when it gathers in corners, and creeps along walls.'

Uncle Joseph looked all round the room inquiringly; and smiled to himself as he took two candles from the cupboard and lighted them. 'You are like the children,' he said, playfully, while he pulled down the window-blind. 'You are afraid of the dark.'

Sarah did not appear to hear him. Her eyes were fixed on the corner of the room which she had pointed out the moment before. When he resumed his place by her side, she never looked round, but laid her hand on his arm, and said to him suddenly:—

'Uncle! Do you believe that the dead can come back to this world, and follow the living everywhere, and see what they do in it?'

The old man started. 'Sarah!' he said, 'why do you talk so? Why do you ask me such a question?'

'Are there lonely hours,' she went on, still never looking away from the corner, still not seeming to hear him, 'when you are sometimes frightened without knowing why,—frightened all over in an instant, from head to foot? Tell me, uncle, have you ever felt the cold steal round and round the roots of your hair, and crawl bit by bit down your back? I have felt that, even in the summer. I have been out of doors, alone on a wide heath, in the heat and brightness of noon, and have felt as if chilly fingers were touching me—chilly, damp, softly-creeping fingers. It says in the New Testament that the dead came once out of their graves, and went into the holy city. The dead! Have they rested, rested always, rested for ever, since that time?'

Uncle Joseph's simple nature recoiled in bewilderment from the dark and daring speculations to which his niece's questions led. Without saying a word, he tried to draw away the arm which she still held; but the only result of the effort was to make her tighten her grasp, and bend forward in her chair so as to look closer still into the corner of the room.

'My mistress was dying,' she said, 'my mistress was very near her grave, when she made me take my oath on the Bible. She made me swear never to destroy the letter; and I did not destroy it. She made me swear not to take it away with me, if I left the house; and I did not take it away. She would have made me swear for the third time, to give it to my master, but death was too quick for her—death stopped her from fastening that third oath on my conscience. But she threatened me, uncle, with the dead dampness on her forehead, and the dead whiteness on her cheeks—she threatened to come to me from the other world, if I thwarted her—and I *have* thwarted her!'

She stopped, suddenly removed her hand from the old man's arm, and made a strange gesture with it towards the part of the room on which her eyes remained fixed. 'Rest, mistress, rest,' she whispered under her breath 'Is my master alive now? Rest, till the drowned rise. Tell him the Secret when the sea gives up her dead.'

'Sarah! Sarah! you are changed, you are ill, you frighten me!' cried Uncle Joseph, starting to his feet.

She turned round slowly, and looked at him with eyes void of all expression, with eyes that seemed to be staring through him vacantly at something beyond.

'Gott im Himmel! what does she see?' He looked round as the exclamation escaped him. 'Sarah! what is it! Are you faint? Are you ill? Are you dreaming with your eyes open?'

He took her by both arms and shook her. At the instant when she felt the touch of his hands, she started violently and trembled all over. Their natural expression flew back into her eyes with the rapidity of a flash of light. Without saying a word, she hastily resumed her seat and began stirring the cold tea round and round in her cup, round and round so fast that the liquid overflowed into the saucer.

'Come! she gets more like herself,' said Uncle Joseph, watching her.

'More like myself?' she repeated, vacantly.

'So! so!' said the old man, trying to soothe her. 'You are ill—what the English call, out of sort. They are good doctors here. Wait till to-morrow, you shall have the best.'

'I want no doctors. Don't speak of doctors. I can't bear them; they look at me with such curious eyes; they are always prying into me, as if they wanted to find out something. What have we been stopping for? I had so much to say; and we seem to have been stopping just when we ought to have been going on. I am in grief and terror, Uncle Joseph; in grief and terror again about the Secret——'

'No more of that!' pleaded the old man. 'No more to-night at least!'

'Why not?'

'Because you will be ill again with talking about it. You will be looking into that corner, and dreaming with your eyes open. You are too ill—yes, yes, Sarah; you are too ill.'

'I'm not ill! Oh, why does everybody keep telling me that I am ill? Let me talk about it, uncle. I have come to talk about it; I can't rest till I have told you.'

She spoke with a changing colour and an embarrassed manner, now apparently conscious for the first time that she had allowed words and actions to escape her which it would have been more prudent to have restrained.

'Don't notice me again,' she said, with her soft voice, and her gentle, pleading manner. 'Don't notice me if I talk or look as I ought not. I lose myself sometimes, without knowing it; and I suppose I lost myself just now. It means nothing, Uncle Joseph—nothing indeed.'

Endeavouring thus to reassure the old man, she again altered the position of her chair, so as to place her back towards the part of the room to which her face had been hitherto turned.

'Well, well, it is good to hear that,' said Uncle Joseph; 'but speak no more about the past time, for fear you should lose yourself again. Let us hear about what is now. Yes, yes, give me my way. Leave the Long Ago to me, and take you the present time. I can go back through the sixteen years as well as you. Ah! you doubt it? Hear me tell you what happened when we last met—hear me prove myself in three words: You leave your place at the old house—you run away here—you stop in hiding with me, while your master and his servants are hunting after you—you start off, when your road is clear, to work for your living, as far away from Cornwall as you can get—I beg and pray you to stop with me, but you are afraid of your master, and away you go. There! that is the whole story of your trouble the last time you came to this house. Leave it so; and tell me what is the cause of your trouble now.'

'The past cause of my trouble, Uncle Joseph, and the present cause of my trouble are the same. The Secret——'

'What! you will go back to that!'

'I must go back to it.'

'And why?'

'Because the Secret is written in a letter——'

'Yes; and what of that?'

'And the letter is in danger of being discovered. It is, uncle,—it is! Sixteen years it has lain hidden—and now, after all that long time, the dreadful chance of its being dragged to light has come like a judgment. The one person in all the world who ought never to set eyes on that letter is the very person who is most likely to find it!'

'So! so! Are you very certain, Sarah? How do you know it?'

'I know it from her own lips. Chance brought us together——'

'Us? us? What do you mean by us?'

'I mean——uncle, you remember that Captain Treverton was my master when I lived at Porthgenna Tower?'

'I had forgotten his name. But, no matter——go on.'

'When I left my place, Miss Treverton was a little girl of five years old. She is a married woman now—so beautiful, so clever, such a sweet, youthful, happy face! And she has a child as lovely as herself. Oh, uncle, if you could see her! I would give so much if you could only see her!'

Uncle Joseph kissed his hand and shrugged his shoulders; expressing by the first action, homage to the lady's beauty, and by the second, resignation under the misfortune of not being able to see her. 'Well, well,' he said, philosophically, 'put this shining woman by, and let us go on.'

'Her name is Frankland now,' said Sarah. 'A prettier name than Treverton, a much prettier name, I think. Her husband is fond of her—I am sure he is. How can he have any heart at all, and not be fond of her?'

'So! so!' exclaimed Uncle Joseph, looking very much perplexed. 'Good, if he is fond of her—very good. But what labyrinth are we getting into now? Wherefore all this about a husband and a wife? My word of honour, Sarah, but your explanation explains nothing—it only softens my brains!'

'I must speak of her and of Mr Frankland, uncle. Porthgenna Tower belongs to her husband now; and they are both going to live there.'

'Ah! we are getting back into the straight road at last.'

'They are going to live in the very house that holds the Secret; they are going to repair that very part of it where the letter is hidden. She will go into the old rooms—I heard her say so; she will search about in them to amuse her curiosity; workmen will clear them out, and she will stand by in her idle hours, looking on.'

'But she suspects nothing of the Secret?'

'God forbid she ever should!'

'And there are many rooms in the house? And the letter in which the Secret is written is hidden in one of the many? Why should she hit on that one?'

'Because I always say the wrong thing! because I always get frightened and lose myself at the wrong time! The letter is hidden in a room called the Myrtle Room, and I was foolish enough, weak enough, crazed enough, to warn her against going into it.'

'Ah, Sarah! Sarah! that was a mistake indeed.'

'I can't tell what possessed me—I seemed to lose my senses

when I heard her talking so innocently of amusing herself by searching through the old rooms, and when I thought of what she might find there. It was getting on towards night, too; the horrible twilight was gathering in the corners and creeping along the walls. I longed to light the candles, and yet I did not dare, for fear she should see the truth in my face. And when I did light them it was worse. Oh, I don't know how I did it! I don't know why I did it! I could have torn my tongue out for saying the words, and still I said them. Other people can think for the best; other people can act for the best; other people have had a heavy weight laid on their minds, and have not dropped under it as I have. Help me, uncle, for the sake of old times when we were happy—help me with a word of advice.'

'I will help you; I live to help you, Sarah! No, no, no—you must not look so forlorn; you must not look at me with those crying eyes. Come! I will advise this minute—but say in what; only say in what.'

'Have I not told you?'

'No; you have not told me a word yet.'

'I will tell you now——'

She paused, looked away distrustfully towards the door leading into the shop, listened a little, and resumed:—'I am not at the end of my journey yet, Uncle Joseph—I am here on my way to Porthgenna Tower—on my way to the Myrtle Room—on my way, step by step, to the place where the letter lies hid. I dare not destroy it; I dare not remove it; but run what risk I may, I must take it out of the Myrtle Room.'

Uncle Joseph said nothing, but he shook his head despondingly.

'I must,' she repeated; 'before Mrs Frankland gets to Porthgenna, I must take that letter out of the Myrtle Room. There are places in the old house where I may hide it again—places that she would never think of—places that she would never notice. Only let me get it out of the one room that she is sure to search in, and I know where to hide it from her and from every one for ever.'

Uncle Joseph reflected, and shook his head again—then said:—'One word, Sarah; does Mrs Frankland know which is the Myrtle Room?'

'I did my best to destroy all trace of that name when I hid the letter; I hope and believe she does not. But she may find out—

remember the words I was crazed enough to speak; they will set her seeking for the Myrtle Room; they are sure to do that.'

'And if she finds it? And if she sees the letter?'

'It will cause misery to innocent people; it will bring death to *me*. Don't push your chair from me, uncle! It is not shameful death I speak of. The worst injury I have done is injury to myself; the worst death I have to fear is the death that releases a worn-out spirit and cures a broken heart.'

'Enough—enough so,' said the old man. 'I ask for no secret, Sarah, that is not yours to give. It is all dark to me—very dark, very confused. I look away from it; I look only towards you. Not with doubt, my child, but with pity, and with sorrow, too—sorrow that ever you went near that house of Porthgenna—sorrow that you are now going to it again.'

'I have no choice, uncle, but to go. If every step on the road to Porthgenna took me nearer and nearer to my death, I must still tread it. Knowing what I know, I can't rest, I can't sleep—my very breath won't come freely—till I have got that letter out of the Myrtle Room. How to do it—oh, Uncle Joseph, how to do it, without being suspected, without being discovered by anybody—that is what I would almost give my life to know! You are a man; you are older and wiser than I am; no living creature ever asked you for help in vain—help *me* now! my only friend in all the world, help me a little with a word of advice!'

Uncle Joseph rose from his chair, and folded his arms resolutely, and looked his niece full in the face.

'You will go?' he said. 'Cost what it may, you will go? Say, for the last time, Sarah, is it yes, or no?'

'Yes! For the last time, I say, Yes.'

'Good. And you will go soon?'

'I must go to-morrow. I dare not waste a single day; hours even may be precious for anything I can tell.'

'You promise me, my child, that the hiding of this Secret does good, and that the finding of it will do no harm?'

'If it was the last word I had to speak in this world, I would say, Yes!'

'You promise me, also, that you want nothing but to take the letter out of the Myrtle Room, and put it away somewhere else?'

'Nothing but that.'

'And it is yours to take and yours to put? No person has a better right to touch it than you?'

'Now that my master is dead, no person.'

'Good. You have given me my resolution. I have done. Sit you there, Sarah; and wonder, if you like, but say nothing.' With these words, Uncle Joseph stepped lightly to the door leading into the shop, opened it, and called to the man behind the counter.

'Samuel, my friend,' he said. 'To-morrow I go a little ways into the country with my niece, who is this lady here. You keep shop and take orders, and be just as careful as you always are, till I get back. If anybody comes and asks for Mr Buschmann, say he has gone a little ways into the country, and will be back in a few days. That is all. Shut up the shop, Samuel, my friend, for the night; and go to your supper. I wish you good appetite, nice victuals, and sound sleep.'

Before Samuel could thank his master, the door was shut again. Before Sarah could say a word, Uncle Joseph's hand was on her lips, and Uncle Joseph's handkerchief was wiping away the tears that were now falling fast from her eyes.

'I will have no more talking, and no more crying,' said the old man. 'I am a German, and I glory in the obstinacy of six Englishmen, all rolled into one. To-night you sleep here, to-morrow we talk again of all this. You want me to help you with a word of advice. I will help you with myself, which is bet-ter than advice, and I say no more till I fetch my pipe down from the wall there, and ask him to make me think. I smoke and think to-night—I talk and do to-morrow. And you, you go up to bed; you take Uncle Max's music-box in your hand, and you let Mozart sing the cradle-song before you go to sleep. Yes, yes, my child, there is always comfort in Mozart—better comfort than in crying. What is there to cry about, or to thank about? Is it so great a wonder that I will not let my sister's child go alone to make a venture in the dark? I said Sarah's sorrow was my sorrow, and Sarah's joy my joy; and now, if there is no way of escape—if it must indeed be done—I also say: Sarah's risk to-morrow is Uncle Joseph's risk to-morrow, too! Good night, my child—good night.'

THE next morning wrought no change in the resolution at which Uncle Joseph had arrived overnight. Out of the amazement and confusion produced in his mind by his niece's avowal of the object that had brought her to Cornwall, he had contrived to extract one clear and definite conclusion—that she was obstinately bent on placing herself in a situation of uncertainty, if not of absolute peril. Once persuaded of this, his kindly instincts all sprang into action, his natural firmness on the side of self-sacrifice asserted itself, and his determination not to let Sarah proceed on her journey alone, followed as a matter of course.

Strong in the self-denying generosity of his purpose—though strong in nothing else—when he and his niece met in the morning, and when Sarah spoke self-reproachfully of the sacrifice that he was making, of the serious hazards to which he was exposing himself for her sake, he refused to listen to her just as obstinately as he had refused the previous night. There was no need, he said, to speak another word on that subject. If she had abandoned her intention of going to Porthgenna, she had only to say so. If she had not, it was mere waste of breath to talk any more, for he was deaf in both ears to everything in the shape of a remonstrance that she could possibly address to him. Having expressed himself in these uncompromising terms, Uncle Joseph abruptly dismissed the subject, and tried to turn the conversation to a cheerful everyday topic, by asking his niece how she had passed the night.

'I was too anxious to sleep,' she answered. 'I can't fight with my fears and misgivings as some people can. All night long they keep me waking and thinking as if it was day.'

'Thinking about what?' asked Uncle Joseph. 'About the letter that is hidden? about the house of Porthgenna? about the Myrtle Room?'

'About how to get into the Myrtle Room,' she said. 'The more I try to plan and ponder, and settle beforehand what I shall do, the more confused and helpless I seem to be. All last night, uncle, I was trying to think of some excuse for getting inside the doors of Porthgenna Tower—and yet, if I was standing on the house-step at this moment, I should not know what to say when the servant and I first came face to face. How are we to persuade them to let us in? How am I to slip out of sight, even if we do get in? Can't you tell me?—you will try, Uncle Joseph—I am sure you will try. Only help me so far, and I think I can answer for the rest. If they keep the keys where they used to keep them in my time, ten minutes to myself is all I should want—ten minutes, only ten short minutes, to make the end of my life easier to me than the beginning has been; to help me to grow old quietly and resignedly, if it is God's will that I should live out my years. O, how happy people must be who have all the courage they want; who are quick and clever, and have their wits about them! You are readier than I am, uncle; you said last night that you would think about how to advise me for the best—what did your thoughts end in? You will make me so much easier if you will only tell me that.'

Uncle Joseph nodded assentingly, assumed a look of the profoundest gravity, and slowly laid his fore-finger along the side of his nose.

'What did I promise you last night?' he said. 'Was it not to take my pipe, and ask him to make me think? Good, I smoke three pipes, and think three thoughts. My first thought is—Wait! My second thought is again—Wait! My third thought is yet once more—Wait! You say you will be easy, Sarah, if I tell you the end of all my thoughts. Good, I have told you. There is the end—you are easy—it is all right.'

'Wait?' repeated Sarah, with a look of bewilderment which suggested anything rather than a mind at ease. 'I am afraid, uncle, I don't quite understand. Wait for what? Wait till when?'

'Wait till we arrive at the house, to be sure! Wait till we are got outside the door; then is time enough to think how we are to get in,' said Uncle Joseph, with an air of conviction, 'You understand now?'

'Yes—at least I understand better than I did. But there is still another difficulty left. Uncle! I must tell you more than I intended ever to tell anybody—I must tell you that the letter is locked up.'

'Locked up in a room?'

'Worse than that—locked up in something inside the room. The key that opens the door—even if I get it—the key that opens the door of the room is not all I want. There is another key besides that, a little key—' She stopped, with a confused, startled look.

'A little key that you have lost?' asked Uncle Joseph.

'I threw it down the well in the village, on the morning when I made my escape from Porthgenna. Oh, if I had only kept it about me! If it had only crossed my mind that I might want it again!'

'Well, well; there is no help for that now. Tell me, Sarah, what the something is which the letter is hidden in.'

'I am afraid of the very walls hearing me.'

'What nonsense! Come! whisper it to me.'

She looked all round her distrustfully, and then whispered into the old man's ear. He listened eagerly, and laughed when she was silent again. 'Bah!' he cried. 'If that is all, make yourself happy. As you wicked English people say, it is as easy as lying. Why, my child, you can burst him open for yourself.'

'Burst it open? How?'

Uncle Joseph went to the window-seat, which was made on the old-fashioned plan, to serve the purpose of a chest as well as a seat. He opened the lid, searched among some tools which lay in the receptacle beneath, and took out a chisel. 'See,' he said, demonstrating on the top of the window-seat the use to which the tool was to be put. 'You push him in so—crick! Then you pull him up so—crack! It is the business of one little moment—crick! crack!—and the lock is done for. Take the chisel yourself, wrap him up in a bit of that stout paper there, and put him in your pocket. What are you waiting for? Do you want me to show you again, or do you think you can do it now for yourself?'

'I should like you to show me again, Uncle Joseph, but not now—not till we have got to the end of our journey.'

'Good. Then I may finish my packing up, and go ask about the coach. First and foremost, Mozart must put on his great coat, and travel with us.' He took up the musical box, and placed it carefully in a leather case, which he slung by a strap over one shoulder. 'Next, there is my pipe, the tobacco to feed him with, and the matches to set him alight. Last, here is my old German knapsack, which I pack last night. See! here is shirt, nightcap, comb, pocket-handkerchief, sock. Say I am an emperor, and what do I want more than that? Good. I have Mozart, I have the pipe, I have the knapsack. I have—stop! stop! there is the old leather purse; he must not be forgotten. Look! here he is. Listen! Ting, ting, ting! He jingles; he has in his inside, money. Aha, my friend, my good Leather, you shall be lighter and leaner before you come home again. So, so—it is all complete; we are ready for the march now, from our tops to our toes. Good-bye, Sarah, my child, for a little half-hour; you shall wait here and amuse yourself while I go ask for the coach.'

When Uncle Joseph came back, he brought his niece information that a coach would pass through Truro in an hour's time, which would set them down at a stage not more than five or six miles distant from the regular post-town* of Porthgenna. The only direct conveyance to the post-town was a night-coach which carried the letter-bags, and which stopped to change horses at Truro at the very inconvenient hour of two o'clock in the morning. Being of opinion that to travel at bed-time was to make a toil of a pleasure, Uncle Joseph recommended taking places in the day-coach, and hiring any conveyance that could be afterwards obtained to carry his niece and himself on to the post-town. By this arrangement they would not only secure their own comfort, but gain the additional advantage of losing as little time as possible at Truro before proceeding on their journey to Porthgenna.

The plan thus proposed, was the plan followed. When the coach stopped to change horses, Uncle Joseph and his niece were waiting to take their places by it. They found all the inside seats but one disengaged, were set down two hours afterwards at the stage that was nearest to the destination for which they were bound, hired a pony-chaise there, and reached the post-town between one and two o'clock in the afternoon.

Dismissing their conveyance at the inn, from motives of caution which were urged by Sarah, they set forth to walk across the moor to Porthgenna. On their way out of the town, they met the postman returning from his morning's delivery of letters in the surrounding district. His bag had been much heavier, and his walk much longer, that morning than usual. Among the extra letters that had taken him out of his ordinary course, was one addressed to the housekeeper at Porthgenna Tower, which he had delivered early in the morning, when he first started on his rounds.

Throughout the whole journey, Uncle Joseph had not made a single reference to the object for which it had been undertaken. Possessing a child's simplicity of nature, he was also endowed with a child's elasticity of disposition. The doubts and forebodings which troubled his niece's spirit, and kept her silent, and thoughtful, and sad, cast no darkening shadow over the natural sunshine of his mind. If he had really been travelling for pleasure alone, he could not have enjoyed more thoroughly than he did the different sights and events of the journey. All the happiness which the passing minute had to give him, he took as readily and gratefully as if there was no uncertainty in the future, no doubt, difficulty, or danger lying in wait for him at the journey's end. Before he had been half-an-hour in the coach, he had begun to tell the third inside passenger—a rigid old lady, who stared at him in speechless amazement—the whole history of the musical box, ending the narrative by setting it playing, in defiance of all the noise that the rolling wheels could make. When they left the coach, he was just as sociable afterwards with the driver of the chaise, vaunting the superiority of German beer over Cornish cider, and making his remarks upon the objects which they passed on the road with the pleasantest familiarity, and the heartiest enjoyment of his own jokes. It was not till he and Sarah were well out of the little town, and away by themselves on the great moor which stretched beyond it, that his manner altered, and his talk ceased altogether. After walking on in silence for some little time, with his niece's arm in his, he suddenly stopped, looked her earnestly and kindly in the face, and laid his hand on hers.

'There is yet one thing more I want to ask you, my child,' he said. 'The journey has put it out of my head, but it has been in my heart all the time. When we leave this place of Porthgenna, and get back to my house, you will not go away? you will not leave Uncle Joseph again? Are you in service still, Sarah? Are you not your own master yet?'

'I was in service a few days since,' she answered. 'But I am free now. I have lost my place.'

'Aha! You have lost your place; and why?'

'Because I would not hear an innocent person unjustly blamed. Because——'

She checked herself. But the few words she had said were spoken with such a suddenly-heightened colour, and with such an extraordinary emphasis and resolution of tone, that the old man opened his eyes as widely as possible, and looked at his niece in undisguised astonishment.

'So! so! so!' he exclaimed. 'What! You have had a quarrel, Sarah?'

'Hush! Don't ask me any more questions now!' she pleaded earnestly. 'I am too anxious and too frightened to answer. Uncle! this is Porthgenna Moor—this is the road I passed over, sixteen years ago, when I ran away to you. O! let us get on, pray let us get on! I can't think of anything now but the house we are so near, and the risk we are going to run.'

They went on quickly, in silence. Half-an-hour's rapid walking brought them to the highest elevation on the moor, and gave the whole western prospect grandly to their view.

There, below them, was the dark, lonesome, spacious structure of Porthgenna Tower, with the sunlight already stealing round towards the windows of the west front! There was the path winding away to it gracefully over the brown moor, in curves of dazzling white! There, lower down, was the solitary old church, with the peaceful burial-ground nestling by its side! There, lower still, were the little scattered roofs of the fishermen's cottages! And there, beyond all, was the change-less glory of the sea, with its old seething lines of white foam, with the old winding margin of its yellow shores! Sixteen long years—such years of sorrow, such years of suffering, such years of change, counted by the pulses of the living heart!—had passed over the dead tranquillity of Porthgenna, and had altered it as little as if they had all been contained within the lapse of a single day!

The moments when the spirit within us is most deeply
stirred, are almost invariably the moments also when its outward manifestations are hardest to detect. Our own thoughts
rise above us; our own feelings lie deeper than we can reach.
How seldom words can help us, when their help is most
wanted! How often our tears are dried up when we most long
for them to relieve us! Was there ever a strong emotion in this
world that could adequately express its own strength? What
third person, brought face to face with the old man and his
niece, as they now stood together on the moor, would have
suspected, to look at them, that the one was contemplating the
landscape with nothing more than a stranger's curiosity, and
that the other was viewing it through the recollections of half a
life-time? The eyes of both were dry, the tongues of both were
silent, the faces of both were set with equal attention towards
the prospect. Even between themselves there was no real
sympathy, no intelligible appeal from one spirit to the other.
The old man's quiet admiration of the view was not more
briefly and readily expressed, when they moved forward and
spoke to each other, than the customary phrases of assent
by which his niece replied to the little that he said. How many
moments there are in this mortal life, when, with all our
boasted powers of speech, the words of our vocabulary treach-
erously fade out, and the page presents nothing to us but the
sight of a perfect blank!

Slowly descending the slope of the moor, the uncle and niece
drew nearer and nearer to Porthgenna Tower. They were
within a quarter of an hour's walk of the house when Sarah
stopped at a place where a second path intersected the main
foot-track which they had hitherto been following. On the left
hand, as they now stood, the cross-path ran on until it was lost
to the eye in the expanse of the moor. On the right hand it led
straight to the church.

'What do we stop for now?' asked Uncle Joseph, looking first
in one direction and then in the other.

'Would you mind waiting for me here a little while, uncle?
I can't pass the church path——' she paused, in some trouble
how to express herself—'without wishing (as I don't know
what may happen after we get to the house), without wishing to

see—to look at something——' She stopped again, and turned her face wistfully towards the church. The tears which had never wetted her eyes at the first view of Porthgenna, were beginning to rise in them now.

Uncle Joseph's natural delicacy warned him that it would be best to abstain from asking her for any explanations.

'Go you where you like, to see what you like,' he said, patting her on the shoulder. 'I shall stop here to make myself happy with my pipe; and Mozart shall come out of his cage, and sing a little in this fine fresh air.' He unslung the leather case from his shoulder while he spoke, took out the musical box, and set it ringing its tiny peal to the second of the two airs which it was constructed to play—the minuet in Don Giovanni.* Sarah left him looking about carefully, not for a seat for himself, but for a smooth bit of rock to place the box upon. When he had found this, he lit his pipe, and sat down to his music and his smoking, like an epicure to a good dinner. 'Aha!' he exclaimed to himself, looking round as composedly at the wild prospect on all sides of him, as if he was still in his own little parlour at Truro—'Aha! Here is a fine big music-room, my friend Mozart, for you to sing in! Ouf! there is wind enough in this place to blow your pretty dance-tune out to sea, and give the sailor-people a taste of it as they roll about in their ships.'

Meanwhile, Sarah walked on rapidly towards the church, and entered the inclosure of the little burial-ground. Towards that same part of it, to which she had directed her steps on the morning of her mistress's death, she now turned her face again, after a lapse of sixteen years. Here, at least, the march of time had left its palpable track—its footprints whose marks were graves. How many a little spot of ground, empty when she last saw it, had its mound and its headstone now! The one grave that she had come to see—the grave which had stood apart in the byegone days, had companion-graves on the right hand and on the left. She could not have singled it out but for the weather-stains on the headstone, which told of storm and rain passing over it, that had not passed over the rest. The mound was still kept in shape; but the grass grew long, and waved a dreary welcome to her, as the wind swept through it. She knelt down by the stone, and tried to read the inscription. The black

paint which had once made the carved words distinct was all
flayed off from them now. To any other eyes but hers, the very
name of the dead man would have been hard to trace. She
sighed heavily as she followed the letters of the inscription
mechanically, one by one, with her finger:—

SACRED TO THE MEMORY

OF

HUGH POLWHEAL,

AGED 26 YEARS.

HE MET WITH HIS DEATH

THROUGH THE FALL OF A ROCK

IN

PORTHGENNA MINE,

DECEMBER 17TH, 1823.

Her hand lingered over the letters after it had followed them
to the last line; and she bent forward and pressed her lips on the
stone.

'Better so!' she said to herself, as she rose from her knees,
and looked down at the inscription for the last time. 'Better it
should fade out so! Fewer strangers' eyes will see it; fewer
strangers' feet will follow where mine have been—he will lie all
the quieter in the place of his rest!'

She brushed the tears from her eyes, and gathered a few
blades of grass from the grave—then left the churchyard. Outside the hedge that surrounded the enclosure, she stopped for a
moment, and drew from the bosom of her dress the little book
of Wesley's Hymns, which she had taken with her from the desk
in her bedroom on the morning of her flight from Porthgenna.
The withered remains of the grass that she had plucked from the
grave sixteen years ago, lay between the pages still. She added to
them the fresh fragments that she had just gathered, replaced
the book in the bosom of her dress, and hastened back over the
moor to the spot where the old man was waiting for her.

She found him packing up the musical-box again in its
leather case. 'A good wind,' he said, holding up the palm of his
hand to the fresh breeze that was sweeping over the moor—'A
very good wind indeed, if you take him by himself—but a bitter
bad wind if you take him with Mozart. He blows off the tune as
if it was the hat on my head. You come back, my child, just at

the nick of time—just when my pipe is done, and Mozart is ready to travel along the road once more. Ah, have you got the crying look in your eyes again, Sarah! What have you met with to make you cry? So! so! I see—the fewer questions I ask just now, the better you will like me. Good. I have done. No! I have a last question yet. What are we standing here for? why do we not go on?'

'Yes, yes; you are right, Uncle Joseph; let us go on at once. I shall lose all the little courage I have, if we stay here much longer looking at the house.'

They proceeded down the path without another moment of delay. When they had reached the end of it, they stood oppo-site the eastern boundary wall of Porthgenna Tower. The principal entrance to the house, which had been very rarely used of late years, was in the west front, and was approached by a terrace road that overlooked the sea. The smaller entrance, which was generally used, was situated on the south side of the building, and led through the servants' offices to the great hall and the west staircase. Sarah's old experience of Porthgenna guided her instinctively towards this part of the house. She led her companion on, until they gained the southern angle of the east wall—then stopped and looked about her. Since they had passed the postman and had entered on the moor, they had not set eyes on a living creature; and still, though they were now under the very walls of Porthgenna, neither man, woman, nor child—not even a domestic animal—appeared in view.

'It is very lonely here,' said Sarah, looking round her distrustfully; 'much lonelier than it used to be.'

'Is it only to tell me what I can see for myself that you are stopping now?' asked Uncle Joseph, whose inveterate cheerful-ness would have been proof against the solitude of Sahara itself.

'No, no!' she answered, in a quick anxious whisper. 'But the bell we must ring at is so close—only round there—I should like to know what we are to say when we come face to face with the servant. You told me it was time enough to think about that when we were at the door. Uncle! we are all but at the door now. What shall we do?'

'The first thing to do,' said Uncle Joseph, shrugging his shoulders, 'is surely to ring.'

'Yes—but when the servant comes, what are we to say?'

'Say?' repeated Uncle Joseph, knitting his eyebrows quite fiercely with the effort of thinking, and rapping his forehead with his forefinger, just under his hat. 'Say? Stop, stop, stop, stop! Ah, I have got it! I know! Make yourself quite easy, Sarah. The moment the door is opened, all the speaking to the servant shall be done by me.'

'O, how you relieve me! What shall you say?'

'Say? This;—"How do you do? We have come to see the house."'

When he had disclosed that remarkable expedient for effecting an entrance into Porthgenna Tower, he spread out both his hands interrogatively, drew back several paces from his niece, and looked at her with the serenely self-satisfied air of a man who has leapt, at one mental bound, from a doubt to a discovery. Sarah gazed at him in astonishment. The expression of absolute conviction on his face staggered her. The poorest of all the poor excuses for gaining admission into the house, which she herself had thought of, and had rejected, during the previous night, seemed like the very perfection of artifice by comparison with such a childishly simple expedient as that suggested by Uncle Joseph. And yet there he stood, apparently quite convinced that he had hit on the means of smoothing away all obstacles at once. Not knowing what to say, not believing sufficiently in the validity of her own doubts to venture on openly expressing an opinion either one way or the other, she took the last refuge that was now left open to her—she endeavoured to gain time.

'It is very, very good of you, uncle, to take all the difficulty of speaking to the servant on your own shoulders,' she said; the hidden despondency at her heart expressing itself, in spite of her, in the faintness of her voice, and the forlorn perplexity of her eyes. 'But would you mind waiting a little before we ring at the door, and walking up and down for a few minutes by the side of this wall, where nobody is likely to see us? I want to get a little more time to prepare myself for the trial that I have to go through; and—and in case the servant makes any difficulties about letting us in—I mean difficulties that we cannot just now anticipate—would it not be as well to think of something else to say at the door? Perhaps, if you were to consider again——'

'There is not the least need,' interposed Uncle Joseph. 'I have only to speak to the servant, and—crick! crack!—you will see that we shall get in. But I will walk up and down as long as you please. There is no reason, because I have done all my thinking in one moment, that you should have done all your thinking in one moment too. No, no, no—no reason at all.' Saying those words with a patronising air, and a self-satisfied smile, which would have been irresistibly comical under any less critical circumstances, the old man again offered his arm to his niece, and led her back over the broken ground that lay under the eastern wall of Porthgenna Tower.

While Sarah was waiting in doubt outside the walls, it happened, by a curious coincidence, that another person, vested with the highest domestic authority, was also waiting in doubt inside the walls. This person was no other than the housekeeper of Porthgenna Tower; and the cause of her perplexity was nothing less than the letter which had been delivered by the postman that very morning.

It was a letter from Mrs Frankland, which had been written after she had held a long conversation with her husband and Mr Orridge, on receiving the last fragments of information which the doctor was able to communicate in reference to Mrs Jazeph.

The housekeeper had read the letter through over and over again, and was more puzzled and astonished by it at every fresh reading. She was now waiting for the return of the steward, Mr Munder, from his occupations out of doors, with the intention of taking his opinion on the singular communication which she had received from her mistress.

While Sarah and her uncle were still walking up and down outside the eastern wall, Mr Munder entered the housekeeper's room. He was one of those tall, grave, benevolent-looking men, with a conical head, a deep voice, a slow step, and a heavy manner, who passively contrive to get a great reputation for wisdom without the trouble of saying or doing anything to deserve it. All round the Porthgenna neighbourhood, the steward was popularly spoken of as a remarkably sound, sensible man; and the housekeeper, although a sharp woman in other matters, in this one respect shared to a large extent in the general delusion.

'Good morning, Mrs Pentreath,' said Mr Munder. 'Any news to-day?' What a weight and importance his deep voice and his impressively slow method of using it, gave to those two insignificant sentences!

'News, Mr Munder, that will astonish you,' replied the housekeeper. 'I have received a letter this morning from Mrs Frankland, which is, without any exception, the most mystifying thing of the sort I ever met with. I am told to communicate the letter to you; and I have been waiting the whole morning to hear your opinion of it. Pray sit down, and give me all your attention—for I do positively assure you that the letter requires it.'

Mr Munder sat down, and became the picture of attention immediately—not of ordinary attention, which can be wearied, but of judicial attention, which knows no fatigue, and is superior alike to the power of dulness and the power of time. The housekeeper, without wasting the precious minutes— Mr Munder's minutes, which ranked next on the scale of importance to a prime minister's!—opened her mistress's letter, and, resisting the natural temptation to make a few more prefatory remarks on it, immediately favoured the steward with the first paragraph, in the following terms:—

'MRS PENTREATH,

'You must be tired of receiving letters from me, fixing a day for the arrival of Mr Frankland and myself. On this, the third occasion of my writing to you about our plans, it will be best, I think, to make no third appointment, but merely to say that we shall leave West Winston for Porthgenna the moment I can get the doctor's permission to travel.'

'So far,' remarked Mrs Pentreath, placing the letter on her lap, and smoothing it out rather irritably while she spoke—'so far, there is nothing of much consequence. The letter certainly seems to me (between ourselves) to be written in rather poor language—too much like common talking to come up to my idea of what a lady's style of composition ought to be—but that is a matter of opinion. I can't say, and I should be the last person to wish to say, that the beginning of Mrs Frankland's letter is not, upon the whole, perfectly clear. It is the middle and the end that I wish to consult you about, Mr Munder.'

'Just so,' said Mr Munder. Only two words, but more meaning in them than two hundred in the mouth of an ordinary man! The housekeeper cleared her throat with extraordinary loudness and elaboration, and read on thus:—

'My principal object in writing these lines is to request, by Mr Frankland's desire, that you and Mr Munder will endeavour to ascertain, as privately as possible, whether a person now travelling in Cornwall—in whom we happen to be much interested—has been yet seen in the neighbourhood of Porthgenna. The person in question is known to us by the name of Mrs Jazeph. She is an elderly woman, of quiet lady-like manners, looking nervous and in delicate health. She dresses, according to our experience of her, with extreme propriety and neatness, and in dark colours. Her eyes have a singular expression of timidity, her voice is particularly soft and low, and her manner is frequently marked by extreme hesitation. I am thus particular in describing her, in case she should not be travelling under the name by which we know her.

'For reasons, which it is not necessary to state, both my husband and myself think it probable that, at some former period of her life, Mrs Jazeph may have been connected with the Porthgenna neighbourhood. Whether this be the fact or no, it is indisputably certain that she is familiar with the interior of Porthgenna Tower, and that she has an interest of some kind, quite incomprehensible to us, in the house. Coupling these facts with the knowledge we have of her being now in Cornwall, we think it just within the range of possibility, that you, or Mr Munder, or some other person in our employment, may meet with her; and we are particularly anxious, if she should by any chance ask to see the house, not only that you should show her over it with perfect readiness and civility, but also that you should take private and particular notice of her conduct from the time when she enters the building to the time when she leaves it. Do not let her out of your sight for a moment; and, if possible, pray get some trustworthy person to follow her unperceived, and ascertain where she goes to, after she has quitted the house. It is of the most vital importance that these instructions (strange as they may seem to you) should be implicitly obeyed to the very letter.

'I have only room and time to add, that we know nothing to the discredit of this person, and that we particularly desire you will manage

matters with sufficient discretion (in case you meet with her) to prevent her from having any suspicion that you are acting under orders, or
that you have any especial interest in watching her movements. You
will be good enough to communicate this letter to the steward, and you
are at liberty to repeat the instructions in it to any other trustworthy
person, if necessary.

'Yours truly,
'ROSAMOND FRANKLAND.
'P. S.—I have left my room, and the baby is getting on charmingly.'

'There!' said the housekeeper. 'Who is to make head or
tail of that, I should like to know! Did you ever, in all your experience, Mr Munder, meet with such a letter before? Here is a
very heavy responsibility laid on our shoulders, without one
word of explanation. I have been puzzling my brains about
what their interest in this mysterious woman can be, the whole
morning; and the more I think, the less comes of it. What is
your opinion, Mr Munder? We ought to do something immediately. Is there any course in particular which you feel
disposed to point out?'

Mr Munder coughed dubiously, crossed his right leg over
his left, put his head critically on one side, coughed for the
second time, and looked at the housekeeper. If it had belonged
to any other man in the world, Mrs Pentreath would have
considered that the face which now confronted hers expressed
nothing but the most profound and vacant bewilderment.
But it was Mr Munder's face, and it was only to be looked at
with sentiments of respectful expectation.

'I rather think—' began Mr Munder.

'Yes?' said the housekeeper, eagerly.

Before another word could be spoken, the maid-servant
entered the room to lay the cloth for Mrs Pentreath's
dinner.

'There, there! never mind now, Betsey,' said the housekeeper, impatiently. 'Don't lay the cloth till I ring for you.
Mr Munder and I have something very important to talk about,
and we can't be interrupted just yet.'

She had hardly said the word, before an interruption of the
most unexpected kind happened. The door-bell rang. This
was a very unusual occurrence at Porthgenna Tower. The

few persons who had any occasion to come to the house on domestic business, always entered by a small side gate, which was left on the latch in the day-time.

'Who in the world can that be!' exclaimed Mrs Pentreath, hastening to the window, which commanded a side view of the lower door steps.

The first object that met her eye when she looked out, was a lady standing on the lowest step—a lady dressed very neatly in quiet, dark colours.

'Good Heavens, Mr Munder!' cried the housekeeper, hurrying back to the table, and snatching up Mrs Frankland's letter, which she had left on it. 'There is a stranger waiting at the door at this very moment! a lady! or, at least, a woman—and dressed neatly, dressed in dark colours! You might knock me down, Mr Munder, with a feather! Stop, Betsey;—stop where you are!'

'I was only going, ma'am, to answer the door,' said Betsey, in amazement.

'Stop where you are,' reiterated Mr Pentreath, composing herself by a great effort. 'I happen to have certain reasons, on this particular occasion, for descending out of my own place and putting myself into yours. Stand out of the way, you staring fool! I am going up-stairs to answer that ring at the door myself.'

CHAPTER III

INSIDE THE HOUSE

MRS PENTREATH'S surprise at seeing a lady through the window was doubled by her amazement at seeing a gentleman, when she opened the door. Waiting close to the bell-handle, after he had rung, instead of rejoining his niece on the step, Uncle Joseph stood near enough to the house to be out of the range of view from Mrs Pentreath's window. To the housekeeper's excited imagination, he appeared on the threshold with the suddenness of an apparition—the apparition of a little rosy-faced old gentleman, smiling, bowing, and taking off his hat with a superb flourish of politeness, which had something quite superhuman in the sweep and the dexterity of it.

'How do you do? We have come to see the house,' said Uncle Joseph, trying his infallible expedient for gaining admission, the instant the door was open.

Mrs Pentreath was struck speechless. Who was this familiar old gentleman with the foreign accent and the fantastic bow? and what did he mean by talking to her as if she was his intimate friend? Mrs Frankland's letter said not so much, from beginning to end, as one word about him.

'How do you do? We have come to see the house,' repeated Uncle Joseph, giving his irresistible form of salutation the benefit of a second trial.

'So you said just now, sir,' remarked Mrs Pentreath, recovering self-possession enough to use her tongue in her own defence. 'Does the lady,' she continued, looking down over the old man's shoulder at the step on which his niece was standing; 'does the lady wish to see the house too?'

Sarah's gently-spoken reply in the affirmative, short as it was, convinced the housekeeper that the woman described in Mrs Frankland's letter really and truly stood before her. Besides the neat, quiet dress, there was now the softly-toned voice, and, when she looked up for a moment, there were the timid eyes also to identify her by! In relation to this one of the two strangers, Mrs Pentreath, however agitated and surprised she might be, could no longer feel any uncertainty about the course she ought to adopt. But in relation to the other visitor, the incomprehensible old foreigner, she was beset by the most bewildering doubts. Would it be safest to hold to the letter of Mrs Frankland's instructions, and ask him to wait outside while the lady was being shown over the house? or would it be best to act on her own responsibility, and to risk giving him admission as well as his companion? This was a difficult point to decide, and therefore one which it was necessary to submit to the superior sagacity of Mr Munder.

'Will you step in for a moment, and wait here while I speak to the steward?' said Mrs Pentreath, pointedly neglecting to notice the familiar old foreigner, and addressing herself straight through him to the lady on the steps below.

'Thank you very much,' said Uncle Joseph, smiling and bowing, impervious to rebuke. 'What did I tell you?' he whispered triumphantly to his niece, as she passed him on her way into the house.

Mrs Pentreath's first impulse was to go downstairs at once, and speak to Mr Munder. But a timely recollection of that part of Mrs Frankland's letter which enjoined her not to lose sight of the lady in the quiet dress, brought her to a stand-still the next moment. She was the more easily recalled to a remembrance of this particular injunction, by a curious alteration in the conduct of the lady herself, who seemed to lose all her diffidence, and to become surprisingly impatient to lead the way into the interior of the house, the moment she had stepped across the threshold.

'Betsey!' cried Mrs Pentreath, cautiously calling to the servant after she had only retired a few paces from the visitors, 'Betsey! ask Mr Munder to be so kind as to step this way.'

Mr Munder presented himself with great deliberation, and with a certain lowering dignity in his face. He had been accustomed to be treated with deference, and he was not pleased with the housekeeper for unceremoniously leaving him the moment she heard the ring at the bell, without giving him time to pronounce an opinion on Mrs Frankland's letter. Accordingly, when Mrs Pentreath, in a high state of excitement, drew him aside out of hearing, and confided to him, in a whisper, the astounding intelligence that the lady in whom Mr and Mrs Frankland were so mysteriously interested, was, at that moment, actually standing before him in the house, he received her communication with an air of the most provoking indifference. It was worse still, when she proceeded to state her difficulties—warily keeping her eye on the two strangers all the while. Appeal as respectfully as she might to Mr Munder's superior wisdom for guidance, he persisted in listening with a disparaging frown, and ended by irritably contradicting her when she ventured to add, in conclusion, that her own ideas inclined her to assume no responsibility, and to beg the foreign gentleman to wait outside while the lady, in conformity with

Mrs Frankland's instructions, was being shown over the house.

'Such may be your opinion, ma'am,' said Mr Munder severely. 'It is not mine.'

The housekeeper looked aghast. 'Perhaps,' she suggested deferentially, 'you think that the foreign old gentleman would be likely to insist on going over the house with the lady?'

'Of course I think so,' said Mr Munder. (He had thought nothing of the sort; his only idea just then being the idea of asserting his own supremacy by setting himself steadily in opposition to any preconceived arrangements of Mrs Pentreath.)

'Then you would take the responsibility of showing them both over the house, seeing that they have both come to the door together!' asked the housekeeper.

'Of course I would,' answered the steward, with the promptitude of resolution which distinguishes all superior men.

'Well, Mr Munder, I am always glad to be guided by your opinion, and I will be guided by it now,' said Mrs Pentreath.

'But, as there will be two people to look after—for I would not trust the foreigner out of sight on any consideration whatever—I must really beg you to share the trouble of showing them over the house along with me. I am so excited and nervous, that I don't feel as if I had all my wits about me—I never was placed in such a position as this before—I am in the midst of mysteries that I don't understand—and, in short, if I can't count on your assistance, I won't answer for it that I shall not make some mistake. I should be very sorry to make a mistake, not only on my own account, but—' Here the housekeeper stopped, and looked hard at Mr Munder.

'Go on, ma'am,' said Mr Munder, with cruel composure.

'Not only on my own account,' resumed Mrs Pentreath, demurely, 'but on yours; for Mrs Frankland's letter certainly casts the responsibility of conducting this delicate business on your shoulders, as well as on mine.'

Mr Munder recoiled a few steps, turned red, opened his lips indignantly, hesitated, and closed them again. He was fairly caught in a trap of his own setting. He could not retreat from the responsibility of directing the housekeeper's conduct, the moment after he had voluntarily assumed it; and he could not deny that Mrs Frankland's letter positively and repeatedly referred to him by name. There was only one way of getting out of the difficulty with dignity, and Mr Munder unblushingly took that way, the moment he had recovered self-possession enough to collect himself for the effort.

'I am perfectly amazed, Mrs Pentreath,' he began, with the gravest dignity. 'Yes, I repeat, I am perfectly amazed that you should think me capable of leaving you to go over the house alone, under such remarkable circumstances as those we are now placed in. No, ma'am! whatever my other faults may be, shrinking from my share of a responsibility is not one of them. I don't require to be reminded of Mrs Frankland's letter; and—no!—I don't require any apologies. I am quite ready, ma'am—quite ready to show the way up-stairs whenever you are.'

'The sooner the better, Mr Munder—for there is that audacious old foreigner actually chattering to Betsey now, as if he had known her all his life!'

The assertion was quite true. Uncle Joseph was exercising his gift of familiarity on the maid-servant (who had lingered to stare at the strangers, instead of going back to the kitchen), just as he had already exercised it on the old lady passenger in the stage-coach, and on the driver of the pony-chaise which took his niece and himself to the post-town of Porthgenna. While the housekeeper and the steward were holding their private conference, he was keeping Betsey in ecstasies of suppressed giggling by the odd questions that he asked about the house, and about how she got on with her work in it. His enquiries had naturally led from the south side of the building, by which he and his companions had entered, to the west side, which they were shortly to explore; and, thence, round to the north side, which was forbidden ground to everybody in the house. When Mrs Pentreath came forward with the steward, she overheard this exchange of question and answer passing between the foreigner and the maid:—

'But tell me, Betzee, my dear,' said Uncle Joseph. 'Why does nobody ever go into these mouldy old rooms?'

'Because there's a ghost in them,' answered Betsey, with a burst of laughter, as if a series of haunted rooms and a series of excellent jokes meant precisely the same thing.

'Hold your tongue directly, and go back to the kitchen,' cried Mrs Pentreath, indignantly. 'The ignorant people about here,' she continued, still pointedly overlooking Uncle Joseph, and addressing herself only to Sarah, 'tell absurd stories about some old rooms on the unrepaired side of the house, which have not been inhabited for more than half a century past—absurd stories about a ghost; and my servant is foolish enough to believe them.'

'No, I'm not,' said Betsey, retiring, under protest, to the lower regions. 'I don't believe a word about the ghost—at least, not in the day-time.' Adding that important saving clause in a whisper, Betsey unwillingly withdrew from the scene.

Mrs Pentreath observed, with some surprise, that the mysterious lady in the quiet dress turned very pale at the mention of the ghost story, and made no remark on it whatever. While she was still wondering what this meant, Mr Munder emerged into dignified prominence, and loftily addressed himself, not to Uncle Joseph, and not to Sarah, but to the empty air between them.

'If you wish to see the house,' he said, 'you will have the goodness to follow me.'

With those words, Mr Munder turned solemnly into the passage that led to the foot of the west staircase, walking with that peculiar, slow strut in which all serious-minded English people indulge when they go out to take a little exercise on Sunday. The housekeeper, adapting her pace with feminine pliancy to the pace of the steward, walked the national Sabbatarian Polonaise* by his side, as if she was out with him for a mouthful of fresh air between the services.

'As I am a living sinner, this going over the house is like going to a funeral!' whispered Uncle Joseph to his niece. He drew her arm into his, and felt, as he did so, that she was trembling.

'What is the matter?' he asked, under his breath.

'Uncle! there is something unnatural about the readiness of these people to show us over the house,' was the faintly-whispered answer. 'What were they talking about just now, out of our hearing? Why did that woman keep her eyes fixed so constantly on me?'

Before the old man could answer, the housekeeper looked

round, and begged, with the severest emphasis, that they would be good enough to follow. In less than another minute they were all standing at the foot of the west staircase.

'Aha!' cried Uncle Joseph, as easy and talkative as ever, even in the presence of Mr Munder himself. 'A fine big house, and a very good staircase.'

'We are not accustomed to hear either the house or the staircase spoken of in these terms, sir,' said Mr Munder, resolving to nip the foreigner's familiarity in the bud. 'The Guide to West Cornwall* which you would have done well to make yourself acquainted with before you came here, describes Porthgenna Tower as a Mansion, and uses the word Spacious in speaking of the west staircase. I regret to find, sir, that you have not consulted the Guide Book to West Cornwall.'

'And why?' rejoined the unabashed German. 'What do I want with a book, when I have got you for my guide? Ah, dear sir, but you are not just to yourself! Is not a living guide like you, who talks and walks about, better for me than dead leaves of print and paper? Ah, no, no! I shall not hear another word— I shall not hear you do any more injustice to yourself.' Here Uncle Joseph made another fantastic bow, looked up smiling into the steward's face, and shook his head several times with an air of friendly reproach.

Mr Munder felt paralysed. He could not have been treated with more easy and indifferent familiarity if this obscure foreign stranger had been an English duke. He had often heard of the climax of audacity; and here it was visibly embodied in one small, elderly individual, who did not rise quite five feet from the ground he stood on!

While the steward was swelling with a sense of injury too large for utterance, the housekeeper, followed by Sarah, was slowly ascending the stairs. Uncle Joseph, seeing them go up, hastened to join his niece, and Mr Munder, after waiting a little while on the mat to recover himself, followed the audacious foreigner with the intention of watching his conduct narrowly, and chastising his insolence at the first opportunity with stinging words of rebuke.

The procession up the stairs thus formed was not, however, closed by the steward; it was further adorned and completed by

Betsey, the servant-maid, who stole out of the kitchen to follow the strange visitors over the house, as closely as she could without attracting the notice of Mrs Pentreath. Betsey had her share of her natural human curiosity and love of change. No such event as the arrival of strangers had ever before enlivened the dreary monotony of Porthgenna Tower within her experience; and she was resolved not to stay alone in the kitchen while there was a chance of hearing a stray word of the conversation, or catching a chance glimpse of the proceedings among the company up-stairs.

In the meantime the housekeeper had led the way as far as the first-floor landing, on either side of which the principal rooms in the west front were situated. Sharpened by fear and suspicion, Sarah's eyes immediately detected the repairs which had been effected in the banisters and stairs of the second flight.

'You have had workmen in the house?' she said quickly to Mrs Pentreath.

'You mean on the stairs?' returned the housekeeper. 'Yes, we have had workmen there.'

'And nowhere else?'

'No. But they are wanted in other places badly enough. Even here, on the best side of the house, half the bedrooms up-stairs are hardly fit to sleep in. They were anything but comfortable, as I have heard, even in the late Mrs Treverton's time; and since she died——'

The housekeeper stopped with a frown, and a look of surprise. The lady in the quiet dress, instead of sustaining the reputation for good manners which had been conferred on her in Mrs Frankland's letter, was guilty of the unpardonable discourtesy of turning away from Mrs Pentreath before she had done speaking. Determined not to allow herself to be impertinently silenced in that way, she coldly and distinctly repeated her last words:—

'And since Mrs Treverton died——'

She was interrupted for the second time. The strange lady, quickly turning round again, confronted her with a very pale face and a very eager look, and asked, in the most abrupt manner, an utterly irrelevant question.

'Tell me about that ghost-story,' she said. 'Do they say it is the ghost of a man, or of a woman?'

'I was speaking of the late Mrs Treverton,' said the house-keeper, in her severest tones of reproof, 'and not of the ghost-story about the north rooms. You would have known that, if you had done me the favour to listen to what I said.'

'I beg your pardon; I beg your pardon a thousand times for seeming inattentive! It struck me just then—or, at least, I wanted to know——'

'If you care to know about anything so absurd,' said Mrs Pentreath, mollified by the evident sincerity of the apology that had been offered to her, 'the ghost, according to the story, is the ghost of a woman.'

The strange lady's face grew whiter than ever; and she turned away once more to the open window on the landing.

'How hot it is!' she said, putting her head out into the air.

'Hot, with a north-east wind!' exclaimed Mrs Pentreath, in amazement.

Here Uncle Joseph came forward with a polite request to know when they were going to look over the rooms. For the last few minutes he had been asking all sorts of questions of Mr Munder; and, having received no answers which were not of the shortest and most ungracious kind, had given up talking to the steward in despair.

Mrs Pentreath prepared to lead the way into the breakfast-room, library, and drawing-room. All three communicated with each other, and each room had a second door opening on a long passage, the entrance to which was on the right-hand side of the first-floor landing. Before leading the way into these rooms, the housekeeper touched Sarah on the shoulder to intimate that it was time to be moving on.

'As for the ghost-story,' resumed Mrs Pentreath, while she opened the breakfast-room door, 'you must apply to the ignorant people who believe in it, if you want to hear it all told. Whether the ghost is an old ghost or a new ghost, and why she is supposed to walk, is more than I can tell you.' In spite of the housekeeper's affectation of indifference towards the popular superstition, she had heard enough of the ghost-story to frighten her, though she would not confess it. Inside the house, or outside the house, nobody much less willing to venture into the north rooms alone could in real truth have been found than Mrs Pentreath herself.

While the housekeeper was drawing up the blinds in the breakfast-parlour, and while Mr Munder was opening the door that led out of it into the library, Uncle Joseph stole to his niece's side, and spoke a few words of encouragement to her in his quaint, kindly way.

'Courage!' he whispered. 'Keep your wits about you, Sarah, and catch your little opportunity whenever you can.'

'My thoughts! My thoughts!' she answered in the same low key. 'This house rouses them all against me. O, why did I ever venture into it again!'

'You had better look at the view from the window now,' said Mrs Pentreath, after she had drawn up the blind. 'It is very much admired.'

While affairs were in this stage of progress on the first floor of the house, Betsey, who had been hitherto stealing up by a stair at a time from the hall, and listening with all her ears in the intervals of the ascent, finding that no sound of voices now reached her, bethought herself of returning to the kitchen again, and of looking after the housekeeper's dinner, which was being kept warm by the fire. She descended to the lower regions, wondering what part of the house the strangers would want to see next, and puzzling her brains to find out some excuse for attaching herself to the exploring party.

After the view from the breakfast-room window had been duly contemplated, the library was next entered. In this room, Mrs Pentreath, having some leisure to look about her, and employing that leisure in observing the conduct of the steward, arrived at the unpleasant conviction that Mr Munder was by no means to be depended on to assist her in the important business of watching the proceedings of the two strangers. Doubly stimulated to assert his own dignity by the disrespectfully easy manner in which he had been treated by Uncle Joseph, the sole object of Mr Munder's ambition seemed to be to divest himself as completely as possible of the character of guide, which the unscrupulous foreigner sought to confer on him. He sauntered heavily about the rooms, with the air of a casual visitor, staring out of window, peeping into books on tables, frowning at himself in the chimney-glasses—looking, in short, anywhere but where he ought to look. The housekeeper, exasperated by this affectation of indifference, whispered to him irritably to keep his eye on the foreigner, as it was quite as much as she could do to look after the lady in the quiet dress.

'Very good; very good,' said Mr Munder, with sulky carelessness. 'And where are you going to next, ma'am, after we have been into the drawing-room? Back again, through the library, into the breakfast-room? or out at once into the passage? Be good enough to settle which, as you seem to be in the way of settling everything.'

'Into the passage to be sure,' answered Mrs Pentreath, 'to show the next three rooms beyond these.'

Mr Munder sauntered out of the library, through the door-way of communication, into the drawing-room, unlocked the door leading into the passage—then, to the great disgust of the housekeeper, strolled to the fireplace and looked at himself in the glass over it, just as attentively as he had looked at himself in the library mirror, hardly a minute before.

'This is the west drawing-room,' said Mrs Pentreath, calling to the visitors. 'The carving of the stone chimney-piece,' she added, with the mischievous intention of bringing them into the closest proximity to the steward, 'is considered the finest thing in the whole apartment.'

Driven from the looking-glass by this manœuvre, Mr Munder provokingly sauntered to the window, and looked out. Sarah, still pale and silent—but with a certain unwonted resoluteness just gathering, as it were, in the lines about her lips—stopped thoughtfully by the chimney-piece, when the housekeeper pointed it out to her. Uncle Joseph, looking all round the room in his discursive manner, spied, in the furthest corner of it from the door that led into the passage, a beautiful maple-wood table and cabinet, of a very peculiar pattern. His workmanlike enthusiasm was instantly aroused; and he darted across the room to examine the make of the cabinet, closely. The table beneath, projected a little way in front of it, and, of all the objects in the world, what should he see reposing on the flat space of the projection, but a magnificent musical-box at least three times the size of his own!

'Aïe! Aïe!! Aïe!!!' cried Uncle Joseph in an ascending scale of admiration, which ended at the very top of his voice. 'Open him! set him going! let me hear what he plays!' He stopped for want of words to express his impatience, and drummed with both hands on the lid of the musical-box, in a burst of uncontrollable enthusiasm.

'Mr Munder!' exclaimed the housekeeper, hurrying across the room in great indignation. 'Why don't you look? why don't you stop him? He's breaking open the musical-box. Be quiet, sir! How dare you touch me?'

'Set him going! set him going!' reiterated Uncle Joseph, dropping Mrs Pentreath's arm, which he had seized in his agitation. 'Look here! this by my side is a music-box, too! Set him going! Does he play Mozart? He is three times bigger than ever I saw! See! see! this box of mine—this tiny bit of box that looks nothing by the side of yours—it was given to my own brother by the king of all the music-composers that ever lived, by the divine Mozart himself. Set the big box going, and you shall hear the little baby-box pipe after! Ah, dear and good madam, if you love me——.'

'Sir!!!' exclaimed the housekeeper, reddening with virtuous indignation to the very roots of her hair.

'What do you mean, sir, by addressing such outrageous language as that to a respectable female?' inquired Mr Munder, approaching to the rescue. 'Do you think we want your foreign noises, and your foreign morals, and your foreign profanity here? Yes, sir! profanity. Any man who calls any human individual, whether musical or otherwise, "divine," is a profane man. Who are you, you extremely audacious person? Are you an infidel?'

Before Uncle Joseph could say a word in vindication of his principles; before Mr Munder could relieve himself of any more indignation, they were both startled into momentary silence by an exclamation of alarm from the housekeeper.

'Where is she?' cried Mrs Pentreath, standing in the middle of the drawing-room, and looking with bewildered eyes all around her.

The lady in the quiet dress had vanished.

She was not in the library, not in the breakfast-room, not in the passage outside. After searching in those three places, the housekeeper came back to Mr Munder with a look of downright terror in her face, and stood staring at him for a moment perfectly helpless and perfectly silent. As soon as she recovered herself she turned fiercely on Uncle Joseph.

'Where is she? I insist on knowing what has become of her! You cunning, wicked, impudent old man! where is she?' cried Mrs Pentreath, with no colour in her cheeks, and no mercy in her eyes.

'I suppose she is looking about the house by herself,' said Uncle Joseph. 'We shall find her surely as we take our walks through the other rooms.' Simple as he was, the old man had, nevertheless, acuteness enough to perceive that he had accidentally rendered the very service to his niece of which she stood in need. If he had been the most artful of mankind, he could have devised no better means of diverting Mrs Pentreath's attention from Sarah to himself than the very means which he had just used in perfect innocence, at the very moment when his thoughts were farthest away from the real object with which he and his niece had entered the house. 'So! so!' thought Uncle Joseph to himself, 'while these two angry people were scolding me for nothing, Sarah has slipped away to the room where the letter is. Good! I have only to wait till she comes back, and to let the two angry people go on scolding me as long as they please.'

'What are we to do? Mr Munder! what on earth are we to do?' asked the housekeeper. 'We can't waste the precious minutes staring at each other here. This woman must be found. Stop! she asked questions about the stairs—she looked up at the second floor, the moment we got on the landing. Mr Munder! wait here, and don't let that foreigner out of your sight for a moment. Wait here while I run up and look into the second-floor passage. All the bedroom doors are locked— I defy her to hide herself if she has gone up there.' With those words, the housekeeper ran out of the drawing room, and breathlessly ascended the second flight of stairs.

While Mrs Pentreath was searching on the west side of the house, Sarah was hurrying, at the top of her speed, along the lonely passages that led to the north rooms.

Terrified into decisive action by the desperate nature of the situation, she had slipped out of the drawing-room into the passage the instant she saw Mrs Pentreath's back turned on her. Without stopping to think, without attempting to compose herself, she ran down the stairs of the first floor, and made straight for the housekeeper's room. She had no excuses ready, if she had found anybody there, or if she had met anybody on the way. She had formed no plan where to seek for them next, if the keys of the north rooms were not hanging in the place where she still expected to find them. Her mind was lost in confusion, her temples throbbed as if they would burst with the heat at her brain. The one blind, wild, headlong purpose of getting into the Myrtle Room drove her on, gave unnatural swiftness to her trembling feet, unnatural strength to her shaking hands, unnatural courage to her sinking heart.

She ran into the housekeeper's room, without even the ordinary caution of waiting for a moment to listen outside the door. No one was there. One glance at the well-remembered nail in the wall showed her the keys still hanging to it in a bunch, as they had hung in the long past time. She had them in her possession in a moment; and was away again, along the solitary passages that led to the north rooms, threading their turnings and windings as if she had left them but the day before; never pausing to listen or to look behind her, never slackening her speed till she was at the top of the back staircase, and had her hand on the locked door that led into the north hall.

As she turned over the bunch to find the first key that was required, she discovered—what her hurry had hitherto prevented her from noticing—the numbered labels which the builder had methodically attached to all the keys, when he had been sent to Porthgenna by Mr Frankland to survey the house. At the first sight of them, her searching hands paused in their work instantaneously, and she shivered all over, as if a sudden chill had struck her.

If she had been less violently agitated, the discovery of the new labels and the suspicions to which the sight of them instantly gave rise would, in all probability, have checked her further progress. But the confusion of her mind was now too great to allow her to piece together even the veriest fragments of thoughts. Vaguely conscious of a new terror, of a sharpened distrust that doubled and trebled the headlong impatience which had driven her on thus far, she desperately resumed her search through the bunch of keys.

One of them had no label; it was larger than the rest—it was the key that fitted the door of communication before which she stood. She turned it in the rusty lock with a strength which, at any other time, she would have been utterly incapable of exerting; she opened the door with a blow of her hand, which burst it away at one stroke from the jambs to which it stuck. Panting for breath, she flew across the forsaken north hall, without stopping for one second to push the door to behind her. The creeping creatures, the noisome house-reptiles that possessed the place, crawled away, shadow-like, on either side of her towards the walls. She never noticed them, never turned away for them. Across the hall, and up the stairs at the end of it, she ran, till she gained the open landing at the top—and there, she suddenly checked herself in front of the first door.

The first door of the long range of rooms that opened on the landing; the door that fronted the topmost of the flight of stairs. She stopped; she looked at it—it was not the door she had come to open; and yet she could not tear herself away from it. Scrawled on the panel in white chalk was the figure—'I.' And when she looked down at the bunch of keys in her hands, there was the figure 'I.' on a label, answering to it.

She tried to think, to follow out any one of all the thronging suspicions that beset her, to the conclusion at which it might point. The effort was useless; her mind was gone: her bodily senses of seeing and hearing—senses which had now become painfully and incomprehensibly sharpened—seemed to be the sole relics of intelligence that she had left to guide her. She put her hand over her eyes, and waited a little so, and then went on slowly along the landing, looking at the doors.

No. 'II.,' No. 'III.,' No. 'IV.,' traced on the panels in the same white chalk, and answering to the numbered labels on the keys, the figures on which were written in ink. No. 'IV.' the middle room of the first floor range of eight. She stopped there again, trembling from head to foot. It was the door of the Myrtle Room.

Did the chalked numbers stop there? She looked on, down the landing. No. The four doors remaining were regularly numbered on to 'VIII.'

She came back again to the door of the Myrtle Room, sought out the key labelled with the figure 'IV.'—hesitated—and looked back distrustfully over the deserted hall.

The canvasses of the old family pictures, which she had seen bulging out from their frames, in the past time when she hid the letter, had, for the most part, rotted away from them now, and lay in great black ragged strips on the floor of the hall. Islands and continents of damp spread like the map of some strange region over the lofty vaulted ceiling. Cobwebs, heavy with dust, hung down in festoons from broken cornices. Dirt stains lay on the stone pavement, like gross reflections of the damp stains on the ceiling. The broad flight of stairs leading up to the open landing before the rooms of the first floor, had sunk down bodily towards one side. The banisters which protected the outer edge of the landing were broken away into ragged gaps. The light of day was stained, the air of heaven was stilled, the sounds of earth were silenced in the north hall.

Silenced? Were *all* sounds silenced? Or was there something stirring that just touched the sense of hearing, that just deepened the dismal stillness, and no more?

Sarah listened, keeping her face still set towards the hall— listened, and heard a faint sound behind her. Was it outside the door on which her back was turned? Or was it inside—in the Myrtle Room?

Inside. With the first conviction of that, all thought, all sensation left her. She forgot the suspicious numbering of the doors; she became insensible to the lapse of time, unconscious of the risk of discovery. All exercise of her other faculties was now merged in the exercise of the one faculty of listening.

It was a still, faint, stealthily-rustling sound; and it moved to and fro at intervals, to and fro softly, now at one end, now at the other of the Myrtle Room. There were moments when it grew suddenly distinct—other moments when it died away in gradations too light to follow. Sometimes it seemed to sweep over the floor at a bound—sometimes it crept with slow, continuous rustlings that just wavered on the verge of absolute silence.

Her feet still rooted to the spot on which she stood, Sarah turned her head slowly, inch by inch, towards the door of the Myrtle Room. A moment before, while she was as yet unconscious of the faint sound moving to and fro within it, she had been drawing her breath heavily and quickly. She might have been dead now, her bosom was so still, her breathing so noiseless. The same mysterious change came over her face which had altered it when the darkness began to gather in the little parlour at Truro. The same fearful look of inquiry which she had then fixed on the vacant corner of the room, was in her eyes now, as they slowly turned on the door.

'Mistress!' she whispered. 'Am I too late? *Are you there before me?*'

The stealthily-rustling sound inside, paused—renewed itself—died away again faintly; away at the lower end of the room.

Her eyes still remained fixed on the Myrtle Room, strained, and opened wider and wider—opened as if they would look through the very door itself—opened as if they were watching for the opaque wood to turn transparent, and show what was behind it.

'Over the lonesome floor, over the lonesome floor—how light it moves!' she whispered again. 'Mistress! does the black dress I made for you rustle no louder than that?'

The sound stopped again—then suddenly advanced at one stealthy sweep, close to the inside of the door.

If she could have moved at that moment; if she could have looked down to the line of open space between the bottom of the door and the flooring below, when the faintly rustling sound came nearest to her, she might have seen the insignificant cause that produced it lying self-betrayed under the door, partly outside, partly inside, in the shape of a fragment of faded red paper from the wall of the Myrtle Room. Time and damp had loosened the paper all round the apartment. Two or three yards of it had been torn off by the builder, while he was examining the walls—sometimes in large pieces, sometimes in small pieces, just as it happened to come away—and had been thrown down by him on the bare, boarded floor, to become the sport of the wind, whenever it happened to blow through the broken panes of glass in the window. If she had only moved! If she had only looked down for one little second of time!

She was past moving and past looking: the paroxysm of superstitious horror that possessed her, held her still in every limb and every feature. She never started, she uttered no cry, when the rustling noise came nearest. The one outward sign which showed how the terror of its approach shook her to the very soul, expressed itself only in the changed action of her right hand, in which she still held the keys. At the instant when the wind wafted the fragment of paper closest to the door, her fingers lost their power of contraction, and became as nerveless and helpless as if she had fainted. The heavy bunch of keys slipped from her suddenly-loosened grasp, dropped at her side on the outer edge of the landing, rolled off through a gap in the broken banister, and fell on the stone pavement below, with a crash which made the sleeping echoes shriek again, as if they were sentient beings writhing under the torture of sound!

The crash of the falling keys, ringing and ringing again through the stillness, woke her, as it were, to instant conscious-ness of present events and present perils. She started, staggered backward, and raised both her hands wildly to her head—paused so for a few seconds—then made for the top of the stairs with the purpose of descending into the hall to recover the keys.

Before she had advanced three paces, the shrill sound of a woman's scream came from the door of communication at the opposite end of the hall. The scream was twice repeated at a greater distance off, and was followed by a confused noise of rapidly advancing voices and footsteps.

She staggered desperately, a few paces farther, and reached the first of the row of doors that opened on the landing. There nature sank exhausted: her knees gave way under her—her breath, her sight, her hearing all seemed to fail her together at the same instant—and she dropped down senseless on the floor at the head of the stairs.

CHAPTER IV

MR MUNDER ON THE SEAT OF JUDGMENT

THE murmuring voices and the hurrying footsteps came nearer and nearer, then stopped altogether. After an interval of silence, one voice called out loudly, 'Sarah! Sarah! where are you?' and the next instant Uncle Joseph appeared alone in the doorway that led into the north hall, looking eagerly all round him.

At first, the prostrate figure on the landing at the head of the stairs escaped his view. But the second time he looked in that direction, the dark dress, and the arm that lay just over the edge of the top stair, caught his eye. With a loud cry of terror and recognition, he flew across the hall, and ascended the stairs. Just as he was kneeling by Sarah's side, and raising her head on his arm, the steward, the house-keeper, and the maid, all three crowded together after him into the doorway.

'Water!' shouted the old man, gesticulating at them wildly with his disengaged hand. 'She is here—she has fallen down—she is in a faint! Water! water!'

Mr Munder looked at Mrs Pentreath, Mrs Pentreath looked at Betsey, Betsey looked at the ground. All three stood stock-still; all three seemed equally incapable of walking across the hall. If the science of physiognomy be not an entire delusion, the cause of this amazing unanimity was legibly written in their faces; in other words, they all three looked equally afraid of the ghost.

'Water, I say! Water!' reiterated Uncle Joseph, shaking his fist at them. 'She is in a faint! Are you three at the door there, and not one heart of mercy among you? Water! water! water! Must I scream myself into fits before I can make you hear?'

'I'll get the water, ma'am,' said Betsey, 'if you or Mr Munder will please to take it from here to the top of the stairs.'

She ran to the kitchen, and came back with a glass of water, which she offered, with a respectful curtsey, first to the house-keeper, and then to the steward.

'How dare you ask us to carry things for you?' said Mrs Pentreath, backing out of the doorway.

'Yes! how dare you ask us?' added Mr Munder, backing after Mrs Pentreath.

'Water!' shouted the old man for the third time. He drew his niece backward a little, so that she could be supported against the wall behind her. 'Water! or I trample down this dungeon of a place about your ears!' he shouted, stamping with impatience and rage.

'If you please, sir, are you sure it's really the lady who is up there?' asked Betsey, advancing a few paces tremulously with the glass of water.

'Am I sure?' exclaimed Uncle Joseph, descending the stairs to meet her. 'What fool's question is this? Who should it be?'

'The ghost, sir,' said Betsey, advancing more and more slowly. 'The ghost of the north rooms.'

Uncle Joseph met her a few yards in advance of the foot of the stairs, took the glass of water from her with a gesture of contempt, and hastened back to his niece. As Betsey turned to effect her retreat, the bunch of keys lying on the pavement below the landing caught her eye. After a little hesitation she mustered courage enough to pick them up, and then ran with them out of the hall as fast as her feet could carry her.

Meanwhile, Uncle Joseph was moistening his niece's lips with the water, and sprinkling it over her forehead. After a while, her breath began to come and go slowly, in faint sighs, the muscles of her face moved a little, and she feebly opened her eyes. They fixed affrightedly on the old man, without any expression of recognition. He made her drink a little water, and spoke to her gently, and so brought her back at last to herself. Her first words were, 'Don't leave me.' Her first action, when she was able to move, was the action of crouching closer to him.

'No fear, my child,' he said, soothingly; 'I will keep by you. Tell me, Sarah, what has made you faint? What has frightened you so?'

'Oh, don't ask me! For God's sake, don't ask me!'

'There, there! I shall say nothing, then. Another mouthful of water? A little mouthful more?'

'Help me up, uncle; help me to try if I can stand.'

'Not yet—not quite yet; patience for a little longer.'

'O, help me! help me! I want to get away from the sight of those doors. If I can only go as far as the bottom of the stairs I shall be better.'

'So, so,' said Uncle Joseph, assisting her to rise. 'Wait now, and feel your feet on the ground. Lean on me, lean hard, lean heavy. Though I am only a light and a little man, I am solid as a rock. Have you been into the room?' he added, in a whisper. 'Have you got the letter?'

She sighed bitterly, and laid her head on his shoulder with a weary despair.

'Why, Sarah! Sarah!' he exclaimed. 'Have you been all this time away, and not got into the room yet?'

She raised her head as suddenly as she had laid it down, shuddered, and tried feebly to draw him towards the stairs. 'I shall never see the Myrtle Room again—never, never, never more!' she said. 'Let us go; I can walk; I am strong now. Uncle Joseph, if you love me, take me away from this house; away anywhere, so long as we are in the free air and the daylight again; anywhere, so long as we are out of sight of Porthgenna Tower.'

Elevating his eyebrows in astonishment, but considerately refraining from asking any more questions, Uncle Joseph assisted his niece to descend the stairs. She was still so weak, that she was obliged to pause on gaining the bottom of them to recover her strength. Seeing this, and feeling, as he led her afterwards across the hall, that she leaned more and more heavily on his arm at every fresh step, the old man, on arriving within speaking distance of Mr Munder and Mrs Pentreath, asked the housekeeper if she possessed any restorative drops which she would allow him to administer to his niece.

Mrs Pentreath's reply in the affirmative, though not very graciously spoken, was accompanied by an alacrity of action which showed that she was heartily rejoiced to take the first fair excuse for returning to the inhabited quarter of the house. Muttering something about showing the way to the place where the medicine chest was kept, she immediately retraced her steps along the passage to her own room; while Uncle Joseph, disregarding all Sarah's whispered assurances that she was well enough to depart without another moment of delay, followed her silently, leading his niece.

Mr Munder, shaking his head, and looking wofully disconcerted, waited behind to lock the door of communication. When he had done this, and had given the keys to Betsey to carry back to their appointed place, he, in his turn, retired from the scene at a pace indecorously approaching to something like a run. On getting well away from the north hall, however, he regained his self-possession wonderfully. He abruptly slackened his pace, collected his scattered wits, and reflected a little, apparently with perfect satisfaction to himself; for when he entered the housekeeper's room, he had quite recovered his usual complacent solemnity of look and manner. Like the vast majority of densely-stupid men, he felt intense pleasure in hearing himself talk, and he now discerned such an opportunity of indulging in that luxury, after the events that had just happened in the house, as he seldom enjoyed. There is only one kind of speaker who is quite certain never to break down under any stress of circumstances—the man whose capability of talking does not include any dangerous underlying capacity for knowing what he means. Among this favoured order of natural orators, Mr Munder occupied a prominent rank—and he was now vindictively resolved to exercise his abilities on the two strangers, under pretence of asking for an explanation of their conduct, before he could suffer them to quit the house.

On entering the room, he found Uncle Joseph seated with his niece at the lower end of it, engaged in dropping some sal volatile into a glass of water. At the upper end stood the housekeeper with an open medicine chest on the table before her. To this part of the room Mr Munder slowly advanced, with a portentous countenance; drew an arm-chair up to the table; sat himself down in it with extreme deliberation and care in the matter of settling his coat-tails; and immediately became, to all outward appearance, the model of a Lord Chief Justice in plain clothes.

Mrs Pentreath, conscious from these preparations that something extraordinary was about to happen, seated herself a little behind the steward. Betsey restored the keys to their place on the nail in the wall, and was about to retire modestly to her proper kitchen sphere, when she was stopped by Mr Munder.

'Wait, if you please,' said the steward; 'I shall have occasion to call on you presently, young woman, to make a plain statement.'

Obedient Betsey waited near the door, terrified by the idea that she must have done something wrong, and that the steward was armed with inscrutable legal power, to try, sentence, and punish her for the offence on the spot.

'Now, sir,' said Mr Munder, addressing Uncle Joseph as if he was the Speaker of the House of Commons, 'if you have done with that sal volatile, and if the person by your side has sufficiently recovered her senses to listen, I should wish to say a word or two to both of you.'

At this exordium, Sarah tried affrightedly to rise from her chair; but her uncle caught her by the hand, and pressed her back in it.

'Wait and rest,' he whispered. 'I shall take all the scolding on my own shoulder, and do all the talking with my own tongue. As soon as you are fit to walk again, I promise you this; whether the big man has said his word or two, or has not said it, we will quietly get up and go our ways out of the house.'

'Up to the present moment,' said Mr Munder, 'I have refrained from expressing an opinion. The time has now come, when, holding a position of trust as I do, in this establishment, and being accountable, and indeed responsible, as I am, for what takes place in it, and feeling, as I must, that things cannot be allowed, or even permitted, to rest as they are—it is my duty to say that I think your conduct is very extraordinary.' Directing this forcible conclusion to his sentence straight at Sarah, Mr Munder leaned back in his chair, quite full of words, and quite empty of meaning, to collect himself comfortably for his next effort.

'My only desire,' he resumed, with a plaintive impartiality, 'is to act fairly by all parties. I don't wish to frighten anybody, or to startle anybody, or even to terrify anybody. I wish to unravel, or, if you please, to make out, what I may term, with perfect propriety—events. And when I have done that, I should wish to put it to you, ma'am, and to you, sir, whether—I say, I should wish to put it to you both, calmly, and impartially, and politely, and plainly, and smoothly—and when I say smoothly,

I mean quietly—whether you are not both of you bound to explain yourselves.'

Mr Munder paused, to let that last irresistible appeal work its way to the consciences of the persons whom he addressed. The housekeeper took advantage of the silence to cough, as congregations cough just before the sermon, apparently on the principle of getting rid of bodily infirmities beforehand, in order to give the mind free play for undisturbed intellectual enjoyment. Betsey, following Mrs Pentreath's lead, indulged in a cough on her own account—of the faint, distrustful sort. Uncle Joseph sat perfectly easy and undismayed, still holding his niece's hand in his, and giving it a little squeeze, from time to time, when the steward's oratory became particularly involved and impressive. Sarah never moved, never looked up, never lost the expression of terrified restraint which had taken possession of her face from the first moment when she entered the housekeeper's room.

'Now what are the facts, and circumstances, and events?' proceeded Mr Munder, leaning back in his chair, in calm enjoyment of the sound of his own voice. 'You, ma'am, and you, sir, ring at the bell of the door of this Mansion' (here he looked hard at Uncle Joseph, as much as to say, 'I don't give up that point about the house being a Mansion, you see, even on the judgment seat')—'you are let in, or, rather, admitted. You, sir, assert that you wish to inspect the Mansion (you say "see the house," but, being a foreigner, we are not surprised at your making a little mistake of that sort); you, ma'am, coincide, and even agree, in that request. What follows? You are shown over the Mansion. It is not usual to show strangers over it, but we happen to have certain reasons—'

Sarah started. 'What reasons?' she asked, looking up quickly.

Uncle Joseph felt her hand turn cold, and tremble in his. 'Hush! hush!' he said, 'leave the talking to me.'

At the same moment, Mrs Pentreath pulled Mr Munder warily by the coat-tail, and whispered to him to be careful. 'Mrs Frankland's letter,' she said in his ear, 'tells us particularly not to let it be suspected that we are acting under orders.'

'Don't you fancy, Mrs Pentreath, that I forget what I ought to remember,' rejoined Mr Munder—who had forgotten, nevertheless. 'And don't you imagine that I was going to commit myself' (the very thing which he had just been on the point of doing). 'Leave this business in my hands, if you will be so good. What reasons did you say, ma'am?' he added aloud, addressing himself to Sarah. 'Never you mind about reasons; we have not got to do with them now; we have got to do with facts, and circumstances, and events. I was observing, or remarking, that you, sir, and you, ma'am, were shown over this Mansion. You were conducted, and indeed led, up the west staircase—the Spacious west staircase, sir!—You were shown with politeness, and even with courtesy, through the breakfast-room, the library, and the drawing-room. In that drawing-room, you, sir, indulge in outrageous, and, I will add, in violent language. In that drawing-room, you, ma'am, disappear, or rather, go altogether out of sight. Such conduct as this, so highly unparalleled, so entirely unprecedented, and so very unusual, causes Mrs Pentreath and myself to feel——' Here Mr Munder stopped, at a loss for a word for the first time.

'Astonished,' suggested Mrs Pentreath after a long interval of silence.

'No, ma'am!' retorted Mr Munder. 'Nothing of the sort. We were not at all astonished; we were—surprised. And what followed and succeeded that? What did you and I hear, sir, on the first floor?' (looking sternly at Uncle Joseph). 'And what did you hear, Mrs Pentreath, while you were searching for the missing and absent party on the second floor? What?'

Thus personally appealed to, the housekeeper answered briefly:—'A scream.'

'No! no! no!' said Mr Munder, fretfully tapping his hand on the table. 'A screech, Mrs Pentreath—a screech. And what is the meaning, purport, and upshot of that screech? Young woman!' (here Mr Munder turned, turned suddenly on Betsey)—'we have now traced these extraordinary facts and circumstances as far as you. Have the goodness to step forward, and tell us, in the presence of these two parties, how you came to utter, or give, what Mrs Pentreath calls a scream, but what I call a screech. A plain statement will do, my good girl—quite a plain statement, if you please. And, young woman, one word more—speak up. You understand me? Speak up!'

Covered with confusion by the public and solemn nature of this appeal, Betsey, on starting with her statement, unconsciously followed the oratorical example of no less a person than Mr Munder himself; that is to say, she spoke on the principle of drowning the smallest possible infusion of ideas in the largest possible dilution of words. Extricated from the mesh of verbal entanglement in which she contrived to involve it, her statement may be not unfairly represented as simply consisting of the following facts:—

First, Betsey had to relate that she happened to be just taking the lid off a saucepan, on the kitchen fire, when she heard, in the neighbourhood of the housekeeper's room, a sound of hurried footsteps (vernacularly termed by the witness, a 'scurrying of somebody's feet'). Secondly, Betsey, on leaving the kitchen to ascertain what the sound meant, heard the footsteps retreating rapidly along the passage which led to the north side of the house, and stimulated by curiosity, followed the sound of them, for a certain distance. Thirdly, at a sharp turn in the passage, Betsey stopped short, despairing of overtaking the person whose footsteps she heard, and feeling also a sense of dread (termed by the witness, 'creeping of the flesh') at the idea of venturing alone, even in broad daylight, into the ghostly quarter of the house. Fourthly, while still hesitating at the turn in the passage, Betsey heard 'the lock of a door go,' and, stimulated afresh by curiosity, advanced a few steps farther—then stopped again, debating within herself the difficult and dreadful question: whether it is the usual custom of ghosts, when passing from one place to another, to unlock any closed door which may happen to be in their way, or to save trouble by simply passing through it? Fifthly, after long deliberation, and many false starts, forward towards the north hall and backward towards the kitchen, Betsey decided that it was the immemorial custom of all ghosts to pass through doors, and not to unlock them. Sixthly, fortified by this conviction, Betsey went on boldly close to the door, when she suddenly heard a loud report as of some heavy body falling (graphically termed by the witness a 'banging scrash'). Seventhly, the noise frightened Betsey out of her wits, brought her heart up into her mouth and took away her breath. Eighthly, and lastly, on recovering breath enough to scream (or screech), Betsey did, with might and main, scream (or screech), running back towards the kitchen as fast as her legs would carry her, with all her hair 'standing up on end,' and all her flesh 'in a crawl' from the crown of her head to the soles of her feet.

'Just so! Just so!' said Mr Munder, when the statement came to a close—as if the sight of a young woman with all her hair standing on end and all her flesh in a crawl, were an ordinary result of his experience of female humanity. 'Just so! You may stand back, my good girl—you may stand back. There is nothing to smile at, sir,' he continued, sternly addressing Uncle Joseph, who had been excessively amused by Betsey's manner of delivering her evidence. 'You would be doing better to carry, or rather transport, your mind back to what followed and succeeded the young woman's screech. What did we all do, sir? We rushed to the spot, and we ran to the place. And what did we all see, sir? We saw *you*, ma'am, lying horizontally prostrate, on the top of the landing of the first of the flight of the north stairs; and we saw those keys now hanging up yonder, abstracted, and purloined, and, as it were, snatched, from their place in this room, and lying horizontally prostrate likewise, on the floor of the hall. There are the facts, the circumstances, and the events, laid, or rather placed, before you. What have you got to say to them? I call upon you both solemnly, and, I will add, seriously! In my own name, in the name of Mrs Pentreath, in the name of our employers, in the name of decency, in the name of wonder—what do you mean by it?'

With that conclusion, Mr Munder struck his fist on the table, and waited, with a stare of merciless expectation, for anything in the shape of an answer, an explanation, or a defence which the culprits at the bottom of the room might be disposed to offer.

'Tell him anything,' whispered Sarah to the old man. 'Anything to keep him quiet; anything to make him let us go! After what I have suffered, these people will drive me mad!'

Never very quick at inventing an excuse, and perfectly ignorant besides of what had really happened to his niece while she was alone in the north hall, Uncle Joseph, with the best will in the world to prove himself equal to the emergency, felt considerable difficulty in deciding what he should say or do. Determined, however, at all hazards, to spare Sarah any useless suffering, and to remove her from the house as speedily as possible, he rose to take the responsibility of speaking on himself, looking hard, before he opened his lips, at Mr Munder, who immediately leaned forward on the table with his hand to his ear. Uncle Joseph acknowledged this polite act of attention with one of his fantastic bows; and then replied to the whole of the steward's long harangue, in these six unanswerable words:—

'I wish you good day, sir!'

'How dare you wish me anything of the sort!' cried Mr Munder, jumping out of his chair in violent indignation. 'How dare you trifle with a serious subject and a serious question in that way? Wish me good day, indeed! Do you suppose I am going to let you out of this house without hearing some explanation of the abstracting and purloining and snatching of the keys of the north rooms?'

'Ah! it is that you want to know?' said Uncle Joseph, stimulated to plunge headlong into an excuse by the increasing agitation and terror of his niece. 'See, now! I shall explain. What was it, dear and good sir, that we said when we were first let in? This:—"We have come to see the house." Now, there is a north side to the house, and a west side to the house. Good! That is two sides; and I and my niece are two people; and we divide ourselves in two, to see the two sides. I am the half that goes west, with you and the dear and good lady behind there. My niece here is the other half that goes north, all by herself, and drops the keys, and falls into a faint, because in that old part of the house it is what you call musty-fusty, and there is smells of tombs and spiders, and that is all the explanation, and quite enough, too. I wish you good day, sir.'

'Damme! if ever I met with the like of you before!' roared Mr Munder, entirely forgetting his dignity, his respectability, and his long words, in the exasperation of the moment. 'You are going to have it all your own way, are you, Mr Foreigner? You will walk out of this place when you please, will you, Mr Foreigner? We will see what the justice of the peace for this district has to say to that,' cried Mr Munder, recovering his solemn manner and his lofty phraseology. 'Property in this house is confided to my care; and unless I hear some satisfactory explanation of the purloining of those keys, hanging up there, sir, on that wall, sir, before your eyes, sir—I shall consider it my duty to detain you, and the person with you, until I can get legal advice, and lawful advice, and magisterial advice. Do you hear that, sir?'

Uncle Joseph's ruddy cheeks suddenly deepened in colour, and his face assumed an expression which made the housekeeper rather uneasy, and which had an irresistibly cooling effect on the heat of Mr Munder's anger.

'You will keep us here? *You?*' said the old man, speaking very quietly, and looking very steadily at the steward. 'Now, see. I take this lady (courage, my child, courage! there is nothing to tremble for)—I take this lady with me; I throw that door open, so! I stand and wait before it; and I say to you, "Shut that door against us, if you dare."'

At this defiance, Mr Munder advanced a few steps, and then stopped. If Uncle Joseph's steady look at him had wavered for an instant, he would have closed the door.

'I say again,' repeated the old man, 'shut it against us, if you dare. The laws and customs of your country, sir, have made me an Englishman. If you can talk into one ear of a magistrate, I can talk into the other. If he must listen to you, a citizen of this country, he must listen to me, a citizen of this country also. Say the word, if you please. Do you accuse? or do you threaten? or do you shut the door?'

Before Mr Munder could reply to any one of these three direct questions, the housekeeper begged him to return to his chair, and to speak to her. As he resumed his place, she whispered to him, in warning tones, 'Remember Mrs Frankland's letter!'

At the same moment, Uncle Joseph, considering that he had waited long enough, took a step forward to the door. He was prevented from advancing any farther by his niece, who caught him suddenly by the arm, and said in his ear, 'Look! they are whispering about us again!'

'Well!' said Mr Munder, replying to the housekeeper. 'I do remember Mrs Frankland's letter, ma'am, and what then?'

'Hush! not so loud,' whispered Mrs Pentreath. 'I don't presume, Mr Munder, to differ in opinion with you; but I want to ask one or two questions. Do you think we have any charge that a magistrate would listen to, to bring against these people?'

Mr Munder looked puzzled, and seemed, for once in a way, to be at a loss for an answer.

'Does what you remember of Mrs Frankland's letter,' pursued the housekeeper, 'incline you to think that she would be pleased at a public exposure of what has happened in the house? She tells us to take *private* notice of that woman's conduct, and to follow her *unperceived* when she goes away. I don't venture on the liberty of advising you, Mr Munder, but, as far as regards myself, I wash my hands of all responsibility, if we do anything but follow Mrs Frankland's instructions (as she herself tells us) to the letter.'

Mr Munder hesitated. Uncle Joseph, who had paused for a minute when Sarah directed his attention to the whispering at the upper end of the room, now drew her on slowly with him to the door. 'Betzee, my dear,' he said, addressing the maid, with perfect coolness and composure; 'we are strangers here; will you be so kind to us as to show the way out?'

Betsey looked at the housekeeper, who motioned to her to appeal for orders to the steward. Mr Munder was sorely tempted, for the sake of his own importance, to insist on instantly carrying out the violent measures to which he had threatened to have recourse; but Mrs Pentreath's objections made him pause in spite of himself.

'Betzee, my dear,' repeated Uncle Joseph, 'has all this talking been too much for your ears? has it made you deaf?'

'Wait!' cried Mr Munder, impatiently. 'I insist on your waiting, sir!'

'You insist? Well, well, because you are an uncivil man, is no reason why I should be an uncivil man too. We will wait a little, sir, if you have anything more to say.' Making that concession to the claims of politeness, Uncle Joseph walked gently backwards and forwards with his niece in the passage outside the door. 'Sarah, my child, I have frightened the man of the big words,' he whispered. 'Try not to tremble so much; we shall soon be out in the fresh air again.'

In the mean time, Mr Munder continued his whispered conversation with the housekeeper, making a desperate effort, in the midst of his perplexities, to maintain his customary air of patronage, and his customary assumption of superiority. 'There is a great deal of truth, ma'am,' he softly began, 'a great deal of truth, certainly, in what you say. But you are talking of the woman, while I am talking of the man. Do you mean to tell me that I am to let him go, after what has happened, without at least insisting on his giving me his name and address?'

'Do you put trust enough in the foreigner to believe that he would give you his right name and address if you asked him?' inquired Mrs Pentreath. 'With submission to your better judgment, I must confess that I don't. But supposing you were to detain him and charge him before the magistrate—and how you are to do that, the magistrate's house being, I suppose, about a couple of hours' walk from here, is more than I can tell—you must surely risk offending Mrs Frankland by detaining the woman and charging the woman as well; for, after all, Mr Munder, though I believe the foreigner to be capable of anything, it was the woman who took the keys, was it not?'

'Quite so, quite so!' said Mr Munder, whose sleepy eyes were now opened to this plain and straightforward view of the case for the first time. 'I was, oddly enough, putting that point to myself, Mrs Pentreath, just before you happened to speak of it. Just so, just so!'

'I can't help thinking,' continued the housekeeper, in a mysterious whisper, 'that the best plan, and the plan most in accordance with our instructions, is to let them both go, as if we did not care to demean ourselves by any more quarrelling or arguing with them; and to have them followed to the next place they stop at. The gardener's boy, Jacob, is weeding the broad walk, in the west garden, this afternoon. These people have not seen him about the premises, and need not see him, if they are let out again by the south door. Jacob is a sharp lad, as you know; and, if he was properly instructed, I really don't see——'

'It is a most singular circumstance, Mrs Pentreath,' interposed Mr Munder, with the gravity of consummate assurance; 'but when I first sat down to this table, that idea about Jacob occurred to me. What with the effort of speaking, and the heat of argument, I got led away from it in the most unaccountable manner——'

Here Uncle Joseph, whose stock of patience and politeness was getting exhausted, put his head into the room again.

'I shall have one last word to address to you, sir, in a moment,' said Mr Munder, before the old man could speak. 'Don't you suppose that your blustering and your bullying has had any effect on me. It may do with foreigners, sir; but it won't do with Englishmen, I can tell you.'

Uncle Joseph shrugged his shoulders, smiled, and rejoined his niece in the passage outside. While the housekeeper and the steward had been conferring together, Sarah had been trying hard to persuade her uncle to profit by her knowledge of the passages that led to the south door, and to slip away unperceived. But the old man steadily refused to be guided by her advice. 'I will not go out of a place guiltily,' he said, 'when I have done no harm. Nothing shall persuade me to put myself, or to put you, in the wrong. I am not a man of much wits; but let my conscience guide me, and so long I shall go right. They let us in here, Sarah, of their own accord; and they shall let us out of their own accord also.'

'Mr Munder! Mr Munder!' whispered the housekeeper, interfering to stop a fresh explosion of the steward's indignation, which threatened to break out at the contempt implied by the shrugging of Uncle Joseph's shoulders, 'while you are speaking to that audacious man, shall I slip into the garden and give Jacob his instructions?'

Mr Munder paused before answering—tried hard to see a more dignified way out of the dilemma in which he had placed himself than the way suggested by the housekeeper—failed entirely to discern anything of the sort—swallowed his indignation at one heroic gulp—and replied emphatically in two words: 'Go, ma'am.'

'What does that mean? what has she gone that way for?' said Sarah to her uncle, in a quick, suspicious whisper, as the house-keeper brushed hastily by them, on her way to the west garden.

Before there was time to answer the question, it was followed by another, put by Mr Munder.

'Now, sir!' said the steward, standing in the doorway, with his hands under his coat-tails and his head very high in the air. 'Now, sir, and now, ma'am, for my last words. Am I to have a proper explanation of the abstracting and purloining of those keys, or am I not?'

'Certainly, sir, you are to have the explanation,' replied Uncle Joseph. 'It is, if you please, the same explanation that I had the honour of giving to you a little while ago. Do you wish to hear it again? It is all the explanation we have got about us.'

'Oh! it is, is it?' said Mr Munder. 'Then all I have to say to both of you is——leave the house directly! Directly!' he added, in his most coarsely offensive tones, taking refuge in the insolence of authority, from the dim consciousness of the absurdity of his own position, which would force itself on him even while he spoke. 'Yes, sir!' he continued, growing more and more angry at the composure with which Uncle Joseph listened to him—'Yes, sir! you may bow and scrape, and jabber your broken English somewhere else. I won't put up with you here. I have reflected with myself, and reasoned with myself, and asked myself, calmly—as Englishmen always do—if it is any use making you of importance, and I have come to a conclusion, and that conclusion is—no, it isn't! Don't you go away with a notion that your blusterings and bullyings have had any effect on me. (Show them out, Betsey!) I consider you beneath—aye, and below!—my notice. Language fails, sir, to express my contempt. Leave the house!'

'And I, sir,' returned the object of all this withering derision, with the most exasperating politeness, 'I shall say, for having your contempt, what I could by no means have said for having your respect, which is, briefly—thank you. I, the small foreigner, take the contempt of you, the big Englishman, as the greatest compliment that can be paid from a man of your composition to a man of mine.' With that, Uncle Joseph made a last fantastic bow, took his niece's arm, and followed Betsey along the passages that led to the south door, leaving Mr Munder to compose a fit retort at his leisure.

Ten minutes later, the housekeeper returned breathless to her room, and found the steward walking backwards and forwards in a high state of irritation.

'Pray make your mind easy, Mr Munder,' she said. 'They are both clear of the house at last, and Jacob has got them well in view on the path over the moor.'

CHAPTER V

MOZART PLAYS FAREWELL

EXCEPTING that he took leave of Betsey, the servant-maid, with great cordiality, Uncle Joseph spoke not another word, after his parting reply to Mr Munder, until he and his niece were alone again under the east wall of Porthgenna Tower. There he paused, looked up at the house, then at his companion, then back at the house once more, and at last opened his lips to speak.

'I am sorry, my child,' he said—'I am sorry from my heart. This has been, what you call in England, a bad job.'

Thinking that he referred to the scene which had just passed in the housekeeper's room, Sarah asked his pardon for having been the innocent means of bringing him into angry collision with such a person as Mr Munder.

'No! no! no!' he cried. 'I was not thinking of the man of the big body and the big words. He made me angry, it is not to be denied; but that is all over and gone, now. I put him and his big words away from me, as I kick this stone, here, from the pathway into the road. It is not of your Munders, or your housekeepers, or your Betzees, that I now speak—it is of something that is nearer to you and nearer to me also, because I make of your interest my own interest too. I shall tell you what it is, while we walk on—for I see in your face, Sarah, that you are restless and in fear so long as we stop in the neighbourhood of this dungeon-house. Come! I am ready for the march. There is the path. Let us go back by it, and pick up our little baggages at the inn where we left them, on the other side of this windy wilderness of a place.'

'Yes, yes, uncle! Let us lose no time; let us walk fast. Don't be afraid of tiring me; I am much stronger now.'

They turned into the same path by which they had approached Porthgenna Tower in the afternoon. By the time they had walked over a little more than the first hundred yards of their journey, Jacob, the gardener's boy, stole out from behind the ruinous enclosure at the north side of the house, with his hoe in his hand. The sun had just set, but there was a fine light still over the wide, open surface of the moor; and Jacob paused to let the old man and his niece get farther away from the building before he followed them. The housekeeper's instructions had directed him just to keep them in sight, and no more; and, if he happened to observe that they stopped and turned round to look behind them, he was to stop, too, and pretend to be digging with his hoe, as if he was at work on the moorland. Stimulated by the promise of a sixpence, if he was careful to do exactly as he had been told, Jacob kept his instructions in his memory, and kept his eye on the two strangers, and promised as fairly to earn the reward in prospect for him as a boy could.

'And now, my child, I shall tell you what it is I am sorry for,' resumed Uncle Joseph, as they proceeded along the path. 'I am sorry that we have come out upon this journey, and run our little risk, and had our little scolding, and gained nothing. The word you said in my ear, Sarah, when I was getting you out of the faint (and you should have come out of it sooner, if the muddle-headed people of the dungeon-house had been quicker with the water)—the word you said in my ear was not much, but it was enough to tell me that we have taken this journey in vain. I may hold my tongue, I may make my best face at it, I may be content to walk blindfolded with a mystery that lets no peep of daylight into my eyes—but it is not the less true, that the one thing your heart was most set on doing, when we started on this journey, is the one thing also, that you have not done. I know that, if I know nothing else; and I say again, it is a bad job—yes, yes, upon my life and faith, there is no disguise to put upon it; it is, in your plainest English, a very bad job.'

As he concluded the expression of his sympathy in these quaint terms, the dread and distrust, the watchful terror, that marred the natural softness of Sarah's eyes, disappeared in an expression of sorrowful tenderness, which seemed to give back to them all their beauty.

'Don't be sorry for me, uncle,' she said, stopping, and gently brushing away with her hand some specks of dust that lay on the collar of his coat. 'I have suffered so much and suffered so long, that the heaviest disappointments pass lightly over me now.'

'I won't hear you say it!' cried Uncle Joseph. 'You give me shocks I can't bear when you talk to me in this way. You shall have no more disappointments——no, you shall not! I, Joseph Buschmann, the Obstinate, the Pig-headed, I say it!——'

'The day when I shall have no more disappointments, uncle, is not far off, now. Let me wait a little longer, and endure a little longer: I have learned to be patient, and to hope for nothing. Fearing and failing, fearing and failing—that has been my life, ever since I was a young woman—the life I have become used to by this time. If you are surprised, as I know you must be, at my not possessing myself of the letter, when I had the keys of the Myrtle Room in my hand, and when no one was near to stop me, remember the history of my life, and take that as an explanation. Fearing and failing, fearing and failing—if I told you all the truth, I could tell no more than that. Let us walk on, uncle.'

The resignation in her voice and manner while she spoke was the resignation of despair. It gave her an unnatural self-possession, which altered her, in the eyes of Uncle Joseph, almost past recognition. He looked at her in undisguised alarm.

'No!' he said, 'we will not walk on; we will walk back to the dungeon-house; we will make another plan; we will try to get at this devil's imp of a letter in some other way. I care for no Munders, no housekeepers, no Betzees—I! I care for nothing, but the getting you the one thing you want, and the taking you home again as easy in your mind as I am myself. Come! let us go back.'

'It is too late to go back.'

'How too late? Ah, dismal, dingy, dungeon-house of the devil, how I hate you!' cried Uncle Joseph, looking back over the prospect, and shaking both his fists at Porthgenna Tower.

'It is too late, uncle,' she repeated. 'Too late, because the opportunity is lost; too late, because if I could bring it back, I dare not go near the Myrtle Room again. My last hope was to change the hiding-place of the letter—and that last hope I have given up. I have only one object in life left now; you may help me in it; but I cannot tell you how unless you come on with me at once—unless you say nothing more about going back to Porthgenna Tower.'

Uncle Joseph began to expostulate. His niece stopped him in the middle of a sentence, by touching him on the shoulder, and pointing to a particular spot on the darkening slope of the moor below them.

'Look!' she said, 'there is somebody on the path behind us. Is it a boy or a man?'

Uncle Joseph looked through the fading light, and saw a figure at some little distance. It seemed like the figure of a boy, and he was apparently engaged in digging on the moor.

'Let us turn round, and go on at once,' pleaded Sarah, before the old man could answer her. 'I can't say what I want to say to you, uncle, until we are safe under shelter at the inn.'

They went on, until they reached the highest ground on the moor. There they stopped, and looked back again. The rest of their way lay down hill; and the spot on which they stood was the last point from which a view could be obtained of Porthgenna Tower.

'We have lost sight of the boy,' said Uncle Joseph, looking over the ground below them.

Sarah's younger and sharper eyes bore witness to the truth of her uncle's words—the view over the moor was lonely now, in every direction, as far as she could see. Before going on again, she moved a little away from the old man, and looked at the tower of the ancient house, rising heavy and black in the dim light, with the dark sea-background stretching behind it like a wall. 'Never again!' she whispered to herself. 'Never, never, never again!' Her eyes wandered away to the church, and to the cemetery-inclosure by its side, barely distinguishable now in the shadows of the coming night. 'Wait for me a little longer,' she said, looking towards the burial-ground with straining eyes, and pressing her hand on her bosom, over the place where the book of Hymns lay hid. 'My wanderings are nearly at an end: the day for my coming home again is not far off!'

The tears filled her eyes, and shut out the view. She rejoined her uncle, and taking his arm again, drew him rapidly a few steps along the downward path—then checked herself, as if struck by a sudden suspicion, and walked back a few paces to the highest ridge of the ground. 'I am not sure,' she said, replying to her companion's look of surprise—'I am not sure whether we have seen the last yet of that boy who was digging on the moor.'

As the words passed her lips, a figure stole out from behind one of the large fragments of granite-rock which were scattered over the waste on all sides of them. It was once more the figure of the boy, and again he began to dig, without the slightest apparent reason, on the barren ground at his feet.

'Yes, yes, I see,' said Uncle Joseph, as his niece eagerly directed his attention to the suspicious figure. 'It is the same boy, and he is digging still—and, if you please, what of that?'

Sarah did not attempt to answer. 'Let us get on,' she said, hurriedly. 'Let us get on as fast as we can to the inn.'

They turned again, and took the downward path before them. In less than a minute they had lost sight of Porthgenna Tower, of the old church, and of the whole of the western view. Still, though there was now nothing but the blank darkening moorland to look back at, Sarah persisted in stopping at frequent intervals, as long as there was any light left, to glance behind her. She made no remark, she offered no excuse for thus delaying the journey back to the inn. It was only when they arrived within sight of the lights of the post-town that she ceased looking back, and that she spoke to her companion. The few words she addressed to him amounted to nothing more than a request that he would ask for a private sitting-room, as soon as they reached their place of sojourn for the night.

They ordered beds at the inn, and were shown into the best parlour to wait for supper. The moment they were alone, Sarah drew a chair close to the old man's side, and whispered these words in his ear:—

'Uncle! we have been followed every step of the way from Porthgenna Tower to this place.'

'So! so! And how do you know that?' inquired Uncle Joseph.

'Hush! Somebody may be listening at the door, somebody may be creeping under the window. You noticed that boy who was digging on the moor?——'

'Bah! Why, Sarah! do you frighten yourself, do you try to frighten me about a boy?'

'O, not so loud! not so loud! They have laid a trap for us. Uncle! I suspected it when we first entered the doors of Porthgenna Tower; I am sure of it now. What did all that whispering mean between the housekeeper and the steward, when we first got into the hall? I watched their faces, and I know they were talking about us. They were not half surprised enough at seeing us, not half surprised enough at hearing what we wanted. Don't laugh at me, uncle! There is real danger: it is no fancy of mine. The keys—come closer—the keys of the north rooms have got new labels on them; the doors have all been numbered. Think of that! Think of the whispering when we came in, and the whispering afterwards, in the housekeeper's room, when you got up to go away. You noticed the sudden change in that man's behaviour, after the housekeeper spoke to him—you must have noticed it? They let us in too easily, and they let us out too easily. No, no! I am not deluding myself. There was some secret motive for letting us into the house, and some secret motive for letting us out again. That boy on the moor betrays it, if nothing else does. I saw him following us all the way here, as plainly as I see you. I am not frightened without reason, this time. As surely as we two are together in this room, there is a trap laid for us by the people at Porthgenna Tower!'

'A trap? What trap? And how? and why? and wherefore?' inquired Uncle Joseph, expressing bewilderment by waving both his hands rapidly to and fro close before his eyes.

'They want to make me speak, they want to follow me, they want to find out where I go, they want to ask me questions,' she answered, trembling violently. 'Uncle! you remember what

I told you of those crazed words I said to Mrs Frankland—
I ought to have cut my tongue out rather than have spoken
them! They have done dreadful mischief—I am certain of it—
dreadful mischief already. I have made myself suspected!
I shall be questioned, if Mrs Frankland finds me out again. She
will try to find me out—we shall be inquired after here—we
must destroy all trace of where we go to next—we must make
sure that the people at this inn can answer no questions—O,
Uncle Joseph! whatever we do, let us make sure of that!'

'Good,' said the old man, nodding his head with a perfectly
self-satisfied air. 'Be quite easy, my child, and leave it to me to
make sure. When you are gone to bed, I shall send for the landlord, and I shall say, "Get us a little carriage, if you please, sir,
to take us back again to-morrow to the coach for Truro."'

'No, no, no! we must not hire a carriage here.'

'And I say, yes, yes, yes! We will hire a carriage here, because
I will, first of all, make sure with the landlord. Listen. I shall say
to him, "If there come after us, people, with inquisitive looks in
their eyes and uncomfortable questions in their mouths—if
you please, sir, hold your tongue." Then, I shall wink my eye,
I shall lay my finger, so, to the side of my nose, I shall give one
little laugh that means much—and, crick! crack! I have made
sure of the landlord! and there is an end of it!'

'We must not trust the landlord, uncle: we must not trust
anybody. When we leave this place to-morrow, we must leave
it on foot, and take care that no living soul follows us. Look!
here is a map of West Cornwall hanging up on the wall, with
roads and cross-roads all marked on it. We may find out,
beforehand, what direction we ought to walk in. A night's rest
will give me all the strength I want; and we have no luggage that
we cannot carry. You have nothing but your knapsack, and
I have nothing but the little carpet-bag you lent me. We can
walk six, seven, even ten miles, with resting by the way. Come
here, and look at the map—pray, pray come and look at the
map!'

Protesting against the abandonment of his own project,
which he declared, and sincerely believed, to be perfectly
adapted to meet the emergency in which they were placed,
Uncle Joseph joined his niece in examining the map. A little

beyond the post-town, a cross-road was marked, running
northward at right angles with the highway that led to Truro,
and conducting to another road, which looked large enough to
be a coach-road, and which led through a town of sufficient
importance to have its name printed in capital letters. On
discovering this, Sarah proposed that they should follow the
cross-road (which did not appear on the map to be more than
five or six miles long) on foot, abstaining from taking any conveyance until they had arrived at the town marked in capital
letters. By pursuing this course, they would destroy all trace of
their progress, after leaving the post-town—unless, indeed,
they were followed on foot from this place, as they had been
followed over the moor. In the event of any fresh difficulty of
that sort occurring, Sarah had no better remedy to propose
than lingering on the road till after nightfall, and leaving it to
the darkness to baffle the vigilance of any person who might be
watching in the distance to see where they went.

Uncle Joseph shrugged his shoulders resignedly when his
niece gave her reasons for wishing to continue the journey on
foot. 'There is much tramping through dust, and much looking
behind us, and much spying and peeping, and suspecting, and
roundabout walking in all this,' he said. 'It is by no means so
easy, my child, as making sure of the landlord, and sitting at
our ease on the cushions of the stage coach. But if you will have
it so, so shall it be. What you please, Sarah; what you please—
that is all the opinion of my own that I allow myself to have till
we are back again at Truro, and are resting for good and all at
the end of our journey.'

'At the end of *your* journey, uncle: I dare not say at the end of
mine.'

Those few words changed the old man's face in an instant.
His eyes fixed reproachfully on his niece, his ruddy cheeks lost
their colour, his restless hands dropped suddenly to his sides.
'Sarah!' he said, in a low, quiet tone, which seemed to have no
relation to the voice in which he spoke on ordinary occasions—
'Sarah! have you the heart to leave me again?'

'Have I the courage to stay in Cornwall? That is the question to ask me, uncle. If I had only my own heart to consult,
O! how gladly I should live under your roof—live under it, if

you would let me, to my dying day! But my lot is not cast for
such rest and such happiness as that. The fear that I have of
being questioned by Mrs Frankland drives me away from
Porthgenna, away from Cornwall, away from you. Even my
dread of the letter being found is hardly so great now, as
my dread of being traced and questioned. I have said what
I ought not to have said already. If I find myself in Mrs Frankland's presence again, there is nothing that she might not
draw out of me. O, my God! to think of that kind-hearted,
lovely young woman, who brings happiness with her wherever she goes, bringing terror to *me!* Terror when her pitying
eyes look at me; terror when her kind voice speaks to me;
terror when her tender hand touches mine! Uncle! when
Mrs Frankland comes to Porthgenna, the very children will
crowd about her—every creature in that poor village will be
drawn towards the light of her beauty and her goodness, as if
it was the sunshine of Heaven itself; and I—I, of all living
beings—must shun her as if she was a pestilence! The day
when she comes into Cornwall is the day when I must go out
of it—the day when we two must say farewell. Don't, don't
add to my wretchedness, by asking me if I have the heart to
leave you! For my dead mother's sake, Uncle Joseph, believe
that I am grateful, believe that it is not my own will that takes
me away when I leave you again.' She sank down on a sofa
near her, laid her head, with one long, deep sigh, wearily on
the pillow, and spoke no more.

The tears gathered thick in Uncle Joseph's eyes as he sat
down by her side. He took one of her hands, and patted and
stroked it as though he were soothing a little child. 'I will bear
it as well as I can, Sarah,' he whispered, faintly, 'and I will say
no more. You will write to me sometimes, when I am left all
alone? You will give a little time to Uncle Joseph, for the poor
dead mother's sake?'

She turned towards him suddenly, and threw both her arms
round his neck with a passionate energy that was strangely at
variance with her naturally quiet self-repressed character.
'I will write often, dear; I will write always,' she whispered, with
her head on his bosom. 'If I am ever in any trouble or danger,
you shall know it.' She stopped confusedly, as if the freedom of

her own words and actions terrified her, unclasped her arms, and, turning abruptly away from the old man, hid her face in her hands. The tyranny of the restraint that governed her whole life, was all expressed—how sadly, how eloquently!—in that one little action.

Uncle Joseph rose from the sofa, and walked gently backwards and forwards in the room, looking anxiously at his niece, but not speaking to her. After a while the servant came in to prepare the table for supper. It was a welcome interruption, for it obliged Sarah to make an effort to recover her self-possession. After the meal was over, the uncle and niece separated at once for the night, without venturing to exchange another word on the subject of their approaching separation.

When they met the next morning, the old man had not recovered his spirits. Although he tried to speak as cheerfully as usual, there was something strangely subdued and quiet about him in voice, look, and manner. Sarah's heart smote her as she saw how sadly he was altered by the prospect of their parting. She said a few words of consolation and hope; but he only waved his hand negatively, in his quaint foreign manner, and hastened out of the room to find the landlord and ask for the bill.

Soon after breakfast, to the surprise of the people at the inn, they set forth to continue their journey on foot, Uncle Joseph carrying his knapsack on his back, and his niece's carpet-bag in his hand. When they arrived at the turning that led into the cross-road, they both stopped and looked back. This time they saw nothing to alarm them. There was no living creature visible on the broad highway over which they had been walking for the last quarter of an hour, after leaving the inn.

'The way is clear,' said Uncle Joseph, as they turned into the cross-road. 'Whatever might have happened yesterday, there is nobody following us now.'

'Nobody that we can see,' answered Sarah. 'But I distrust the very stones by the roadside. Let us look back often, uncle, before we allow ourselves to feel secure. The more I think of it, the more I dread the snare that is laid for us by those people at Porthgenna Tower.'

'You say *us*, Sarah. Why should they lay a snare for *me?*'

'Because they have seen you in my company. You will be safer from them when we are parted; and that is another reason, Uncle Joseph, why we should bear the misfortune of our separation as patiently as we can.'

'Are you going far, very far away, Sarah, when you leave me?'

'I dare not stop on my journey till I can feel that I am lost in the great world of London. Don't look at me so sadly! I shall never forget my promise; I shall never forget to write. I have friends—not friends like you, but still friends—to whom I can go. I can feel safe from discovery nowhere but in London. My danger is great—it is, it is, indeed! I know, from what I have seen at Porthgenna, that Mrs Frankland has an interest already in finding me out; and I am certain that this interest will be increased tenfold when she hears (as she is sure to hear) of what happened yesterday in the house. If they *should* trace you to Truro, O, be careful, uncle! be careful how you deal with them; be careful how you answer their questions!'

'I will answer nothing, my child. But tell me—for I want to know all the little chances that there are of your coming back—tell me, if Mrs Frankland finds the letter, what shall you do then?'

At that question Sarah's hand, which had been resting languidly on her uncle's arm while they walked together, closed on it suddenly. 'Even if Mrs Frankland gets into the Myrtle Room,' she said, stopping and looking affrightedly about her while she replied, 'she may not find the letter. It is folded up so small; it is hidden in such an unlikely place.'

'But if she does find it?'

'If she does, there will be more reason than ever for my being miles and miles away.'

As she gave that answer, she raised both her hands to her heart, and pressed them firmly over it. A slight distortion passed rapidly across her features; her eyes closed; her face flushed all over—then turned paler again than ever. She drew out her pocket-handkerchief, and passed it several times over her face, on which the perspiration had gathered thickly. The old man, who had looked behind him when his niece stopped, under the impression that she had just seen somebody following them, observed this latter action, and asked if she felt too hot. She shook her head, and took his arm again to go on, breathing, as he fancied, with some difficulty. He proposed that they should sit down by the roadside and rest a little; but she only answered, 'Not yet.' So they went on for another half hour; then turned to look behind them again, and, still seeing nobody, sat down for a little while to rest on a bank by the wayside.

After stopping twice more at convenient resting-places, they reached the end of the cross-road. On the highway to which it led them, they were overtaken by a man driving an empty cart, who offered to give them a lift as far as the next town. They accepted the proposal gratefully; and, arriving at the town, after a drive of half an hour, were set down at the door of the principal inn. Finding on inquiry at this place that they were too late for the coach, they took a private conveyance, which brought them to Truro late in the afternoon. Throughout the whole of the journey, from the time when they left the post-town of Porthgenna to the time when they stopped, by Sarah's desire, at the coach-office in Truro, they had seen nothing to excite the smallest suspicion that their movements were being observed. None of the people whom they saw in the inhabited places, or whom they passed on the road, appeared to take more than the most casual notice of them.

It was five o'clock when they entered the office at Truro to ask about conveyances running in the direction of Exeter. They were informed that a coach would start in an hour's time, and that another coach would pass through Truro at eight o'clock the next morning.

'You will not go to-night?' pleaded Uncle Joseph. 'You will wait, my child, and rest with me till to-morrow?'

'I had better go, uncle, while I have some little resolution left,' was the sad answer.

'But you are so pale, so tired, so weak.'

'I shall never be stronger than I am now. Don't set my own heart against me! It is hard enough to go without that.'

Uncle Joseph sighed, and said no more. He led the way across the road and down the bye-street to his house. The cheerful man in the shop was polishing a piece of wood behind the counter, sitting in the same position in which Sarah had seen him when she first looked through the window on her arrival at Truro. He had good news for his master of orders received, but Uncle Joseph listened absently to all that his shopman said, and hastened into the little back parlour without the faintest reflection of its customary smile on his face. 'If I had no shop and no orders, I might go away with you, Sarah,' he said when he and his niece were alone. 'Aïe! Aïe! the setting out on this journey has been the only happy part of it. Sit down and rest, my child. I must put my best face upon it, and get you some tea.'

When the tea-tray had been placed on the table, he left the room, and returned, after an absence of some little time, with a basket in his hand. When the porter came to carry the luggage to the coach office, he would not allow the basket to be taken away at the same time, but sat down and placed it between his feet while he occupied himself in pouring out a cup of tea for his niece.

The musical-box still hung at his side in its travelling-case of leather. As soon as he had poured out the cup of tea, he unbuckled the strap, removed the covering from the box, and placed it on the table near him. His eyes wandered hesitatingly towards Sarah, as he did this: he leaned forward, his lips trembling a little, his hand trifling uneasily with the empty leather-case that now lay on his knees, and said to her in low, unsteady tones:—

'You will hear a little farewell song of Mozart? It may be a long time, Sarah, before he can play to you again. A little farewell song, my child, before you go?'

His hand stole up gently from the leather-case to the table, and set the box playing the same air that Sarah had heard on the evening when she entered the parlour, after her journey from Somersetshire, and found him sitting alone listening to the music. What depths of sorrow there were now in those few simple notes! What mournful memories of past times gathered and swelled in the heart at the bidding of that one little plaintive melody! Sarah could not summon the courage to lift her eyes to the old man's face—they might have betrayed to him that she was thinking of the days when the box that he treasured so dearly, played the air they were listening to now, by the bedside of his dying child.

The stop had not been set, and the melody, after it had come to an end, began again. But now, after the first few bars, the notes succeeded one another more and more slowly—the air grew less and less recognisable—dropped at last to three notes, following each other at long intervals—then ceased altogether. The chain that governed the action of the machinery had all run out: Mozart's farewell song was silenced on a sudden, like a voice that had broken down.

The old man started, looked earnestly at his niece, and threw the leather-case over the box as if he desired to shut out the sight of it. 'The music stopped so,' he whispered to himself, in his own language, 'when little Joseph died! Don't go!' he added quickly, in English, almost before Sarah had time to feel surprised at the singular change that had taken place in his voice and manner. 'Don't go! Think better of it, and stop with me.'

'I have no choice, uncle, but to leave you—indeed, indeed I have not! You don't think me ungrateful? Comfort me at the last moment by telling me that!'

He pressed her hand in silence, and kissed her on both cheeks. 'My heart is very heavy for you, Sarah,' he said. 'The fear has come to me that it is not for your own good that you are going away from Uncle Joseph now!'

'I have no choice,' she sadly repeated, 'no choice but to leave you.'

'It is time then to get the parting over.' The cloud of doubt and fear that had altered his face, from the moment when the music came to its untimely end, seemed to darken, when he had said those words. He took up the basket which he had kept so carefully at his feet, and led the way out in silence.

They were barely in time: the driver was mounting to his seat when they got to the coach office. 'God preserve you, my child, and send you back to me soon, safe and well. Take the basket on your lap; there are some little things in it for your journey.' His voice faltered at the last word, and Sarah felt his lips pressed on her hand. The next instant the door was closed, and she saw him dimly through her tears standing among the idlers on the pavement, who were waiting to see the coach drive off.

By the time they were a little way out of the town, she was able to dry her eyes and look into the basket. It contained a pot of jam and a horn spoon, a small inlaid workbox from the stock in the shop, a piece of foreign-looking cheese, a French roll, and a little paper-packet of money, with the words, 'Don't be angry!' written on it, in Uncle Joseph's hand. Sarah closed the cover of the basket again, and drew down her veil. She had not felt the sorrow of the parting in all its bitterness until that moment. Oh, how hard it was to be banished from the sheltering home which was offered to her by the one friend she had left in the world!

While that thought was in her mind, the old man was just closing the door of his lonely parlour. His eyes wandered to the tea-tray on the table and to Sarah's empty cup, and he whispered to himself in his own language again:

'The music stopped so, when little Joseph died!'

BOOK V

CHAPTER I

AN OLD FRIEND AND A NEW SCHEME

IN declaring, positively, that the boy whom she had seen digging on the moor had followed her uncle and herself to the post-town of Porthgenna, Sarah had asserted the literal truth. Jacob had tracked them to the inn, had waited a little while about the door, to ascertain if there was any likelihood of their continuing their journey that evening, and had then returned to Porthgenna Tower to make his report, and to claim his promised reward.

The same night, the housekeeper and the steward devoted themselves to the joint production of a letter to Mrs Frankland, informing her of all that had taken place, from the time when the visitors first made their appearance, to the time when the gardener's boy had followed them to the door of the inn. The composition was plentifully garnished throughout with the flowers of Mr Munder's rhetoric, and was, by a necessary consequence, inordinately long as a narrative, and hopelessly confused as a statement of facts.

It is unnecessary to say that the letter, with all its faults and absurdities, was read by Mrs Frankland with the deepest interest. Her husband and Mr Orridge, to both of whom she communicated its contents, were as much amazed and perplexed by it as she was herself. Although the discovery of Mrs Jazeph's departure for Cornwall had led them to consider it within the range of possibility that she might appear at Porthgenna, and although the housekeeper had been written to by Rosamond under the influence of that idea, neither she nor her husband were quite prepared for such a speedy confirmation of their suspicions as they had now received. Their astonishment, however, on first ascertaining the general purport of the letter, was as nothing compared with their astonishment when they came to those particular passages in it

which referred to Uncle Joseph. The fresh element of compli-
cation imparted to the thickening mystery of Mrs Jazeph and
the Myrtle Room, by the entrance of the foreign stranger on the
scene, and by his intimate connexion with the extraordinary
proceedings that had taken place in the house, fairly baffled
them all. The letter was read again and again; was critically
dissected paragraph by paragraph: was carefully annotated by
the doctor, for the purpose of extricating all the facts that it
contained from the mass of unmeaning words in which
Mr Munder had artfully and lengthily involved them; and was
finally pronounced, after all the pains that had been taken to
render it intelligible, to be the most mysterious and bewildering document that mortal pen had ever produced.

The first practical suggestion, after the letter had been laid
aside in despair, emanated from Rosamond. She proposed
that her husband and herself (the baby included, as a matter
of course) should start at once for Porthgenna, to question
the servants minutely about the proceedings of Mrs Jazeph
and the foreign stranger who had accompanied her, and to
examine the premises on the north side of the house, with a
view to discovering a clue to the locality of the Myrtle Room,
while events were still fresh in the memories of witnesses. The
plan thus advocated, however excellent in itself, was opposed
by Mr Orridge on medical grounds. Mrs Frankland had
caught cold by exposing herself too carelessly to the air, on
first leaving her room, and the doctor refused to grant her permission to travel for at least a week to come, if not for a longer
period.

The next proposal came from Mr Frankland. He declared it
to be perfectly clear to his mind, that the only chance of
penetrating the mystery of the Myrtle Room, rested entirely on
the discovery of some means of communicating with
Mrs Jazeph. He suggested that they should not trouble
themselves to think of anything unconnected with the accomplishment of this purpose; and he proposed that the servant
then in attendance on him at West Winston—a man who had
been in his employment for many years, and whose zeal,
activity, and intelligence could be thoroughly depended on—
should be sent to Porthgenna forthwith, to start the necessary

inquiries, and to examine the premises carefully on the north side of the house.

This advice was immediately acted on. At an hour's notice, the servant started for Cornwall, thoroughly instructed as to what he was to do, and well supplied with money, in case he found it necessary to employ many persons in making the proposed inquiries. In due course of time he sent a report of his proceedings to his master. It proved to be of a most discouraging nature.

All trace of Mrs Jazeph and her companion had been lost at the post-town of Porthgenna. Investigations had been made in every direction, but no reliable information had been obtained. People in totally different parts of the country declared readily enough that they had seen two persons answering to the description of the lady in the dark dress and the old foreigner; but when they were called upon to state the direction in which the two strangers were travelling, the answers received turned out to be of the most puzzling and contradictory kind. No pains had been spared, no necessary expenditure of money had been grudged; but, so far, no results of the slightest value had been obtained. Whether the lady and the foreigner had gone east, west, north or south, was more than Mr Frankland's servant, at the present stage of the proceedings, could take it on himself to say.

The report of the examination of the north rooms was not more satisfactory. Here, again, nothing of any importance could be discovered. The servant had ascertained that there were twenty-two rooms on the uninhabited side of the house:—six on the ground floor opening into the deserted garden: eight on the first floor, and eight above that, on the second story. He had examined all the doors carefully from top to bottom, and had come to the conclusion that none of them had been opened. The evidence afforded by the lady's own actions led to nothing. She had, if the testimony of the servant could be trusted, dropped the keys on the floor of the hall. She was found, as the housekeeper and the steward asserted, lying, in a fainting condition, at the top of the landing of the first flight of stairs. The door opposite to her, in this position, showed no more traces of having been recently opened than any of the

other doors of the other twenty-one rooms. Whether the room
to which she wished to gain access was one of the eight on the
first floor, or whether she had fainted on her way up to the
higher range of eight rooms on the second floor, it was
impossible to determine.

The only conclusions that could be fairly drawn from the
events that had taken place in the house, were two in number.
First, it might be taken for granted, that the lady had been
disturbed before she had been able to use the keys to gain
admission to the Myrtle Room. Secondly, it might be assumed
from the position in which she was found on the stairs, and
from the evidence relating to the dropping of the keys, that the
Myrtle Room was not on the ground floor, but was one of the
sixteen rooms situated on the first and second stories. Beyond
this, the writer of the report had nothing further to mention,
except that he had ventured to decide on waiting at
Porthgenna, in the event of his master having any further
instructions to communicate.

What was to be done next? That was necessarily the first
question suggested by the servant's announcement of the
unsuccessful result of his inquiries at Porthgenna. How it was
to be answered, was not very easy to discover. Mrs Frankland
had nothing to suggest, Mr Frankland had nothing to suggest,
the doctor had nothing to suggest. The more industriously they
all three hunted through their minds for a new idea, the less
chance there seemed to be of their succeeding in finding one.
At last, Rosamond proposed, in despair, that they should seek
the advice of some fourth person who could be depended on;
and asked her husband's permission to write a confidential
statement of their difficulties to the Vicar of Long Beckley.
Doctor Chennery was their oldest friend and adviser; he had
known them both as children; he was well acquainted with the
history of their families: he felt a fatherly interest in their
fortunes; and he possessed that invaluable quality of plain
clear-headed common sense, which marked him out as the
very man who would be most likely, as well as most willing, to
help them.

Mr Frankland readily agreed to his wife's suggestion; and
Rosamond wrote immediately to Doctor Chennery, informing

him of everything that had happened since Mrs Jazeph's first introduction to her, and asking him for his opinion on the course of proceeding which it would be best for her husband and herself to adopt, in the difficulty in which they were now placed. By return of post an answer was received, which amply justified Rosamond's reliance on her old friend. Doctor Chennery not only sympathised heartily with the eager curiosity which Mrs Jazeph's language and conduct had excited in the mind of his correspondent, but he had also a plan of his own to propose for ascertaining the position of the Myrtle Room.

The vicar prefaced his suggestion by expressing a strong opinion against instituting any further search after Mrs Jazeph. Judging by the circumstances, as they were related to him, he considered that it would be the merest waste of time to attempt to find her out. Accordingly, he passed from that part of the subject at once, and devoted himself to the consideration of the more important question, How Mr and Mrs Frankland were to proceed in the endeavour to discover for themselves the mystery of the Myrtle Room?

On this point, Doctor Chennery entertained a conviction of the strongest kind; and he warned Rosamond, beforehand, that she must expect to be very much surprised when he came to the statement of it. Taking it for granted that she and her husband could not hope to find out where the room was, unless they were assisted by some one better acquainted than themselves with the old local arrangements of the interior of Porthgenna Tower, the vicar declared it to be his opinion that there was only one individual living who could afford them the information they wanted, and that this person was no other than Rosamond's own cross-grained relative, Andrew Treverton.

This startling opinion Doctor Chennery supported by two reasons. In the first place, Andrew was the only surviving member of the elder generation who had lived at Porthgenna Tower, in the byegone days when all traditions connected with the north rooms were still fresh in the memories of the inhabitants of the house. The people who lived in it now, were strangers who had been placed in their situations by

Mr Frankland's father; and the servants employed in former days by Captain Treverton were dead or dispersed. The one available person, therefore, whose recollections were likely to be of any service to Mr and Mrs Frankland, was indisputably the brother of the old owner of Porthgenna Tower.

In the second place, there was the chance, even if Andrew Treverton's memory was not to be trusted, that he might possess written or printed information relating to the locality of the Myrtle Room. By his father's will—which had been made when Andrew was a young man just going to college, and which had not been altered at the period of his departure from England, or at any after-time—he had inherited the choice old collection of books in the library at Porthgenna. Supposing that he still preserved these heir-looms, it was highly probable that there might exist among them some plan, or some description of the house as it was in the olden time, which would supply all the information that was wanted. Here, then, was another valid reason for believing that if a clue to the position of the Myrtle Room existed anywhere, Andrew Treverton was the man to lay his hand on it.

Assuming it, therefore, to be proved that the surly old misanthrope was the only person who could be profitably applied to for the requisite information, the next question was, How to communicate with him? The vicar understood perfectly that after Andrew's inexcusably heartless conduct towards her father and mother, it was quite impossible for Rosamond to address any direct application to him. That obstacle, however, might be surmounted by making the necessary communication proceed from Doctor Chennery. Heartily as the vicar disliked Andrew Treverton personally, and strongly as he disapproved of the old misanthrope's principles, he was willing to set aside his own antipathies and objections to serve the interests of his young friends; and he expressed his perfect readiness to write and recall himself to Andrew's recollection, and to ask, as if it was a matter of antiquarian curiosity, for information on the subject of the north side of Porthgenna Tower—including, of course, a special request to be made acquainted with the names by which the rooms had been individually known in former days.

In making this offer, the vicar frankly acknowledged that he thought the chances were very much against his receiving any answer at all to his application, no matter how carefully he might word it, with a view to humouring Andrew's churlish peculiarities. However, considering that, in the present posture of affairs, a forlorn hope was better than no hope at all, he thought it was at least worth while to make the attempt, on the plan which he had just suggested. If Mr and Mrs Frankland could devise any better means of opening communications with Andrew Treverton, or if they had discovered any new method of their own for obtaining the information of which they stood in need, Doctor Chennery was perfectly ready to set aside his own opinions, and to defer to theirs.

A very brief consideration of the vicar's friendly letter convinced Rosamond and her husband that they had no choice but gratefully to accept the offer which it contained. The chances were certainly against the success of the proposed application; but were they more unfavourable than the chances against the success of any unaided investigations at Porthgenna? There was, at least, a faint hope of Doctor Chennery's request for information producing some results; but there seemed no hope at all of penetrating a mystery connected with one room only, by dint of wandering, in perfect ignorance of what to search for, through two ranges of rooms which reached the number of sixteen. Influenced by these considerations, Rosamond wrote back to the vicar to thank him for his kindness, and to beg that he would communicate with Andrew Treverton, as he had proposed, without a moment's delay.

Doctor Chennery immediately occupied himself in the composition of the important letter, taking care to make the application on purely antiquarian grounds, and accounting for his assumed curiosity on the subject of the interior of Porthgenna Tower, by referring to his former knowledge of the Treverton family, and to his natural interest in the old house with which their name and fortunes had been so closely connected. After appealing to Andrew's early recollections for the information that he wanted, he ventured a step farther, and alluded to the library of old books, mentioning his own idea that there might be found among them some plan or verbal description of the house, which might prove to be of the greatest service, in the event of Mr Treverton's memory not having preserved all particulars in connection with the names and positions of the north rooms. In conclusion, he took the liberty of mentioning that the loan of any document of the kind to which he had alluded, or the permission to have extracts made from it, would be thankfully acknowledged as a great favour conferred; and he added, in a postscript, that, in order to save Mr Treverton all trouble, a messenger would call for any answer he might be disposed to give, the day after the delivery of the letter. Having completed the application in these terms, the vicar inclosed it under cover to his man of business in London, with directions that it was to be delivered by a trustworthy person, and that the messenger was to call again the next morning to know if there was any answer.

Three days after this letter had been despatched to its destination—at which time no tidings of any sort had been received from Doctor Chennery—Rosamond at last obtained her medical attendant's permission to travel. Taking leave of Mr Orridge, with many promises to let him know what progress they made towards discovering the Myrtle Room, Mr and Mrs Frankland turned their backs on West Winston, and, for the third time, started on the journey to Porthgenna Tower.

CHAPTER II

THE BEGINNING OF THE END

IT was baking day in the establishment of Mr Andrew Treverton, when the messenger intrusted with Doctor Chennery's letter found his way to the garden-door of the cottage at Bayswater. After he had rung three times, he heard a gruff voice, on the other side of the wall, roaring at him to let the bell alone, and asking who he was, and what the devil he wanted.

'A letter for Mr Treverton,' said the messenger, nervously backing away from the door while he spoke.

'Chuck it over the wall, then, and be off with you!' answered the gruff voice.

The messenger obeyed both injunctions. He was a meek, modest, elderly man; and when Nature mixed up the ingredients of his disposition, the capability of resenting injuries was not among them.

The man with the gruff voice—or, to put it in plainer terms, the man Shrowl—picked up the letter, weighed it in his hand, looked at the address on it with an expression of contemptuous curiosity in his bull-terrier's eyes, put it in his waistcoat pocket, and walked round lazily to the kitchen entrance of the cottage.

In the apartment which would probably have been called the pantry, if the house had belonged to civilised tenants, a handmill had been set up; and, at the moment when Shrowl made his way to this room, Mr Treverton was engaged in asserting his independence of all the millers in England by grinding his own corn. He paused irritably in turning the handle of the mill, when his servant appeared at the door.

'What do you come here for?' he asked. 'When the flour's ready, I'll call for you. Don't let's look at each other oftener than we can help! I never set eyes on you, Shrowl, but I ask myself whether, in the whole range of creation, there is any animal as ugly as man? I saw a cat this morning, on the garden wall, and there wasn't a single point in which you would bear comparison with him. The cat's eyes were clear—yours are muddy. The cat's nose was straight—yours is crooked. The cat's whiskers were clean—yours are dirty. The cat's coat fitted him—yours hangs about you like a sack. I tell you again, Shrowl, the species to which you (and I) belong, is the ugliest on the whole face of creation. Don't let us revolt each other by keeping in company any longer. Go away, you last, worst, infirmest freak of Nature—go away!'

Shrowl listened to this complimentary address with an aspect of surly serenity. When it had come to an end, he took the letter from his waistcoat pocket, without condescending to make any reply. He was, by this time, too thoroughly conscious of his own power over his master to attach the smallest importance to anything Mr Treverton might say to him.

'Now you've done your talking, suppose you take a look at that' said Shrowl, dropping the letter carelessly on a deal table* by his master's side. 'It isn't often that people trouble themselves to send letters to you—is it? I wonder whether your niece has took a fancy to write to you? It was put in the papers, the other day, that she'd got a son and heir. Open the letter, and see if it's an invitation to the christening. The company would be sure to want your smiling face at the table to make 'em jolly. Just let me take a grind at the mill, while you go out and get a silver mug. The son and heir expects a mug you know, and his nurse expects half-a-guinea, and his mamma expects all your fortune. What a pleasure to make the three innocent creatures happy! It's shocking to see you pulling wry faces, like that, over the letter. Lord! lord! where can all your natural affection have gone to?——'

'If I only knew where to lay my hand on a gag, I'd cram it into your infernal mouth!' cried Mr Treverton. 'How dare you talk to me about my niece? You wretch! you know I hate her for her mother's sake. What do you mean by harping perpetually on my fortune? Sooner than leave it to the play-actress's child, I'd even leave it to you; and sooner than leave it to you, I would take every farthing of it out in a boat, and bury it for ever at the bottom of the sea!' Venting his dissatisfaction in these strong terms, Mr Treverton snatched up Doctor Chennery's letter, and tore it open in a humour which by no means promised favourably for the success of the vicar's application.

He read the letter with an ominous scowl on his face, which grew darker and darker as he got nearer and nearer to the end. When he came to the signature his humour changed, and he laughed sardonically. 'Faithfully yours, Robert Chennery,' he repeated to himself. 'Yes! faithfully mine, if I humour your whim. And what if I don't, Parson?' He paused, and looked at the letter again, the scowl reappearing on his face as he did so. 'There's a lie of some kind lurking about under these lines of fair writing,' he muttered suspiciously. '*I* am not one of his congregation: the law gives him no privilege of imposing on *me*. What does he mean by making the attempt?' He stopped again, reflected a little, looked up suddenly at Shrowl, and said to him:—

'Have you lit the oven fire yet?'

'No, I hav'n't,' answered Shrowl.

Mr Treverton examined the letter for the third time—hesitated—then slowly tore it in half, and tossed the two pieces over contemptuously to his servant.

'Light the fire at once,' he said. 'And, if you want paper, there it is for you. Stop!' he added, after Shrowl had picked up the torn letter. 'If anybody comes here to-morrow morning to ask for an answer, tell them I gave you the letter to light the fire with, and say that's the answer.' With those words Mr Treverton returned to the mill, and began to grind at it again, with a grin of malicious satisfaction on his haggard face.

Shrowl withdrew into the kitchen, closed the door, and, placing the torn pieces of the letter together on the dresser, applied himself, with the coolest deliberation, to the business of reading it. When he had gone slowly and carefully through it, from the address at the beginning to the name at the end, he scratched reflectively for a little while at his ragged beard, then folded the letter up carefully and put it in his pocket.

'I'll have another look at it, later in the day,' he thought to himself, tearing off a piece of an old newspaper to light the fire with. 'It strikes me, just at present, that there may be better things done with this letter than burning it.'

Resolutely abstaining from taking the letter out of his pocket again, until all the duties of the household for that day had been duly performed, Shrowl lit the fire, occupied the morning in making and baking the bread, and patiently took his turn afterwards at digging in the kitchen garden. It was four o'clock in the afternoon before he felt himself at liberty to think of his private affairs, and to venture on retiring into solitude with the object of secretly looking over the letter once more.

A second perusal of Doctor Chennery's unlucky application to Mr Treverton helped to confirm Shrowl in his resolution not to destroy the letter. With great pains and perseverance, and much incidental scratching at his beard, he contrived to make himself master of three distinct points in it, which stood out, in his estimation, as possessing prominent and serious importance.

The first point which he contrived to establish clearly in his mind was, that the person who signed the name of Robert Chennery was desirous of examining a plan, or printed account, of the north side of the interior of a certain old house in Cornwall, called Porthgenna Tower. The second point appeared to resolve itself into this:—that Robert Chennery believed some such plan, or printed account, might be found among the collection of books belonging to Mr Treverton. The third point was, that this same Robert Chennery would receive the loan of the plan or printed account as one of the greatest favours that could be conferred on him. Meditating on the latter fact, with an eye exclusively fixed on the contemplation of his own interests, Shrowl arrived at the conclusion that it might be well worth his while, in a pecuniary point of view, to try if he could not privately place himself in a position to oblige Robert Chennery by searching in secret among his master's books. 'It might be worth a five-pound note to me, if I managed it well,' thought Shrowl, putting the letter back in his pocket again, and ascending the stairs thoughtfully to the lumber-rooms at the top of the house.

These rooms were two in number, were entirely unfurnished, and were littered all over with the rare collection of books which had once adorned the library at Porthgenna Tower. Covered with dust, and scattered in all directions and positions over the floor, lay hundreds and hundreds of volumes, cast out of their packing-cases as coals are cast out of their sacks into a cellar. Ancient books, which students would have treasured as priceless, lay in chaotic equality of neglect side by side with modern publications whose chief merit was the beauty of the binding by which they were enclosed. Into this wilderness of scattered volumes Shrowl now wandered, fortified by the supreme self-possession of ignorance, to search resolutely for one particular book, with no other light to direct him than the faint glimmer of the two guiding words, Porthgenna Tower. Having got them firmly fixed in his mind, his next object was to search until he found them printed on the first page of any one of the hundreds of volumes that lay around him. This was, for the time being, emphatically his business in life, and there he now stood, in the largest of the two attics, doggedly prepared to do it.

He cleared away space enough with his feet to enable him to sit down comfortably on the floor, and then began to look over all the books that lay within arm's length of him. Odd volumes of rare editions of the classics, odd volumes of the English historians, odd volumes of plays by the Elizabethan dramatists, books of travel, books of sermons, books of jests, books of natural history, books of sports, turned up in quaint and rapid succession; but no book containing on the title-page the words 'Porthgenna Tower,' rewarded the searching industry of Shrowl for the first ten minutes after he had sat himself down on the floor.

Before removing to another position, and contending with a fresh accumulation of literary lumber, he paused and considered a little with himself, whether there might not be some easier and more orderly method than any he had yet devised of working his way through the scattered mass of volumes which yet remained to be examined. The result of his reflections was, that it would be less confusing to him if he searched through the books in all parts of the room indifferently, regulating his selection of them solely by their various sizes; disposing of all the largest to begin with; then, after stowing them away together, proceeding to the next largest, and so going on until he came down at last to the pocket-volumes. Accordingly, he cleared away another morsel of vacant space, near the wall, and then, trampling over the books as coolly as if they were so many clods of earth on a ploughed field, picked out the largest of all the volumes that lay on the floor.

It was an atlas, Shrowl turned over the maps, reflected, shook his head, and removed the volume to the vacant space which he had cleared close to the wall.

The next largest book was a magnificently bound collection of engraved portraits of distinguished characters. Shrowl saluted the distinguished characters with a grunt of gothic disapprobation, and carried them off to keep the atlas company against the wall.

The third largest book lay under several others. It projected a little at one end, and it was bound in scarlet morocco. In another position, or bound in a quieter colour, it would probably have escaped notice. Shrowl drew it out with some difficulty, opened it with a portentous frown of distrust, looked at the title-page—and suddenly slapped his thigh with a great oath of exultation. There were the very two words of which he was in search, staring him in the face, as it were, with all the emphasis of the largest capital letters.

He took a step towards the door to make sure that his master was not moving in the house; then checked himself and turned back. 'What do I care,' thought Shrowl, 'whether he sees me or not? If it comes to a tussle betwixt us which is to have his own way, I know who's master and who's servant in the house by this time.' Composing himself with that reflection, he turned to the first leaf of the book with the intention of looking it over carefully page by page, from beginning to end.

The first leaf was a blank. The second leaf had an inscription written at the top of it, in faded ink, which contained these words and initials:—'Rare. Only six copies printed. J. A. T.' Below, on the middle of the leaf, was the printed dedication:— 'To John Arthur Treverton, Esquire, Lord of the Manor of Porthgenna, One of his Majesty's Justices of the Peace, FRS*, &c. &c. &c., this work, in which an attempt is made to describe the ancient and honoured Mansion of his Ancestors—' There were many more lines, filled to bursting with all the largest and most obsequious words to be found in the Dictionary; but Shrowl wisely abstained from giving himself the trouble of reading them, and turned over at once to the title-page.

There were the all-important words:—'The History and Antiquities of PORTHGENNA TOWER. From the period of its first erection, to the present time; comprising interesting genea-logical particulars relating to the Treverton family: with an inquiry into the Origin of Gothic Architecture, and a few thoughts on the Theory of Fortification after the period of the Norman Conquest. By the Reverend Job Dark, DD, Rector of Porthgenna. The whole adorned with Portraits, Views, and Plans, executed in the highest style of Art. Not Published. Printed by Spaldock and Grimes, Truro, 1734.'

That was the title-page. The next leaf contained an engraved view of Porthgenna Tower, from the West. Then came several pages, devoted to The Origin of Gothic Architecture. Then more pages, explaining The Norman Theory of Fortification.

These were succeeded by another engraving—Porthgenna Tower, from the East. After that followed more reading, under the title of The Treverton Family; and then came the third engraving—Porthgenna Tower, from the North. Shrowl paused there, and looked with interest at the leaf opposite the print. It only announced more reading still, about the Erection of the Mansion; and this was succeeded by engravings from family portraits in the gallery at Porthgenna. Placing his left thumb between the leaves to mark the place, Shrowl impatiently turned to the end of the book, to see what he could find there. The last leaf contained a plan of the stables; the leaf before that, presented a plan of the north garden; and on the next leaf, turning backward, was the very thing described in Robert Chennery's letter—a plan of the interior arrangement of the north side of the house!

Shrowl's first impulse, on making this discovery, was to carry the book away to the safest hiding-place he could find for it, preparatory to secretly offering it for sale, when the messenger called the next morning for an answer to the letter. A little reflection, however, convinced him that a proceeding of this sort bore a dangerously close resemblance to the act of thieving, and might get him into trouble if the person with whom he desired to deal asked him any preliminary questions touching his right to the volume which he wanted to dispose of. The only alternative that remained was to make the best copy he could of the Plan, and to traffic with that, as a document which the most scrupulous person in the world need not hesitate to purchase.

Resolving, after some consideration, to undergo the trouble of making the copy rather than run the risk of purloining the book, Shrowl descended to the kitchen, took from one of the drawers of the dresser an old stump of a pen, a bottle of ink, and a crumpled half-sheet of dirty letter-paper; and returned to the garret to copy the Plan as he best might. It was of the simplest kind, and it occupied but a small portion of the page; yet it presented to his eyes a hopelessly involved and intricate appearance, when he now examined it for the second time.

The rooms were represented by rows of small squares, with names neatly printed inside them; and the positions of doors, staircases, and passages, were indicated by parallel lines of various lengths and breadths. After much cogitation, frowning, and pulling at his beard, it occurred to Shrowl that the easiest method of copying the Plan would be to cover it with the letter-paper—which, though hardly half the size of the page, was large enough to spread over the engraving on it—and then to trace the lines which he saw through the paper as carefully as he could with his pen and ink. He puffed, and snorted, and grumbled, and got red in the face over his task; but he accomplished it at last—bating certain drawbacks in the shape of blots and smears—in a sufficiently creditable manner; then stopped to let the ink dry and to draw his breath freely, before he attempted to do anything more.

The next obstacle to be overcome, consisted in the difficulty of copying the names of the rooms, which were printed inside the squares. Fortunately for Shrowl, who was one of the clumsiest of mankind in the use of the pen, none of the names were very long. As it was, he found the greatest difficulty in writing them in sufficiently small characters to fit into the squares. One name in particular—that of The Myrtle Room—presented combinations of letters, in the word 'Myrtle,' which tried his patience and his fingers sorely, when he attempted to reproduce them. Indeed, the result, in this case, when he had done his best, was so illegible, even to his eyes, that he wrote the word over again in larger characters at the top of the page, and connected it by a wavering line with the square which represented the Myrtle Room. The same accident happened to him in two other instances, and was remedied in the same way. With the rest of the names, however, he succeeded better; and, when he had finally completed the business of transcription, by writing the title, 'Plan of the North Side,' his copy presented, on the whole, a more respectable appearance than might have been anticipated. After satisfying himself of its accuracy by a careful comparison of it with the original, he folded it up along with Doctor Chennery's letter, and deposited it in his pocket with a hoarse gasp of relief and a grim smile of satisfaction.

The next morning, the garden-door of the cottage presented itself to the public eye in the totally new aspect of standing hospitably ajar; and one of the bare posts had the advantage of being embellished by the figure of Shrowl, who leaned against it easily, with his legs crossed, his hands in his pockets, and his pipe in his mouth, looking out for the return of the messenger who had delivered Doctor Chennery's letter the day before.

CHAPTER III

APPROACHING THE PRECIPICE

TRAVELLING from London to Porthgenna, Mr and Mrs Frankland had stopped, on the ninth of May, at the West Winston station. On the eleventh of June they left it again to continue their journey to Cornwall. On the thirteenth, after resting two nights upon the road, they arrived, towards the evening, at Porthgenna Tower.

There had been storm and rain all the morning; it had lulled towards the afternoon; and at the hour when they reached the house, the wind had dropped, a thick white fog hid the sea from view, and sudden showers fell drearily from time to time over the sodden land. Not even a solitary idler from the village was hanging about the west terrace, as the carriage containing Mr and Mrs Frankland, the baby, and the two servants, drove up to the house.

No one was waiting with the door open to receive the travellers; for all hope of their arriving on that day had been given up, and the ceaseless thundering of the surf, as the stormy sea surged in on the beach beneath, drowned the roll of the carriage-wheels over the terrace road. The driver was obliged to leave his seat, and ring at the bell for admittance. A minute or more elapsed before the door was opened. With the rain falling sullen and steady on the roof of the carriage, with the raw dampness of the atmosphere penetrating through all coverings and defences, with the booming of the surf sounding threateningly near in the dense obscurity of the fog, the young couple waited for admission to their own home, as strangers might have waited who had called at an ill-chosen time.

When the door was opened at last, the master and mistress, whom the servants would have welcomed with the proper congratulations on any other occasion, were now received with the proper apologies instead. Mr Munder, Mrs Pentreath, Betsey, and Mr Frankland's man, all crowded together in the hall, and all begged pardon confusedly for not having been ready at the door, when the carriage drove up. The appearance of the baby changed the conventional excuses of the housekeeper and the maid into conventional expressions of admiration; but the men remained grave and gloomy, and spoke of the miserable weather apologetically, as if the rain and the fog had been of their own making.

The reason for their persistency in dwelling on this one dreary topic, came out while Mr and Mrs Frankland were being conducted up the west staircase. The storm of the morning had been fatal to three of the Porthgenna fishermen, who had been lost with their boat at sea, and whose deaths had thrown the whole village into mourning. The servants had done nothing but talk of the catastrophe ever since the intelligence of it had reached them, early in the afternoon; and Mr Munder now thought it his duty to explain that the absence of the villagers, on the occasion of the arrival of his master and mistress, was entirely attributable to the effect produced among the little community by the wreck of the fishing boat. Under any less lamentable circumstances, the west terrace would have been crowded, and the appearance of the carriage would have been welcomed with cheers.

'Lenny, I almost wish we had waited a little longer before we came here,' whispered Rosamond, nervously pressing her husband's arm. 'It is very dreary and disheartening to return to my first home on such a day as this. That story of the poor fishermen is a sad story, love, to welcome me back to the place of my birth. Let us send the first thing to-morrow morning, and see what we can do for the poor helpless women and children. I shall not feel easy in my mind, after hearing that story, till we have done something to comfort them.'

'I trust you will approve of the repairs, ma'am,' said the housekeeper, pointing to the staircase which led to the second story.

'The repairs?' said Rosamond, absently. 'Repairs! I never hear the word now, without thinking of the north rooms, and of the plans we devised for getting my poor dear father to live in them. Mrs Pentreath, I have a host of questions to ask you and Mr Munder, about all the extraordinary things that happened when the mysterious lady and the incomprehensible foreigner came here. But tell me first—this is the west front, I suppose?— how far are we from the north rooms? I mean, how long would it take us to get to them, if we wanted to go now to that part of the house?'

'Oh, dear me, ma'am, not five minutes!' answered Mrs Pentreath.

'Not five minutes!' repeated Rosamond, whispering to her husband again. 'Do you hear that, Lenny? In five minutes we might be in the Myrtle Room!'

'Yet,' said Mr Frankland, smiling, 'in our present state of ignorance, we are just as far from it, as if we were at West Winston still!'

'I can't think that, Lenny. It may be only my fancy, but now we are on the spot, I feel as if we had driven the mystery into its last hiding place. We are actually in the house that holds the Secret; and nothing will persuade me that we are not half way already towards finding it out. But don't let us stop on this cold landing. Which way are we to go next?'

'This way, ma'am,' said Mr Munder, seizing the first opportunity of placing himself in a prominent position. 'There is a fire in the drawing-room. Will you allow me the honour of leading and conducting you, sir, to the apartment in question?' he added, officiously stretching out his hand to Mr Frankland.

'Certainly not!' interposed Rosamond sharply. She had noticed with her usual quickness of observation, that Mr Munder wanted the delicacy of feeling which ought to have restrained him from staring curiously at his blind master, in her presence; and she was unfavourably disposed towards him in consequence. 'Wherever the apartment in question may happen to be,' she continued with satirical emphasis, 'I will lead Mr Frankland to it, if you please. If you want to make yourself useful, you had better go on before us, and open the door.'

Outwardly crest-fallen, but inwardly indignant, Mr Munder led the way to the drawing-room. The fire burned brightly, the old-fashioned furniture displayed itself to the most picturesque advantage, the paper on the walls looked comfortably mellow, the carpet, faded as it was, felt soft and warm underfoot. Rosamond led her husband to an easy chair by the fireside, and began to feel at home for the first time.

'This looks really comfortable,' she said. 'When we have shut out that dreary white fog, and the candles are lit, and the tea is on the table, we shall have nothing in the world to complain of. You enjoy this nice warm atmosphere, don't you, Lenny? There is a piano in the room, my dear; I can play to you in the evening at Porthgenna, just as I used in London. Nurse, sit down and make yourself and the baby as comfortable as you can. Before we take our bonnets off, I must go away with Mrs Pentreath, and see about the bedrooms. What is your name, you very rosy, good-natured looking girl? Betsey, is it? Well then, Betsey, suppose you go down and get the tea; and we shall like you all the better, if you can contrive to bring us some cold meat with it.' Giving her orders in those good-humoured terms, and not noticing that her husband looked a little uneasy while she was talking so familiarly to a servant, Rosamond left the room in company with Mrs Pentreath.

When she returned, her face and manner were altered: she looked and spoke seriously and quietly.

'I hope I have arranged everything for the best, Lenny,' she said. 'The airiest and largest room, Mrs Pentreath tells me, is the room in which my mother died. But I thought we had better not make use of that: I felt as if it chilled and saddened me only to look at it. Further on, along the passage, there is a room that was my nursery. I almost fancied, when Mrs Pentreath told me she had heard I used to sleep there, that I remembered the pretty little arched doorway leading into the second room—the night-nursery, it used to be called in former days. I have ordered the fire to be lit there, and the beds to be made. There is a third room on the right hand, which communicates with the day-nursery. I think we might manage to establish ourselves very comfortably in the three rooms—if you felt no objection—though they are not so large or so grandly furnished as the company-bedrooms. I will change the arrangement, if you like—but the house looks rather lonesome and dreary, just at first—and my heart warms to the old nursery—and I think we might at least try it, to begin with, don't you, Lenny?'

Mr Frankland was quite of his wife's opinion, and was ready to accede to any domestic arrangements that she might think fit to make. While he was assuring her of this, the tea came up: and the sight of it helped to restore Rosamond to her usual spirits. When the meal was over, she occupied herself in seeing the baby comfortably established for the night, in the room on the right hand which communicated with the day-nursery. That maternal duty performed, she came back to her husband in the drawing-room; and the conversation between them turned— as it almost always turned, now, when they were alone—on the two perplexing subjects of Mrs Jazeph and the Myrtle Room.

'I wish it was not night,' said Rosamond. 'I should like to begin exploring at once. Mind, Lenny, you must be with me in all my investigations. I lend you my eyes, and you give me your advice. You must never lose patience, and never tell me that you can be of no use. How I do wish we were starting on our voyage of discovery at this very moment! But we may make inquiries, at any rate,' she continued, ringing the bell. 'Let us have the housekeeper and the steward up, and try if we can't make them tell us something more than they told us in their letter.'

The bell was answered by Betsey. Rosamond desired that Mr Munder and Mrs Pentreath might be sent upstairs. Betsey having heard Mrs Frankland express her intention of questioning the housekeeper and the steward, guessed why they were wanted, and smiled mysteriously.

'Did *you* see anything of those strange visitors who behaved so oddly?' asked Rosamond, detecting the smile. 'Yes, I am sure you did. Tell us what you saw. We want to hear everything that happened everything, down to the smallest trifle.'

Appealed to in these direct terms, Betsey contrived, with much circumlocution and confusion, to relate what her own personal experience had been of the proceedings of Mrs Jazeph and her foreign companion. When she had done,

Rosamond stopped her on her way to the door, by asking this question:—

'You say the lady was found lying in a fainting fit at the top of the stairs. Have you any notion, Betsey, why she fainted?'

The servant hesitated.

'Come! come!' said Rosamond. 'You have some notion, I can see. Tell us what it is.'

'I'm afraid you will be angry with me, ma'am,' said Betsey, expressing embarrassment by drawing lines slowly with her forefinger on a table at her side.

'Nonsense! I shall only be angry with you, if you won't speak. Why do you think the lady fainted?'

Betsey drew a very long line with her embarrassed forefinger, wiped it afterwards on her apron, and answered:—

'I think she fainted, if you please, ma'am, because she see the ghost.'

'The ghost! What! is there a ghost in the house? Lenny, here is a romance that we never expected. What sort of ghost is it? Let us have the whole story.'

The whole story, as Betsey told it, was not of a nature to afford her hearers any extraordinary information, or to keep them very long in suspense. The ghost was a lady who had been at a remote period the wife of one of the owners of Porthgenna Tower, and who had been guilty of deceiving her husband in some way unknown. She had been condemned in consequence to walk about the north rooms, as long as ever the walls of them held together. She had long curling light brown hair, and very white teeth, and a dimple in each cheek, and was altogether 'awful beautiful' to look at. Her approach was heralded to any mortal creature who was unfortunate enough to fall in her way, by the blowing of a cold wind; and nobody who had once felt that wind had the slightest chance of ever feeling warm again. That was all Betsey knew about the ghost; and it was in her opinion enough to freeze a person's blood only to think of it.

Rosamond smiled, then looked grave again. 'I wish you could have told us a little more,' she said. 'But, as you cannot, we must try Mrs Pentreath and Mr Munder next. Send them up here, if you please, Betsey, as soon as you get down-stairs.'

The examination of the housekeeper and the steward led to no result whatever. Nothing more than they had already communicated in their letter to Mrs Frankland could be extracted from either of them. Mr Munder's dominant idea was, that the foreigner had entered the doors of Porthgenna Tower with felonious ideas on the subject of the family plate. Mrs Pentreath concurred in that opinion, and mentioned, in connection with it, her own private impression that the lady in the quiet dress was an unfortunate person who had escaped from a madhouse. As to giving a word of advice, or suggesting a plan for solving the mystery, neither the housekeeper nor the steward appeared to think that the rendering of any assistance of that sort lay at all within their province. They took their own practical view of the suspicious conduct of the two strangers, and no mortal power could persuade them to look an inch beyond it.

'O, the stupidity, the provoking, impenetrable, pretentious stupidity of respectable English servants!' exclaimed Rosamond, when she and her husband were alone again. 'No help, Lenny, to be hoped for from either of those two people. We have nothing to trust to now but the examination of the house to-morrow; and that resource may fail us, like all the rest. What can Doctor Chennery be about? Why did we not hear from him before we left West Winston yesterday?'

'Patience, Rosamond, patience. We shall see what the post brings to-morrow.'

'Pray don't talk about patience, dear! My stock of that virtue was never a very large one, and it was all exhausted ten days ago, at least. O, the weeks and weeks I have been vainly asking myself—Why should Mrs Jazeph warn me against going into the Myrtle Room? Is she afraid of my discovering a crime? or afraid of my tumbling through the floor? What did she want to do in the room, when she made that attempt to get into it? Why, in the name of wonder, should she know something about this house that I never knew, that my father never knew, that nobody else——'

'Rosamond!' cried Mr Frankland, suddenly changing colour, and starting in his chair—'I think I can guess who Mrs Jazeph is!'

'Good gracious, Lenny! What do you mean?'

'Something in those last words of yours started the idea in my mind, the instant you spoke. Do you remember, when we were staying at St Swithin's on Sea, and talking about the chances for and against our prevailing on your father to live with us here—do you remember, Rosamond, telling me at that time of certain unpleasant associations which he had with the house, and mentioning among them the mysterious disappearance of a servant on the morning of your mother's death?'

Rosamond turned pale at the question. 'How came we never to think of that before?' she said.

'You told me,' pursued Mr Frankland, 'that this servant left a strange letter behind her, in which she confessed that your mother had charged her with the duty of telling a secret to your father—a secret that she was afraid to divulge, and that she was afraid of being questioned about. I am right, am I not, in stating those two reasons as the reasons she gave for her disappearance?'

'Quite right.'

'And your father never heard of her again?'

'Never!'

'It is a bold guess to make, Rosamond, but the impression is strong on my mind that, on the day when Mrs Jazeph came into your room at West Winston, you and that servant met, and *she* knew it!'

'And the Secret, dear—the Secret she was afraid to tell my father?'

'Must be in some way connected with the Myrtle Room.'

Rosamond said nothing in answer. She rose from her chair, and began to walk agitatedly up and down the room. Hearing the rustle of her dress, Leonard called her to him, and, taking her hand, laid his fingers on her pulse, and then lifted them for a moment to her cheek.

'I wish I had waited until to-morrow morning before I told you my idea about Mrs Jazeph,' he said. 'I have agitated you to no purpose whatever, and have spoilt your chance of a good night's rest.'

'No, no! nothing of the kind. O, Lenny, how this guess of

yours adds to the interest, the fearful, breathless interest, we have in tracing that woman, and in finding out the Myrtle Room. Do you think——?'

'I have done with thinking, for the night, my dear; and you must have done with it too. We have said more than enough about Mrs Jazeph already. Change the subject, and I will talk of anything else you please.'

'It is not so easy to change the subject,' said Rosamond, pouting, and moving away to walk up and down the room again.

'Then let us change the place, and make it easier that way. I know you think me the most provokingly obstinate man in the world, but there is reason in my obstinacy, and you will acknowledge as much when you wake to-morrow morning refreshed by a good night's rest. Come, let us give our anxieties a holiday. Take me into one of the other rooms, and let me try if I can guess what it is like by touching the furniture.'

The reference to his blindness which the last words contained brought Rosamond to his side in a moment. 'You always know best,' she said, putting her arm round his neck and kissing him. 'I was looking cross, love, a minute ago, but the clouds are all gone now. We will change the scene, and explore some other room, as you propose.'

She paused, her eyes suddenly sparkled, her colour rose, and she smiled to herself as if some new fancy had that instant crossed her mind.

'Lenny, I will take you where you shall touch a very remarkable piece of furniture indeed,' she resumed, leading him to the door while she spoke. 'We will see if you can tell me at once what it is like. You must not be impatient, mind; and you must promise to touch nothing till you feel me guiding your hand.'

She drew him after her along the passage, opened the door of the room in which the baby had been put to bed, made a sign to the nurse to be silent, and, leading Leonard up to the cot, guided his hand down gently, so as to let the tips of his fingers touch the child's cheek.

'There, sir!' she cried, her face beaming with happiness as she saw the sudden flush of surprise and pleasure which changed her husband's naturally quiet, subdued expression in an instant. 'What do you say to that piece of furniture? Is it a chair, or a table? Or is it the most precious thing in all the house, in all Cornwall, in all England, in all the world? Kiss it, and see which it is—a bust of a baby by a sculptor, or a living cherub by your wife!' She turned, laughing, to the nurse: 'Hannah, you look so serious that I am sure you must be hungry. Have you had your supper yet?' The woman smiled, and answered that she had arranged to go down-stairs, as soon as one of the servants could relieve her in taking care of the child. 'Go at once,' said Rosamond. 'I will stop here and look after the baby. Get your supper, and come back again in half-an-hour.'

When the nurse had left the room, Rosamond placed a chair for Leonard by the side of the cot, and seated herself on a low stool at his knees. Her variable disposition seemed to change again when she did this; her face grew thoughtful, her eyes softened, as they turned, now on her husband, now on the bed in which the child was sleeping by his side. After a minute or two of silence, she took one of his hands, placed it on his knee, and laid her cheek gently down on it.

'Lenny,' she said, rather sadly, 'I wonder whether we are any of us capable of feeling perfect happiness in this world?'

'What makes you ask that question, my dear?'

'I fancy that I could feel perfect happiness, and yet——'

'And yet, what?'

'And yet, it seems as if, with all my blessings, that blessing was never likely to be granted to me. I should be perfectly happy now, but for one little thing. I suppose you can't guess what that thing is?'

'I would rather you told me, Rosamond.'

'Ever since our child was born, love, I have had a little aching at the heart—especially when we are all three together, as we are now—a little sorrow that I can't quite put away from me, on your account.'

'On my account! Lift up your head, Rosamond, and come nearer to me. I feel something on my hand which tells me that you are crying.'

She rose directly, and laid her face close to his. 'My own

love,' she said, clasping her arms fast round him. 'My own heart's darling, you have never seen our child.'

'Yes, Rosamond, I see him with your eyes.'

'Oh, Lenny! I tell you everything I can—I do my best to lighten the cruel, cruel darkness which shuts you out from that lovely little face lying so close to you! But can I tell you how he looks when he first begins to take notice? can I tell you all the thousand pretty things he will do, when he first tries to walk? God has been very merciful to us—but, oh, how much more heavily the sense of your affliction weighs on me, now when I am more to you than your wife, now when I am the mother of your child!'

'And yet, that affliction ought to weigh lightly on your spirits, Rosamond; for you have made it weigh lightly on mine.'

'Have I? Really and truly, have I? It is something noble to live for, Lenny, if I can live for that! It is some comfort to hear you say, as you said just now, that you see with my eyes. They shall always serve you—oh, always! always!—as faithfully as if they were your own. The veriest trifle of a visible thing that I look at with any interest, you shall as good as look at, too. I might have had my own little harmless secrets, dear, with another husband; but, with you, to have even so much as a thought in secret, seems like taking the basest, the cruellest advantage of your blindness. I do love you so, Lenny! I am so much fonder of you now, than I was when we were first married—I never thought I should be, but I am. You are so much handsomer to me, so much cleverer to me, so much more precious to me, in every way. But I am always telling you that, am I not? Do you get tired of hearing me? No? Are you sure of that? Very, very, very sure?' She stopped, and looked at him earnestly, with a smile on her lips, and the tears still glistening in her eyes. Just then, the child stirred a little in his cot, and drew her attention away. She arranged the bed-clothes over him, watched him in silence for a little while, then sat down again on the stool at Leonard's feet. 'Baby has turned his face quite round towards you now,' she said. 'Shall I tell you exactly how he looks, and what his bed is like, and how the room is furnished?'

Without waiting for an answer, she began to describe the child's appearance and position with the marvellous minuteness of a woman's observation. While she proceeded, her elastic spirits recovered themselves, and its naturally bright happy expression reappeared on her face. By the time the nurse returned to her post, Rosamond was talking with all her accustomed vivacity, and amusing her husband with all her accustomed success.

When they went back to the drawing-room, she opened the piano, and sat down to play. 'I must give you your usual evening concert, Lenny,' she said, 'or I shall be talking again on the forbidden subject of the Myrtle Room.'

She played some of Mr Frankland's favourite airs, with a certain union of feeling and fancifulness in her execution of the music, which seemed to blend the charm of her own disposition with the charm of the melodies which sprang into life under her touch. After playing through the airs she could remember most easily, she ended with the Last Waltz of Weber.* It was Leonard's favourite, and it was always reserved on that account to grace the close of the evening's performance.

She lingered longer than usual over the last plaintive notes of the waltz; then suddenly left the piano, and hastened across the room to the fireplace.

'Surely it has turned much colder within the last minute or two,' she said, kneeling down on the rug, and holding her face and hands over the fire.

'Has it?' returned Leonard. 'I don't feel any change.'

'Perhaps I have caught cold,' said Rosamond. 'Or perhaps,' she added, laughing rather uneasily, 'the wind that goes before the ghostly lady of the north rooms, has been blowing over me. I certainly felt something like a sudden chill, Lenny, while I was playing the last notes of Weber.'

'Nonsense, Rosamond. You are over-fatigued and over-excited. Tell your maid to make you some hot wine and water, and lose no time in getting to bed.'

Rosamond cowered closer over the fire. 'It's lucky I am not superstitious,' she said, 'or I might fancy that I was predestined to see the ghost.'

CHAPTER IV

STANDING ON THE BRINK

THE first night at Porthgenna passed without the slightest noise or interruption of any kind. No ghost, or dream of a ghost, disturbed the soundness of Rosamond's slumbers. She woke in her usual spirits and her usual health, and was out in the west garden before breakfast.

The sky was cloudy and the wind veered about capriciously to all the points of the compass. In the course of her walk, Rosamond met with the gardener, and asked him what he thought about the weather. The man replied that it might rain again before noon, but that, unless he was very much mistaken, it was going to turn to heat in the course of the next four-and-twenty hours.

'Pray did you ever hear of a room on the north side of our old house, called the Myrtle room?' inquired Rosamond. She had resolved, on rising that morning, not to lose a chance of making the all-important discovery for want of asking questions of everybody in the neighbourhood; and she began with the gardener accordingly.

'I never heard tell of it, ma'am,' said the man. 'But it's a likely name enough, considering how the myrtles do grow in these parts.'

'Are there any myrtles growing at the north side of the house?' asked Rosamond, struck with the idea of tracing the mysterious room by searching for it outside the building instead of inside. 'I mean close to the walls,' she added, seeing the man look puzzled, 'under the windows, you know?'

'I never see anything under the windows, in my time, but weeds and rubbish,' replied the gardener.

Just then the breakfast-bell rang. Rosamond returned to the house, determined to explore the north garden, and, if she found any relic of a bed of myrtles, to mark the window above it, and to have the room which that window lighted opened immediately. She confided this new scheme to her husband. He complimented her on her ingenuity, but confessed that he had no great hope of any discoveries being made out of doors, after what the gardener had said about the weeds and rubbish.

As soon as breakfast was over, Rosamond rang the bell, to order the gardener to be in attendance, and to say that the keys of the north rooms would be wanted. The summons was answered by Mr Frankland's servant, who brought up with him the morning's supply of letters, which the postman had just delivered. Rosamond turned them over eagerly, pounced on one with an exclamation of delight, and said to her husband:— 'The Long Beckley postmark! News from the vicar, at last!'

She opened the letter and ran her eye over it—then suddenly dropped it in her lap with her face all in a glow. 'Lenny!' she exclaimed, 'there is news here that is positively enough to turn one's head. I declare the vicar's letter has quite taken away my breath!'

'Read it,' said Mr Frankland, 'pray read it at once.'

Rosamond complied with the request in a very faltering, unsteady voice. Doctor Chennery began his letter by announcing that his application to Andrew Treverton had remained unanswered; but he added that it had, nevertheless, produced results which no one could possibly have anticipated. For information on the subject of those results, he referred Mr and Mrs Frankland to a copy subjoined of a communication marked private, which he had received from his man of business in London.

The communication contained a detailed report of an interview which had taken place between Mr Treverton's servant and the messenger who had called for an answer to Doctor Chennery's letter. Shrowl, it appeared, had opened the interview, by delivering his master's message, had then produced the vicar's torn letter and the copy of the Plan, and had announced his readiness to part with the latter for the consideration of a five-pound note. The messenger had explained that he had no power to treat for the document, and had advised Mr Treverton's servant to wait on Doctor Chennery's agent. After some hesitation, Shrowl had decided to do this, on pretence of going out on an errand—had seen the agent—had been questioned about how he became possessed of the copy—and, finding that there would be no chance of disposing of it unless he answered all inquiries, had related the circumstances under which the copy had been made. After hearing his statement the agent had engaged to apply immediately for instructions to Doctor Chennery; and had written accordingly, mentioning, in a postscript, that he had seen the transcribed Plan, and had ascertained that it really exhibited the positions of doors, stair-cases, and rooms, with the names attached to them.

Resuming his own letter, Doctor Chennery proceeded to say that he must now leave it entirely to Mr and Mrs Frankland to decide what course they ought to adopt. He had already compromised himself a little in his own estimation, by assuming a character which really did not belong to him, when he made his application to Andrew Treverton; and he felt he could personally venture no further in the affair, either by expressing an opinion or giving any advice, now that it had assumed such a totally new aspect. He felt quite sure that his young friends would arrive at the wise and the right decision, after they had maturely considered the matter in all its bearings. In that conviction, he had instructed his man of business not to stir in the affair until he had heard from Mr Frankland, and to be guided entirely by any directions which that gentleman might give.

'Directions!' exclaimed Rosamond, crumpling up the letter in a high state of excitement as soon as she had read to the end of it. 'All the directions we have to give may be written in a minute and read in a second! What in the world does the vicar mean by talking about mature consideration? Of course,' cried Rosamond, looking, womanlike, straight on to the purpose she had in view, without wasting a thought on the means by which it was to be achieved,—'Of course we give the man his five-pound note and get the Plan by return of post!'

Mr Frankland shook his head gravely. 'Quite impossible,' he said. 'If you think for a moment, my dear, you will surely see that it is out of the question to traffic with a servant for information that has been surreptitiously obtained from his master's library.'

'O, dear! dear! don't say that!' pleaded Rosamond, looking quite aghast at the view her husband took of the matter. 'What harm are we doing, if we give the man his five pounds? He has only made a copy of the Plan: he has not stolen anything.'

'He has stolen information, according to my idea of it,' said Leonard.

'Well, but if he has,' persisted Rosamond, 'what harm does it do to his master? In my opinion his master deserves to have the information stolen, for not having had the common politeness to send it to the vicar. We *must* have the Plan—O, Lenny, don't shake your head, please!—we must have it, you know we must! What is the use of being scrupulous with an old wretch (I must call him so, though he *is* my uncle), who won't conform to the commonest usages of society? You can't deal with him—and I am sure the vicar would say so, if he was here—as you would with civilised people, or people in their senses, which everybody says he is not. What use is the Plan of the north rooms to him? And, besides, if it is of any use, he has got the original; so his information is not stolen, after all, because he has got it the whole time—has he not, dear?'

'Rosamond! Rosamond!' said Leonard, smiling at his wife's transparent sophistries, 'you are trying to reason like a Jesuit.'*

'I don't care who I reason like, love, as long as I get the Plan.'

Mr Frankland still shook his head. Finding her arguments of no avail, Rosamond wisely resorted to the immemorial weapon of her sex—Persuasion; using it at such close quarters and to such good purpose, that she finally won her husband's reluctant consent to a species of compromise, which granted her leave to give directions for purchasing the copied Plan, on one condition.

This condition was, that they should send back the Plan to Mr Treverton as soon as it had served their purpose; making a full acknowledgment to him of the manner in which it had been obtained, and pleading in justification of the proceeding his own want of courtesy in withholding information of no consequence in itself, which any one else in his place would have communicated as a matter of course. Rosamond tried hard to obtain the withdrawal, or modification, of this condition; but her husband's sensitive pride was not to be touched, on that point, with impunity, even by her light hand. 'I have done too much violence already to my own convictions,' he said, 'and I will now do no more. If we are to degrade ourselves by dealing with this servant, let us at least prevent him from claiming us as his accomplices. Write in my name, Rosamond, to Doctor Chennery's man of business, and say that we are willing to purchase the transcribed Plan, on the condition that I have stated—which condition he will of course place before the servant in the plainest possible terms.'

'And suppose the servant refuses to risk losing his place, which he must do if he accepts your condition?' said Rosamond, going rather reluctantly to the writing-table.

'Let us not worry ourselves, my dear, by supposing anything. Let us wait and hear what happens, and act accordingly. When you are ready to write, tell me, and I will dictate your letter on this occasion. I wish to make the vicar's man of business understand that we act as we do, knowing, in the first place, that Mr Andrew Treverton cannot be dealt with according to the established usages of society; and knowing, in the second place, that the information which his servant offers to us, is contained in an extract from a printed book, and is in no way, directly or indirectly, connected with Mr Treverton's private affairs. Now that you have made me consent to this compromise, Rosamond, I must justify it as completely as possible to others as well as to myself.'

Seeing that his resolution was firmly settled, Rosamond had tact enough to abstain from saying anything more. The letter was written exactly as Leonard dictated it. When it had been placed in the post-bag, and when the other letters of the morning had been read and answered, Mr Frankland reminded his wife of the intention she had expressed at breakfast-time of visiting the north garden, and requested that she would take him there with her. He candidly acknowledged that since he had been made acquainted with Doctor Chennery's letter, he would give five times the sum demanded by Shrowl for the copy of the Plan, if the Myrtle Room could be discovered, without assistance from any one, before the letter to the vicar's man of business was put into the post. Nothing would give him so much pleasure, he said, as to be able to throw it into the fire, and to send a plain refusal to treat for the Plan in its place.

They went into the north garden, and there Rosamond's own eyes convinced her that she had not the slightest chance of discovering any vestige of a myrtle-bed near any one of the windows. From the garden they returned to the house, and had the door opened that led into the north hall.

They were shown the place on the pavement where the keys had been found, and the place at the top of the first flight of stairs where Mrs Jazeph had been discovered when the alarm was given. At Mr Frankland's suggestion, the door of the room which immediately fronted this spot was opened. It presented a dreary spectacle of dust and dirt and dimness. Some old pictures were piled against one of the walls, some tattered chairs were heaped together in the middle of the floor, some broken china lay on the mantel-piece, and a rotten cabinet, cracked through from top to bottom, stood in one corner. These few relics of the furnishing and fitting-up of the room were all carefully examined, but nothing of the smallest importance—nothing tending in the most remote degree to clear up the mystery of the Myrtle Room—was discovered.

'Shall we have the other doors opened?' inquired Rosamond when they came out on the landing again.

'I think it will be useless,' replied her husband. 'Our only hope of finding out the mystery of the Myrtle Room—if it is as deeply hidden from us as I believe it to be—is by searching for it in that room, and no other. The search, to be effectual, must extend, if we find it necessary, to the pulling up of the floor and wainscots—perhaps even to the dismantling of the walls. We may do that with one room when we know where it is, but we cannot, by any process short of pulling the whole side of the house down, do it with the sixteen rooms, through which our present ignorance condemns us to wander without guide or clue. It is hopeless enough to be looking for we know not what; but let us discover, if we can, where the four walls are within which that unpromising search must begin and end. Surely the floor of the landing must be dusty? Are there no footmarks on it, after Mrs Jazeph's visit, that might lead us to the right door?'

This suggestion led to a search for footsteps on the dusty floor of the landing, but nothing of the sort could be found. Matting had been laid down over the floor at some former period, and the surface, torn, ragged, and rotten with age, was too uneven in every part to allow the dust to lie smoothly on it. Here and there, where there was a hole through to the boards of the landing, Mr Frankland's servant thought he detected marks in the dust which might have been produced by the toe or the heel of a shoe; but these faint and doubtful indications lay yards and yards apart from each other, and to draw any conclusion of the slightest importance from them was simply and plainly impossible. After spending more than an hour in examining the north side of the house, Rosamond was obliged to confess that the servants were right when they predicted, on first opening the door into the hall, that she would discover nothing.

'The letter must go, Lenny,' she said, when they returned to the breakfast-room.

'There is no help for it,' answered her husband. 'Send away the post-bag, and let us say no more about it.'

The letter was despatched by that day's post. In the remote position of Porthgenna, and in the unfinished state of the railroad at that time, two days would elapse before an answer from London could be reasonably hoped for. Feeling that it would be better for Rosamond if this period of suspense was passed out of the house, Mr Frankland proposed to fill up the time by a little excursion along the coast to some places famous for their scenery, which would be likely to interest his wife, and which she might occupy herself pleasantly in describing on the spot for the benefit of her blind husband. This suggestion was immediately acted on. The young couple left Porthgenna, and only returned on the evening of the second day.

On the morning of the third day, the longed-for letter from the vicar's man of business lay on the table when Leonard and Rosamond entered the breakfast-room. Shrowl had decided to accept Mr Frankland's condition—first, because he held that any man must be out of his senses who refused a five-pound note when it was offered to him; secondly, because he believed that his master was too absolutely dependent on him to turn him away for any cause whatever; thirdly, because if Mr Treverton did part with him, he was not sufficiently attached to his place to care at all about losing it. Accordingly, the bargain had been struck in five minutes,—and there was the copy of the Plan, enclosed with the letter of explanation to attest the fact!

Rosamond spread the all-important document out on the table with trembling hands, looked it over eagerly for a few moments, and laid her finger on the square that represented the position of the Myrtle Room.

'Here it is!' she cried. 'O, Lenny, how my heart beats! One, two, three, four—the fourth door on the first-floor landing is the door of the Myrtle Room!'

She would have called at once for the keys of the north rooms; but her husband insisted on her waiting until she had composed herself a little, and until she had taken some breakfast. In spite of all he could say, the meal was hurried over so rapidly, that in ten minutes more his wife's arm was in his, and she was leading him to the staircase.

The gardener's prognostication about the weather had been verified: it had turned to heat—heavy, misty, vaporous, dull heat. One white quivering fog-cloud spread thinly over all the heaven, rolled down seaward on the horizon line, and dulled the sharp edges of the distant moorland view. The sunlight shone pale and trembling; the lightest, highest leaves of flowers at open windows were still; the domestic animals lay about sleepily in dark corners. Chance household noises sounded heavy and loud in the languid airless stillness which the heat seemed to hold over the earth. Down in the servants' hall, the usual bustle of morning work was suspended. When Rosamond looked in, on her way to the housekeeper's room to get the keys, the women were fanning themselves, and the men were sitting with their coats off. They were all talking peevishly about the heat, and all agreeing that such a day as that, in the month of June, they had never known and never heard of before.

Rosamond took the keys, declined the housekeeper's offer to accompany her, and, leading her husband along the passages, unlocked the door of the north hall.

'How unnaturally cool it is here!' she said, as they entered the deserted place.

At the foot of the stairs she stopped, and took a firmer hold of her husband's arm.

'Is anything the matter?' asked Leonard. 'Is the change to the damp coolness of this place affecting you in any way?'

'No, no,' she answered hastily. 'I am far too excited to feel either heat or damp, as I might feel them at other times. But, Lenny, supposing your guess about Mrs Jazeph is right?——'

'Yes?'

'And, supposing we discover the secret of the Myrtle Room, might it not turn out to be something concerning my father or my mother, which we ought not to know? I thought of that, when Mrs Pentreath offered to accompany us, and it determined me to come here alone with you.'

'It is just as likely that the secret might be something we ought to know,' replied Mr Frankland, after a moment's thought. 'In any case, my idea about Mrs Jazeph is, after all, only a guess in the dark. However, Rosamond, if you feel any hesitation——'

'No! come what may of it, Lenny, we can't go back now. Give me your hand again. We have traced the mystery thus far, together; and together we will find it out.'

She ascended the staircase, leading him after her, as she spoke. On the landing, she looked again at the Plan, and satisfied herself that the first impression she had derived from it, of the position of the Myrtle Room, was correct. She counted the doors on to the fourth, and looked out from the bunch the key numbered '4,' and put it into the lock.

Before she turned it she paused, and looked round at her husband.

He was standing by her side, with his patient face turned expectantly towards the door. She put her right hand on the key, turned it slowly in the lock, drew him closer to her with her left hand, and paused again.

'I don't know what has come to me,' she whispered faintly. 'I feel as if I was afraid to push open the door.'

'Your hand is cold, Rosamond. Wait a little—lock the door again—put it off till another day.'

He felt his wife's fingers close tighter and tighter on his hand, while he said those words. Then there was an instant—one memorable, breathless instant, never to be forgotten after-wards—of utter silence. Then he heard the sharp, cracking sound of the opening door, and felt himself drawn forward suddenly into a changed atmosphere, and knew that Rosamond and he were in the Myrtle Room.

CHAPTER V

THE MYRTLE ROOM

A BROAD, square window, with small panes and dark sashes; dreary yellow light, glimmering through the dirt of half a century, crusted on the glass; purer rays striking across the dimness through the fissures of three broken panes; dust floating upward, pouring downward, rolling smoothly round and round in the still atmosphere; lofty, bare, faded red walls; chairs in confusion, tables placed awry; a tall black bookcase, with an open door half dropping from its hinges; a pedestal, with a broken bust lying in fragments at its feet; a ceiling darkened by stains, a floor whitened by dust;—such was the aspect of the Myrtle Room when Rosamond first entered it, leading her husband by the hand.

After passing the doorway, she slowly advanced a few steps, and then stopped, waiting with every sense on the watch, with every faculty strung up to the highest pitch of expectation— waiting in the ominous stillness, in the forlorn solitude, for the vague Something which the room might contain, which might rise visibly before her, which might sound audibly behind her, which might touch her on a sudden from above, from below, from either side. A minute, or more, she breathlessly waited; and nothing appeared, nothing sounded, nothing touched her. The silence and the solitude had their secret to keep, and kept it.

She looked round at her husband. His face, so quiet and composed at other times, expressed doubt and uneasiness now. His disengaged hand was outstretched, and moving backwards and forwards and up and down, in the vain attempt to touch something which might enable him to guess at the position in which he was placed. His look and action, as he stood in that new and strange sphere, the mute appeal which he made so sadly and so unconsciously to his wife's loving help, restored Rosamond's self-possession by recalling her heart to the dearest of all its interests, to the holiest of all its cares. Her eyes, fixed so distrustfully, but the moment before, on the dreary spectacle of neglect and ruin which spread around them, turned fondly to her husband's face, radiant with the unfathomable brightness of pity and love. She bent quickly across him, caught his outstretched arm, and pressed it to his side.

'Don't do that, darling,' she said, gently; 'I don't like to see it. It looks as if you had forgotten that I was with you—as if you were left alone and helpless. What need have you of your sense of touch, when you have got *me?* Did you hear me open the door, Lenny? Do you know that we are in the Myrtle Room?'

'What did you see, Rosamond, when you opened the door? What do you see now?' He asked those questions rapidly and eagerly, in a whisper.

'Nothing but dust and dirt and desolation. The loneliest moor in Cornwall is not so lonely-looking as this room; but there is nothing to alarm us, nothing (except one's own fancy) that suggests an idea of danger of any kind.'

'What made you so long before you spoke to me, Rosamond?'

'I was frightened, love, on first entering the room—not at what I saw, but at my own fanciful ideas of what I might see. I was child enough to be afraid of something starting out of the walls, or of something rising through the floor; in short, of I hardly know what. I have got over those fears, Lenny, but a certain distrust of the room still clings to me. Do you feel it?'

'I feel something like it,' he replied, uneasily. 'I feel as if the night that is always before my eyes was darker to me in this place than in any other. Where are we standing now?'

'Just inside the door.'

'Does the floor look safe to walk on?' He tried it suspiciously with his foot as he put the question.

'Quite safe,' replied Rosamond. 'It would never support the furniture that is on it, if it was so rotten as to be dangerous.

Come across the room with me, and try it.' With these words
she led him slowly to the window.

'The air seems as if it was nearer to me,' he said, bending his
face forward towards the lowest of the broken panes. 'What is
before us now?'

She told him, describing minutely the size and appearance of
the window. He turned from it carelessly, as if that part of the
room had no interest for him. Rosamond still lingered near
the window, to try if she could feel a breath of the outer
atmosphere. There was a momentary silence, which was
broken by her husband.

'What are you doing now?' he asked anxiously.

'I am looking out at one of the broken panes of glass, and
trying to get some air,' answered Rosamond. 'The shadow of
the house is below me, resting on the lonely garden; but there
is no coolness breathing up from it. I see the tall weeds rising
straight and still, and the tangled wild-flowers interlacing
themselves heavily. There is a tree near me, and the leaves look
as if they were all struck motionless. Away to the left, there is a
peep of white sea and tawny sand quivering in the yellow heat.
There are no clouds; there is no blue sky. The mist quenches
the brightness of the sunlight, and lets nothing but the fire of it
through. There is something threatening in the sky, and the
earth seems to know it!'

'But the room! the room!' said Leonard, drawing her aside
from the window. 'Never mind the view; tell me what the room
is like, exactly what it is like. I shall not feel easy about you,
Rosamond, if you don't describe everything to me just as it is.'

'My darling! You know you can depend on my describing
everything. I am only doubting where to begin, and how to
make sure of seeing for you, what you are likely to think most
worth looking at. Here is an old ottoman against the wall—the
wall where the window is. I will take off my apron, and dust the
seat for you; and then you can sit down, and listen comfortably
while I tell you, before we think of anything else, what the room
is like, to begin with. First of all, I suppose, I must make you
understand how large it is?'

'Yes, that is the first thing. Try if you can compare it with any
room that I was familiar with, before I lost my sight.'

Rosamond looked backwards and forwards, from wall to wall—then went to the fire-place, and walked slowly down the length of the room, counting her steps. Pacing over the dusty floor with a dainty regularity and a childish satisfaction in looking down at the gay pink rosettes on her morning shoes; holding up her crisp, bright muslin dress out of the dirt, and showing the fanciful embroidery of her petticoat, and the glossy stockings that fitted her little feet and ankles like a second skin, she moved through the dreariness, the desolation, the dingy ruin of the scene around her, the most charming living contrast to its dead gloom that youth, health, and beauty could present.

Arrived at the bottom of the room, she reflected a little, and said to her husband:—

'Do you remember the blue drawing-room, Lenny, in your father's house at Long Beckley? I think this room is quite as large, if not larger.'

'What are the walls like?' asked Leonard, placing his hand on the wall behind him while he spoke. 'They are covered with paper, are they not?'

'Yes; with faded red paper, except on one side, where strips have been torn off and thrown on the floor. There is wainscoting round the walls. It is cracked in many places, and has ragged holes in it, which seem to have been made by the rats and mice.'

'Are there any pictures on the walls?'

'No. There is an empty frame over the fire-place. And, opposite—I mean just above where I am standing now—there is a small mirror, cracked in the centre, with broken branches for candlesticks projecting on either side of it. Above that, again, there is a stag's head and antlers; some of the face has dropped away, and a perfect maze of cobwebs is stretched between the horns. On the other walls there are large nails, with more cobwebs hanging down from them heavy with dirt—but no pictures anywhere. Now you know everything about the walls. What is the next thing? The floor?'

'I think, Rosamond, my feet have told me already what the floor is like?'

'They may have told you that it is bare, dear; but I can tell you more than that. It slopes down from every side towards the middle of the room. It is covered thick with dust, which is swept about—I suppose by the wind blowing through the broken panes—into strange, wavy, feathery shapes that quite hide the floor beneath. Lenny! suppose these boards should be made to take up anywhere! If we discover nothing to-day, we will have them swept to-morrow. In the meantime, I must go on telling you about the room, must I not? You know already what the size of it is, what the window is like, what the walls are like, what the floor is like. Is there anything else before we come to the furniture? O, yes! the ceiling—for that completes the shell of the room. I can't see much of it, it is so high. There are great cracks and stains from one end to the other, and the plaster has come away in patches in some places. The centre ornament seems to be made of alternate rows of small plaster cabbages and large plaster lozenges. Two bits of chain hang down from the middle, which, I suppose, once held a chandelier. The cornice is so dingy that I can hardly tell what pattern it represents. It is very broad and heavy, and it looks in some places as if it had once been coloured, and that is all I can say about it. Do you fell as if you thoroughly understood the whole room now, Lenny?'

'Thoroughly, my love; I have the same clear picture of it in my mind which you always give me of everything you see. You need waste no more time on me. We may now devote ourselves to the purpose for which we came here.'

At those last words, the smile which had been dawning on Rosamond's face when her husband addressed her, vanished from it in a moment. She stole close to his side, and, bending down over him, with her arm on his shoulder, said, in low, whispering tones:—

'When we had the other room opened, opposite the landing, we began by examining the furniture. We thought—if you remember—that the mystery of the Myrtle Room might be connected with hidden valuables that had been stolen, or hidden papers that ought to have been destroyed, or hidden stains and traces of some crime, which even a chair or a table might betray. Shall we examine the furniture here?'

'Is there much of it, Rosamond?'

'More than there was in the other room,' she answered.

'More than you can examine in one morning?'

'No; I think not.'

'Then begin with the furniture, if you have no better plan to propose. I am but a helpless adviser at such a crisis as this: I must leave the responsibilities of decision, after all, to rest on your shoulders. Yours are the eyes that look, and the hands that search; and, if the secret of Mrs Jazeph's reason for warning you against entering this room, is to be found by seeking in the room, *you* will find it——'

'And you will know it, Lenny, as soon as it is found. I won't hear you talk, love, as if there was any difference between us, or any superiority in my position over yours. Now, let me see. What shall I begin with? The tall bookcase opposite the window? or the dingy old writing-table, in the recess behind the fire-place? Those are the two largest pieces of furniture that I can see in the room.'

'Begin with the book-case, my dear, as you seem to have noticed that first.'

Rosamond advanced a few steps towards the bookcase—then stopped, and looked aside suddenly to the lower end of the room.

'Lenny! I forgot one thing, when I was telling you about the walls,' she said. 'There are two doors in the room besides the door we came in at. They are both in the wall to the right, as I stand now with my back to the window. Each is at the same distance from the corner, and each is of the same size and appearance. Don't you think we ought to open them, and see where they lead to?'

'Certainly. But are the keys in the locks?'

Rosamond approached more closely to the doors, and answered in the affirmative.

'Open them, then,' said Leonard. 'Stop! not by yourself. Take me with you. I don't like the idea of sitting here, and leaving you to open those doors by yourself.'

Rosamond retraced her steps to the place where he was sitting, and then led him with her to the door that was farthest from the window. 'Suppose there should be some dreadful sight behind it!' she said, trembling a little, as she stretched out her hand towards the key.

'Try to suppose (what is much more probable) that it only leads into another room,' suggested Leonard.

Rosamond threw the door wide open, suddenly. Her husband was right. It merely led into the next room.

They passed on to the second door. 'Can this one serve the same purpose as the other?' said Rosamond, slowly and distrustfully turning the key.

She opened it as she had opened the first door, put her head inside it for an instant, drew back, shuddering, and closed it again violently, with a faint exclamation of disgust.

'Don't be alarmed, Lenny,' she said leading him away abruptly. 'The door only opens on a large, empty cupboard. But there are quantities of horrible, crawling brown creatures about the wall inside. I have shut them in again in their darkness and their secresy; and now I am going to take you back to your seat, before we find out, next, what the book-case contains.'

The door of the upper part of the book-case, hanging open and half-dropping from its hinges, showed the emptiness of the shelves on one side at a glance. The corresponding door, when Rosamond pulled it open, disclosed exactly the same spectacle of barrenness on the other side. Over every shelf there spread the same dreary accumulation of dust and dirt, without a vestige of a book, without even a stray scrap of paper, lying anywhere in a corner to attract the eye, from top to bottom.

The lower portion of the book-case was divided into three cupboards. In the door of one of the three, the rusty key remained in the lock. Rosamond turned it with some difficulty and looked into the cupboard. At the back of it were scattered a pack of playing cards, brown with dirt. A morsel of torn, tangled muslin lay among them, which, when Rosamond spread it out, proved to be the remains of a clergyman's band. In one corner she found a broken corkscrew, and the winch of a fishing-rod; in another, some stumps of tobacco pipes, a few old medicine bottles, and a dog's-eared pedlar's song-book. These were all the objects that the cupboard contained. After Rosamond had scrupulously described each one of them to her husband, just as she found it, she went on to the second cupboard. On trying the door, it turned out not to be locked.

On looking inside, she discovered nothing but some pieces of blackened cotton wool, and the remains of a jeweller's packing-case.

The third door was locked, but the rusty key from the first cupboard opened it. Inside, there was but one object—a small wooden box, banded round with a piece of tape, the two edges of which were fastened together by a seal. Rosamond's flagging interest rallied instantly at this discovery. She described the box to her husband, and asked if he thought she was justified in breaking the seal.

'Can you see anything written on the cover?' he inquired.

Rosamond carried the box to the window, blew the dust off the top of it, and read, on a parchment label nailed to the cover: PAPERS. JOHN ARTHUR TREVERTON. 1760.

'I think you may take the responsibility of breaking the seal,' said Leonard. 'If those papers had been of any family import-ance, they could scarcely have been left forgotten in an old book-case by your father and his executors.'

Rosamond broke the seal, then looked up doubtfully at her husband before she opened the box. 'It seems a mere waste of time to look into this,' she said. 'How can a box that has not been opened since seventeen hundred and sixty help us to discover the mystery of Mrs Jazeph and the Myrtle Room?'

'But do we know that it has not been opened since then?' said Leonard. 'Might not the tape and seal have been put round it by anybody at some more recent period of time? You can judge best, because you can see if there is any inscription on the tape, or any signs to form an opinion by, upon the seal.'

'The seal is a blank, Lenny, except that it has a flower like a Forget-me-not* in the middle. I can see no mark of a pen on either side of the tape. Anybody in the world might have opened the box before me,' she continued, forcing up the lid easily with her hands, 'for the lock is no protection to it. The wood of the cover is so rotten that I have pulled the staple out, and left it sticking by itself in the lock below.'

On examination, the box proved to be full of papers. At the top of the uppermost packet were written these words: 'Election expenses. I won by four votes. Price fifty pounds each. J. A. Treverton.' The next layer of papers had no inscription. Rosamond opened them, and read on the first leaf:—'Birthday Ode. Respectfully addressed to the Mæcenas* of modern times in his poetic retirement at Porthgenna.' Below this production, appeared a collection of old bills, old notes of invitation, old doctor's prescriptions, and old leaves of betting-books, tied together with a piece of whipcord. Last of all, there lay on the bottom of the box, one thin leaf of paper, the visible side of which presented a perfect blank. Rosamond took it up, turned it to look at the other side, and saw some faint ink lines crossing each other in various directions, and having letters of the alphabet attached to them in certain places. She had made her husband acquainted with the contents of all the other papers, as a matter of course; and when she had described this last paper to him, he explained to her that the lines and letters represented a mathematical problem.

'The book-case tells us nothing,' said Rosamond, slowly putting the papers back in the box. 'Shall we try the writing-table by the fire-place, next?'

'What does it look like, Rosamond?'

'It has two rows of drawers down each side; and the whole top is made in an odd, old-fashioned way to slope upwards, like a very large writing-desk.'

'Does the top open?'

Rosamond went to the table, examined it narrowly, and then tried to raise the top. 'It is made to open, for I see the keyhole,' she said. 'But it is locked. And all the drawers,' she continued, trying them one after another, 'are locked too.'

'Is there no key in any of them?' asked Leonard.

'Not a sign of one. But the top feels so loose that I really think it might be forced open—as I forced the little box open just now—by a pair of stronger hands than I can boast of. Let me take you to the table, dear; it may give way to your strength, though it will not to mine.'

She placed her husband's hands carefully under the ledge formed by the overhanging top of the table. He exerted his whole strength to force it up; but, in this case, the wood was sound, the lock held, and all his efforts were in vain.

'Must we send for a locksmith?' asked Rosamond, with a look of disappointment.

'If the table is of any value, we must,' returned her husband. 'If not, a screw-driver and a hammer will open both the top and the drawers, in anybody's hands.'

'In that case, Lenny, I wish we had brought them with us when we came into the room; for the only value of the table lies in the secrets that it may be hiding from us. I shall not feel satisfied until you and I know what there is inside of it.'

While saying these words, she took her husband's hand to lead him back to his seat. As they passed before the fire-place, he stepped upon the bare stone hearth; and, feeling some new substance under his feet, instinctively stretched out the hand that was free. It touched a marble tablet, with figures on it in basso-relievo,* which had been let into the middle of the chimney-piece. He stopped immediately, and asked what the object was that his fingers had accidentally touched.

'A piece of sculpture,' said Rosamond. 'I did not notice it before. It is not very large, and not particularly attractive, according to my taste. So far as I can tell, it seems to be intended to represent——'

Leonard stopped her before she could say any more. 'Let me try, for once, if I can't make a discovery for myself,' he said, a little impatiently. 'Let me try if my fingers won't tell me what this sculpture is meant to represent.'

He passed his hands carefully over the basso-relievo (Rosamond watching their slightest movement with silent interest, the while), considered a little, and said:—

'Is there not a figure of a man sitting down, in the right-hand corner? And are there not rocks and trees, very stiffly done, high up, at the left-hand side?'

Rosamond looked at him tenderly, and smiled. 'My poor dear!' she said. 'Your man sitting down is, in reality, a miniature copy of the famous ancient statue of Niobe* and her child; your rocks are marble imitations of clouds, and your stiffly done trees are arrows darting out from some invisible Jupiter or Apollo*, or other heathen god. Ah, Lenny, Lenny! you can't trust your touch, love, as you can trust me!'

A momentary shade of vexation passed across his face; but it vanished the instant she took his hand again, to lead him back to his seat. He drew her to him gently, and kissed her cheek.

'You are right, Rosamond,' he said. 'The one faithful friend to me in my blindness, who never fails, is my wife.'

Seeing him look a little saddened, and feeling, with the quick intuition of a woman's affection, that he was thinking of the days when he had enjoyed the blessing of sight, Rosamond returned abruptly, as soon as she saw him seated once more on the ottoman, to the subject of the Myrtle Room.

'Where shall I look next, dear?' she said. 'The bookcase we have examined. The writing-table we must wait to examine. What else is there, that has a cupboard or a drawer in it?' She looked round her in perplexity: then walked away towards the part of the room to which her attention had been last drawn—the part where the fire-place was situated.

'I thought I noticed something here, Lenny, when I passed just now with you,' she said, approaching the second recess behind the mantel-piece, corresponding with the recess in which the writing-table stood.

She looked into the place closely, and detected in a corner, darkened by the shadow of the heavy projecting mantel-piece, a narrow, rickety little table, made of the commonest maho-gany—the frailest, poorest, least conspicuous piece of furniture in the whole room. She pushed it out contemptuously into the light with her foot. It ran on clumsy old-fashioned castors, and creaked wearily as it moved.

'Lenny, I have found another table,' said Rosamond. 'A miserable, forlorn-looking little thing, lost in a corner. I have just pushed it into the light, and I have discovered one drawer in it.' She paused, and tried to open the drawer; but it resisted her. 'Another lock!' she exclaimed impatiently. 'Even this wretched thing is closed against us!'

She pushed the table sharply away with her hand. It swayed on its frail legs, tottered, and fell over on the floor—fell as heavily as a table of twice its size—fell with a shock that rang through the room, and repeated itself again and again in the echoes of the lonesome north hall.

Rosamond ran to her husband, seeing him start from his seat in alarm, and told him what had happened. 'You call it a little table,' he replied, in astonishment. 'It fell like one of the largest pieces of furniture in the room!'

'Surely there must have been something heavy in the drawer!' said Rosamond, approaching the table with her spirits still fluttered by the shock of its unnaturally heavy fall. After waiting for a few moments to give the dust which it had raised, and which still hung over it in thick lazy clouds, time to disperse, she stooped down and examined it. It was cracked across the top from end to end, and the lock had been broken away from its fastenings by the fall.

She set the table up again carefully, drew out the drawer, and, after a glance at its contents, turned to her husband. 'I knew it,' she said, 'I knew there must have been something heavy in the drawer. It is full of pieces of copper-ore, like those specimens of my father's, Lenny, from Porthgenna mine. Wait! I think I feel something else, as far away at the back here as my hand can reach.'

She extricated from the lumps of ore at the back of the drawer, a small circular picture-frame of black wood, about the size of an ordinary hand-glass. It came out with the front part downwards, and with the area which its circle enclosed filled up by a thin piece of wood, of the sort which is used at the backs of small frames to keep drawings and engravings steady in them. This piece of wood (only secured to the back of the frame by one nail) had been forced out of its place, probably by the overthrow of the table; and when Rosamond took the frame out of the drawer, she observed between it and the dislodged piece of wood, the end of morsel of paper, apparently folded many times over, so as to occupy the smallest possible space. She drew out the piece of paper, laid it aside on the table without unfolding it, replaced the piece of wood in its proper position, and then turned the frame round, to see if there was a picture in front.

There was a picture—a picture painted in oils, darkened, but not much faded, by age. It represented the head of a woman, and the figure, as far as the bosom.

The instant Rosamond's eyes fell on it, she shuddered, and hurriedly advanced towards her husband with the picture in her hand.

'Well, what have you found now?' he inquired, hearing her approach.

'A picture,' she answered, faintly, stopping to look at it again.

Leonard's sensitive ear detected a change in her voice. 'Is there anything that alarms you in the picture?' he asked, half in jest, half in earnest.

'There is something that startles me—something that seems to have turned me cold for the moment, hot as the day is,' said Rosamond. 'Do you remember the description the servant-girl gave us, on the night when we arrived here, of the ghost of the north rooms?'

'Yes, I remember it perfectly.'

'Lenny! that description and this picture are exactly alike! Here is the curling, light-brown hair. Here is the dimple on each cheek. Here are the bright regular teeth. Here is that leering, wicked, fatal beauty which the girl tried to describe, and did describe, when she said it was awful!'

Leonard smiled. 'That vivid fancy of yours, my dear, takes strange flights sometimes,' he said, quietly.

'Fancy!' repeated Rosamond to herself. 'How can it be fancy when I see the face? how can it be fancy when I feel——' She stopped, shuddered again, and, returning hastily to the table, placed the picture on it, face downwards. As she did so, the morsel of folded paper which she had removed from the back of the frame caught her eye.

'There may be some account of the picture in this,' she said, and stretched out her hand to it.

It was getting on towards noon. The heat weighed heavier on the air, and the stillness of all things was more intense than ever, as she took up the paper from the table.

Fold by fold she opened it, and saw that there were written characters inside, traced in ink that had faded to a light yellow hue. She smoothed it out carefully on the table—then took it up again and looked at the first line of the writing.

The first line contained only three words—words which told her that the paper with the writing on it was not a description of a picture, but a letter—words which made her start and change colour the moment her eye fell upon them. Without attempting to read any further, she hastily turned over the leaf to find out the place where the writing ended.

It ended at the bottom of the third page; but there was a break in the lines, near the foot of the second page, and in that break there were two names signed. She looked at the uppermost of the two—started again—and turned back instantly to the first page.

Line by line, and word by word, she read through the writing; her natural complexion fading out gradually the while, and a dull, equal whiteness overspreading all her face in its stead. When she had come to the end of the third page, the hand in which she held the letter dropped to her side, and she turned her head slowly towards Leonard. In that position she stood,—no tears moistening her eyes, no change passing over her features, no word escaping her lips, no movement varying the position of her limbs—in that position she stood, with the fatal letter crumpled up in her cold fingers, looking steadfastly, speechlessly, breathlessly at her blind husband.

He was still sitting as she had seen him a few minutes before, with his legs crossed, his hands clasped together in front of them, and his head turned expectantly in the direction in which he had last heard the sound of his wife's voice. But, in a few moments, the intense stillness in the room forced itself upon his attention. He changed his position—listened for a little, turning his head uneasily from side to side—and then called to his wife.

'Rosamond!'

At the sound of his voice her lips moved, and her fingers closed faster on the paper that they held; but she neither stepped forward nor spoke.

'Rosamond!'

Her lips moved again—faint traces of expression began to pass shadow-like over the blank whiteness of her face—she advanced one step, hesitated, looked at the letter, and stopped.

Hearing no answer, he rose surprised and uneasy. Moving his poor, helpless, wandering hands to and fro before him in the air, he walked forward a few paces, straight out from the wall against which he had been sitting. A chair, which his hands were not held low enough to touch, stood in his way; and, as he still advanced, he struck his knee sharply against it.

A cry burst from Rosamond's lips, as if the pain of the blow had passed, at the instant of its infliction, from her husband to herself. She was by his side in a moment. 'You are not hurt, Lenny,' she said faintly.

'No, no.' He tried to press his hand on the place where he had struck himself, but she knelt down quickly, and put her own hand there instead; nestling her head against him, while she was on her knees, in a strangely hesitating timid way. He lightly laid the hand which she had intercepted on her shoulder. The moment it touched her, her eyes began to soften; the tears rose in them, and fell slowly one by one down her cheeks.

'I thought you had left me,' he said. 'There was such a silence that I fancied you had gone out of the room.'

'Will you come out of it with me, now?' Her strength seemed to fail her, while she asked the question; her head drooped on her breast, and she let the letter fall on the floor at her side.

'Are you tired already, Rosamond? Your voice sounds as if you were.'

'I want to leave the room,' she said, still in the same low, faint, constrained tone. 'Is your knee easier, dear? Can you walk, now?'

'Certainly. There is nothing in the world the matter with my knee. If you are tired, Rosamond—as I know you are, though you may not confess it—the sooner we leave the room the better.'

She appeared not to hear the last words he said. Her fingers were working feverishly about her neck and bosom; two bright red spots were beginning to burn in her pale cheeks; her eyes were fixed vacantly on the letter at her side; her hands wavered about it before she picked it up. For a few seconds she waited on her knees, looking at it intently, with her head turned away from her husband—then rose and walked to the fireplace. Among the dust, ashes, and other rubbish at the back of the grate, were scattered some old torn pieces of paper. They caught her eye, and held it fixed on them. She looked and looked, slowly bending down nearer and nearer to the grate. For one moment she held the letter out over the rubbish in both hands—the next she drew back shuddering violently, and turned round so as to face her husband again.

At the sight of him a faint inarticulate exclamation, half sigh, half sob, burst from her. 'Oh, no, no!' she whispered to herself, clasping her hands together, fervently, and looking at him with fond, mournful eyes. 'Never, never, Lenny—come of it what may!'

'Were you speaking to me, Rosamond?'

'Yes, love. I was saying—' She paused, and, with trembling fingers, folded up the paper again, exactly in the form in which she had found it.

'Where are you?' he asked. 'Your voice sounds away from me at the other end of the room again. Where are you?'

She ran to him, flushed, and trembling, and tearful; took him by the arm; and, without an instant of hesitation, without the faintest sign of irresolution in her face, placed the folded paper boldly in his hand. 'Keep that, Lenny,' she said, turning deadly pale, but still not losing her firmness. 'Keep that, and ask me to read it to you as soon as we are out of the Myrtle Room.'

'What is it?' he asked.

'The last thing I have found, love,' she replied, looking at him earnestly, with a deep sigh of relief.

'Is it of any importance?'

Instead of answering, she suddenly caught him to her bosom, clung to him with all the fervour of her impulsive nature, and breathlessly and passionately covered his face with kisses.

'Gently! gently!' said Leonard, laughing. 'You take away my breath.'

She drew back, and stood looking at him in silence, with a hand laid on each of his shoulders. 'Oh, my angel!' she murmured tenderly. 'I would give all I have in the world, if I could only know how much you love me!'

'Surely,' he returned, still laughing, 'surely, Rosamond, you ought to know by this time!'

'I shall know soon.' She spoke those words in tones so quiet and low that they were barely audible. Interpreting the change in her voice as a fresh indication of fatigue, Leonard invited her to lead him away by holding out his hand. She took it in silence, and guided him slowly to the door.

CHAPTER VI

THE TELLING OF THE SECRET

On their way back to the inhabited side of the house, Rosamond made no further reference to the subject of the folded paper which she had placed in her husband's hands.

All her attention, while they were returning to the west front, seemed to be absorbed in the one act of jealously watching every inch of ground that Leonard walked over, to make sure that it was safe and smooth before she suffered him to set his foot on it. Careful and considerate as she had always been, from the first day of their married life, whenever she led him from one place to another, she was now unduly, almost absurdly, anxious to preserve him from the remotest possibility of an accident. Finding that he was the nearest to the outside of the open landing, when they left the Myrtle Room, she insisted on changing places, so that he might be nearest to the wall. While they were descending the stairs, she stopped him in the middle, to inquire if he felt any pain in the knee which he had struck against the chair. At the last step she brought him to a stand-still again, while she moved away the torn and tangled remains of an old mat, for fear one of his feet should catch in it. Walking across the north hall, she intreated that he would take her arm and lean heavily upon her, because she felt sure that his knee was not quite free from stiffness yet. Even at the short flight of stairs which connected the entrance to the hall with the passages leading to the west side of the house, she twice stopped him on the way down, to place his foot on the sound parts of the steps, which she represented as dangerously worn away in more places than one. He laughed good-humouredly at her excessive anxiety to save him from all danger of stumbling, and asked if there was any likelihood, with their numerous stoppages, of getting back to the west side of the house in time for lunch. She was not ready, as usual, with her retort; his laugh found no pleasant echo in hers: she only answered that it was impossible to be too anxious about him; and then went on in silence, till they reached the door of the housekeeper's room.

Leaving him for a moment outside, she went in to give the keys back again to Mrs Pentreath.

'Dear me, ma'am!' exclaimed the housekeeper, 'you look quite overcome by the heat of the day, and the close air of those old rooms. Can I get you a glass of water, or may I give you my bottle of salts?'

Rosamond declined both offers.

'May I be allowed to ask, ma'am, if anything has been found this time in the north rooms?' inquired Mrs Pentreath, hanging up the bunch of keys.

'Only some old papers,' replied Rosamond, turning away.

'I beg pardon, again, ma'am,' pursued the housekeeper; 'but, in case any of the gentry of the neighbourhood should call to-day?'

'We are engaged. No matter who it may be, we are both engaged.' Answering briefly in these terms, Rosamond left Mrs Pentreath, and rejoined her husband.

With the same excess of attention and care which she had shown on the way to the housekeeper's room, she now led him up the west staircase. The library door happening to stand open, they passed through it on their way to the drawing-room, which was the larger and cooler apartment of the two. Having guided Leonard to a seat, Rosamond returned to the library, and took from the table a tray containing a bottle of water, and a tumbler, which she had noticed when she passed through.

'I may feel faint as well as frightened,' she said quickly to herself, turning round with the tray in her hand to return to the drawing-room.

After she had put the water down on a table in a corner, she noiselessly locked the door leading into the library, then the door leading into the passage. Leonard, hearing her moving about, advised her to keep quiet on the sofa. She patted him gently on the cheek, and was about to make some suitable answer, when she accidentally beheld her face reflected in the looking-glass under which he was sitting. The sight of her own white cheeks and startled eyes suspended the words on her lips. She hastened away to the window, to catch any breath of air that might be wafted towards her from the sea.

The heat-mist still hid the horizon. Nearer, the oily, colour-less surface of the water was just visible, heaving slowly from time to time in one vast monotonous wave that rolled itself out smoothly and endlessly till it was lost in the white obscurity of the mist. Close on the shore, the noisy surf was hushed. No sound came from the beach except at long, wearily long intervals, when a quick thump, and a still splash, just audible and no more, announced the fall of one tiny, mimic wave upon the parching sand. On the terrace in front of the house, the changeless hum of summer insects was all that told of life and movement. Not a human figure was to be seen anywhere on the shore; no sign of a sail loomed shadowy through the heat at sea; no breath of air waved the light tendrils of the creepers that twined up the house-wall, or refreshed the drooping flowers ranged in the windows. Rosamond turned away from the outer prospect, after a moment's weary contemplation of it. As she looked into the room again, her husband spoke to her.

'What precious thing lies hidden in this paper?' he asked, producing the letter, and smiling as he opened it. 'Surely there must be something besides writing—some inestimable powder, or some bank-note of fabulous value—wrapped up in all these folds?'

Rosamond's heart sank within her, as he opened the letter and passed his finger over the writing inside, with a mock expression of anxiety, and a light jest about sharing all treasures discovered at Porthgenna with his wife.

'I will read it to you directly, Lenny,' she said, dropping into the nearest seat, and languidly pushing her hair back from her temples. 'But put it away for a few minutes now, and let us talk of anything else you like that does not remind us of the Myrtle Room. I am very capricious, am I not, to be so suddenly weary of the very subject that I have been fondest of talking about for so many weeks past? Tell me, love,' she added, rising abruptly and going to the back of his chair: 'do I get worse with my whims and fancies and faults?—or am I improved, since the time when we were first married?'

He tossed the letter aside carelessly on a table which was always placed by the arm of his chair, and shook his forefinger at her with a frown of comic reproof. 'Oh fie, Rosamond! are you trying to entrap me into paying you compliments?'

The light tone that he persisted in adopting seemed absolutely to terrify her. She shrank away from his chair, and sat down again at a little distance from him.

'I remember I used to offend you,' she continued, quickly and confusedly. 'No, no, not to offend—only to vex you a little—by talking too familiarly to the servants. You might almost have fancied, at first, if you had not known me so well, that it was a habit with me because I had once been a servant myself. Suppose I had been a servant—the servant who had helped to nurse you in your illnesses, the servant who led you about in your blindness more carefully than anyone else— would you have thought much, then, of the difference between us? would you——'

She stopped. The smile had vanished from Leonard's face, and he had turned a little away from her. 'What is the use, Rosamond, of supposing events that never could have happened?' he asked rather impatiently.

She went to the side-table, poured out some of the water she had brought from the library, and drank it eagerly; then walked to the window and plucked a few of the flowers that were placed there. She threw some of them away again the next moment; but kept the rest in her hand, thoughtfully arranging them so as to contrast their colours with the best effect. When this was done, she put them into her bosom, looked down absently at them, took them out again, and, returning to her husband, placed the little nosegay in the buttonhole of his coat.

'Something to make you look gay and bright, love—as I always wish to see you,' she said, seating herself in her favourite attitude at his feet, and looking up at him sadly, with her arms resting on his knees.

'What are you thinking about, Rosamond?' he asked, after an interval of silence.

'I was only wondering, Lenny, whether any woman in the world could be as fond of you as I am. I feel almost afraid that there are others who would ask nothing better than to live and die for you, as well as me. There is something in your face, in your voice, in all your ways—something besides the interest of your sad, sad affliction—that would draw any woman's heart to you, I think. If I was to die—'

'If you were to die!' He started as he repeated the words after her, and, leaning forward, anxiously laid his hand upon her forehead. 'You are thinking and talking very strangely, this morning, Rosamond! Are you not well?'

She rose on her knees and looked closer at him, her face brightening a little, and a faint smile just playing round her lips. 'I wonder if you will always be as anxious about me, and as fond of me, as you are now?' she whispered, kissing his hand as she removed it from her forehead. He leaned back again in the chair and told her jestingly not to look too far into the future. The words, lightly as they were spoken, struck deep into her heart. 'There are times, Lenny,' she said, 'when all one's happiness in the present depends upon one's certainty of the future.' She looked at the letter, which her husband had left open on a table near him, as she spoke; and, after a momentary struggle with herself, took it in her hand to read it. At the first word her voice failed her; the deadly paleness overspread her face again; she threw the letter back on the table, and walked away to the other end of the room.

'The future?' asked Leonard. 'What future, Rosamond, can you possibly mean?'

'Suppose I meant our future at Porthgenna?' she said, moistening her dry lips with a few drops of water. 'Shall we stay here as long as we thought we should, and be as happy as we have been everywhere else? You told me on the journey that I should find it dull, and that I should be driven to try all sorts of extraordinary occupations to amuse myself. You said you expected that I should begin with gardening and end by writing a novel. A novel!' She approached her husband again, and watched his face eagerly while she went on. 'Why not? More women write novels now than men. What is to prevent me from trying? The first great requisite, I suppose, is to have an idea of a story; and that I have got.' She advanced a few steps further, reached the table on which the letter lay, and placed her hand on it, keeping her eyes still fixed intently on Leonard's face.

'And what is your idea, Rosamond?' he asked.

'This,' she replied. 'I mean to make the main interest of the story centre in two young married people. They shall be very fond of each other—as fond as we are, Lenny—and they shall be in our rank of life. After they have been happily married some time, and when they have got one child to make them love each other more dearly than ever, a terrible discovery shall fall upon them like a thunderbolt. The husband shall have chosen for his wife a young lady bearing as ancient a family name as——'

'As your name?' suggested Leonard.

'As the name of the Treverton family,' she continued, after a pause, during which her hand had been restlessly moving the letter to and fro on the table. 'The husband shall be well-born—as well-born as you, Lenny—and the terrible discovery shall be, that his wife has no right to the ancient name that she bore when he married her.'

'I can't say, my love, that I approve of your idea. Your story will decoy the reader into feeling an interest in a woman who turns out to be an impostor.'

'No!' cried Rosamond, warmly. 'A true woman—a woman who never stooped to a deception—a woman full of faults and failings, but a teller of the truth at all hazards and all sacrifices. Hear me out, Lenny, before you judge.' Hot tears rushed into her eyes; but she dashed them away passionately, and went on. 'The wife shall grow up to womanhood, and shall marry, in total ignorance—mind that!—in total ignorance of her real history. The sudden disclosure of the truth shall overwhelm her—she shall find herself struck by a calamity which she had no hand in bringing about. She shall be staggered in her very reason by the discovery; it shall burst upon her when she has no one but herself to depend on; she shall have the power of keeping it a secret from her husband with perfect impunity; she shall be tried, she shall be shaken in her mortal frailness, by one moment of fearful temptation; she shall conquer it, and, of her own free will, she shall tell her husband all that she knows herself. Now, Lenny, what do you call that woman? an impostor?'

'No: a victim.'

'Who goes of her own accord to the sacrifice? and who *is* to be sacrificed?'

'I never said that.'

'What would you do with her, Lenny, if you were writing the story? I mean, how would you make her husband behave to her? It is a question in which a man's nature is concerned, and a woman is not competent to decide it. I am perplexed about how to end the story. How would you end it, love?' As she ceased, her voice sank sadly to its gentlest pleading tones. She came close to him, and twined her fingers in his hair fondly. 'How would you end it, love?' she repeated, stooping down till her trembling lips just touched his forehead.

He moved uneasily in his chair, and replied, 'I am not a writer of novels, Rosamond.'

'But how would you act, Lenny, if you were that husband?'

'It is hard for me to say,' he answered. 'I have not your vivid imagination, my dear: I have no power of putting myself, at a moment's notice, into a position that is not my own, and of knowing how I should act in it.'

'But suppose your wife was close to you—as close as I am now? Suppose she had just told you the dreadful secret, and was standing before you—as I am standing now—with the happiness of her whole life to come depending on one kind word from your lips? Oh, Lenny, you would not let her drop broken-hearted at your feet? You would know, let her birth be what it might, that she was still the same faithful creature who had cherished, and served, and trusted, and worshipped you since her marriage-day, and who asked nothing in return but to lay her head on your bosom, and to hear you say that you loved her? You would know that she had nerved herself to tell the fatal secret, because, in her loyalty and love to her husband, she would rather die forsaken and despised, than live, deceiving him? You would know all this, and you would open your arms to the mother of your child, to the wife of your first love, though she was the lowliest of all lowly-born women in the estimation of the world? Oh, you would, Lenny, I know you would!'

'Rosamond! how your hands tremble; how your voice alters! You are agitating yourself about this supposed story of yours, as if you were talking of real events.'

'You would take her to your heart, Lenny? You would open your arms to her without an instant of unworthy doubt?'

'Hush! hush! I hope I should.'

'Hope? only hope? Oh, think again, love, think again; and say you *know* you should!'

'Must I, Rosamond? Then I do say it.'

She drew back as the words passed his lips, and took the letter from the table.

'You have not yet asked me, Lenny, to read the letter that I found in the Myrtle Room. I offer to read it now, of my own accord.'

She trembled a little as she spoke those few decisive words, but her utterance of them was clear and steady, as if her consciousness of being now irrevocably pledged to make the disclosure, had strengthened her at last to dare all hazards and end all suspense.

Her husband turned towards the place from which the sound of her voice had reached him, with a mixed expression of perplexity and surprise in his face. 'You pass so suddenly from one subject to another,' he said, 'that I hardly know how to follow you. What in the world, Rosamond, takes you, at one jump, from a romantic argument about a situation in a novel, to the plain, practical business of reading an old letter?'

'Perhaps there is a closer connection between the two than you suspect,' she answered.

'A closer connection? What connection? I don't understand.'

'The letter will explain.'

'Why the letter? Why should *you* not explain?'

She stole one anxious look at his face, and saw that a sense of something serious to come was now overshadowing his mind for the first time.

'Rosamond!' he exclaimed, 'there is some mystery—'

'There are no mysteries between us two,' she interposed quickly. 'There never have been any, love; there never shall be.' She moved a little nearer to him to take her old favourite place on his knee, then checked herself, and drew back again to the table. Warning tears in her eyes bade her distrust her own firmness, and read the letter where she could not feel the beating of his heart.

'Did I tell you,' she resumed, after waiting an instant to compose herself, 'where I found the folded piece of paper which I put into your hand in the Myrtle Room?'

'No,' he replied, 'I think not.'

'I found it at the back of the frame of that picture—the picture of the ghostly woman with the wicked face. I opened it immediately, and saw that it was a letter. The address inside, the first line under it, and one of the two signatures which it contained, were in a handwriting that I knew.'

'Whose?'

'The handwriting of the late Mrs Treverton.'

'Of your mother?'

'Of the late Mrs Treverton.'

'Gracious God, Rosamond! why do you speak of her in that way?'

'Let me read, and you will know. You have seen, with my eyes, what the Myrtle Room is like; you have seen, with my eyes, every object which the search through it brought to light, you must now see, with my eyes, what this letter contains. It is the Secret of the Myrtle Room.'

She bent close over the faint, faded writing, and read these words:—

'To my husband—

'We have parted, Arthur, for ever, and I have not had the courage to embitter our farewell by confessing that I have deceived you— cruelly and basely deceived you. But a few minutes since, you were weeping by my bedside, and speaking of our child. My wronged, my beloved husband, the little daughter of your heart is not yours, is not mine. She is a love-child, whom I have imposed on you for mine. Her father was a miner at Porthgenna, her mother is my maid, Sarah Leeson.'

Rosamond paused, but never raised her head from the letter. She heard her husband lay his hand suddenly on the table; she heard him start to his feet; she heard him draw his breath heavily in one quick gasp; she heard him whisper to himself the instant after, 'A love-child!' With a fearful, painful distinctness she heard those three words. The tone in which he whispered them turned her cold. But she never moved, for there was more to read; and while more remained, if her life had depended on it, she could not have looked up.

In a moment more she went on, and read these lines next:—

'I have many heavy sins to answer for, but this one sin you must pardon, Arthur; for I committed it through fondness for you. That fond- ness told me a secret which you sought to hide from me. That fondness told me that your barren wife would never make your heart all her own until she had borne you a child; and your lips proved it true. Your first words, when you came back from sea, and when the infant was placed in your arms, were:—"I have never loved you, Rosamond, as I love you now." If you had not said that, I should never have kept my guilty secret.

'I can add no more, for death is very near me. How the fraud was committed, and what my other motives were, I must leave you to discover from the mother of the child, who writes this under my dictation, and who is charged to give it to you when I am no more. You will be merciful to the poor little creature who bears my name. Be merciful also to her unhappy parent: she is only guilty of too blindly obeying me. If there is anything that mitigates the bitterness of my remorse, it is the remembrance that my act of deceit saved the most faithful and the most affectionate of women from shame that she had not deserved. Remember me forgivingly, Arthur,—words may tell how I have sinned against you; no words can tell how I have loved you!'

She had struggled on thus far, and had reached the last line on the second page of the letter, when she paused again, and then tried to read the first of the two signatures—'Rosamond Treverton.' She faintly repeated two syllables of that familiar Christian name—the name that was on her husband's lips every hour of the day!—and strove to articulate the third, but her voice failed her. All the sacred household memories which that ruthless letter had profaned for ever, seemed to tear themselves away from her heart at the same moment. With a low, moaning cry she dropped her arms on the table, and laid her head down on them, and hid her face.

She heard nothing, she was conscious of nothing, until she felt a touch on her shoulder—a light touch from a hand that trembled. Every pulse in her body bounded in answer to it, and she looked up.

Her husband had guided himself near to her by the table. The tears were glistening in his dim, sightless eyes. As she rose and touched him, his arms opened, and closed fast round her.

'My own Rosamond!' he said, 'come to me and be comforted!'

BOOK VI

CHAPTER I

UNCLE JOSEPH

THE day and the night had passed, and the new morning had come, before the husband and wife could trust themselves to speak calmly of the Secret, and to face resignedly the duties and the sacrifices which the discovery of it imposed on them.

Leonard's first question referred to those lines in the letter which Rosamond had informed him were in a handwriting that she knew. Finding that he was at a loss to understand what means she could have of forming an opinion on this point, she explained that, after Captain Treverton's death, many letters had naturally fallen into her possession, which had been written by Mrs Treverton to her husband. They treated of ordinary domestic subjects, and she had read them often enough to become thoroughly acquainted with the peculiarities of Mrs Treverton's handwriting. It was remarkably large, firm, and masculine in character; and the address, the line under it, and the uppermost of the two signatures in the letter which had been found in the Myrtle Room, exactly resembled it in every particular.

The next question related to the body of the letter. The writing of this, of the second signature ('Sarah Leeson'), and of the additional lines on the third page, also signed by Sarah Leeson, proclaimed itself in each case to be the production of the same person. While stating that fact to her husband, Rosamond did not forget to explain to him that, while reading the letter on the previous day, her strength and courage had failed her before she got to the end of it. She added that the postscript which she had thus omitted to read, was of importance, because it mentioned the circumstances under which the Secret had been hidden; and begged that he would listen while she made him acquainted with its contents without any further delay.

Sitting as close to his side, now, as if they were enjoying their first honeymoon-days over again, she read these last lines—the lines which her mother had written sixteen years before, on the morning when she fled from Porthgenna Tower:—

'If this paper should ever be found (which I pray with my whole heart it never may be), I wish to state that I have come to the resolution of hiding it, because I dare not show the writing that it contains to my master, to whom it is addressed. In doing what I now propose to do, though I am acting against my mistress's last wishes, I am not breaking the solemn engagement which she obliged me to make before her on her death bed. That engagement forbids me to destroy this letter, or to take it away with me if I leave the house. I shall do neither,—my purpose is to conceal it in the place, of all others, where I think there is least chance of its ever being found again. Any hardship or misfortune which may follow as a consequence of this deceitful proceeding on my part, will fall on myself. Others, I believe, in my conscience, will be the happier for the hiding of the dreadful secret which this letter contains.'

'There can be no doubt, now,' said Leonard, when his wife had read to the end; 'Mrs Jazeph, Sarah Leeson, and the servant who disappeared from Porthgenna Tower, are one and the same person.'

'Poor creature!' said Rosamond, sighing as she put down the letter. 'We know now why she warned me so anxiously not to go into the Myrtle Room. Who can say what she must have suffered when she came as a stranger to my bedside? Oh, what would I not give if I had been less hasty with her! It is dreadful to remember that I spoke to her as a servant whom I expected to obey me; it is worse still to feel that I cannot, even now, think of her as a child should think of a mother. How can I ever tell her that I know the Secret? how—' She paused, with a heart-sick consciousness of the slur that was cast on her birth; she paused, shrinking as she thought of the name her husband had given to her, and of her own parentage, which the laws of society disdained to recognise.

'Why do you stop?' asked Leonard.

'I was afraid—' she began, and paused again.

'Afraid,' he said, finishing the sentence for her, 'that words of pity for that unhappy woman might wound my sensitive pride, by reminding me of the circumstances of your birth? Rosamond! I should be unworthy of your matchless truthfulness towards me, if I, on my side, did not acknowledge that this discovery *has* wounded me as only a proud man can be wounded. My pride has been born and bred in me. My pride, even while I am now speaking to you, takes advantage of my first moments of composure, and deludes me into doubting, in the face of all probability, whether the words you have read to me, can, after all, be words of truth. But, strong as that inborn and inbred feeling is—hard as it may be for me to discipline and master it as I ought, and must and will,—there is another feeling in my heart that is stronger yet.' He felt for her hand, and took it in his; then added: 'From the hour when you first devoted your life to your blind husband—from the hour when you won all his gratitude, as you had already won all his love, you took a place in his heart, Rosamond, from which nothing, not even such a shock as has now assailed us, can move you! High as I have always held the worth of rank in my estimation, I have learnt, even before the event of yesterday, to hold the worth of my wife, let her parentage be what it may, higher still.'

'Oh, Lenny, Lenny, I can't hear you praise me, if you talk in the same breath as if I had made a sacrifice in marrying you! But for my blind husband I might never have deserved what you have just said of me. When I first read that fearful letter, I had one moment of vile, ungrateful doubt if your love for me would hold out against the discovery of the Secret. I had one moment of horrible temptation, that drew me away from you when I ought to have put the letter into your hand. It was the sight of you, waiting for me to speak again, so innocent of all knowledge of what had happened close by you, that brought me back to my senses, and told me what I ought to do. It was the sight of my blind husband that made me conquer the temptation to destroy that letter, in the first hour of discovering it. Oh, if I had been the hardest-hearted of women, could I have ever taken your hand again,—could I kiss you, could I lie down by your side, and hear you fall asleep, night after night, feeling that I had abused your blind dependence on me, to serve my own selfish interests? Knowing that I had only succeeded in my deceit because your affliction made you incapable of suspecting deception? No, no; I can hardly believe that the basest of women could be guilty of such baseness as that; and I can claim nothing more for myself than the credit of having been true to my trust. You said yesterday, love, in the Myrtle Room, that the one faithful friend to you in your blindness, who never failed, was your wife. It is reward enough and consolation enough for me, now that the worst is over, to know that you can say so still.'

'Yes, Rosamond, the worst is over; but we must not forget that there may be hard trials still to meet.'

'Hard trials, love? To what trials do you refer?'

'Perhaps, Rosamond, I over-rate the courage that the sacrifice demands; but, to *me* at least, it will be a hard sacrifice of my own feelings to make strangers partakers in the know-ledge that we now possess.'

Rosamond looked at her husband in astonishment. 'Why need we tell the Secret to anyone?' she asked.

'Assuming that we can satisfy ourselves of the genuineness of that letter,' he answered, 'we shall have no choice but to tell it to strangers. You cannot forget the circumstances under which your father—under which Captain Treverton——'

'Call him my father,' said Rosamond, sadly. 'Remember how he loved me, and how I loved him, and say "my father," still.'

'I am afraid I must say "Captain Treverton" now,' returned Leonard, 'or I shall hardly be able to explain simply and plainly what it is very necessary that you should know. Captain Treverton died without leaving a will. His only property was the purchase-money of this house and estate; and you inherited it, as his next of kin—'

Rosamond started back in her chair and clasped her hands in dismay. 'Oh, Lenny,' she said simply, 'I have thought so much of you, since I found the letter, that I never remembered this!'

'It is time to remember it, my love. If you are not Captain Treverton's daughter, you have no right to one farthing of the fortune that you possess; and it must be restored at once to the person who *is* Captain Treverton's next of kin—or, in other words, to his brother.'

'To that man!' exclaimed Rosamond. 'To that man who is a stranger to us, who holds our very name in contempt! Are we to be made poor that he may be made rich?——'

'We are to do what is honourable and just, at any sacrifice of our own interests and ourselves,' said Leonard, firmly. 'I believe, Rosamond, that my consent, as your husband, is necessary, according to the law, to effect this restitution. If Mr Andrew Treverton was the bitterest enemy I had on earth, and if the restoring of this money utterly ruined us both in our worldly circumstances, I would give it back of my own accord to the last farthing—and so would you!'

The blood mantled in his cheeks as he spoke. Rosamond looked at him admiringly in silence. 'Who would have him less proud,' she thought fondly, 'when his pride speaks in such words as those!'

'You understand now,' continued Leonard, 'that we have duties to perform which will oblige us to seek help from others, and which will therefore render it impossible to keep the Secret to ourselves? If we search all England for her, Sarah Leeson must be found. Our future actions depend upon her answers to our inquiries, upon her testimony to the genuineness of that letter. Although I am resolved beforehand to shield myself behind no technical quibbles and delays—although I want nothing but evidence that is morally conclusive, however legally imperfect it may be—it is still impossible to proceed without seeking advice immediately. The lawyer who always managed Captain Treverton's affairs, and who now manages ours, is the proper person to direct us in instituting a search; and to assist us, if necessary, in making the restitution.'

'How quietly and firmly you speak of it, Lenny! Will not the abandoning of my fortune be a dreadful loss to us?'

'We must think of it as a gain to our consciences, Rosamond; and must alter our way of life resignedly to suit our altered means. But we need speak no more of that until we are assured of the necessity of restoring the money. My immediate anxiety, and your immediate anxiety, must turn now on the discovery of Sarah Leeson—no! on the discovery of your mother; I must learn to call her by that name, or I shall not learn to pity and forgive her.'

Rosamond nestled closer to her husband's side. 'Every word you say, love, does my heart good,' she whispered, laying her head on his shoulder. 'You will help me and strengthen me, when the time comes, to meet my mother as I ought? Oh, how pale and worn and weary she was when she stood by my bedside, and looked at me and my child! Will it be long before we find her? Is she far away from us, I wonder? or nearer, much nearer, than we think?'

Before Leonard could answer, he was interrupted by a knock at the door, and Rosamond was surprised by the appearance of the maid-servant. Betsey was flushed, excited, and out of breath; but she contrived to deliver intelligibly a brief message from Mr Munder, the steward, requesting permission to speak to Mr Frankland, or to Mrs Frankland, on business of importance.

'What is it? What does he want?' asked Rosamond.

'I think, ma'am, he wants to know whether he had better send for the constable or not,' answered Betsey.

'Send for the constable!' repeated Rosamond. 'Are there thieves in the house in broad daylight?'

'Mr Munder says he don't know but what it may be worse than thieves,' replied Betsey. 'It's the foreigner again, if you please, ma'am. He come up and rung at the door as bold as brass, and asked if he could see Mrs Frankland.'

'The foreigner!' exclaimed Rosamond, laying her hand eagerly on her husband's arm.

'Yes, ma'am,' said Betsey. 'Him as come here to go over the house along with the lady——'

Rosamond, with characteristic impulsiveness, started to her feet. 'Let me go down!' she began.

'Wait,' interposed Leonard, catching her by the hand. 'There is not the least need for you to go down stairs. Show the foreigner up here,' he continued, addressing himself to Betsey, 'and tell Mr Munder that we will take the management of this business into our own hands.'

Rosamond sat down again by her husband's side. 'This is a very strange accident,' she said, in a low, serious tone. 'It must be something more than mere chance that puts the clue into our hands, at the moment when we least expected to find it.'

The door opened for the second time, and there appeared, modestly, on the threshold, a little old man, with rosy cheeks and long white hair. A small leather case was slung by a strap at his side, and the stem of a pipe peeped out of the breast-pocket of his coat. He advanced one step into the room, stopped, raised both his hands with his felt hat crumpled up in them to his heart, and made five fantastic bows in quick succession—two to Mrs Frankland, two to her husband, and one to Mrs Frankland, again, as an act of separate and special homage to the lady. Never had Rosamond seen a more complete embodiment in human form of perfect innocence and perfect harmlessness, than the foreigner who was described in the housekeeper's letter as an audacious vagabond, and who was dreaded by Mr Munder as something worse than a thief!

'Madam, and good sir,' said the old man, advancing a little nearer at Mrs Frankland's invitation, 'I ask your pardon for intruding myself. My name is Joseph Buschmann. I live in the town of Truro, where I work in cabinets and tea-caddies, and other shining woods. I am also, if you please, the same little foreign man who was scolded by the big major-domo when I came to see the house. All that I ask of your kindness is, that you will let me say for my errand here and for myself, and for another person who is very near to my love,—one little word. I will be but few minutes, madam and good sir, and then I will go my ways again, with my best wishes and my best thanks.'

'Pray, consider, Mr Buschmann, that our time is your time,' said Leonard. 'We have no engagement whatever which need oblige you to shorten your visit. I must tell you, beforehand, in order to prevent any embarrassment on either side, that I have the misfortune to be blind. I can promise you, however, my best attention as far as listening goes. Rosamond, is Mr Buschmann seated?'

Mr Buschmann was still standing near the door, and was expressing sympathy by bowing to Mr Frankland again, and crumpling his felt hat once more over his heart.

'Pray come nearer, and sit down,' said Rosamond. 'And don't imagine for one moment that any opinion of the steward's has the least influence on us, or that we feel it at all necessary for you to apologise for what took place the last time you came to this house. We have an interest—a very great interest,' she added, with her usual hearty frankness, 'in hearing anything that you have to tell us. You are the person of all others whom we are, just at this time—' She stopped, feeling her foot touched by her husband's, and rightly interpreting the action as a warning not to speak too unrestrainedly to the visitor, before he had explained his object in coming to the house.

Looking very much pleased, and a little surprised also, when he heard Rosamond's last words, Uncle Joseph drew a chair near to the table by which Mr and Mrs Frankland were sitting, crumpled his felt hat up smaller than ever, and put it in one of his side pockets, drew from the other a little packet of letters, placed them on his knees as he sat down, patted them gently with both hands, and entered on his explanation in these terms:—

'Madam and good sir,' he began, 'before I can say comfortably my little word, I must, with your leave, travel backwards to the last time when I came to this house in company with my niece.'

'Your niece!' exclaimed Rosamond and Leonard, both speaking together.

'My niece, Sarah,' said Uncle Joseph, 'the only child of my sister Agatha. It is for the love of Sarah, if you please, that I am here now. She is the one last morsel of my flesh and blood that is left to me in the world. The rest, they are all gone! My wife, my little Joseph, my brother Max, my sister Agatha and the husband she married, the good and noble Englishman, Leeson—they are all, all gone!'

'Leeson,' said Rosamond, pressing her husband's hand significantly under the table. 'Your niece's name is Sarah Leeson?'

Uncle Joseph sighed and shook his head. 'One day,' he said, 'of all the days in the year the evilmost for Sarah, she changed that name. Of the man she married—who is dead now, madam—it is little or nothing that I know but this:—His name was Jazeph, and he used her ill, for which I think him the First Scoundrel! Yes,' exclaimed Uncle Joseph, with the nearest approach to anger and bitterness which his nature was capable of making, and with an idea that he was using one of the strongest superlatives in the language. 'Yes! if he was to come to life again at this very moment of time, I would say it of him to his face:—Englishman Jazeph, you are the First Scoundrel!'

Rosamond pressed her husband's hand for the second time. If their own convictions had not already identified Mrs Jazeph with Sarah Leeson, the old man's last words must have amply sufficed to assure them that both names had been borne by the same person.

'Well, then, I shall now travel backwards to the time when I was here with Sarah, my niece,' resumed Uncle Joseph. 'I must, if you please, speak the truth in this business, or, now that I am already backwards where I want to be, I shall stick fast in my place, and get on no more for the rest of my life. Sir and good madam, will you have the great kindness to forgive me and Sarah, my niece, if I confess that it was not to see the house that we came here, and rang at the bell, and gave deal of trouble, and wasted much breath of the big major-domo's with the scolding that we got. It was only to do one curious little thing, that we came together to this place—or, no, it was all about a secret of Sarah's, which is still as black and dark to me as the middle of the blackest and darkest night that ever was in the world—and, as I nothing knew about it, except that there was no harm in it to anybody or anything, and that Sarah was determined to go, and that I could not let her go by herself; as also for the good reason that she told me, she had the best right of anybody to take the letter and to hide it again, seeing that she was afraid of its being found if longer in that room she left it, which was the room where she had hidden it before—Why, so it happened, that I—no, that she—no, no, that I—Ach Gott!' cried Uncle Joseph, striking his forehead in despair, and relieving himself by an invocation in his own language. 'I am lost in my own muddlement; and whereabouts the right place is, and how I am to get myself back into it, as I am a living sinner is more than I know!'

'There is not the least need to go back on our account,' said Rosamond, forgetting all caution and self-restraint in her anxiety to restore the old man's confidence and composure. 'Pray don't try to repeat your explanations. We know already—'

'We will suppose,' said Leonard, interposing abruptly before his wife could add another word, 'that we know already everything you can desire to tell us in relation to your niece's secret, and to your motives for desiring to see the house.'

'You will suppose that!' exclaimed Uncle Joseph, looking greatly relieved. 'Ah! I thank you, sir, and you, good madam, a thousand times for helping me out of my own muddlement with a "Suppose." I am all over confusion from my tops to my toes; but I can go on now, I think, and lose myself no more. So! Let us say it in this way: I and Sarah, my niece, are *in* the house—that is the first "Suppose." I and Sarah, my niece, are *out* of the house—that is the second "Suppose." Good! now we go on once more. On my way back to my own home at Truro, I am frightened for Sarah, because of the faint she fell into on your stairs here, and because of a look in her face that it makes me heavy at my heart to see. Also, I am sorry for her sake, because she has not done that one curious little thing which she came into the house to do. I fret about these same matters, but I console myself too; and my comfort is that Sarah will stop with me in my house at Truro, and that I shall make her happy and well again, as soon as we are settled in our life together. Judge, then, sir, what a blow falls on me, when I hear that she will not make her home where I make mine. Judge you, also, good madam, what my surprise must be, when I ask for her reason, and she tells me she must leave Uncle Joseph, because she is afraid of being found out by *you*.' He stopped, and looking anxiously at Rosamond's face, saw it sadden and turn away from him, after he had spoken his last words. 'Are you sorry, madam, for Sarah, my niece? do you pity her?' he asked with a little hesitation and trembling in his voice.

'I pity her with my whole heart,' said Rosamond, warmly.

'And with my whole heart for that pity I thank you!' rejoined Uncle Joseph. 'Ah, madam, your kindness gives me the courage to go on, and to tell you that we parted from each other

on the day of our getting back to Truro! When she came to see
me this time, it was years and years, long and lonely and very
many, since we two had met. I was afraid that many more
would pass again, and I tried to make her stop with me to the
very last. But she had still the same fear to drive her away;
the fear of being found and put to the question by you. So, with
the tears in her eyes (and in mine), and the grief at her heart
(and at mine), she went away to hide herself in the empty
bigness of the great city, London, which swallows up all people
and all things that pour into it, and which has now swallowed
up Sarah, my niece, with the rest. "My child, you will write
sometimes to Uncle Joseph," I said, and she answered me, "I
will write often." It is three weeks now since that time, and
here, on my knee, are four letters she has written to me. I shall
ask your leave to put them down open before you, because they
will help me to get on farther yet with what I must say, and
because I see in your face, madam, that you are indeed sorry for
Sarah, my niece, from your heart.'

He untied the packet of letters, opened them, kissed them
one by one, and put them down in a row on the table, smoothing them out carefully with his hand, and taking great pains to
arrange them all in a perfectly straight line. A glance at the first
of the little series showed Rosamond that the handwriting in it
was the same as the handwriting in the body of the letter which
had been found in the Myrtle Room.

'There is not much to read,' said Uncle Joseph. 'But if you
will look through them first, madam, I can tell you after, all the
reason for showing them that I have.'

The old man was right. There was very little to read in the
letters, and they grew progressively shorter as they became
more recent in date. All four were written in the formal,
conventionally correct style of a person taking up the pen with
a fear of making mistakes in spelling and grammar, and were
equally destitute of any personal particulars relative to the
writer; all four anxiously entreated that Uncle Joseph would
not be uneasy, inquired after his health, and expressed
gratitude and love for him as warmly as their timid restraints of
style would permit; all four contained these two questions
relating to Rosamond:—First, had Mrs Frankland arrived yet

at Porthgenna Tower? Secondly, if she had arrived, what had Uncle Joseph heard about her?—And, finally, all four gave the same instructions for addressing an answer:—'Please direct to me, "S. J., Post Office, Smith Street, London," '—followed by the same apology, 'Excuse my not giving my address, in case of accidents; for even in London I am still afraid of being followed and found out. I send every morning for letters; so I am sure to get your answer.'

'I told you, madam,' said the old man, when Rosamond raised her head from the letters, 'that I was frightened and sorry for Sarah when she left me. Now see, if you please, why I get more frightened and more sorry yet, when I have all the four letters that she writes to me. They begin here, with the first, at my left hand; and they grow shorter, and shorter, and shorter, as they get nearer to my right, till the last is but eight little lines. Again, see, if you please. The writing of the first letter, here, at my left hand, is very fine—I mean it is very fine to me, because I love Sarah, and because I write very badly myself—but it is not so good in the second letter, it shakes a little, it blots a little, it crooks itself a little in the last lines. In the third it is worse—more shake, more blot, more crook. In the fourth, where there is least to do, there is still more shake, still more blot, still more crook, than in all the other three put together. I see this; I remember that she was weak, and worn, and weary when she left me, and I say to myself, "She is ill, though she will not tell it, for the writing betrays her!"'

Rosamond looked down again at the letters, and followed the significant changes for the worse in the handwriting, line by line, as the old man pointed them out.

'I say to myself that,' he continued, 'I wait, and think a little; and I hear my own heart whisper to me, "Go you, Uncle Joseph, to London, and, while there is yet time, bring her back to be cured, and comforted and made happy in your own home!" After that, I wait, and think a little again—not about leaving my business; I would leave it for ever sooner than Sarah should come to harm—but about what I am to do to get her to come back. That thought makes me look at the letters again; the letters show me always the same questions about Mistress Frankland; I see it plainly as my own hand before me, that

I shall never get Sarah, my niece, back, unless I can make easy her mind about those questions of Mistress Frankland's that she dreads as if there was death to her in every one of them. I see it! it makes my pipe go out; it drives me up from my chair; it puts my hat on my head; it brings me here, where I have once intruded myself already, and where I have no right, I know, to intrude myself again; it makes me beg and pray now, of your compassion for my niece, and of your goodness for me, that you will not deny me the means of bringing Sarah back. If I may only say to her, I have seen Mistress Frankland, and she has told me with her own lips that she will ask none of those questions that you fear so much—if I may only say that, Sarah will come back with me, and I shall thank you every day of my life for making me a happy man!'

The simple eloquence of his words, the innocent earnestness of his manner, touched Rosamond to the heart. 'I will do anything, I will promise anything,' she answered eagerly, 'to help you to bring her back! If she will only let me see her, I promise not to say one word that she would not wish me to say; I promise not to ask one question—no, not one—that it will pain her to answer. Oh, what comforting message can I send besides! what can I say!'——she stopped confusedly, feeling her husband's foot touching hers again.

'Ah, say no more! say no more!' cried Uncle Joseph, tying up his little packet of letters, with his eyes sparkling and his ruddy face all in a glow. 'Enough said to bring Sarah back! enough said to make me grateful for all my life! Oh, I am so happy, so happy, so happy, my skin is too small to hold me!' He tossed up the packet of letters into the air, caught it, kissed it, and put it back again in his pocket, all in an instant.

'You are not going?' said Rosamond. 'Surely you are not going yet?'

'It is my loss to go away from here, which I must put up with, because it is also my gain to get sooner to Sarah,' replied Uncle Joseph. 'For that reason only, I shall ask your pardon if I take my leave with my heart full of thanks, and go my ways home again.'

'When do you propose to start for London, Mr Buschmann?' inquired Leonard.

'To-morrow, in the morning, early, sir,' replied Uncle Joseph. 'I shall finish the work that I must do to-night, and shall leave the rest to Samuel (who is my very good friend, and my shopman too), and shall then go to Sarah by the first coach.'

'May I ask for your niece's address in London, in case we wish to write to you?'

'She gives me no address, sir, but the post-office; for even at the great distance of London, the same fear that she had all the way from this house, still sticks to her. But here is the place where I shall get my own bed,' continued the old man, producing a small shop card. 'It is the house of a countryman of my own, a fine baker of buns, sir, and a very good man indeed.'

'Have you thought of any plan for finding out your niece's address?' inquired Rosamond, copying the direction on the card while she spoke.

'Ah, yes,—for I am always quick at making my plans,' said Uncle Joseph. 'I shall present myself to the master of the post, and to him I shall say just this and no more: "Good morning, sir. I am the man who writes the letters to S. J. She is my niece, if you please; and all that I want to know is, Where does she live?" There is something like a plan, I think? A-ha!' He spread out both his hands interrogatively, and looked at Mrs Frankland with a self-satisfied smile.

'I am afraid,' said Rosamond, partly amused, partly touched by his simplicity, 'that the people at the post office are not at all likely to be trusted with the address. I think you would do better to take a letter with you, directed to "S. J.;" to deliver it in the morning when letters are received from the country; to wait near the door, and then to follow the person who is sent by your niece (as she tells you herself) to ask for letters for S. J.'

'You think that is better?' said Uncle Joseph, secretly convinced that his own idea was unquestionably the most ingenious of the two. 'Good! The least little word that you say to me, madame, is a command that I follow with all my heart.' He took the crumpled felt hat out of his pocket, and advanced to say farewell, when Mr Frankland spoke to him again.

'If you find your niece well, and willing to travel,' said Leonard, 'you will bring her back to Truro at once? And you will let us know when you are both at home again?'

'At once, sir,' said Uncle Joseph. 'To both these questions, I say at once.'

'If a week from this time passes,' continued Leonard, 'and we hear nothing from you, we must conclude, then, either that some unforeseen obstacle stands in the way of your return, or that your fears on your niece's account have been but too well founded, and that she is not able to travel?'

'Yes, sir; so let it be. But I hope you will hear from me before the week is out.'

'Oh, so do I! most earnestly, most anxiously!' said Rosamond. 'You remember my message?'

'I have got it here, every word of it,' said Uncle Joseph, touching his heart. He raised the hand which Rosamond held out to him, to his lips. 'I shall try to thank you better when I have come back,' he said. 'For all your kindness to me and to my niece, God bless you both, and keep you happy, till we meet again.' With these words, he hastened to the door, waved his hand gaily with the old crumpled hat in it, and went out.

'Dear, simple, warm-hearted old man!' said Rosamond, as the door closed. 'I wanted to tell him everything, Lenny. Why did you stop me?'

'My love, it is that very simplicity which you admire, and which I admire, too, that makes me cautious. At the first sound of his voice I felt as warmly towards him as you do; but the more I heard him talk, the more convinced I became that it would be rash to trust him, at first, for fear of his disclosing too abruptly to your mother that we know her secret. Our chance of winning her confidence and obtaining an interview with her, depends, I can see, upon our own tact in dealing with her exaggerated suspicions and her nervous fears. That good old man, with the best and kindest intentions in the world, might ruin everything. He will have done all that we can hope for, and all that we can wish, if he only succeeds in bringing her back to Truro.'

'But if he fails—if anything happens—if she is really ill?'

'Let us wait till the week is over, Rosamond. It will be time enough, then, to decide what we shall do next.'

CHAPTER II

WAITING AND HOPING

THE week of expectation passed, and no tidings from Uncle Joseph reached Porthgenna Tower.

On the eighth day, Mr Frankland sent a messenger to Truro, with orders to find out the cabinet-maker's shop kept by Mr Buschmann, and to inquire of the person left in charge there, whether he had received any news from his master. The messenger returned in the afternoon, and brought word that Mr Buschmann had written one short note to his shopman since his departure, announcing that he had arrived safely towards nightfall in London; that he had met with a hospitable welcome from his countryman, the German baker; and that he had discovered his niece's address, but had been prevented from seeing her by an obstacle which he hoped would be removed at his next visit. Since the delivery of that note, no further communication had been received from him, and nothing therefore was known of the period at which he might be expected to return.

The one fragment of intelligence thus obtained was not of a nature to relieve the depression of spirits which the doubt and suspense of the past week had produced in Mrs Frankland. Her husband endeavoured to combat the oppression of mind from which she was suffering, by reminding her that the ominous silence of Uncle Joseph might be just as probably occasioned by his niece's unwillingness as by her inability to return with him to Truro. Remembering the obstacle at which the old man's letter hinted, and taking also into consideration her excessive sensitiveness and her unreasoning timidity, he declared it to be quite possible that Mrs Frankland's message, instead of re-assuring her, might only inspire her with fresh apprehensions, and might consequently strengthen her resolution to keep herself out of reach of all communications from Porthgenna Tower.

Rosamond listened patiently while this view of the case was placed before her, and acknowledged that the reasonableness of it was beyond dispute; but her readiness in admitting that her husband might be right and that she might be wrong, was accompanied by no change for the better in the condition of her spirits. The interpretation which the old man had placed upon the alteration for the worse in Mrs Jazeph's handwriting, had produced a vivid impression on her mind, which had been strengthened by her own recollection of her mother's pale, worn face, when they met as strangers at West Winston. Reason, therefore, as convincingly as he might, Mr Frankland was unable to shake his wife's conviction that the obstacle mentioned in Uncle Joseph's letter, and the silence which he had maintained since, were referable alike to the illness of his niece.

The return of the messenger from Truro suggested, besides this topic of discussion, another question of much greater importance. After having waited one day beyond the week that had been appointed, what was the proper course of action for Mr and Mrs Frankland now to adopt, in the absence of any information from London or from Truro to decide their future proceedings?

Leonard's first idea was to write immediately to Uncle Joseph, at the address which he had given on the occasion of his visit to Porthgenna Tower. When this project was communicated to Rosamond, she opposed it, on the ground that the necessary delay before the answer to the letter could arrive would involve a serious waste of time, when it might, for aught they knew to the contrary, be of the last importance to them not to risk the loss of a single day. If illness prevented Mrs Jazeph from travelling, it would be necessary to see her at once, because that illness might increase. If she were only suspicious of their motives, it was equally important to open personal communications with her before she could find an opportunity of raising some fresh obstacle, and of concealing herself again in some place of refuge which Uncle Joseph himself might not be able to trace.

The truth of these conclusions was obvious, but Leonard hesitated to adopt them, because they involved the necessity of a journey to London. If he went there without his wife, his blindness placed him at the mercy of strangers and servants, in conducting investigations of the most delicate and most private nature. If Rosamond accompanied him, it would be necessary to risk all kinds of delays and inconveniences by taking the child with them on a long and wearisome journey of more than two hundred and fifty miles.

Rosamond met both these difficulties with her usual direct-ness and decision. The idea of her husband travelling anywhere under any circumstances, in his helpless, dependent state, without having her to attend on him, she dismissed at once as too preposterous for consideration. The second objection of subjecting the child to the chances and fatigues of a long jour-ney, she met by proposing that they should travel to Exeter at their own time, and in their own conveyance, and that they should afterwards insure plenty of comfort and plenty of room by taking a carriage to themselves, when they reached the railroad at Exeter. After thus smoothing away the difficulties which seemed to set themselves in opposition to the journey, she again reverted to the absolute necessity of undertaking it. She reminded Leonard of the serious interest that they both had in immediately obtaining Mrs Jazeph's testimony to the genuineness of the letter which had been found in the Myrtle Room, as well as in ascertaining all the details of the extraordi-nary fraud which had been practised by Mrs Treverton on her husband. She pleaded also her own natural anxiety to make all the atonement in her power for the pain she must have unconsciously inflicted, in the bedroom at West Winston, on the person of all others whose failings and sorrows she was most bound to respect; and having thus stated the motives which urged her husband and herself to lose no time in communicating personally with Mrs Jazeph, she again drew the inevitable conclusion, that there was no alternative, in the position in which they were now placed, but to start forthwith on the journey to London.

A little further consideration satisfied Leonard that the emergency was of such a nature as to render all attempts to meet it by half measures impossible. He felt that his own con-victions agreed with his wife's; and he resolved accordingly to act at once, without further indecision or further delay. Before the evening was over, the servants at Porthgenna were amazed by receiving directions to pack the trunks for travelling, and to order horses at the post-town for an early hour the next morning.

On the first day of the journey, the travellers started as soon as the carriage was ready, rested on the road towards noon, and remained for the night at Liskeard. On the second day, they arrived at Exeter, and slept there. On the third day, they reached London by the railway, between six and seven o'clock in the evening.*

When they were comfortably settled for the night at their hotel, and when an hour's rest and quiet had enabled them to recover a little after the fatigues of the journey, Rosamond wrote two notes under her husband's direction. The first was addressed to Mr Buschmann: it simply informed him of their arrival, and of their earnest desire to see him at the hotel as early as possible the next morning; and it concluded by cautioning him to wait until he had seen them, before he announced their presence in London to his niece.

The second note was addressed to the family solicitor, Mr Nixon,—the same gentleman who, more than a year since, had written, at Mrs Frankland's request, the letter which informed Andrew Treverton of his brother's decease, and of the circumstances under which the captain had died. All that Rosamond now wrote, in her husband's name and her own, to ask of Mr Nixon, was that he would endeavour to call at their hotel on his way to business the next morning, to give his opinion on a private matter of great importance, which had obliged them to undertake the journey from Porthgenna to London. This note, and the note to Uncle Joseph, were sent to their respective addresses by a messenger, on the evening when they were written.

The first visitor who arrived the next morning was the solicitor,—a clear-headed, fluent, polite old gentleman, who had known Captain Treverton and his father before him. He came to the hotel fully expecting to be consulted on some difficulties connected with the Porthgenna estate, which the local agent was perhaps unable to settle, and which might be of too confused and intricate a nature to be easily expressed in writing. When he heard what the emergency really was, and when the letter that had been found in the Myrtle Room was placed in his hands, it is not too much to say that, for the first time in the course of a long life and a varied practice among all sorts and conditions of clients, sheer astonishment utterly paralysed Mr Nixon's faculties, and bereft him, for some moments, of the power of uttering a single word.

When, however, Mr Frankland proceeded from making the disclosure to announcing his resolution to give up the purchase-money of Porthgenna Tower, if the genuineness of the letter could be proved to his own satisfaction, the old lawyer recovered the use of his tongue immediately, and protested against his client's intention with the sincere warmth of a man who thoroughly understood the advantage of being rich, and who knew what it was to gain and to lose a fortune of forty thousand pounds.

Leonard listened with patient attention, while Mr Nixon argued from his professional point of view, against regarding the letter, taken by itself, as a genuine document, and against accepting Mrs Jazeph's evidence, taken with it, as decisive on the subject of Mrs Frankland's real parentage. He expatiated on the improbability of Mrs Treverton's alleged fraud upon her husband having been committed without other persons, besides her maid and herself, being in the secret. He declared it to be in accordance with all received experience of human nature, that one or more of those other persons must have spoken of the secret either from malice or from want of caution, and that the consequent exposure of the truth must, in the course of so long a period as twenty-two years, have come to the knowledge of some among the many people in the West of England as well as in London, who knew the Treverton family personally or by reputation. From this objection he passed to another which admitted the possible genuineness of the letter, as a written document; but which pleaded the probability of its having been produced under the influence of some mental delusion on Mrs Treverton's part, which her maid might have had an interest in humouring at the time, though she might have hesitated, after her mistress's death, at risking the possible consequences of attempting to profit by the imposture. Having stated this theory, as one which not only explained the writing of the letter but the hiding of it also, Mr Nixon further observed, in reference to Mrs Jazeph, that any evidence she might give was of little or no value in a legal point of view, from the difficulty—or, he might say, the impossibility—of satisfactorily identifying the infant mentioned in the letter, with the lady whom he had now the honour of addressing as Mrs Frankland, and whom no unsubstantiated document in existence should induce him to believe to be any other than the daughter of his old friend and client, Captain Treverton.

Having heard the lawyer's objections to the end, Leonard admitted their ingenuity, but acknowledged, at the same time, that they had produced no alteration in his impression on the subject of the letter, or in his convictions as to the course of duty which he felt bound to follow. He would wait, he said, for Mrs Jazeph's testimony before he acted decisively; but if that testimony were of such a nature, and were given in such a manner, as to satisfy him that his wife had no moral right to the fortune that she possessed, he would restore it at once to the person who had—Mr Andrew Treverton.

Finding that no fresh arguments or suggestions could shake Mr Frankland's resolution, and that no separate appeal to Rosamond had the slightest effect in stimulating her to use her influence for the purpose of inducing her husband to alter his determination; and feeling convinced, moreover, from all that he heard, that Mr Frankland would, if he was opposed by many more objections, either employ another professional adviser, or risk committing some fatal legal error by acting for himself in the matter of restoring the money; Mr Nixon at last consented, under protest, to give his client what help he needed in case it became necessary to hold communication with Andrew Treverton. He listened with polite resignation to Leonard's brief statement of the questions that he intended to put to Mrs Jazeph; and said, with the slightest possible dash of sarcasm, when it came to his turn to speak, that they were excellent questions in a moral point of view, and would doubtless produce answers which would be full of interest of the most romantic kind. 'But,' he added, 'as you have one child already, Mr Frankland, and as you may, perhaps, if I may venture on suggesting such a thing, have more in the course of years; and as those children, when they grow up, may hear of the loss of their mother's fortune, and may wish to know why it was sacrificed, I should recommend—resting the matter on family grounds alone, and not going further to make a legal point of it also—that you procure from Mrs Jazeph, besides the vivâ voce* evidence you propose to extract (against the admissibility of which, in this case, I again protest), a written declaration, which you may leave behind you at your death, and which may justify you in the eyes of your children, in case the necessity for such justification should arise at some future period.'

This advice was too plainly valuable to be neglected. At Leonard's request, Mr Nixon drew out at once a form of declaration, affirming the genuineness of the letter addressed by the late Mrs Treverton, on her death-bed, to her husband, since also deceased, and bearing witness to the truth of the statements therein contained, both as regarded the fraud practised on Captain Treverton and the asserted parentage of the child. Telling Mr Frankland that he would do well to have Mrs Jazeph's signature to this document attested by the names of two competent witnesses, Mr Nixon handed the declaration to Rosamond to read aloud to her husband, and, finding that no objection was made to any part of it, and that he could be of no further use in the present early stage of the proceedings, rose to take his leave. Leonard engaged to communicate with him again, in the course of the day, if necessary; and he retired, reiterating his protest to the last, and declaring that he had never met with such an extraordinary case and such a self-willed client before in the whole course of his practice.

Nearly an hour elapsed after the departure of the lawyer before any second visitor was announced. At the expiration of that time, the welcome sound of footsteps was heard approaching the door, and Uncle Joseph entered the room.

Rosamond's observation, stimulated by anxiety, detected a change in his look and manner, the moment he appeared. His face was harassed and fatigued, and his gait, as he advanced into the room, had lost the briskness and activity which so quaintly distinguished it when she saw him, for the first time, at Porthgenna Tower. He tried to add to his first words of greeting an apology for being late: but Rosamond interrupted him, in her eagerness to ask the first important question.

'We know that you have discovered her address,' she said, anxiously, 'but we know nothing more. Is she as you feared to find her? Is she ill?'

The old man shook his head sadly. 'When I showed you her letter,' he said, 'what did I tell you? She is so ill, madam, that not even the message your kindness gave to me will do her any good.'

Those few simple words struck Rosamond's heart with a strange fear, which silenced her against her own will, when she tried to speak again. Uncle Joseph understood the anxious look she fixed on him, and the quick sign she made towards the chair standing nearest to the sofa on which she and her husband were sitting. There he took his place, and there he confided to them all that he had to tell.

He had followed, he said, the advice which Rosamond had given to him at Porthgenna, by taking a letter addressed to 'S. J.' to the post-office, the morning after his arrival in London. The messenger—a maid servant—had called to inquire, as was anticipated, and had left the post-office with his letter in her hand. He had followed her to a lodging-house in a street near, had seen her let herself in at the door, and had then knocked and inquired for Mrs Jazeph. The door was answered by an old woman, who looked like the landlady; and the reply was that no one of that name lived there. He had then explained that he wished to see the person for whom letters were sent to the neighbouring post-office, addressed to 'S. J.;' but the old woman had answered, in the surliest way, that they had nothing to do with anonymous people or their friends in that house, and had closed the door in his face. Upon this, he had gone back to his friend, the German baker, to get advice; and had been recommended to return, after allowing some little time to elapse, to ask if he could see the servant who waited on the lodgers, to describe his niece's appearance, and to put half-a-crown into the girl's hand to help her to understand what he wanted. He had followed these directions, and had discovered that his niece was lying ill in the house, under the assumed name of 'Mrs James.' A little persuasion (after the present of the half crown) had induced the girl to go upstairs and announce his name. After that, there were no more obstacles to be overcome; and he was conducted immediately to the room occupied by his niece.

He was inexpressibly shocked and startled, when he saw her, by the violent nervous agitation which she manifested as he approached her bedside. But he did not lose heart and hope, until he had communicated Mrs Frankland's message, and had found that it failed altogether in producing the re-assuring effect on her spirits which he had trusted and believed that it would exercise. Instead of soothing, it seemed to excite and alarm her afresh. Among a host of minute inquiries about Mrs Frankland's looks, about her manner towards him, about the exact words she had spoken, all of which he was able to answer more or less to her satisfaction, she had addressed two questions to him, to which he was utterly unable to reply. The first of the questions was, Whether Mrs Frankland had said anything about the Secret? The second was, Whether she had spoken any chance word to lead to the suspicion that she had found out the situation of the Myrtle Room?

The doctor in attendance had come in, the old man added, while he was still sitting by his niece's bedside, and still trying ineffectually to induce her to accept the friendly and re-assuring language of Mrs Frankland's message. After making some inquiries and talking a little while on indifferent matters, the doctor had privately taken him aside; had informed him that the pain over the region of the heart and the difficulty in breathing, which were the symptoms of which his niece complained, were more serious in their nature than persons uninstructed in medical matters might be disposed to think; and had begged him to give her no more messages from any one, unless he felt perfectly sure beforehand that they would have the effect of clearing her mind, at once and for ever, from the secret anxieties that now harassed it—anxieties which he might rest assured were aggravating her malady day by day, and rendering all the medical help that could be given of little or no avail.

Upon this, after sitting longer with his niece, and after holding counsel with himself, he had resolved to write privately to Mrs Frankland that evening, after getting back to his friend's house. The letter had taken him longer to compose than anyone accustomed to writing would believe. At last, after delays in making a fair copy from many rough drafts, and delays in leaving his task to attend on his niece, he had completed a letter narrating what had happened since his arrival in London, in language which he hoped might be understood. Judging by comparison of dates, this letter must have crossed Mr and Mrs Frankland on the road. It contained nothing more than he had just been relating with his own lips— except that it also communicated, as a proof that distance had not diminished the fear which tormented his niece's mind, the explanation she had given to him of her concealment of her name, and of her choice of an abode among strangers, when she had friends in London to whom she might have gone. That explanation it was perhaps needless to have lengthened the letter by repeating, for it only involved his saying over again, in substance, what he had already said in speaking of the motive which had forced Sarah to part from him at Truro.

With last words such as those, the sad and simple story of the old man came to an end. After waiting a little to recover her self-possession and to steady her voice, Rosamond touched her husband to draw his attention to herself, and whispered to him—

'I may say all, now, that I wished to say at Porthgenna?'

'All,' he answered. 'If you can trust yourself, Rosamond, it is fittest that he should hear it from your lips.'

After the first natural burst of astonishment was over, the effect of the disclosure of the Secret on Uncle Joseph exhibited the most striking contrast that can be imagined to the effect of it on Mr Nixon. No shadow of doubt darkened the old man's face, not a word of objection dropped from his lips. The one emotion excited in him was simple, unreflecting, unalloyed delight. He sprang to his feet with all his natural activity, his eyes sparkled again with all their natural brightness: one moment, he clapped his hands like a child; the next, he caught up his hat, and entreated Rosamond to let him lead her at once to his niece's bedside. 'If you will only tell Sarah what you have just told me,' he cried, hurrying across the room to open the door, 'you will give her back her courage, you will raise her up from her bed, you will cure her before the day is out!'

A warning word from Mr Frankland stopped him on a sudden, and brought him back, silent and attentive, to the chair that he had left the moment before.

'Think a little of what the doctor told you,' said Leonard. 'The sudden surprise which has made you so happy, might do fatal mischief to your niece. Before we take the responsibility of speaking to her on a subject which is sure to agitate her violently, however careful we may be in introducing it, we ought first, I think, for safety's sake, to apply to the doctor for advice.'

Rosamond warmly seconded her husband's suggestion, and, with her characteristic impatience of delay, proposed that they should find out the medical man immediately. Uncle Joseph announced—a little unwillingly, as it seemed—in answer to her inquiries, that he knew the place of the doctor's residence, and that he was generally to be found at home before one o'clock in the afternoon. It was then just half-past twelve; and Rosamond, with her husband's approval, rang the bell at once to send for a cab.

She was about to leave the room to put on her bonnet, after giving the necessary order, when the old man stopped her by asking, with some appearance of hesitation and confusion, if it was considered necessary that he should go to the doctor with Mr and Mrs Frankland; adding, before the question could be answered, that he would greatly prefer, if there was no objection to it on their parts, being left to wait at the hotel to receive any instructions they might wish to give him on their return. Leonard immediately complied with his request, without inquiring into his reasons for making it; but Rosamond's curiosity was aroused, and she asked why he preferred remaining by himself at the hotel to going with them to the doctor.

'I like him not,' said the old man. 'When he speaks about Sarah, he looks and talks as if he thought she would never get up from her bed again.' Answering in those brief words, he walked away uneasily to the window, as if he desired to say no more.

The residence of the doctor was at some little distance, but Mr and Mrs Frankland arrived there before one o'clock, and found him at home. He was a young man, with a mild, grave

face, and a quiet subdued manner. Daily contact with suffering and sorrow had perhaps prematurely steadied and
saddened his character. Merely introducing her husband and
herself to him, as persons who were deeply interested in his
patient at the lodging-house, Rosamond left it to Leonard to
ask the first questions relating to the condition of her mother's
health.

The doctor's answer was ominously prefaced by a few polite
words which were evidently intended to prepare his hearers for
a less hopeful report than they might have come there expecting to receive. Carefully divesting the subject of all professional
technicalities, he told them that his patient was undoubtedly
affected with serious disease of the heart. The exact nature of
this disease he candidly acknowledged to be a matter of doubt,
which various medical men might decide in various ways.
According to the opinion which he had himself formed from
the symptoms, he believed that the patient's malady was connected with the artery which conveys blood directly from the
heart through the system. Having found her singularly unwilling to answer questions relating to the nature of her past life, he
could only guess that the disease was of long standing; that it
was originally produced by some great mental shock, followed
by long wearing anxiety (of which her face showed palpable
traces); and that it had been seriously aggravated by the fatigue
of a journey to London, which she acknowledged she had
undertaken at a time when great nervous exhaustion rendered
her totally unfit to travel. Speaking according to this view of the
case, it was his painful duty to tell her friends, that any violent
emotion would unquestionably put her life in danger. At the
same time, if the mental uneasiness from which she was now
suffering could be removed, and if she could be placed in a
quiet, comfortable country home, among people who would be
unremittingly careful in keeping her composed, and in suffering her to want for nothing, there was reason to hope that the
progress of the disease might be arrested, and that her life
might be spared for some years to come.

Rosamond's heart bounded at the picture of the future
which her fancy drew from the suggestions that lay hidden in
the doctor's last words. 'She can command every advantage

you have mentioned, and more, if more is required!' she interposed eagerly, before her husband could speak again. 'Oh, sir, if rest among kind friends is all that her poor weary heart wants, thank God we can give it!'

'We can give it,' said Leonard, continuing the sentence for his wife, 'if the doctor will sanction our making a communication to his patient, which is of a nature to relieve her of all anxiety, but which, it is necessary to add, she is at present quite unprepared to receive.'

'May I ask,' said the doctor, 'who is to be entrusted with the responsibility of making the communication you mention?'

'There are two persons who could be entrusted with it,' answered Leonard. 'One is the old man whom you have seen by your patient's bedside. The other is my wife.'

'In that case,' rejoined the doctor, looking at Rosamond, 'there can be no doubt that this lady is the fittest person to undertake the duty.' He paused, and reflected for a moment; then added:—'May I inquire, however, before I venture on guiding your decision one way or the other, whether the lady is as familiarly known to my patient, and is on the same intimate terms with her, as the old man?'

'I am afraid I must answer No to both those questions,' replied Leonard. 'And I ought, perhaps, to tell you, at the same time, that your patient believes my wife to be now in Cornwall. Her first appearance in the sick room would, I fear, cause great surprise to the sufferer, and possibly some little alarm as well.'

'Under those circumstances,' said the doctor, 'the risk of trusting the old man, simple as he is, seems to be infinitely the least risk of the two—for the plain reason that his presence can cause her no surprise. However unskilfully he may break the news, he will have the great advantage over this lady of not appearing unexpectedly at the bedside. If the hazardous experiment must be tried,—and I assume that it must, from what you have said,—you have no choice, I think, but to trust it, with proper cautions and instructions, to the old man to carry out.'

After arriving at that conclusion, there was no more to be said on either side. The interview terminated, and Rosamond and her husband hastened back to give Uncle Joseph his instructions at the hotel.

As they approached the door of their sitting-room they were surprised by hearing the sound of music inside. On entering, they found the old man crouched up on a stool, listening to a shabby little musical box which was placed on a table close by him, and which was playing an air that Rosamond recognised immediately as the 'Batti, batti' of Mozart.

'I hope you will pardon me for making music to keep myself company while you were away,' said Uncle Joseph, starting up in some little confusion, and touching the stop of the box. 'This is, if you please, of all my friends and companions the oldest that is left. The divine Mozart, the king of all the composers that ever lived, gave it with his own hand, madam, to my brother, when Max was a boy in the music-school at Vienna. Since my niece left me in Cornwall, I have not had the heart to make Mozart sing to me out of this little bit of box until to-day. Now that you have made me happy about Sarah again, my ears ache once more for the tiny *ting-ting* that has always the same friendly sound to my heart, travel where I may. But enough so!' said the old man, placing the box in the leather case by his side, which Rosamond had noticed there when she first saw him at Porthgenna. 'I shall put back my singing-bird into his cage, and shall ask, when that is done, if you will be pleased to tell me what it is that the doctor has said?'

Rosamond answered his request by relating the substance of the conversation which had passed between her husband and the doctor. She then, with many preparatory cautions, proceeded to instruct the old man how to disclose the discovery of the Secret to his niece. She told him that the circumstances in connection with it must be first stated, not as events that had really happened, but as events that might be supposed to have happened. She put the words that he would have to speak, into his mouth, choosing the fewest and the plainest that would answer the purpose; she showed him how he might glide almost imperceptibly from referring to the discovery as a thing that might be supposed, to referring to it as a thing that had really happened; and she impressed upon him, as most important of all, to keep perpetually before his niece's mind the fact that the discovery of the Secret had not awakened one bitter feeling or one resentful thought, towards her, in the minds of either of the persons who had been so deeply interested in finding it out.

Uncle Joseph listened with unwavering attention until Rosamond had done; then rose from his seat, fixed his eyes intently on her face, and detected an expression of anxiety and doubt in it which he rightly interpreted as referring to himself.

'May I make you sure, before I go away, that I shall forget nothing?' he asked, very earnestly. 'I have no head to invent, it is true; but I have something in me that can remember, and the more especially when it is for Sarah's sake. If you please, listen now, and hear if I can say to you over again all that you have said to me?'

Standing before Rosamond, with something in his look and manner strangely and touchingly suggestive of the long past days of his childhood, and of the time when he had said his earliest lessons at his mother's knee, he now repeated, from first to last, the instructions that had been given to him, with a verbal exactness, with an easy readiness of memory, which, in a man of his age, was nothing less than astonishing. 'Have I kept it all as I should?' he asked simply, when he had come to an end. 'And may I go my ways now, and take my good news to Sarah's bedside?'

It was still necessary to detain him, while Rosamond and her husband consulted together on the best and safest means of following up the avowal that the Secret was discovered, by the announcement of their own presence in London.

After some consideration, Leonard asked his wife to produce the document which the lawyer had drawn out that morning, and to write a few lines, from his dictation, on the blank side of the paper, requesting Mrs Jazeph to read the form of declaration, and to affix her signature to it, if she felt that it required her, in every particular, to affirm nothing that was not the exact truth. When this had been done, and when the leaf on which Mrs Frankland had written, had been folded outwards, so that it might be the first page to catch the eye, Leonard directed that the paper should be given to the old man, and explained to him what he was to do with it, in these words:—

'When you have broken the news about the Secret to your niece,' he said, 'and when you have allowed her full time to compose herself, if she asks questions about my wife and myself (as I believe she will), hand that paper to her for answer, and beg her to read it. Whether she is willing to sign it, or not, she is sure to inquire how you came by it. Tell her in return that you have received it from Mrs Frankland—using the word "received," so that she may believe at first that it was sent to you from Porthgenna by post. If you find that she signs the declaration, and that she is not much agitated after doing so, then tell her in the same gradual way in which you tell the truth about the discovery of the Secret, that my wife gave the paper to you with her own hands, and that she is now in London——'

'Waiting and longing to see her,' added Rosamond. 'You, who forget nothing, will not, I am sure, forget to say that?'

The little compliment to his powers of memory made Uncle Joseph colour with pleasure, as if he was a boy again. Promising to prove worthy of the trust reposed in him, and engaging to come back and relieve Mrs Frankland of all suspense before the day was out, he took his leave, and went forth hopefully on his momentous errand.

Rosamond watched him from the window, threading his way in and out among the throng of passengers on the pavement, until he was lost to view. How nimbly the light little figure sped away out of sight! How gaily the unclouded sunlight poured down on the cheerful bustle in the street! The whole being of the great city basked in the summer glory of the day; all its mighty pulses beat high; and all its myriad voices whispered of hope!

CHAPTER III

THE STORY OF THE PAST

THE afternoon wore away, and the evening came, and still there were no signs of Uncle Joseph's return.

Towards seven o'clock, Rosamond was summoned by the

nurse, who reported that the child was awake and fretful. After soothing and quieting him, she took him back with her to the sitting-room; having first, with her usual consideration for the comfort of any servant whom she employed, sent the nurse down stairs, with a leisure hour at her own disposal, after the duties of the day. 'I don't like to be away from you, Lenny, at this anxious time,' she said, when she rejoined her husband; 'so I have brought the child in here. He is not likely to be trouble-some again; and the having him to take care of is really a relief to me in our present state of suspense.'

The clock on the mantel-piece chimed the half-hour past seven. The carriages in the street were following one another more and more rapidly, filled with people in full dress, on their way to dinner, or on their way to the opera. The hawkers were shouting proclamations of news in the neighbouring square, with the second editions of the evening papers under their arms. People who had been serving behind the counter all day, were standing at the shop door to get a breath of fresh air. Working men were trooping homeward, now singly, now together, in weary, shambling gangs. Idlers, who had come out after dinner, were lighting cigars at corners of streets, and look-ing about them, uncertain which way they should turn their steps next. It was just that transitional period of the evening at which the street-life of the day is almost over, and the street-life of the night has not quite begun—just the time, also, at which Rosamond, after vainly trying to find relief from the weariness of waiting by looking out of window, was becoming more and more deeply absorbed in her own anxious thoughts—when her attention was abruptly recalled to events in the little world about her by the opening of the room door. She looked up immediately from the child lying asleep on her lap, and saw that Uncle Joseph had returned at last.

The old man came in silently, with the form of declaration which he had taken away with him by Mr Frankland's desire, open in his hand. As he approached nearer to the window, Rosamond noticed that his face looked as if it had grown strangely older during the few hours of his absence. He came close up to her, and still not saying a word, laid his trembling forefinger low down on the open paper, and held it before her so that she could look at the place thus indicated without rising from her chair.

His silence and the change in his face struck her with a sudden dread which made her hesitate before she spoke to him. 'Have you told her all?' she asked, after a moment's delay, putting the question in low, whispering tones, and not heeding the paper.

'This answers that I have,' he said, still pointing to the declaration. 'See! here is the name, signed in the place that was left for it—signed by her own hand.'

Rosamond glanced at the paper. There indeed was the signature, 'S. Jazeph;' and underneath it were added, in faintly traced lines of parenthesis, these explanatory words: 'Formerly, Sarah Leeson.'

'Why don't you speak?' exclaimed Rosamond, looking at him in growing alarm. 'Why don't you tell us how she bore it?'

'Ah! don't ask me, don't ask me!' he answered, shrinking back from her hand, as she tried in her eagerness to lay it on his arm. 'I forgot nothing. I said the words as you taught me to say them—I went the roundabout way to the truth with my tongue; but my face took the short cut, and got to the end first. Pray, of your goodness to me, ask nothing about it! Be satisfied, if you please, with knowing that she is better, and quieter, and happier now. The bad is over and past, and the good is all to come. If I tell you how she looked, if I tell you what she said, if I tell you all that happened when first she knew the truth, the fright will catch me round the heart again, and all the sobbing and crying that I have swallowed down will rise once more and choke me. I must keep my head clear and my eyes dry—or, how shall I say to you all the things that I have promised Sarah, as I love my own soul and hers, to tell, before I lay myself down to rest to-night?' He stopped, took out a coarse little cotton pocket-handkerchief, with a flaring white pattern on a dull blue ground, and dried a few tears that had risen in his eyes while he was speaking. 'My life has had so much happiness in it,' he said, self-reproachfully, looking at Rosamond, 'that my courage, when it is wanted for the time of trouble, is not easy to find. And yet, I am German! all my nation are philosophers— why is it that I alone am as soft in my brains, and as weak in my heart, as the pretty little baby, there, that is lying asleep in your lap?'

'Don't speak again; don't tell us anything till you feel more composed,' said Rosamond. 'We are relieved from our worst suspense now that we know you have left her quieter and better. I will ask no more questions,—at least,' she added after a pause, 'I will only ask one.'—She stopped; and her eyes wandered inquiringly towards Leonard. He had hitherto been listening with silent interest to all that had passed; but he now interposed gently, and advised his wife to wait a little before she ventured on saying anything more.

'It is such an easy question to answer,' pleaded Rosamond. 'I only wanted to hear whether she has got my message— whether she knows that I am waiting and longing to see her, if she will but let me come?'

'Yes, yes,' said the old man, nodding to Rosamond with an air of relief. 'That question is easy; easier even than you think, for it brings me straight to the beginning of all that I have got to say.'

He had been hitherto walking restlessly about the room; sitting down one moment, and getting up the next. He now placed a chair for himself, midway between Rosamond—who was sitting, with the child, near the window—and her husband, who occupied the sofa at the lower end of the room. In this position, which enabled him to address himself alternately to Mr and Mrs Frankland without difficulty, he soon recovered composure enough to open his heart unreservedly to the interest of his subject.

'When the worst was over and past,' he said, addressing Rosamond—'when she could listen and when I could speak, the first words of comfort that I said to her were the words of your message. Straight she looked at me, with doubting fearing eyes. "Was her husband there to hear her?" she says. "Did he look angry? did he look sorry? did he change ever so little, when you got that message from her?" And I said, "No: no change, no anger, no sorrow, nothing like it." And she said again, "Has it made between them no misery? has it nothing wrenched away of all the love and all the happiness that binds them the one to the other?" And once more I answer to that, "No! no misery, no wrench. See now! I shall go my ways at once to the good wife, and fetch her here to answer for the good husband with her own tongue." While I speak those words there flies out over all her face a look—no, not a look—a light, like a sunflash. While I can count one, it lasts; before I can count two, it is gone; the face is all dark again; it is turned away from me on the pillow, and I see the hand that is outside the bed begin to crumple up the sheet. "I shall go my ways, then, and fetch the good wife," I say again. And she says, "No, not yet. I must not see her, I dare not see her till she knows—" and there she stops, and the hand crumples up the sheet again, and softly, softly, I say to her, "Knows what?" and she answers me, "What I, her mother, cannot tell her to her face, for shame." And I say, "So, so, my child! tell it not, then—tell it not at all." She shakes her head at me, and wrings her two hands together, like this, on the bed-cover. "I *must* tell it," she says. "I must rid my heart of all that has been gnawing, gnawing, gnawing at it, or how shall I feel the blessing that the seeing her will bring to me, if my conscience is only clear?" Then she stops a little, and lifts up her two hands, so, and cries out loud, "Oh, will God's mercy show me no way of telling it that will spare me before my child!" And I say, "Hush, then! there is a way. Tell it to Uncle Joseph, who is the same as father to you! Tell it to Uncle Joseph, whose little son died in your arms, whose tears your hand wiped away, in the grief time long ago! tell it, my child, to *me;* and *I* shall take the risk, and the shame (if there is shame) of telling it again. I, with nothing to speak for me but my white hair; I, with nothing to help me but my heart that means no harm—I shall go to that good and true woman, with the burden of her mother's grief to lay before her; and, in my soul of souls I believe it, she will not turn away!" '

He paused, and looked at Rosamond. Her head was bent down over her child; her tears were dropping slowly, one by one, on the bosom of his little white dress. Waiting a moment to collect herself before she spoke, she held out her hand to the old man, and firmly and gratefully met the look he fixed on her. 'O, go on, go on!' she said. 'Let me prove to you that your generous confidence in me is not misplaced.'

'I knew it was not, from the first, as surely as I know it now!' said Uncle Joseph. 'And Sarah, when I had spoken to her, she knew it too. She was silent for a little; she cried for a little; she leant over from the pillow and kissed me here, on my cheek, as I sat by the bedside; and then she looked back, back, back, in her mind, to the Long Ago, and very quietly, very slowly, with her eyes looking into my eyes, and her hand resting so in mine, she spoke the words to me that I must now speak again to you, who sit here to-day as her judge, before you go to her to-morrow, as her child.'

'Not as her judge!' said Rosamond. 'I cannot, I must not hear you say that.'

'I speak her words, not mine,' rejoined the old man gravely. 'Wait, before you bid me change them for others—wait, till you know the end.'

He drew his chair a little nearer to Rosamond, paused for a minute or two, to arrange his recollections, and to separate them one from the other; then resumed:

'As Sarah began with me,' he said, 'so I, for my part, must begin also,—which means to say, that I go down now through the years that are past, to the time when my niece went out to her first service. You know that the sea-captain, the brave and good man Treverton, took for his wife an artist on the stage— what they call play-actress, here? A grand big woman, and a handsome; with a life, and a spirit, and a will in her, that is not often seen: a woman of the sort who can say, We will do this thing, or that thing—and do it in the spite and face of all the scruples, all the obstacles, all the oppositions in the world. To this lady there comes for maid to wait upon her, Sarah, my niece,—a young girl, then, pretty, and kind, and gentle, and very, very shy. Out of many others who want the place, and who are bolder and bigger and quicker girls, Mistress Treverton, nevertheless, picks Sarah. This is strange, but it is stranger yet, that Sarah, on her part, when she comes out of her first fears, and doubts, and pains of shyness about herself, gets to be fond with all her heart of that grand and handsome mistress, who has a life, and a spirit, and a will of the sort that is not often seen. This is strange to say, but it is also, as I know from Sarah's own lips, every word of it true.'

'True beyond a doubt,' said Leonard. 'Most strong attachments are formed between people who are unlike each other.'

'So the life they led in that ancient house of Porthgenna began happily for them all,' continued the old man. 'The love that the mistress had for her husband was so full in her heart, that it overflowed in kindness to everybody who was about her, and to Sarah, her maid, before all the rest. She would have nobody but Sarah to read to her, to work for her, to dress her in the morning and the evening, and to undress her at night. She was as familiar as a sister might have been with Sarah, when they two were alone, in the long days of rain. It was the game of her idle time—the laugh that she liked most—to astonish the poor country maid, who had never so much as seen what a theatre's inside was like, by dressing in fine clothes, and painting her face, and speaking and doing all that she had done on the theatre-scene, in the days that were before her marriage. The more she puzzled Sarah with these jokes and pranks of masquerade, the better she was always pleased. For a year this easy, happy life went on in the ancient house,—happy for all the servants,—happier still for the master and mistress, but for the want of one thing to make the whole complete, one little blessing, that was always hoped for, and that never came—the same, if you please, as the blessing in the long white frock, with the plump delicate face and the tiny arms, that I see before me now.'

He paused, to point the allusion by nodding and smiling at the child in Rosamond's lap; then resumed.

'As the new year gets on,' he said, 'Sarah sees in the mistress a change. The good sea-captain is a man who loves children, and is fond of getting to the house all the little boys and girls of his friends round about. He plays with them, he kisses them, he makes them presents—he is the best friend the little boys and girls have ever had. The mistress, who should be their best friend too, looks on and says nothing; looks on, red sometimes, and sometimes pale; goes away into her room where Sarah is at work for her, and walks about, and finds fault; and one day lets the evil temper fly out of her at her tongue, and says, "Why have I got no child for my husband to be fond of? Why must he kiss and play always with the children of other women? They take his love away for something that is not mine. I hate those children and their mothers too!" It is her passion that speaks then, but it speaks what is near the truth for all that. She will not make friends with any of those mothers; the ladies she is familiar-fond with, are the ladies who have no children, or the ladies whose families are all upgrown. You think that was wrong of the mistress?'

He put the question to Rosamond, who was toying thoughtfully with one of the baby's hands which was resting in hers. 'I think Mrs Treverton was very much to be pitied,' she answered, gently lifting the child's hand to her lips.

'Then I, for my part, think so too,' said Uncle Joseph. 'To be pitied?—yes! To be more pitied some months after, when there is still no child and no hope of a child, and the good sea-captain says, one day, "I rust here, I get old with much idleness, I want to be on the sea again. I shall ask for a ship." And he asks for a ship, and they give it him, and he goes away on his cruises— with much kissing and fondness at parting from his wife—but still he goes away. And when he is gone, the mistress comes in again where Sarah is at work for her on a fine new gown, and snatches it away, and casts it down on the floor, and throws after it all the fine jewels she has got on her table, and stamps and cries with the misery and the passion that is in her. "I would give all those fine things, and go in rags for the rest of my life to have a child!" she says. "I am losing my husband's love; he would never have gone away from me if I had brought him a child!" Then she looks in the glass, and says between her teeth, "Yes! yes! I am a fine woman with a fine figure, and I would change places with the ugliest, crookedest wretch in all creation, if I could only have a child!" And then she tells Sarah that the captain's brother spoke the vilest of all vile words of her, when she was married, because she was an artist on the stage; and she says, "If I have no child, who but he—the rascal-monster that I wish I could kill!—who but he will come to possess all that the captain has got?" And then she cries again, and says, "I am losing his love—ah, I know it, I know it!—I am losing his love!" Nothing that Sarah can say will alter her thoughts about that. And the months go on, and the sea-captain comes back, and still there is always the same secret grief growing and growing in the mistress's heart—growing and growing till it is now the third year since the marriage, and there is no hope yet of a child; and once more the sea-captain gets tired on the land, and goes off again for his cruises—long cruises, this time; away, away, away, at the other end of the world.'

Here Uncle Joseph paused once more, apparently hesitating a little about how he should go on with the narrative. His mind seemed to be soon relieved of its doubts, but his face saddened, and his tones sank lower, when he addressed Rosamond again.

'I must, if you please, go away from the mistress now,' he said, 'and get back to Sarah, my niece, and say one word also of a mining man, with the Cornish name of Polwheal. This was a young man that worked well and got good wage, and kept a good character. He lived with his mother in the little village that is near the ancient house; and, seeing Sarah from time to time, took much fancy to her, and she to him. So the end came that the marriage-promise was between them given and taken; as it happened, about the time when the sea-captain was back after his first cruises, and just when he was thinking of going away in a ship again. Against the marriage-promise nor he nor the lady his wife had a word to object, for the miner, Polwheal, had good wage and kept a good character. Only the mistress said that the loss of Sarah would be sad to her—very sad; and Sarah answered that there was yet no hurry to part. So the weeks go on, and the sea-captain sails away again for his long cruises; and about the same time also the mistress finds out that Sarah frets and looks not like herself, and that the miner, Polwheal, he lurks here and lurks there, round about the house; and she says to herself, "So! so! Am I standing too much in the way of this marriage? For Sarah's sake, that shall not be!" And she calls for them both one evening, and talks to them kindly, and sends away to put up the banns* next morning the young man Polwheal. That night, it is his turn to go down into the Porthgenna mine, and work after the hours of the day. With his heart all light, down into that dark he goes. When he rises to the world again, it is the dead body of him that is drawn up—the dead body, with all the young life, by the fall of a rock, crushed out in a moment. The news flies here; the news flies there. With no break, with no warning, with no comfort near, it comes on a sudden to Sarah, my niece. When to her sweetheart that evening she had said good-bye, she was a young, pretty girl; when six little weeks after, she, from the sick-bed where the shock threw her, got up,—all her youth was gone, all her hair was grey, and in her eyes the fright-look was fixed that has never left them since.'

The simple words drew the picture of the miner's death, and of all that followed it, with a startling distinctness—with a fearful reality. Rosamond shuddered and looked at her husband. 'Oh, Lenny!' she murmured, 'the first news of your blindness was a sore trial to me—but what was it to this!'

'Pity her!' said the old man. 'Pity her for what she suffered then! Pity her for what came after, that was worse! Yet five, six, seven weeks pass, after the death of the mining-man, and Sarah, in the body suffers less, but in the mind suffers more. The mistress, who is kind and good to her as any sister could be, finds out, little by little, something in her face which is not the pain-look, nor the fright-look, nor the grief-look; something which the eyes can see, but which the tongue cannot put into words. She looks and thinks, looks and thinks, till there steals into her mind a doubt which makes her tremble at herself, which drives her straight forward into Sarah's room, which sets her eyes searching through and through Sarah to her inmost heart. "There is something on your mind besides your grief for the dead and gone," she says, and catches Sarah by both the arms before she can turn away, and looks her in the face, front to front, with curious eyes that search and suspect steadily. "The miner-man, Polwheal," she says; "my mind misgives me about the miner-man, Polwheal. Sarah! I have been more friend to you than mistress. As your friend I ask you, now—tell me all the truth?" The question waits; but no word of answer! only Sarah struggles to get away, and the mistress holds her tighter yet, and goes on and says, "I know that the marriage-promise passed between you and miner Polwheal: I know that if ever there was truth in man, there was truth in him; I know that he went out from this place to put the banns up, for you and for him, in the church. Have secrets from all the world besides, Sarah, but have none from *me*. Tell me, this minute, tell me the truth! Of all the lost creatures in this big, wide world, are you—?" Before she can say the words that are next to come, Sarah falls on her knees, and cries out suddenly to be let go away to hide and die, and be heard of no more. That was all the answer she gave. It was enough for the truth then; it is enough for the truth now.'

He sighed bitterly, and ceased speaking for a little while. No voice broke the reverent silence that followed his last words. The one living sound that stirred in the stillness of the room, was the light breathing of the child as he lay asleep in his mother's arms.

'That was all the answer,' repeated the old man, 'and the mistress who heard it says nothing for some time after, but still looks straight forward into Sarah's face, and grows paler and paler the longer she looks—paler and paler, till on a sudden she starts, and at one flash the red flies back into her face. "No," she says, whispering and looking at the door, "once your friend, Sarah, always your friend. Stay in this house, keep your own counsel, do as I bid you, and leave the rest to me." And with that she turns round quick on her heel, and falls to walking up and down the room,—faster, faster, faster, till she is out of breath. Then she pulls the bell with an angry jerk, and calls out loud at the door. "The horses! I want to ride;" then turns upon Sarah, "My gown for riding in! Pluck up your heart, poor creature! On my life and honour I will save you. My gown, my gown, then; I am mad for a gallop in the open air!" And she goes out, in a fever of the blood, and gallops, gallops, till the horse reeks again, and the groom-man who rides after her wonders if she is mad. When she comes back, for all that ride in the air, she is not tired. The whole evening after, she is now walking about the room, and now striking loud tunes all mixed up together on the piano. At the bed-time, she cannot rest. Twice, three times in the night she frightens Sarah by coming in to see how she does, and by saying always those same words over again, "Keep your own counsel, do as I bid you, and leave the rest to me." In the morning, she lies late, sleeps, gets up very pale and quiet, and says to Sarah, "No word more between us two of what happened yesterday—no word till the time comes when you fear the eyes of every stranger who looks at you. Then I shall speak again. Till that time let us be as we were before I put the question yesterday, and before you told the truth!"'

At this point he broke the thread of the narrative again, explaining as he did so, that his memory was growing confused about a question of time, which he wished to state correctly in introducing the series of events that were next to be described.

'Ah, well! well!' he said, shaking his head, after vainly endeavouring to pursue the lost recollection. 'For once, I must acknowledge that I forget. Whether it was two months, or whether it was three, after the mistress said those last words to Sarah, I know not—but at the end of the one time, or of the other, she, one morning, orders her carriage and goes away alone to Truro. In the evening she comes back with two large, flat baskets. On the cover of the one there is a card, and written on it are the letters "S. L." On the cover of the other there is a card, and written on it are the letters "R. T." The baskets are taken into the mistress's room, and Sarah is called, and the mistress says to her, "Open the basket with S. L. on it; for those are the letters of your name, and the things in it are yours." Inside, there is first a box, which holds a grand bonnet of black lace; then, a fine, dark shawl; then black silk of the best kind, enough to make a gown; then linen and stuff for the under garments, all of the finest sort. "Make up those things to fit yourself," says the mistress. "You are so much littler than I, that to make the things up, new, is less trouble, than from my fit to yours, to alter old gowns." Sarah, to all this, says in astonishment, "Why?" And the mistress answers, "I will have no questions. Remember what I said; keep your own counsel, and leave the rest to me!" So she goes out; and the next thing she does is to send for the doctor to see her. He asks what is the matter; gets for answer that Mistress Treverton feels strangely, and not like herself; also that she thinks the soft air of Cornwall makes her weak. The days pass, and the doctor comes and goes, and, say what he may, those two answers are always the only two that he can get. All this time, Sarah is at work; and when she has done, the mistress says, "Now for the other basket, with R. T. on it; for those are the letters of my name, and the things in it are mine." Inside this, there is first a box which holds a common bonnet of black straw; then a coarse dark shawl; then a gown of good common black stuff; then linen, and other things for the under garments, that are only of the sort called second best. "Make up all that rubbish," says the mistress, "to fit me. No questions! You have always done as I told you; do as I tell you now, or you are a lost woman." When the rubbish is made up, she tries it on, and looks in the glass, and laughs in a way that is wild and desperate to hear. "Do I make a fine, buxom, comely servant-woman?" she says. "Ha! but I have acted that part times enough in my past days on the theatre-scene." And then she takes off the clothes again, and bids Sarah pack them up at once in one trunk, and pack the things she has made for herself in another. "The doctor orders me to go away out of this damp, soft Cornwall climate, to where the air is fresh, and dry, and cheerful-keen!" she says, and laughs again, till the room rings with it. At the same time, Sarah begins to pack, and takes some knick-knack things off the table, and among them a brooch which has on it the likeness of the sea-captain's face. The mistress sees her, turns white in the cheeks, trembles all over, snatches the brooch away, and locks it up in the cabinet in a great hurry, as if the look of it frightened her. "I shall leave that behind me," she says, and turns round on her heel, and goes quickly out of the room. You guess now, what the thing was that Mistress Treverton had it in her mind to do?'

He addressed the question to Rosamond first, and then repeated it to Leonard. They both answered in the affirmative, and entreated him to go on.

'You guess?' he said. 'It is more than Sarah, at that time, could do. What with the misery in her own mind, and the strange ways and strange words of her mistress, the wits that were in her were all confused. Nevertheless, what her mistress has said to her, that she has always done; and together alone those two from the house of Porthgenna drive away. Not a word says the mistress till they have got to the journey's end for the first day, and are stopping at their inn among strangers for the night. Then at last she speaks out, "Put you on, Sarah, the good linen and the good gown to-morrow," she says, "but keep the common bonnet and the common shawl, till we get into the carriage again. I shall put on the coarse linen and the coarse gown, and keep the good bonnet and shawl. We shall pass so the people at the inn, on our way to the carriage, without very much risk of surprising them by our change of gowns. When we are out on the road again, we can change bonnets and shawls in the carriage—and then, it is all done. You are the married lady, Mrs Treverton, and I am your maid who waits on you, Sarah Leeson." At that, the glimmering on Sarah's mind breaks in at last: she shakes with the fright it gives her, and all she can say is, "Oh, mistress! for the love of Heaven, what is it you mean to do?" "I mean," the mistress answers, "to save you, my faithful servant, from disgrace and ruin; to prevent every penny that the captain has got from going to that rascal-monster, his brother, who slandered me; and, last and most, I mean to keep my husband from going away to sea again, by making him love me as he has never loved me yet. Must I say more, you poor, afflicted, frightened creature—or is it enough so?" And all that Sarah can answer, is to cry bitter tears, and to say faintly, "No." "Do you doubt," says the mistress, and grips her by the arm, and looks her close in the face with fierce eyes—"Do you doubt which is best, to cast yourself into the world forsaken, and disgraced, and ruined, or to save yourself from shame, and make a friend of me for the rest of your life? You weak, wavering, baby-woman, if you cannot decide for yourself, I shall for you. As I will, so it shall be! To-morrow, and the day after, and the day after that, we go on and on, up to the north, where my good fool of a doctor says the air is cheerful-keen—up to the north, where nobody knows me or has heard my name. I, the maid, shall spread the report that you, the lady, are weak in your health. No strangers shall you see, but the doctor and the nurse, when the time to call them comes. Who they may be, I know not; but this I do know, that the one and the other will serve our purpose without the least suspicion of what it is; and that when we get back to Cornwall again, the secret between us two will to no third person have been trusted, and will remain a Dead Secret to the end of the world!" With all the strength of the strong will that is in her, at the hush of night and in a house of strangers, she speaks those words to the woman of all women the most frightened, the most afflicted, the most helpless, the most ashamed. What need to say the end? On that night Sarah first stooped her shoulders to the burthen that has weighed heavier and heavier on them with every year, for all her after-life.'

'How many days did they travel towards the north?' asked Rosamond, eagerly. 'Where did the journey end? In England or in Scotland?'

'In England,' answered Uncle Joseph. 'But the name of the place escapes my foreign tongue. It was a little town by the side of the sea—the great sea that washes between my country and yours. There they stopped, and there they waited till the time came to send for the doctor and the nurse. And as Mistress Treverton had said it should be, so, from the first to the last, it was. The doctor and the nurse, and the people of the house were all strangers; and to this day, if they still live, they believe that Sarah was the sea-captain's wife, and that Mistress Treverton was the maid who waited on her. Not till they were far back on their way home with the child, did the two change gowns again, and return each to her proper place. The first friend at Porthgenna that the mistress sends for to show the child to, when she gets back, is the doctor who lives there. "Did you think what was the matter with me, when you sent me away to change the air?" she says, and laughs. And the doctor, he laughs too, and says, "Yes, surely! but I was too cunning to say what I thought in those early days, because, at such times, there is always fear of a mistake. And you found the fine dry air so good for you that you stopped?" he says. "Well, that was right! right for yourself and right also for the child." And the doctor laughs again and the mistress with him, and Sarah, who stands by and hears them, feels as if her heart would burst within her, with the horror, and the misery, and the shame of that deceit. When the doctor's back is turned, she goes down on her knees, and begs and prays with all her soul that the mistress will repent, and send her away with her child, to be heard of at Porthgenna no more. The mistress, with that tyrant-will of hers, has but four words of answer to give:—"It is too late!" Five weeks after, the sea-captain comes back, and the "Too late" is a truth that no repentance can ever alter more. The mistress's cunning hand that has guided the deceit from the first, guides it always to the last—guides it so that the captain, for the love of her and of the child, goes back to the sea no more—guides it till the time when she lays her down on the bed to die, and leaves all the burden of the secret, and all the guilt of the confession, to Sarah—to Sarah, who, under the tyranny of that tyrant-will, has lived in the house, for five long years, a stranger to her own child!'

'Five years!' murmured Rosamond, raising the baby gently in her arms, till his face touched hers. 'Oh me! five long years a stranger to the blood of her blood, to the heart of her heart!'

'And all the years after!' said the old man. 'The lonesome years and years among strangers, with no sight of the child that was growing up, with no heart to pour the story of her sorrow into the ear of any living creature, not even into mine! "Better," I said to her, when she could speak to me no more, and when her face was turned away again on the pillow: "a thousand times better, my child, if you had told the Secret!" "Could I tell it," she said, "to the master who trusted me? Could I tell it afterwards to the child, whose birth was a reproach to me? Could she listen to the story of her mother's shame, told by her mother's lips? How will she listen to it now, Uncle Joseph, when she hears it from *you?* Remember the life she has led, and the high place she has held in the world. How can she forgive me? How can she ever look at me in kindness again?"'

'You never left her!' cried Rosamond, interposing before he could say more; 'surely, surely, you never left her with that thought in her heart!'

Uncle Joseph's head drooped on his breast. 'What words of mine could change it?' he asked, sadly.

'Oh, Lenny, do you hear that? I must leave you, and leave the baby. I must go to her, or those last words about me will break my heart.' The passionate tears burst from her eyes as she spoke; and she rose hastily from her seat, with the child in her arms.

'Not to night,' said Uncle Joseph. 'She said to me at parting, "I can bear no more to-night; give me till the morning to get as strong as I can."'

'Oh, go back then yourself!' cried Rosamond. 'Go, for God's sake, without wasting another moment, and make her think of me as she ought! Tell her how I listened to you, with my own child sleeping on my bosom all the time—tell her—oh, no, no! words are too cold for it!—Come here, come close, Uncle Joseph (I shall always call you so now); come close to me and kiss my child—*her* grandchild—Kiss him on this cheek, because it has lain nearest to my heart. And now, go back, kind and dear old man—go back to her bedside, and say nothing but that *I* sent that kiss to *her!*'

CHAPTER IV

THE CLOSE OF DAY

THE night, with its wakeful anxieties, wore away at last; and the morning light dawned hopefully, for it brought with it the promise of an end to Rosamond's suspense.

The first event of the day was the arrival of Mr Nixon, who had received a note on the previous evening, written by Leonard's desire, to invite him to breakfast. Before the lawyer withdrew, he had settled with Mr and Mrs Frankland all the preliminary arrangements that were necessary to effect the restoration of the purchase-money of Porthgenna Tower, and had dispatched a messenger with a letter to Bayswater, announcing his intention of calling upon Andrew Treverton that afternoon, on private business of importance relating to the personal estate of his late brother.

Towards noon, Uncle Joseph arrived at the hotel to take Rosamond with him to the house where her mother lay ill.

He came in, talking, in the highest spirits, of the wonderful change for the better that had been wrought in his niece by the affectionate message which he had taken to her on the previous evening. He declared that it had made her look happier, stronger, younger, all in a moment; that it had given her the longest, quietest, sweetest night's sleep she had enjoyed for years and years past; and, last, best triumph of all, that its good influence had been acknowledged, not an hour since, by the doctor himself.

Rosamond listened thankfully, but it was with a wandering attention, with a mind ill at ease. When she had taken leave of her husband, and when she and Uncle Joseph were out in the street together, there was something in the prospect of the approaching interview between her mother and herself, which, in spite of her efforts to resist the sensation, almost daunted her. If they could have come together, and have recognised each other without time to think what should be first said or done on either side, the meeting would have been nothing more than the natural result of the discovery of the Secret. But, as it was, the waiting, the doubting, the mournful story of the past, which had filled up the emptiness of the last day of suspense, all had their depressing effect on Rosamond's impulsive disposition. Without a thought in her heart which was not tender, compassionate, and true towards her mother, she now felt, nevertheless, a vague sense of embarrassment, which increased to positive uneasiness the nearer she and the old man drew to their short journey's end. As they stopped at last at the house-door, she was shocked to find herself thinking beforehand, of what first words it would be best to say, of what first things it would be best to do, as if she had been about to visit a total stranger, whose favourable opinion she wished to secure, and whose readiness to receive her cordially was a matter of doubt.

The first person whom they saw after the door was opened, was the doctor. He advanced towards them from a little empty room at the end of the hall, and asked permission to speak with Mrs Frankland for a few minutes. Leaving Rosamond to her interview with the doctor, Uncle Joseph gaily ascended the stairs to tell his niece of her arrival, with an activity which might well have been envied by many a man of half his years.

'Is she worse? Is there any danger in my seeing her?' asked Rosamond, as the doctor led her into the empty room.

'Quite the contrary,' he replied. 'She is much better this morning; and the improvement, I find, is mainly due to the composing and cheering influence on her mind of a message which she received from you last night. It is the discovery of this which makes me anxious to speak to you now on the subject of one particular symptom of her mental condition which surprised and alarmed me when I first discovered it, and which has perplexed me very much ever since. She is suffering—not to detain you, and to put the matter at once in the plainest terms—under a mental hallucination of a very extraordinary kind, which, so far as I have observed it, affects her, generally, towards the close of the day, when the light gets obscure. At such times, there is an expression in her eyes, as if she fancied some person had walked suddenly into the room. She looks and talks at perfect vacancy, as you or I might look or talk at some one who was really standing and listening to us. The old man, her uncle, tells me that he first observed this when she came to see him (in Cornwall, I think he said) a short time since. She was speaking to him then on private affairs of her own, when she suddenly stopped, just as the evening was closing in, startled him by a question on the old superstitious subject of the re-appearance of the dead, and then looking away at a shadowed corner of the room, began to talk at it—exactly as I have seen her look and heard her talk upstairs. Whether she fancies that she is pursued by an apparition, or whether she imagines that some living person enters her room at certain times, is more than I can say; and the old man gives me no help in guessing at the truth. Can you throw any light on the matter?'

'I hear of it now for the first time,' answered Rosamond, looking at the doctor in amazement and alarm.

'Perhaps,' he rejoined, 'she may be more communicative with you than she is with me. If you could manage to be by her bedside at dusk to-day or to-morrow, and if you think you are not likely to be frightened by it, I should very much wish you to see and hear her, when she is under the influence of her delusion. I have tried in vain to draw her attention away from it, at the time, or to get her to speak of it afterwards. You have evidently considerable influence over her, and you might therefore succeed where I have failed. In her state of health, I attach great importance to clearing her mind of everything that clouds and oppresses it, and especially of such a serious hallucination as that which I have been describing. If you could succeed in combating it, you would be doing her the greatest service, and would be materially helping my efforts to improve her health. Do you mind trying the experiment?'

Rosamond promised to devote herself unreservedly to this service, or to any other which was for the patient's good. The doctor thanked her, and led the way back into the hall again.

Uncle Joseph was descending the stairs as they came out of the room. 'She is ready and longing to see you,' he whispered in Rosamond's ear.

'I am sure I need not impress on you again the very serious necessity of keeping her composed,' said the doctor, taking his leave. 'It is, I assure you, no exaggeration to say that her life depends on it.'

Rosamond bowed to him in silence, and in silence followed the old man up the stairs.

At the door of a back room on the second floor, Uncle Joseph stopped.

'She is there,' he whispered eagerly. 'I leave you to go in by yourself, for it is best that you should be alone with her at first. I shall walk about the streets in the fine warm sunshine, and think of you both, and come back after a little. Go in; and the blessing and the mercy of God go with you!' He lifted her hand to his lips, and softly and quickly descended the stairs again.

Rosamond stood alone before the door. A momentary tremor shook her from head to foot as she stretched out her hand to knock at it. The same sweet voice that she had last heard in her bedroom at West Winston, answered her now. As its tones fell on her ear, a thought of her child stole quietly into her heart, and stilled its quick throbbing. She opened the door at once, and went in.

Neither the look of the room inside, nor the view from the window; neither its characteristic ornaments, nor its prominent pieces of furniture; none of the objects in it or about it, which would have caught her quick observation at other times, struck it now. From the moment when she opened the door, she saw nothing but the pillows of the bed, the head resting on them, and the face turned towards hers. As she stepped across the threshold, that face changed; the eyelids drooped a little, and the pale cheeks were tinged suddenly with burning red.

Was her mother ashamed to look at her?

The bare doubt freed Rosamond in an instant from all the self-distrust, all the embarrassment, all the hesitation about choosing her words and directing her actions which had fettered her generous impulses up to this time. She ran to the bed, raised the worn shrinking figure in her arms, and laid the

poor weary head gently on her warm, young bosom. 'I have
come at last, mother, to take my turn at nursing you,' she said.
Her heart swelled as those simple words came from it—her
eyes overflowed—she could say no more.

'Don't cry!' murmured the faint, sweet voice timidly. 'I have
no right to bring you here, and make you sorry. Don't, don't
cry!'

'Oh, hush! hush! I shall do nothing but cry if you talk to me
like that!' said Rosamond. 'Let us forget that we have ever
been parted—call me by my name—speak to me as I shall
speak to my own child, if God spares me to see him grow up.
Say "Rosamond," and—oh, pray, pray,—tell me to do something for you!' She tore asunder, passionately, the strings of her
bonnet, and threw it from her on the nearest chair. 'Look! here
is your glass of lemonade on the table. Say "Rosamond, bring
me my lemonade!" say it familiarly, mother! say it as if you
knew that I was bound to obey you!'

She repeated the words after her daughter, but still not in
steady tones—repeated them with a sad, wondering smile, and
with a lingering of the voice on the name of Rosamond, as if it
was a luxury to her to utter it.

'You made me so happy with that message and with the kiss
you sent me from your child,' she said, when Rosamond had
given her the lemonade, and was seated quietly by the bedside
again. 'It was such a kind way of saying that you pardoned me!
It gave me all the courage I wanted to speak to you as I am
speaking now. Perhaps my illness has changed me—but I don't
feel frightened and strange with you; as I thought I should, at
our first meeting after you knew the Secret. I think I shall soon
get well enough to see your child. Is he like what you were at his
age? If he is, he must be very, very——' She stopped. 'I may
think of that,' she added, after waiting a little, 'but I had better
not talk of it, or I shall cry too; and I want to have done with
sorrow now.'

While she spoke those words, while her eyes were fixed with
wistful eagerness on her daughter's face, the whole instinct of
neatness was still mechanically at work in her weak, wasted
fingers. Rosamond had tossed her gloves from her on the bed
but the minute before; and already her mother had taken them

up, and was smoothing them out carefully and folding them neatly together, all the while she spoke.

'Call me "mother" again,' she said, as Rosamond took the gloves from her and thanked her with a kiss for folding them up. 'I have never heard you call me "mother," till now—never, never till now, from the day when you were born!'

Rosamond checked the tears that were rising in her eyes again, and repeated the word.

'It is all the happiness I want, to lie here, and look at you, and hear you say that! Is there any other woman in the world, my love, who has a face so beautiful and so kind as yours?' She paused and smiled faintly. 'I can't look at those sweet rosy lips now,' she said, 'without thinking how many kisses they owe me!'

'If you had only let me pay the debt before!' said Rosamond, taking her mother's hand, as she was accustomed to take her child's, and placing it on her neck. 'If you had only spoken the first time we met, when you came to nurse me! How sorrowfully I have thought of that since! O, mother, did I distress you much, in my ignorance? Did it make you cry when you thought of me after that?'

'Distress me! All my distress, Rosamond, has been of my own making, not of yours. My kind, thoughtful love! you said, "Don't be hard on her"—do you remember? When I was being sent away, deservedly sent away, dear, for frightening you, you said to your husband, "Don't be hard on her!" Only five words—but, oh, what a comfort it was to me, afterwards, to think that you had said them! I did want to kiss you so, Rosamond, when I was brushing your hair: I had such a hard fight of it to keep from crying out loud when I heard you, behind the bed-curtains, wishing your little child goodnight. My heart was in my mouth, choking me all that time. I took your part afterwards, when I went back to my mistress— I wouldn't hear her say a harsh word of you. I could have looked a hundred mistresses in the face then, and contradicted them all. Oh, no, no, no! you never distressed me. My worst grief at going away was years and years before I came to nurse you at West Winston. It was when I left my place at Porthgenna; when I stole into your nursery, on that dreadful morning, and when I saw you with both your little arms round my master's neck. The doll you had taken to bed with you was in one of your hands; and your head was resting on the captain's bosom—just as mine rests now—oh, so happily, Rosamond—on yours. I heard the last words he was speaking to you! words you were too young to remember. "Hush! Rosie dear," he said, "don't cry any more for poor mamma. Think of poor papa, and try to comfort him!" There, my love—there was the bitterest distress, and the hardest to bear! I, your own mother, standing like a spy, and hearing him say that to the child I dared not own! "Think of poor papa!" My own Rosamond! you know, now, what father *I* thought of when he said those words! How could I tell him the Secret? how could I give him the letter, with his wife dead that morning—with nobody but you to comfort him—with the awful truth crushing down upon my heart, at every word he spoke, as heavily as ever the rock crushed down upon the father you never saw!'

'Don't speak of it now!' said Rosamond. 'Don't let us refer again to the past: I know all I ought to know, all I wish to know of it. We will talk of the future, mother, and of happier times to come. Let me tell you about my husband. If any words can praise him as he ought to be praised, and thank him as he ought to be thanked, I am sure mine ought—I am sure yours will! Let me tell you what he said and what he did when I read him the letter that I found in the Myrtle Room. Yes, yes, do let me!'

Warned by a remembrance of the doctor's last injunctions; trembling in secret, as she felt under her hand the heavy, toilsome, irregular heaving of her mother's heart, as she saw the rapid changes of colour from pale to red, and from red to pale again that fluttered across her mother's face, she resolved to let no more words pass between them which were of a nature to recal painfully the sorrow and the suffering of the years that were gone. After describing the interview between her husband and herself which ended in the disclosure of the Secret, she led her mother, with compassionate abruptness, to speak of the future, of the time when she would be able to travel again, of the happiness of returning together to Cornwall, of the little festival they might hold on arriving at Uncle Joseph's house in Truro, and of the time after that, when they might go on still further to Porthgenna, or perhaps to some other place where new scenes and new faces might help them to forget all sad associations which it was best to think of no more.

Rosamond was still speaking on these topics; her mother was still listening to her with growing interest in every word that she said, when Uncle Joseph returned. He brought in with him a basket of flowers and a basket of fruit, which he held up in triumph at the foot of his niece's bed.

'I have been walking about, my child, in the fine bright sunshine,' he said, 'and waiting to give your face plenty of time to look happy, so that I might see it again as I want to see it always, for the rest of my life. Aha, Sarah! it is I who have brought the right doctor to cure you!' he added gaily, looking at Rosamond. 'She has made you better already; wait but a little while longer, and she shall get you up from your bed again, with your two cheeks as red, and your heart as light, and your tongue as fast to chatter as mine. See! the fine flowers, and the fruit I have bought that is nice to your eyes, and nice to your nose, and nicest of all to put into your mouth. It is festival-time with us to-day, and we must make the room bright, bright, bright, all over. And then, there is your dinner to come soon; I have seen it on the dish—a cherub among chicken-fowls! And, after that, there is your fine sound sleep, with Mozart to sing the cradle-song, and with me to sit for watch, and to go down-stairs when you wake up again, and fetch your cup of tea. Ah, my child, my child, what a fine thing it is to have come at last to this festival-day!'

With a bright look at Rosamond, and with both his hands full of flowers, he turned away from his niece to begin decorating the room. Except when she thanked the old man for the presents he had brought, her attention had never wandered, all the while he had been speaking, from her daughter's face; and her first words, when he was silent again, were addressed to Rosamond alone.

'While I am happy with *my* child,' she said, 'I am keeping you from *yours*. I, of all persons, ought to be the last to part you from each other too long. Go back now, my love, to your husband and your child; and leave me to my grateful thoughts and my dreams of better times.'

'If you please answer Yes to that, for your mother's sake,' said Uncle Joseph, before Rosamond could reply. 'The doctor says, she must take her repose in the day as well as her repose in the night. And how shall I get her to close her eyes, so long as she has the temptation to keep them open upon *you?*'

Rosamond felt the truth of those last words, and consented to go back for a few hours to the hotel, on the understanding that she was to resume her place at the bedside in the evening. After making this arrangement, she waited long enough in the room to see the meal brought up which Uncle Joseph had announced, and to aid the old man in encouraging her mother to partake of it. When the tray had been removed, and when the pillows of the bed had been comfortably arranged by her own hands, she at last prevailed on herself to take leave.

Her mother's arms lingered round her neck; her mother's cheek nestled fondly against hers. 'Go, my dear, go now, or I shall get too selfish to part with you even for a few hours,' murmured the sweet voice, in its lowest, softest tones. 'My own Rosamond! I have no words to bless you that are good enough; no words to thank you that will speak as gratefully for me as they ought! Happiness has been long in reaching me,—but, oh how mercifully it has come at last!'

Before she passed the door, Rosamond stopped and looked back into the room. The table, the mantel-piece, the little framed prints on the wall were bright with flowers; the musical-box was just playing the first sweet notes of the air from Mozart; Uncle Joseph was seated already in his accustomed place by the bed, with the basket of fruit on his knees; the pale, worn face on the pillow was tenderly lighted up by a smile: peace and comfort, and repose, all mingled together happily in the picture of the sick room, all joined in leading Rosamond's thoughts to dwell quietly on the hope of a happier time.

Three hours passed. The last glory of the sun was lighting the long summer day to its rest in the western heaven, when Rosamond returned to her mother's bedside.

She entered the room softly. The one window in it looked towards the west, and on that side of the bed the chair was placed which Uncle Joseph had occupied when she left him, and in which she now found him still seated on her return. He raised his finger to his lips, and looked towards the bed, as she opened the door. Her mother was asleep, with her hand resting in the hand of the old man.

As Rosamond noiselessly advanced, she saw that Uncle Joseph's eyes looked dim and weary. The constraint of the position that he occupied, which made it impossible for him to move without the risk of awakening his niece, seemed to be beginning to fatigue him. Rosamond removed her bonnet and shawl, and made a sign to him to rise and let her take his place.

'Yes, yes!' she whispered, seeing him reply by a shake of the head. 'Let me take my turn, while you go out a little and enjoy the cool evening air. There is no fear of waking her: her hand is not clasping yours, but only resting in it—let me steal mine into its place gently, and we shall not disturb her.'

She slipped her hand under her mother's while she spoke. Uncle Joseph smiled as he rose from his chair, and resigned his place to her. 'You will have your way,' he said; 'you are too quick and sharp for an old man like me.'

'Has she been long asleep?' asked Rosamond.

'Nearly two hours,' answered Uncle Joseph. 'But it has not been the good sleep I wanted for her;—a dreaming, talking, restless sleep. It is only ten little minutes, since she has been so quiet as you see her now.'

'Surely you let in too much light?' whispered Rosamond, looking round at the window, through which the glow of the evening sky poured warmly into the room.

'No, no!' he hastily rejoined. 'Asleep or awake, she always wants the light. If I go away for a little while, as you tell me, and if it gets on to be dusk before I come back, light both those candles on the chimney-piece. I shall try to be here again before that; but if the time slips by too fast for me, and if it so happens that she wakes and talks strangely, and looks much away from you into that far corner of the room there, remember that the matches and the candles are together on the chimney-piece, and that the sooner you light them after the dim twilight-time, the better it will be.' With those words he stole on tiptoe to the door and went out.

His parting directions recalled Rosamond to a remembrance of what had passed between the doctor and herself that morning. She looked round again anxiously to the window.

The sun was just sinking beyond the distant house-tops: the close of day was not far off.

As she turned her head once more towards the bed, a momentary chill crept over her. She trembled a little, partly at the sensation itself, partly at the recollection it aroused of that other chill which had struck her in the solitude of the Myrtle Room.

Stirred by the mysterious sympathies of touch, her mother's hand at the same instant moved in hers, and over the sad peacefulness of the weary face there fluttered a momentary trouble—the flying shadow of a dream. The pale, parted lips opened, closed, quivered, opened again; the toiling breath came and went quickly and more quickly; the head moved uneasily on the pillow; the eyelids half unclosed themselves; low, faint, moaning sounds poured rapidly from the lips—changed ere long to half-articulated sentences—then merged softly into intelligible speech, and uttered these words:—

'Swear that you will not destroy this paper! Swear that you will not take this paper away with you if you leave the house!'

The words that followed these were whispered so rapidly and so low that Rosamond's ear failed to catch them. They were followed by a short silence. Then the dreaming voice spoke again suddenly, and spoke louder.

'Where? where? where?' it said. 'In the bookcase? In the table-drawer?—Stop! stop! In the picture of the ghost——'

The last words struck cold on Rosamond's heart. She drew back suddenly with a movement of alarm,—checked herself the instant after, and bent down over the pillow again. But it was too late. Her hand had moved abruptly when she drew back, and her mother woke with a start and a faint cry,—with vacant, terror-stricken eyes, and with the perspiration standing thick on her forehead.

'Mother!' cried Rosamond, raising her on the pillow. 'I have come back. Don't you know me?'

'Mother?' she repeated in mournful, questioning tones. 'Mother?' At the second repetition of the word a bright flush of delight and surprise broke out on her face, and she clasped both arms suddenly round her daughter's neck. 'Oh, my own Rosamond!' she said. 'If I had ever been used to waking up and seeing your dear face look at me, I should have known you sooner, in spite of my dream! Did you wake me, my love? or did I wake myself?'

'I am afraid I woke you, mother.'

'Don't say "afraid." I would wake from the sweetest sleep that ever woman had, to see your face and to hear you say "Mother" to me. You have delivered me, my love, from the terror of one of my dreadful dreams. Oh, Rosamond, I think I should live to be happy in your love, if I could only get Porthgenna Tower out of my mind—if I could only never remember again the bedchamber where my mistress died, and the room where I hid the letter——'

'We will try and forget Porthgenna Tower now,' said Rosamond. 'Shall we talk about other places where I have lived, which you have never seen? Or shall I read to you, mother? Have you got any book here that you are fond of?'

She looked across the bed, at the table on the other side. There was nothing on it but some bottles of medicine, a few of Uncle Joseph's flowers in a glass of water, and a little oblong work-box. She looked round at the chest of drawers behind her—there were no books placed on the top of it. Before she turned towards the bed again, her eyes wandered aside to the window. The sun was lost beyond the distant housetops: the close of day was nearer at hand.

'If I could forget! O, me, if I could only forget!' said her mother, sighing wearily and beating her hand on the coverlid of the bed.

'Are you well enough, dear, to amuse yourself with work?' asked Rosamond, pointing to the little oblong box on the table, and trying to lead the conversation to a harmless, every-day topic, by asking questions about it. 'What work do you do? May I look at it?'

Her face lost its weary, suffering look, and brightened once more into a smile. 'There is no work there,' she said. 'All the treasures I had in the world, till you came to see me, are shut up in that one little box. Open it, my love, and look inside.'

Rosamond obeyed, placing the box on the bed where her mother could see it easily. The first object that she discovered inside was a little book, in dark, worn binding. It was an old copy of Wesley's Hymns. Some withered blades of grass lay between its pages; and on one of its blank leaves was this inscription:—'Sarah Leeson, her book. The gift of Hugh Polwheal.'

'Look at it, my dear,' said her mother. 'I want you to know it again. When my time comes to leave you, Rosamond, lay it on my bosom with your own dear hands, and put a little morsel of your hair with it, and bury me, in the grave in Porthgenna churchyard, where *he* has been waiting for me to come to him so many weary years. The other things in the box, Rosamond, belong to you; they are little stolen keepsakes that used to remind me of my child, when I was alone in the world. Perhaps, years and years hence, when your brown hair begins to grow grey like mine, you may like to show these poor trifles to your children when you talk about me. Don't mind telling them, Rosamond, how your mother sinned and how she suffered—you can always let these little trifles speak for her at the end. The least of them will show that she always loved you.'

She took out of the box a morsel of neatly-folded white paper, which had been placed under the book of Wesley's Hymns, opened it, and showed her daughter a few faded laburnum leaves that lay inside. 'I took these from your bed, Rosamond, when I came, as a stranger, to nurse you at West Winston. I tried to take a ribbon out of your trunk, love, after I had taken the flowers—a ribbon that I knew had been round your neck. But the doctor came near at the time, and frightened me.'

She folded the paper up again, laid it aside on the table, and drew from the box next a small print which had been taken from the illustrations to a pocket-book. It represented a little girl, in a gipsy-hat, sitting by the water-side, and weaving a daisy chain. As a design, it was worthless; as a print, it had not even the mechanical merit of being a good impression. Underneath it a line was written in faintly pencilled letters:— 'Rosamond when I last saw her.'

'It was never pretty enough for you,' she said. 'But still there was something in it that helped me to remember what my own love was like, when she was a little girl.'

She put the engraving aside with the laburnum leaves, and took from the box a leaf of a copy-book, folded in two, out of which there dropped a tiny strip of paper, covered with small printed letters. She looked at the strip of paper first. 'The advertisement of your marriage, Rosamond,' she said. 'I used to be fond of reading it over and over again to myself when I was alone, and trying to fancy how you looked and what dress you wore. If I had only known when you were going to be married, I would have ventured into the church, my love, to look at you and at your husband. But that was not to be,—and perhaps it was best so, for the seeing you in that stolen way might only have made my trials harder to bear afterwards. I have had no other keepsake to remind me of you, Rosamond, except this leaf out of your first copy-book. The nurse-maid at Porthgenna tore up the rest one day to light the fire, and I took this leaf when she was not looking. See! you had not got as far as words then,—you could only do up-strokes and down-strokes. O me! how many times I have sat looking at this one leaf of paper, and trying to fancy that I saw your small child's hand travelling over it, with the pen held tight in the rosy little fingers. I think I have cried oftener, my darling, over that first copy of yours than over all my other keepsakes put together.'

Rosamond turned aside her face towards the window to hide the tears which she could restrain no longer.

As she wiped them away, the first sight of the darkening sky warned her that the twilight dimness was coming soon. How dull and faint the glow in the west looked now! how near it was to the close of day!

When she turned towards the bed again, her mother was still looking at the leaf of the copy-book.

'That nurse-maid who tore up all the rest of it to light the fire,' she said, 'was a kind friend to me, in those early days at Porthgenna. She used sometimes to let me put you to bed, Rosamond; and never asked questions, or teased me, as the rest of them did. She risked the loss of her place by being so good to me. My mistress was afraid of my betraying myself and betraying her if I was much in the nursery, and she gave orders that I was not to go there, because it was not my place. None of the other women-servants were so often stopped from playing with you and kissing you, Rosamond, as I was. But the nursemaid—God bless and prosper her for it!—stood my friend. I often lifted you into your little cot, my love, and wished you good-night, when my mistress thought I was at work in her room. You used to say you liked your nurse better than you liked me, but you never told me so fretfully; and you always put your laughing lips up to mine whenever I asked you for a kiss!'

Rosamond laid her head gently on the pillow by the side of her mother's. 'Try to think less of the past, dear, and more of the future,' she whispered pleadingly; 'try to think of the time when my child will help you to recall those old days without their sorrow,—the time when you will teach him to put his lips up to yours, as I used to put mine.'

'I will try, Rosamond,—but my only thoughts of the future, for years and years past, have been thoughts of meeting you in heaven. If my sins are forgiven, how shall we meet there? Shall you be like my little child to me,—the child I never saw again after she was five years old? I wonder if the mercy of God will recompense me for our long separation on earth? I wonder if you will first appear to me in the happy world, with your child's face, and be what you should have been to me on earth, my little angel that I can carry in my arms? If we pray in heaven, shall I teach you your prayers there, as some comfort to me for never having taught them to you here?'

She paused, smiled sadly, and, closing her eyes, gave herself in silence to the dream-thoughts that were still floating in her mind. Thinking that she might sink to rest again if she was left undisturbed, Rosamond neither moved nor spoke. After watching the peaceful face for some time, she became conscious that the light was fading on it slowly. As that conviction impressed itself on her, she looked round at the window once more.

The western clouds wore their quiet twilight-colours already: the close of day had come.

The moment she moved in the chair, she felt her mother's

hand on her shoulder. When she turned again towards the bed, she saw her mother's eyes open and looking at her—looking at her, as she thought, with a change in their expression, a change to vacancy.

'Why do I talk of heaven?' she said, turning her face suddenly towards the darkening sky, and speaking in low, muttering tones. 'How do I know I am fit to go there? And yet, Rosamond, I am not guilty of breaking my oath to my mistress. You can say for me that I never destroyed the letter, and that I never took it away with me when I left the house. I tried to get it out of the Myrtle Room; but I only wanted to hide it somewhere else. I never thought to take it away from the house: I never meant to break my oath.'

'It will be dark soon, mother. Let me get up for one moment to light the candles.'

Her hand crept softly upward, and clung fast round Rosamond's neck.

'I never swore to give him the letter,' she said. 'There was no crime in the hiding of it. You found it in a picture, Rosamond? They used to call it a picture of the Porthgenna ghost. Nobody knew how old it was, or when it came into the house. My mistress hated it, because the painted face had a strange likeness to hers. She told me, when first I lived at Porthgenna, to take it down from the wall and destroy it. I was afraid to do that; so I hid it away, before ever you were born, in the Myrtle Room. You found the letter at the back of the picture, Rosamond? And yet that was a likely place to hide it in. Nobody had ever found the picture. Why should anybody find the letter that was hid in it?'

'Let me get a light, mother! I am sure you would like to have a light!'

'No! no light now. Give the darkness time to gather down there in the corner of the room. Lift me up close to you, and let me whisper.'

The clinging arm tightened its grasp as Rosamond raised her in the bed. The fading light from the window fell full on her face, and was reflected dimly in her vacant eyes.

'I am waiting for something that comes at dusk, before the candles are lit,' she whispered in low, breathless tones. 'My mistress!—down there!' And she pointed away to the farthest corner of the room near the door.

'Mother! for God's sake, what is it! what has changed you so?'

'That's right! say, "Mother." *If she does come*, she can't stop when she hears you call me "Mother," when she sees us together at last, loving and knowing each other in spite of her. Oh, my kind, tender, pitying child! if you can only deliver me from her, how long I may live yet!—how happy we may both be!'

'Don't talk so! don't look so! Tell me quietly—dear, dear mother, tell me quietly——'

'Hush! hush! I am going to tell you. She threatened me on her death-bed, if I thwarted her: she said she would come to me from the other world. Rosamond! I *have* thwarted her and she has kept her promise—all my life since, she has kept her promise! Look! Down there!'

Her left arm was still clasped round Rosamond's neck. She stretched her right arm out towards the far corner of the room, and shook her hand slowly at the empty air,

'Look!' she said. 'There she is as she always comes to me, at the close of day,—with the coarse, black dress on, that my guilty hands made for her,—with the smile that there was on her face when she asked me if she looked like a servant. Mistress! mistress! Oh, rest at last! the Secret is ours no longer! Rest at last! my child is my own again! Rest, at last; and come between us no more!'

She ceased, panting for breath; and laid her hot, throbbing cheek against the cheek of her daughter. 'Call me "Mother" again!' she whispered. 'Say it loud; and send her away from me for ever!'

Rosamond mastered the terror that shook her in every limb, and pronounced the word.

Her mother leaned forward a little, still gasping heavily for breath, and looked with straining eyes into the quiet twilight dimness at the lower end of the room.

'*Gone!!!*' she cried suddenly, with a scream of exultation. 'Oh, merciful, merciful God! gone at last!'

The next instant she sprang up on her knees in the bed. For

one awful moment her eyes shone in the grey twilight with a radiant unearthly beauty, as they fastened their last look of fondness on her daughter's face. 'Oh, my love! my angel!' she murmured, 'how happy we shall be together now!' As she said the words, she twined her arms round Rosamond's neck, and pressed her lips rapturously on the lips of her child.

The kiss lingered till her head sank forward gently on Rosamond's bosom—lingered, till the time of God's mercy came, and the weary heart rested at last.

CHAPTER V

FORTY THOUSAND POUNDS

No popular saying is more commonly accepted than the maxim which asserts, that Time is the great consoler;* and, probably no popular saying more imperfectly expresses the truth. The work that we must do, the responsibilities that we must undertake, the example that we must set to others,—these are the great consolers, for these apply the first remedies to the malady of grief. Time possesses nothing but the negative virtue of helping it to wear itself out. Who that has observed at all, has not perceived that those among us who soonest recover from the shock of a great grief for the dead are those who have most duties to perform towards the living? When the shadow of calamity rests on our houses, the question with us is, not how much time will suffice to bring back the sunshine to us again but how much occupation have we got to force us forward into the place where the sunshine is waiting for us to come? Time may claim many victories, but not the victory over grief. The great consolation for the loss of the dead who are gone is to be found in the great necessity of thinking of the living who remain.

The history of Rosamond's daily life, now that the darkness of a heavy affliction had fallen on it, was in itself the sufficient illustration of this truth. It was not the slow lapse of time that helped to raise her up again, but the necessity which would not wait for time—the necessity which made her remember what was due to the husband who sorrowed with her, to the child whose young life was linked to hers, and to the old man whose helpless grief found no support but in the comfort she could give, learnt no lesson of resignation but from the example she could set.

From the first the responsibility of sustaining him had rested on her shoulders alone. Before the close of day had been counted out by the first hour of the night, she had been torn from the bedside by the necessity of meeting him at the door, and preparing him to know that he was entering the chamber of death. To guide the dreadful truth gradually and gently, till it stood face to face with him, to support him under the shock of recognising it, to help his mind to recover after the inevitable blow had struck it at last—these were the sacred duties which claimed all the devotion that Rosamond had to give, and which forbade her heart, for his sake, to dwell selfishly on its own grief.

He looked like a man whose faculties had been stunned past recovery. He would sit for hours with the musical-box by his side, patting it absently from time to time, and whispering to himself as he looked at it, but never attempting to set it playing. It was the one memorial left that reminded him of all the joys and sorrows, the simple family interests and affections of his past life. When Rosamond first sat by his side and took his hand to comfort him, he looked backwards and forwards with forlorn eyes from her compassionate face to the musical-box, and vacantly repeated to himself the same words over and over again: 'They are all gone—my brother Max, my wife, my little Joseph, my sister Agatha, and Sarah my niece! I and my little bit of box are left alone together in the world. Mozart can sing no more. He has sung to the last of them now!'

The second day there was no change in him. On the third, Rosamond placed the book of Hymns reverently on her mother's bosom, laid a lock of her own hair round it, and kissed the sad, peaceful face for the last time.

The old man was with her at that silent leave-taking, and followed her away, when it was over. By the side of the coffin, and, afterwards, when she took him back with her to her husband, he was still sunk in the same apathy of grief which had overwhelmed him from the first. But when they began to speak of the removal of the remains the next day to Porthgenna churchyard, they noticed that his dim eyes brightened suddenly, and that his wandering attention followed every word they said. After a while, he rose from his chair, approached Rosamond, and looked anxiously in her face. 'I think I could bear it better if you would let me go with her?' he said. 'We two should have gone back to Cornwall together, if she had lived. Will you let us still go back together now that she has died?'

Rosamond gently remonstrated, and tried to make him see that it was best to leave the remains to be removed under the charge of her husband's servant, whose fidelity could be depended on, and whose position made him the fittest person to be charged with cares and responsibilities which near relations were not capable of undertaking with sufficient composure. She told him that her husband intended to stop in London, to give her one day of rest and quiet, which she absolutely needed, and that they then proposed to return to Cornwall in time to be at Porthgenna before the funeral took place; and she begged earnestly that he would not think of separating his lot from theirs at a time of trouble and trial, when they ought to be all three most closely united by the ties of mutual sympathy and mutual sorrow.

He listened silently and submissively while Rosamond was speaking, but he only repeated his simple petition when she had done. The one idea in his mind, now, was the idea of going back to Cornwall with all that was left on earth of his sister's child. Leonard and Rosamond both saw that it would be useless to oppose it, both felt that it would be cruelty to keep him with them, and kindness to let him go away. After privately charging the servant to spare him all trouble and difficulty, to humour him by acceding to any wishes that he might express, and to give him all possible protection and help without obtruding either officiously on his attention, they left him free to follow the one purpose of his heart which still connected him with the interests and events of the passing day. 'I shall thank you better soon,' he said at leave-taking, 'for letting me go away out of this din of London with all that is left to me of Sarah, my niece. I will dry up my tears as well as I can, and try to have more courage when we meet again.'

On the next day, when they were alone, Rosamond and her husband sought refuge from the oppression of the present, in speaking together of the future, and of the influence which the change in their fortunes ought to be allowed to exercise on their plans and projects for the time to come. After exhausting this topic, the conversation turned next on the subject of their friends, and on the necessity of communicating to some of the oldest of their associates the events which had followed the discovery in the Myrtle Room.

The first name on their lips while they were considering this question, was the name of Doctor Chennery; and Rosamond, dreading the effect on her spirits of allowing her mind to remain unoccupied, volunteered to write to the vicar at once, referring briefly to what had happened since they had last communicated with him, and asking him to fulfil, that year, an engagement of long standing, which he had made with her husband and herself, to spend his autumn holiday with them at Porthgenna Tower. Rosamond's heart yearned for a sight of her old friend; and she knew him well enough to be assured that a hint at the affliction which had befallen her, and at the hard trial which she had undergone, would be more than enough to bring them together the moment Doctor Chennery could make his arrangements for leaving home.

The writing of this letter suggested recollections which called to mind another friend, whose intimacy with Leonard and Rosamond was of recent date, but whose connection with the earlier among the train of circumstances which had led to the discovery of the Secret, entitled him to a certain share in their confidence. This friend was Mr Orridge, the doctor at West Winston, who had accidentally been the means of bringing Rosamond's mother to her bedside. To him she now wrote, acknowledging the promise which she had made, on leaving West Winston, to communicate the result of their search for the Myrtle Room; and informing him that it had terminated in the discovery of some very sad events, of a family nature, which were now numbered with the events of the past. More than this, it was not necessary to say to a friend who occupied such a position towards them as that held by Mr Orridge.

Rosamond had written the address of this second letter, and was absently drawing lines on the blotting-paper with her pen, when she was startled by hearing a contention of angry voices in the passage outside. Almost before she had time to wonder what the noise meant, the door was violently pushed open, and a tall, shabbily dressed, elderly man, with a peevish, haggard face, and a ragged grey beard, stalked in, followed indignantly by the head waiter of the hotel.

'I have three times told this person,' began the waiter, with a strong emphasis on the word 'person,' 'that Mr and Mrs Frankland——'

'Were not at home,' broke in the shabbily dressed man, finishing the sentence for the waiter. 'Yes, you told me that; and I told you that the gift of speech was only used by mankind for the purpose of telling lies, and that consequently I didn't believe you. You *have* told a lie. Here are Mr and Mrs Frankland both at home. I come on business, and I mean to have five minutes' talk with them. I sit down unasked, and I announce my own name—Andrew Treverton.'

With those words, he took his seat coolly on the nearest chair. Leonard's cheeks reddened with anger while he was speaking, but Rosamond interposed before her husband could say a word.

'It is useless, love, to be angry with him,' she whispered. 'The quiet way is the best way with a man like that.' She made a sign to the waiter, which gave him permission to leave the room—then turned to Mr Treverton. 'You have forced your presence on us, sir,' she said quietly, 'at a time when a very sad affliction makes us quite unfit for contentions of any kind. We are willing to show more consideration for your age than you have shown for our grief. If you have anything to say to my husband, he is ready to control himself and to hear you quietly, for my sake.'

'And I shall be short with him and with you, for my own sake,' rejoined Mr Treverton. 'No woman has ever yet had the chance of sharpening her tongue long on me, or ever shall. I have come here to say three things. First, your lawyer has told me all about the discovery in the Myrtle Room, and how you made it. Secondly, I have got your money. Thirdly, I mean to keep it. What do you think of that?'

'I think you need not give yourself the trouble of remaining in the room any longer, if your only object in coming here is to tell us what we know already,' replied Leonard. 'We know you have got the money; and we never doubted that you meant to keep it.'

'You are quite sure of that, I suppose?' said Mr Treverton. 'Quite sure you have no lingering hope that any future twists and turns of the law will take the money out of my pocket again and put it back into yours? It is only fair to tell you that there is not the shadow of a chance of any such thing ever happening, or of my ever turning generous and rewarding you of my own accord for the sacrifice you have made. I have been to Doctors' Commons,* I have taken out a grant of administration, I have got the money legally, I have lodged it safe at my banker's, and I have never had one kind feeling in my heart since I was born. That was my brother's character of me, and he knew more of my disposition, of course, than anyone else. Once again, I tell you both, not a farthing of all that large fortune will ever return to either of you.'

'And once again I tell *you*,' said Leonard, 'that we have no desire to hear what we know already. It is a relief to my conscience and to my wife's to have resigned a fortune which we had no right to possess; and I speak for her as well as for myself when I tell you that your attempt to attach an interested motive to our renunciation of that money, is an insult to us both which you ought to have been ashamed to offer.'

'That is your opinion, is it?' said Mr Treverton. 'You, who have lost the money, speak to me, who have got it, in that manner, do you? Pray, do you approve of your husband's treating a rich man who might make both your fortunes, in that way?' he inquired, addressing himself sharply to Rosamond.

'Most assuredly I approve of it,' she answered. 'I never agreed with him more heartily in my life than I agree with him now.'

'O!' said Mr Treverton. 'Then it seems you care no more for the loss of the money than he does?'

'He has told you already,' said Rosamond, 'that it is as great a relief to my conscience as to his, to have given it up.'

Mr Treverton carefully placed a thick stick which he carried with him, upright between his knees, crossed his hands on the top of it, rested his chin on them, and, in that investigating position, stared steadily in Rosamond's face.

'I rather wish I had brought Shrowl here with me,' he said to himself. 'I should like him to have seen this. It staggers *me*, and I rather think it would have staggered *him*. Both these people,' continued Mr Treverton, looking perplexedly from Rosamond to Leonard, and from Leonard back again to Rosamond, 'are, to all outward appearance, human beings. They walk on their hind legs, they express ideas readily by uttering articulate sounds, they have the usual allowance of features, and in respect of weight, height, and size, they appear to me to be mere average human creatures of the regular civilised sort. And yet, there they sit, taking the loss of a fortune of forty thousand pounds as easily as Crœsus, King of Lydia,* might have taken the loss of a half-penny!'

He rose, put on his hat, tucked the thick stick under his arm, and advanced a few steps towards Rosamond.

'I am going now,' he said. 'Would you like to shake hands?'

Rosamond turned her back on him contemptuously.

Mr Treverton chuckled with an air of supreme satisfaction.

Meanwhile, Leonard, who sat near the fireplace, and whose colour was rising angrily once more, had been feeling for the bell-rope, and had just succeeded in getting it into his hand, as Mr Treverton approached the door.

'Don't ring, Lenny,' said Rosamond. 'He is going of his own accord.'

Mr Treverton stepped out into the passage—then glanced back into the room with an expression of puzzled curiosity on his face, as if he was looking into a cage which contained two animals of a species that he had never heard of before. 'I have seen some strange sights in my time,' he said to himself. 'I have had some queer experience of this trumpery little planet, and of the creatures who inhabit it—but I never was staggered yet by any human phenomenon, as I am staggered now by those two.' He shut the door without saying another word, and Rosamond heard him chuckle to himself again as he walked away along the passage.

Ten minutes afterwards the waiter brought up a sealed letter addressed to Mrs Frankland. It had been written, he said, in the coffee-room of the hotel, by the 'person' who had intruded himself into Mr and Mrs Frankland's presence. After giving it to the waiter to deliver, he had gone away in a hurry, swinging his thick stick complacently, and laughing to himself.

Rosamond opened the letter.

On one side of it was a crossed cheque,* drawn in her name, for Forty Thousand pounds.

On the other side, were these lines of explanation:—

Take your money back again. First, because you and your husband are the only two people I have ever met with who are not likely to be made rascals by being made rich. Secondly, because you have told the truth, when letting it out meant losing money, and keeping it in, saving a fortune. Thirdly, because you are *not* the child of the player-woman. Fourthly, because you can't help yourself—for I shall leave it to you at my death, if you won't have it now. Good-bye. Don't come and see me, don't write grateful letters to me, don't invite me into the country, don't praise my generosity, and, above all things, don't have anything more to do with Shrowl.

ANDREW TREVERTON.

The first thing Rosamond did, when she and her husband had a little recovered from their astonishment, was to disobey the injunction which forbade her to address any grateful letters to Mr Treverton. The messenger who was sent with her note to Bayswater, returned without an answer, and reported that he had received directions from an invisible man, with a gruff voice, to throw it over the garden-wall and to go away immediately after, unless he wanted to have his head broken.

Mr Nixon, to whom Leonard immediately sent word of what had happened, volunteered to go to Bayswater the same evening, and make an attempt to see Mr Treverton on Mr and Mrs Frankland's behalf. He found Timon of London more approachable than he had anticipated. The misanthrope was, for once in his life, in a good humour. This extraordinary change in him had been produced by the sense of satisfaction which he experienced in having just turned Shrowl out of his situation, on the ground that his master was not fit company for him after having committed such an act of folly as giving Mrs Frankland back her forty thousand pounds.

'I told him,' said Mr Treverton, chuckling over his recollection of the parting-scene between his servant and himself—'I told him that I could not possibly expect to merit his continued approval after what I had done, and that I could not think of detaining him in his place, under the circumstances. I begged him to view my conduct as leniently as he could, because the first cause that led to it was, after all, his copying the plan of Porthgenna, which guided Mrs Frankland to the discovery in the Myrtle Room. I congratulated him on having got a reward of five pounds for being the means of restoring a fortune of forty thousand; and I bowed him out with a polite humility that half drove him mad. Shrowl and I have had a good many tussles in our time; he was always even with me till to-day, and now I've thrown him on his back at last!'

Although Mr Treverton was willing to talk of the defeat and dismissal of Shrowl as long as the lawyer would listen to him, he was perfectly unmanageable on the subject of Mrs Frankland, when Mr Nixon tried to turn the conversation to that topic. He would hear no messages—he would give no promise of any sort for the future. All that he could be prevailed on to say about himself and his own projects, was, that he intended to give up the house at Bayswater, and to travel again for the purpose of studying human nature, in different countries, on a plan that he had not tried yet—the plan of endeavouring to find out the good that there might be in people as well as the bad. He said the idea had been suggested to his mind by his anxiety to ascertain whether Mr and Mrs Frankland were perfectly exceptional human beings or not. At present, he was disposed to think that they were, and that his travels were not likely to lead to anything at all remarkable in the shape of a satisfactory result. Mr Nixon pleaded hard for something in the shape of a friendly message to take back, along with the news of his intended departure. The request produced nothing but a sardonic chuckle, followed by this parting speech, delivered to the lawyer at the garden-gate.

'Tell those two superhuman people,' said Timon of London, 'that I may give up my travels in disgust when they least expect it; and that I may possibly come back to look at them again—I don't personally care about either of them—but I should like to get one satisfactory sensation more out of the lamentable spectacle of humanity before I die.'

CHAPTER VI

THE DAWN OF A NEW LIFE

FOUR days afterwards, Rosamond and Leonard and Uncle Joseph met together in the cemetery of the church of Porthgenna.

The earth to which we all return had closed over Her: the weary pilgrimage of Sarah Leeson had come to its quiet end at last. The miner's grave from which she had twice plucked in secret her few memorial fragments of grass, had given her the home, in death, which, in life, she had never known. The roar of the surf was stilled to a low murmur before it reached the place of her rest; and the wind that swept joyously over the open moor, paused a little when it met the old trees that watched over the graves, and wound onward softly through the myrtle hedge which held them all embraced alike in its circle of lustrous green.

Some hours had passed since the last words of the burial service had been read. The fresh turf was heaped already over the mound, and the old headstone with the miner's epitaph on it had been raised once more in its former place at the head of the grave. Rosamond was reading the inscription softly to her husband. Uncle Joseph had walked a little apart from them while she was thus engaged, and had knelt down by himself at the foot of the mound. He was fondly smoothing and patting the newly-laid turf,—as he had often smoothed Sarah's hair in the long past days of her youth,—as he had often patted her hand in the after-time, when her heart was weary and her hair was grey.

'Shall we add any new words to the old worn letters as they stand now?' said Rosamond, when she had read the inscription to the end. 'There is a blank space left on the stone. Shall we fill it, love, with the initials of my mother's name, and the date of her death? I feel something in my heart which seems to tell me to do that, and to do no more.'

'So let it be, Rosamond,' said her husband. 'That short and simple inscription is the fittest and the best.'

She looked away, as he gave that answer, to the foot of the grave, and left him for a moment to approach the old man. 'Take my hand, Uncle Joseph,' she said, and touched him gently on the shoulder. 'Take my hand, and let us go back together to the house.'

He rose as she spoke, and looked at her doubtfully. The musical-box, enclosed in its well-worn leather case, lay on the grave near the place where he had been kneeling. Rosamond took it up from the grass, and slung it in the old place at his side, which it had always occupied when he was away from home. He sighed a little as he thanked her. 'Mozart can sing no more,' he said. 'He has sung to the last of them now!'

'Don't say to the last, yet,' said Rosamond, 'don't say to the last, Uncle Joseph, while I am alive. Surely Mozart will sing to *me*, for my mother's sake?'

A smile—the first she had seen since the time of their grief—trembled faintly round his lips. 'There is comfort in that,' he said; 'there is comfort for Uncle Joseph still, in hearing that.'

'Take my hand,' she repeated softly. 'Come home with us now.'

He looked down wistfully at the grave. 'I will follow you,' he said, 'if you will go on before me to the gate.'

Rosamond took her husband's arm, and guided him to the path that led out of the churchyard. As they passed from sight, Uncle Joseph knelt down once more at the foot of the grave, and pressed his lips on the fresh turf.

'Good-bye, my child,' he whispered, and laid his cheek for a moment against the grass, before he rose again.

At the gate, Rosamond was waiting for him. Her right hand was resting on her husband's arm; her left hand was held out for Uncle Joseph to take.

'How cool the breeze is!' said Leonard. 'How pleasantly the sea sounds! Surely this is a fine summer day?'

'The calmest and loveliest of the year,' said Rosamond. 'The only clouds on the sky are clouds of shining white; the only shadows over the moor lie light as down on the heather. O, Lenny, it is such a different day from that day of dull oppression and misty heat when we found the letter in the Myrtle Room! Even the dark tower of our old house, yonder, looks its brightest and best, as if it waited to welcome us to the beginning of a new life. I will make it a happy life to you, and to Uncle Joseph, if I can—happy as the sunshine we are walking in now. You shall never repent, love, if *I* can help it, that you have married a wife who has no claim of her own to the honours of a family name.'

'I can never repent my marriage, Rosamond, because I can never forget the lesson that my wife has taught me.'

'What lesson, Lenny?'

'An old one, my dear, which some of us can never learn too often. The highest honours, Rosamond, are those which no accident can take away—the honours that are conferred by LOVE and TRUTH.'

THE END

EXPLANATORY NOTES

5 *third time, in the present form*: the novel first appeared in periodical form in *Household Words* from 3 January 1857 to 13 June 1857, and then in a two-volume edition published by Bradbury and Evans in June 1857. Its appearance in a one-volume edition published by Sampson Low in 1861 marked its third publication.

periodical publication . . . weeks: *The Dead Secret* was the first of Collins's novels written for serial publication, appearing in *Household Words* and then in *Harper's Weekly* (NY) and *Littell's Living Age* (Boston). See Note on the Text.

the end: Collins's departure from the conventional suppression of secrets until the end of the story created controversy among critics. By the conclusion of Book I of *The Dead Secret*, the secret has become apparent. He would follow this open treatment of mystery, with the occasional false lead, in *The Woman in White*, as well as *The Moonstone*.

9 *Cornwall*: the county in south-west England, which was one of Collins's favourite haunts, first visited in the summer of 1850 and described in detail in *Rambles Beyond Railways* (1851) and in the dramatic conclusion to *Basil* (1852).

14 *Light!—give me more light*: an example of the theatrical as both reference and method in the novel. Collins alludes to the moment in *Hamlet* when Claudius disrupts the performance of 'The Mousetrap' crying out 'Give me some light. Away!' as he witnesses his own crime in Act III, Scene ii.

15 *plays*: prompt-books used by actors to study their lines.

19 *Sign as I tell you*: Collins repeats this scene in his next novel, *The Woman in White*, when Sir Percivale Glyde commands Laurie Fairlie to sign a document giving him control of her fortune without letting her read it. See 'Miss Halcombe's Narrative'.

21 *Swear!*: an echo of the Ghost's charge to Hamlet's followers in Act I, Scene v of the play, ordering them not to report his sighting.

29 *myrtle*: *Myrtus communus*, an aromatic evergreen shrub whose solitary flowers are white or pink. The first of numerous references to the plant in the novel, myrtle is the emblem of love and the symbol of Venus, as well as the aptly if ironically named room where Sarah Leeson will shortly hide the letter dictated to her by Mrs Treverton.

30 *Porthgenna Tower*: the name of the Treverton estate, which includes the village as well as a mine and fisheries. The tower itself is at one point in the novel called 'feudal' (p. 58); the original for the home may have been Lanhydrock House or Lanherne House, both located on the Cornish coast. See Introduction.

33 *housewife*: a pocket-case for needles, pins, threads, and scissors, popular in the eighteenth and early nineteenth centuries.

35 *Wesley's Hymns*: this collection of Methodist hymns by Charles Wesley (1701–88), composer of 'Jesu, Lover of my Soul', and 'Hark, the herald angels sing', is most likely *A Pocket Hymn Book for the Use of Christians of All Denominations Used at the Methodist Preaching Houses in town and country*, first published in 1787. It contained 250 hymns and was a redaction of *A Collection of Hymns for the Use of the People called Methodists*, first published in 1780, with 504 hymns. Sarah Leeson carries the hymnal throughout the novel.

36 *Polwheal*: Collins's source for the name is likely that of Richard Polwhele, a Cornish author who published a multi-volume *History of Cornwall* (1803–08) cited by Collins in *Rambles Beyond Railways*. See Introduction.

37 *Truro*: Originally spelt 'Triueru', meaning town where three roads meet, Truro was the largest town in south-west Cornwall in the nineteenth century and acknowledged to be the unofficial capital of the region, although Bodmin was the actual County Town. In 1877 it became a city and from 1880 to 1910 the cathedral, the only one in Cornwall, was constructed.

39 *Protestant Loyola*: a Protestant clergyman with the ascetic and austere look of a monastic Jesuit of the Society of Jesus, the order founded by the Spanish monk St Ignatius Loyola in 1534.

42 *execution of Charles the First*: king of England from 1625 to 1649, whose beheading on 30 January 1649 marked the collapse of the constitutional monarchy and the nadir of the English Civil War.

43 *Thirty-nine Articles*: usually appended to the *Book of Common Prayer*, they are concise doctrinal statements established in 1571 of a confessional-liturgical nature, dealing with the fundamentals of faith in the Church of England. Subscription to the Articles was required of all clerics of the church.

Privy Council: originally, the British Sovereign's private counsellors; more recently, an office concerned with formulating orders in council and officiating through committees, the most important having been the judicial which heard appeals from

ecclesiastical courts, colonial courts, and occasionally common-
wealth countries. After George I, the Privy Council became a
formal body increasingly composed of honorary appointees.

43 *Exeter Hall*: a classical building in the Strand, London, used for
religious and scientific gatherings, built between 1829 and 1831;
temporary occupants included the Bible Society, the Sacred
Harmonic Society, and the Temperance Society who was distressed to find that the cellars were let to a wine merchant.

49 *so thick a drop serene*: *Paradise Lost*, iii. 25. The passage, from the
narrator's invocation, relates to his temporary lack of sight but
also serenity caused by the grandeur of God's radiant light.

53 *Herod*: refers to the massacre of all infants under two years old
ordered by King Herod after the birth of Jesus (Matthew 2: 16).

58 *Popish priest*: a derogatory term for an Anglican priest with High
Church sympathies marked by Catholic preferences expressed
through an emphasis on tradition, sacraments, and authority.
Identified with the Oxford Movement (1833–45) and Edward
Pusey, such feared 'popery' or Anglo-Catholicism, which elevated clericalism, upset the Evangelicals and more traditional
members of the Church of England.

61 *Hebe*: the daughter of Zeus and Hera, often represented as the
cup-bearer to the gods and thought to be the goddess of youth.
She became the bride of Hercules.

65 *St Swithin's . . . English prose*: a fictitious church fabricated by
Collins; *Smallridge's Sermons*: George Smalridge (1663–1719),
bishop of Bristol, popular preacher and writer well known in
London during the reign of Queen Anne. Addison, Steel, and
Swift wrote of him. His *Sixty Sermons* first appeared in 1726;
they were reprinted in Oxford in 1824 and again in 1832; *Klopstock's Messiah*: Friedrich Klopstock (1724–1803), German
poet inspired by Virgil and Milton. He began his lengthy
religious epic, *Der Messias*, in 1745 and finished it in 1773. The
poem, written in hexameters, was intended to rival *Paradise
Lost*.

73 *Radical*: in 1844, the time of this scene, a Radical was one who
sought extensive social and political change, believing in the
inalienable rights and freedoms of individuals. Radicalism
became a political movement marked by mass meetings and peti-
tions for parliamentary reforms, while opposing oligarchic
attitudes and aristocratic ideals. The Reform Bill of 1832 signalled
one of the major achievements of the radical movement.

74 *Tory*: a colloquial term originating in the eighteenth century for one who desires to maintain social differences and political divisions for purposes of social order and security of the propertied classes. Often contrasted with the 'Whigs', who sought moderate Parliamentary reform and who formed the government in 1830, guiding the passage of the Reform Bill of 1832.

80 *Timon of Athens*: Athenian who, because of the supposed ingratitude of his friends, became a misanthrope. Shakespeare based his play *Timon of Athens* on his story as told by Plutarch and Lucian.

Oxford Street: one of the longest shopping streets in central London.

83 *letting his beard grow*: the social and professional status of Victorians was often marked, as Collins notes, by the presence and length of their beards, which went in and out of fashion. In the 1840s they were out of style; when the Radical politician G. F. Muntz appeared in Parliament with a full beard many thought he used it as a means to insult Parliamentary institutions. The artist James Ward felt compelled to publish a mid-Victorian defence of his beard with eighteen arguments. Beards gradually became acceptable when officers returned from the Crimean War (1854–6) and paraded about Piccadilly displaying their masculinity.

Collins himself attempted a moustache in 1853 which, according to Dickens, was unsuccessful. This effort, however, blossomed into a distinctive, full-grown, luxuriant brown beard from approximately 1857 on, grown partly to hide the oddities of his small chin and balance his disproportionate limbs and protruding forehead. The lengthy beard, which appears in his mature portraits and photographs, also enhanced his flamboyant appearance and claim to literary authority despite his diminutive stature.

Dr Johnson: Samuel Johnson (1709–1784) eighteenth-century man of letters and author of the first authoritative English dictionary; Boswell's *Life of Johnson* depicts him as a man of sharp disputation, careful argument, and devastating wit; in short, a dangerous verbal combatant.

86 *Petticoat Lane*: one of the largest Victorian street markets specializing in second-hand goods, located in the East End of London; its name was derived in the early seventeenth century from the sale of used clothes; around 1830 the street was renamed Middlesex Street, although the area still retains its original designation.

98 *fly*: a one-horse carriage for hire.

110 *pony-chaise*: open-topped horse-drawn carriage with two wheels, for one or two occupants.

115 *chemisette*: a short-sleeved shirt.

125 *Seven Wonders of the World*: the seven pre-eminent sights of the ancient world generally thought to be the Pyramids of Egypt, the Hanging Gardens of Babylon, the statue of Zeus by Phidias at Olympus, the Temple of Artemis at Ephesus, the Mausoleum of Halicarnassus, the Colossus of Rhodes, and the Pharos of Alexandria, the most famous lighthouse in the ancient world.

147 *Batti, Batti*: 'Batti, batti, o bel Masetto', an aria sung by Zerlina from Act I of Mozart's *Don Giovanni* (1787), in which she pleads with her fiancé to believe that nothing occurred between herself and Don Giovanni.

165 *post-town*: closest town with a post office to Porthgenna Tower.

169 *minuet in Don Giovanni*: an aristocratic dance occurring in the Finale to Act I of the opera.

182 *national Sabbatarian Polonaise*: Sunday walk between religious services followed by those strict observers of Sunday laws called Sabbatarians. The polonaise is a dance of Polish origin in triple time.

183 *Guide to West Cornwall*: a fictitious guide-book. Collins actually relied on John Murray's *A Handbook for Travellers in Cornwall*, the last of the volumes in Murray's popular Victorian series.

234 *deal table*: a small table made of fir or pine, so called because it is made of 'deals', plain unfinished planks of wood.

238 *FRS*: Fellow of the Royal Society, founded in 1660, the oldest scientific society in Great Britain whose Transactions became one of the important records of scientific advances in England. Scientific experiments were often conducted at the regular meetings.

252 *Last Waltz of Weber*: Carl Maria von Weber (1786–1826), the most popular German Romantic composer of his time, who wrote operas, chamber music, and piano pieces. The 'Last Waltz' was part of his *Six Favourite Waltzes* (1812) written for Marie Louise, Queen of France.

256 *Jesuit*: member of the Society of Jesus founded by St Ignatius Loyola and St Francis Xavier in 1534, noted for skill in debate and austere living. Part of the order's training originates in Loyola's *Spiritual Exercises*.

269 *Forget-me-not*: *Myosotis scorpioides*, sometimes called scorpion grass, is a perennial plant with pink flower buds that become blue as they expand. A symbol of constancy, it supposedly received its popular name from the last words of a knight who was drowned in an attempt to procure the flower for his lady.

270 *Maecenas of modern times*: Gaius Maecenas (d. 8 BCE), counsellor to the Emperor Augustus, was a famous Roman literary patron whose circle included Virgil, Horace, and Propertius.

271 *basso-relievo*: low relief; a method of moulding or carving in which the figures or design stand out shallowly from the surface.

Niobe: daughter of Tantalus and wife of Amphion, who boasted of her superiority as a mother—she had twelve children—to the goddess Leto. Seeking revenge for this insult, the twins of Leto, Apollo and Artemis, killed all of Niobe's children with arrows, causing Niobe to weep for them until she turned into a column of stone. Homer describes the tragedy in *Iliad* xxiv. The massacre of her children became a frequent subject of Greek sculpture.

Jupiter or Apollo: Jupiter is the Roman name for Zeus, the God of Weather, gatherer of storms, hurler of thunderbolts. He is the father of Apollo and Artemis, twins by Leto. Apollo is the god of music, prophecy, and light, embodying male beauty and moral excellence.

306 *six and seven o'clock in the evening*: the itinerary follows a north-easterly journey from the south-west coast of Cornwall, possibly near Portreth, through Truro, to Liskeard, a market town, where they spend the night. They continued on to Exeter in Devon, a major rail junction for the London–Plymouth route. After a night's rest they journey north by train to London.

309 *vivâ voce*: oral, from the medieval Latin meaning 'with living voice'.

326 *banns*: a notice read out on three successive Sundays in a parish church announcing an intended marriage and giving the opportunity for objections.

351 *Time is the great consoler*: Collins's version of a classical tag restated by the Victorians: 'Time is a physician that heals every grief' (Diphilus); 'Time heals what reason cannot' (Seneca); 'Time is the great physician' (Disraeli, in *Henrietta Temple*, 1837).

356 *Doctors' Commons*: colloquial name for the College of Advocates and Doctors of Law on grounds near St Paul's Cathedral on Paternoster Row. In the year following the Court of Probate Act

of 1857, the college was dissolved. For a description of Doctors' Commons see *David Copperfield*, ch. 23.

357 *Crœsus, King of Lydia*: the last King of Lydia, *c.*560–546 BCE, known for his great wealth. The rise of Persia led him to battle with Cyrus, their King, but he was defeated because he misunderstood the oracle at Delphi when she told him that if he crossed the river Halys a great kingdom would be destroyed. It was his own.

358 *crossed cheque*: a term from English banking meaning to draw two parallel transverse lines across the face of a cheque often with or without adding between them the name of a bank and the words 'not negotiable'. The cheque is then payable only through a bank to the person named on it.

The Oxford World's Classics Website

www.worldsclassics.co.uk

- Information about new titles
- Explore the full range of Oxford World's Classics
- Links to other literary sites and the main OUP webpage
- Imaginative competitions, with bookish prizes
- Peruse the Oxford World's Classics Magazine
- Articles by editors
- Extracts from Introductions
- A forum for discussion and feedback on the series
- Special information for teachers and lecturers

www.worldsclassics.co.uk

American Literature

British and Irish Literature

Children's Literature

Classics and Ancient Literature

Colonial Literature

Eastern Literature

European Literature

History

Medieval Literature

Oxford English Drama

Poetry

Philosophy

Politics

Religion

The Oxford Shakespeare

A complete list of Oxford Paperbacks, including Oxford World's Classics, Oxford Shakespeare, Oxford Drama, and Oxford Paperback Reference, is available in the UK from the Academic Division Publicity Department, Oxford University Press, Great Clarendon Street, Oxford OX2 6DP.

In the USA, complete lists are available from the Paperbacks Marketing Manager, Oxford University Press, 198 Madison Avenue, New York, NY 10016.

Oxford Paperbacks are available from all good bookshops. In case of difficulty, customers in the UK can order direct from Oxford University Press Bookshop, Freepost, 116 High Street, Oxford OX1 4BR, enclosing full payment. Please add 10 per cent of published price for postage and packing.